ECHOED IN MY BONES

Twisted Road Publications

www.twistedroadpublications.com

ECHOED IN MY BONES

A Novel By

Lisa A. Sturm

For the beautiful women and teens of Irvington, Newark,

Orange, East Orange, Elizabeth, and Plainfield, New Jersey

who shared their lives with me.

It had been almost two years since Lakisha had seen her mother—
she remembered only a soft cheek pressed against hers and dark eyes
that seemed ready to cry. Then, the summer before kindergarten,
Maizy returned. She scooped Lakisha up off the thinning living-
room carpet, squeezed her against a bony chest fragrant with
lavender powder, and kissed her cheek with a cinnamon-gum
mouth.

She reached into a blue-and-white striped bag and Lakisha
stared at her slender, scarred arm. After a moment of fishing, Maizy
pulled out a doll in clear plastic. "It's from the South," she said, like
that made it special, and handed it to Lakisha. Aunt Dottie and
Grandma Louema had given her other dolls, used toys with knotted
hair or missing clothing. But this one, a brand-new doll all her own,
she pressed against her ribs, her eyes lifting to her mother and
beyond, as if it were Judgment Day and she had been deemed
worthy.

"It's a Topsy-Turvy Doll—it changes," explained Maizy,
pulling off the wrapping. Then Lakisha saw it was true. When she
held it up one way, it was a black girl with a long red and white
polka-dot dress and matching checked headscarf. When she turned
the doll upside down and flipped the dress, it was fair-skinned with
two blonde braids, a light-blue dress and matching bonnet.

"I love it!" Lakisha's heart felt like a balloon filled to bursting,
and she tried not to let her mother or the rag doll escape her sight.
That night, Maizy climbed into bed with her, and Lakisha tucked
herself beneath her mother's arm. She held a fist-full of Maizy's

braids in one hand, and in the other she clutched the doll: the special one from the South, who unlike most people around her, had the ability to change.

Eleven years later, Lakisha leaned back on a birthing bed, her limbs still shaking from hours of pushing, her hospital gown plastered against her sweaty skin. She fingered the mattress until she found the topsy-turvy doll, now frayed and stained from years of loving. She pressed the raggedy treasure to her face, inhaling a memory—the scent of her mother. All that remained of Maizy was an image; soft skin over fragile bones, and track-marked arms that could hold you in a way that made everything bad in the world disappear.

The door swung open and banged on a rubber stopper. "You should've called me when you went into labor!" Aunt Dottie plowed into the room, her black umbrella trailing raindrops as it bounced against wide hips. "Damn Newark traffic; it's a mess. Too bad your Grandma Louema didn't live to see this—crazy about babies she was...even though you are way too young!" She shook herself, sending a small shower onto the speckled linoleum.

Dottie's meaty body twisted around taking in the monitors and bloodied sheets peeking out of a laundry bin. "You all done? Where..." Dottie took a few steps toward a nurse who was moving back and forth between two pieces of equipment that resembled giant toaster ovens. Then she lifted a palm to her hazelnut cheek. "Lord!"

"I had twins. It's all right, Auntie."

"Uh, oh. This is not good!"

Dottie had a knack for turning situations sour; like her fat fists perpetually clutched lemons, and she stood ready to juice away anything sweet. The obstetrician who had delivered the babies entered the room, trailed by a few others in white lab coats who looked like students. The small group peered over the nurse's shoulder as she worked. Their murmurings registered surprise, and a few glanced at Lakisha with wide-eyes before leaving.

"What is it?" Lakisha's throat was parched, her voice gravel. She felt a wave of heat rise in her chest. "What's wrong?" Maybe this time, Dottie was right. She hadn't heard anything about the second baby other than that it was a girl—hadn't even seen her. Did she have two heads? Eleven toes? A birthmark that looked like Jesus on her forehead? The first girl had a mark above her right cheek that resembled a half-moon. Lakisha hoped it wouldn't make her ugly. But whatever was going on with the second one had to be even worse. "Auntie, bring me that baby you're looking at!"

Dottie was usually the one who did the bossing, but this time she obeyed. Lakisha stared down at the small bundle. She unwrapped the infant and blinked several times, hoping to see something different. It couldn't be…this had to be a mistake. She shoved it back into Dottie's arms.

"Just a little surprise from the gene pool," explained the nurse. "Most of us got some mix of blood. Blond hair can be pretty."

Lakisha shook her head, trying to dismiss the truth that now clawed its way up into her throat. "There's no way that one—"

"Don't worry about the coloring. Babies can change—"

Lakisha stiffened. Her panicked eyes gripped the nurse, "No, no! That one's not mine!" She paused for a beat, "The other one either!" She turned to Aunt Dottie, "You understand what's happened, right? You have to help me! If they're a set, I can't keep them—they can't be mine! They can't be…oh, Theo." She collapsed into the mattress.

PART ONE
The Color of Loss

Thirteen Years Later:
Jasmine

Outside the barred window, a teenage boy called to his friend on the street and an ambulance siren wailed. Jasmine peeked out through the slatted blinds to make sure no one on her block was bleeding. It was Sunday morning, Jasmine's favorite time of the week. She found her foster mom, Treasure, in the kitchen, bent over a skillet of frying bacon and eggs. The steam rose up from the wide pan, making Treasure's heart-shaped face dewy.

"I was motivated today," Treasure said pointing to the flour, buttermilk, and other ingredients that sat on the counter next to a large wooden board. "Go ahead and wash your hands, roll up your sleeves, and get started on the biscuits. You remember the recipe?"

"Uh, you taught me to multiply using it, remember?" Then she put a hand on her hip and began wagging an index finger through the air in mock imitation of her mother. "Let's double the recipe! Two cups of flour become four, one teaspoon of salt becomes...hmmm...what is it?"

Grabbing the dishtowel tucked into the top of her sweatpants, Treasure swiped at Jasmine's legs and laughed. "Well I'm glad you listen to some of what I say. Now before you get started, come on over here and give me a hug. Since I picked up more night-shifts, I feel like I barely see you. Tell me, what's been going on?"

Jasmine wrapped her arms around Treasure's solid center and breathed in the sleepy smell of laundered bed sheets and coconut hair cream. Beneath that was the sterile scent of antiseptic that followed Treasure home from the hospital, reminding Jasmine that her mother would soon have to return to her patients. Her grip tightened.

Before Jasmine could answer, William shuffled into the room, scowling. Outside the kitchen window a bank of clouds drifted by, eclipsing the sunlight that had been dancing on the stained-glass ornaments that lined the sill. "I don't know why you two get up so early when you could sleep late."

Jasmine turned her back to avoid his gaze. Her stomach clenched. She heard William muttering endearments to Treasure and flinched at the sound of his loud pucker when they kissed. Then he was approaching. She realized there were things on the counter that needed to be put away and got busy.

"Good morning, Jasmine."

"Morning." She sensed him right behind her, but kept her face buried in the open refrigerator. She used to let him kiss her, but that was before everything changed; back when Treasure only had day-shifts and William still had his job working security at the Newark jail. It was before her feelings about William had become such a mess. That was back when her biggest concerns were remembering to wear her Nikes on gym day and figuring out why Bryanna invited only Crystal to go with her to shop for new jeans at the Livingston Mall. If only she had an invisibility cloak like Dumbledore had given to Harry Potter during his first year at Hogwarts. Then she'd have the power to disappear.

Once William was back at Treasure's side discussing the day, Jasmine shoved the baking sheet into the wall oven, set the timer, and slipped back to her bedroom. She tossed herself on the mattress and stared up at a crack in the plaster that spread like a vine across the ceiling and down the side wall, waiting for her heartbeat to steady.

Yesterday, she'd gone to her after-school girls' club. She'd joined because the end of year trip was to Great Adventure, but yesterday's presentation made her tremble. She thought of leaving, but what if she missed something important: a suggestion, an explanation, a way to make it stop? The speaker wore a thin, creamy sweater with flared sleeves, and when she lifted her arms up, her delicate shoulders seemed to sprout wings. "Your body, your choice!" she declared. "You decide who touches you, no one else!"

Jasmine wanted to stand up and shout, *Amen*, like folks did at church.

"If it doesn't feel right, tell someone. Call us. We're here to help you."

Some of the girls looked embarrassed and squirmed against the ancient wooden chairs and chewing gum-stained floor-tiles. The angel-woman handed each of them a pamphlet with her business card stapled to the back. She was a social worker. But Jasmine already had one of those. In fact, she'd had a string of them through the years, and she didn't know if she wanted to start up with a new one. *Is it really my body, my choice?*

Her mind drifted to her favorite fantasy: she and Treasure living on their own. They'd own a new brick townhouse in downtown Newark, with two bedrooms and a little spare room where she and Treasure would make crafts, paint, and write poetry. The house would have wide windows facing south, making their lucky bamboo and spider plants flourish. Freed from William and his pet allergies, they'd adopt two cats: an orange and white calico, and a Bengal that looked like a small leopard.

Her best friend, Marleeka, would live next door, and the corner house would be home to the cute guy she'd met on the city bus who wore a fake tiger's tooth around his neck, a jaguar belt buckle, and dreadlocks. He said his name was Drake and gave her an easy way of remembering it, "Dimples, Dreads, Drake."

After school, she and Drake would sit on her front stoop telling stories, and when daylight faded, they'd walk the streets with their hands tucked around each other, feeling safe in the darkness. They'd join a group bathed in lamplight, and Jasmine would summon her courage. There, she'd speak the poetry of pain that echoed in her bones, and for a few moments she'd feel weightless. Drake's soft lips would brush against hers, making her spirit want to twist with his in the moonlit sky.

Feeling inspired, she opened the bottom drawer of her desk, and tugged a spiral notebook from underneath a short stack of concert programs from the years she spent in the Pentecostal church choir. Leafing through pages stiff with ink, Jasmine looked over the poem she had written the previous night:

> *You come to my bed,*
> *Eyes fierce in your head.*
> *Ash taste, cold lips,*
> *Liquor-stink mouth, on my hips.*
> *With stiff limbs I push—*
> *I push, prod, and plead.*
> *But I know that don't matter*
> *When you got your need.*
> *Broken glass promises litter the floor,*
> *Cutting my feet as I flee for the door.*
> *But your fingers they fan, they fumble—*
> *Finally fuck.*
> *You're supposed to be Dad?*
> *Shit foster-family luck!*

It wasn't a poem she would share, at least not now while she lived with William, but it still felt good writing it. She had more than one book packed with poems about things she'd seen, troubles she'd narrowly avoided, and others she hadn't. She sat for several minutes with the notebook open and a pen poised over the paper.

> *What to do?*
> *Who to tell?*

What will happen?
Life in Hell?
Where to turn?
Punishment paid?
If my lips part the truth,
What could possibly come after that?
will I end...
In the grave?

She closed the book and buried it in the back corner of the drawer. Then she curled up on the lime-green beanbag chair that sat beneath the small room's only window. Opening her dog-eared copy of *Harry Potter and the Sorcerer's Stone,* Jasmine began reading it again from the beginning, anticipating the moment of Harry's release from the cupboard beneath the staircase.

Two weeks later, Jasmine sat on the living room sofa next to Miss Darlene, her latest Family Services social worker. Jasmine didn't know why, but she had never been officially adopted. A prior case worker had let slip that she suspected money had something to do with it. "It wouldn't take much for your foster parents to complete the adoption, but then they'd lose the monthly board payment," she'd said. "This should've been caught years ago." Though she too had been transferred before the adoption was finalized.

Miss Darlene, who was stuffed into her too-tight polyester pantsuit and black Life Stride flats, reminded Jasmine of a sausage. Her hair was cut in a short practical pixie, similar to Treasure's, but she had some blonde highlights tossed in. Jasmine fingered one of her own shoulder-length locks, still straight from the last time Treasure had ironed it.

Jasmine loved spending time with Treasure, even now that she had turned thirteen. When Treasure was getting ready to go out, she'd always invite Jasmine into the bathroom, so she could learn how to properly style a human-hair wig and apply eye shadow and liner, and she still drove Jasmine to the Irvington Library every other Sunday so that she could pick out some new books to supplement what Treasure called her *comfort reading* of Harry Potter.

Treasure was in her room preparing for her night shift, and William would be home any minute. She'd have to spend the night alone with him. There was no telling what his mood might be or if he'd begin downing his Jack Daniel's, or if anything else might—

"Jasmine, I'm gonna get going." Miss Darlene gathered her clipboard and folder and placed them in her briefcase. She stood up, but then paused.

With eyes fixed on the banged-up wood coffee table, Jasmine knocked at the side of her head with her fist, as if that might force a decision.

"Honey, are you sure you're okay?" When there was no response, Miss Darlene sat back down and sighed. She scanned the apartment, looking from the living room decorated with framed Monet and Van Gogh posters, toward the well-stocked kitchen and two cozy bedrooms. Perhaps she was checking to see if Treasure was within earshot. "Jasmine, I know I'm kind of new, and we haven't spoken that many times, but if there's something you need to tell me, if something is going on that's upsetting you—we can talk about it."

Jasmine's mind travelled back to her days of innocence, before the earth seemed to tilt off its axis. She remembered a cloudless spring afternoon in Branch Brook Park, racing through the ball fields, zipping down the slide, and swinging across the jungle gym.

Later, she'd sat between Treasure and William, eating a tuna salad sandwich and babbling on and on about the latest *Clifford* book she was reading and how she wanted to get her own big red dog. She asked, "Do dogs really come in red? Because I never seen one."

They both giggled, leaned in on either side of her and gave her a squeeze, saying she was the tuna in their sandwich and they were the bread.

"We'll have to keep our eyes peeled for some red dogs—see if we can find one. Meantime you keep reading," Treasure had said. "There's nothing in the world that's more important than learning."

But now she was thinking that there *were* things that were more important, things that Treasure wasn't paying attention to. If she had been home more, she might have noticed.

Jasmine brought her mind back to the social worker sitting next to her. She kept her knuckles moving against her head, but still couldn't find the words. The night-time visits had been going on for well over a year. She had thought about telling someone so many times, but in the end, had always decided against it. What if the social worker thought it was her fault? More than once, Treasure had vetoed her choice of tops at the mall saying, *you don't want boys to think you're looking for something.* What if Treasure blamed her? There was something else too; something that made her cringe and feel disgusted with herself. Sometimes…once he was touching her…her body would…respond. When she thought of this, her hands would ball into fists and start punishing her flesh for its betrayal. *Maybe it is my fault.*

Still, the angel-woman at the girls' group said she should always be able to say no. She'd told them that adults have more power than teens, and that this inequity means it's wrong for adults to touch them, even if their bodies were developing. According to her, what William did was a crime. Would they send him to jail or at least make him leave the apartment? Treasure would be devastated. She knew Treasure loved her, but the thing was—she loved William too.

Miss Darlene cleared her throat. "Well, I have to get going. I guess we can discuss it next time." That's what the case worker said, but still she stayed glued to her seat, staring straight ahead at the off-white paint on the walls and the beige carpet.

"Sometimes he hurts me."

"Who hurts you?" Miss Darlene asked, and after a few beats added, "I can't help you if you don't tell me who."

"William." Her voice was so soft, Miss Darlene leaned in to hear it.

"William? You mean some boy named William…or…?"

Jasmine started to tear up. "I mean…my daddy."

The case worker exhaled like she was blowing out candles. She glanced at her watch. "I'm glad you told me. Here is what's gonna happen…" her eyes darted around like she herself wasn't sure, then she called, "Treasure!"

Jasmine jerked like she'd just touched a live wire.

Miss Darlene seemed not to notice. "Jasmine and I are heading into her room for some girl talk. Just wanted you to know I'm still here."

"Okay!" Treasure's voice sang out.

Jasmine crumpled as she tried to breathe.

"Did you think we were all gonna talk together? I'm smarter than that! Come on." She led Jasmine into the second bedroom, sat down at the foot of the bed, and waited for Jasmine to join her. Jasmine plopped down at the opposite end and hugged her pillow. Being where everything had happened made her squirm.

"Normally we'd get out of the house to discuss this, but I'm short on time, so we'll bend the rules a bit. You don't mind, right?"

Jasmine shrugged and fidgeted. Her eyes latched onto the buttons of Miss Darlene's blouse that looked like they were about to pop off. Did she have a choice?

"So, tell me, how does William hurt you?"

"He…he comes in sometimes at night, when my mom is at work." It was all too humiliating. How could she speak it?

"And what does he do in your room…at night?"

Jasmine's head and neck began to shake, and soon her whole torso was trembling. "It started as just touching me over my pajamas. Then it got worse…he started…." Her face fell into her hands.

"I know this is upsetting. If you want, you can just point with your finger at where he touched you or...." Miss Darlene looked around the small room. "Do you have a doll?"

Jasmine pulled open her closet door. Tossing things around at the bottom, she came up holding a dark-skinned Barbie wearing Capri pants and a sleeveless top.

"Perfect! Let me have her. Okay, so let's pretend that this doll is you. Can you point to where William touched you?"

Jasmine rolled her eyes.

"I know this may seem babyish, but even for teens like you, it can help because you don't have to say the words. Ready? So where did he touch you?"

Jasmine took the doll and stroked its nylon hair, like she was trying to prepare her plastic friend for what was to come. She put fingers on the doll's breasts, and then spread the doll's legs and pointed.

"Did you always have on clothing?"

Jasmine shook her head.

"So, he touched you...."

Jasmine was busy stripping the doll down and running her fingers roughly over the dolls naked body.

"And did he put anything...I'm sorry to have to ask you this, but did he put anything inside you? Did he put anything in your mouth, your vagina, anywhere else?"

Something caught at the back of Jasmine's throat and emotion puddled in her eyes. "His penis..." she pointed to the doll's mouth. "His fingers..." she spread the doll's legs wide and tapped at the space between them.

Miss Darlene was blowing out more invisible candles, and then looked right and left while batting her fan of fake lashes. "Honey, I know this is difficult, but I have to ask. Did he do anything else? You know, like put his penis inside of you?"

Jasmine felt her cheeks turn to ripe apples. The rims around her chestnut eyes felt swollen and too weak to contain her tears.

"I'm so sorry to make you talk about it, but it's important that I know… everything."

"He didn't do none of that." She focused on the floor, hoping the questioning was over.

"Okay, thank heaven for small things. Honey, you did the right thing by telling me. It was absolutely the best thing you could have done." She gave Jasmine's shoulder a few soft pats. "That's all I need to know for now. The rest we'll hear about when the prosecutor gets involved." Miss Darlene stood up and straightened her too-tight suit.

"Prosecutor?"

The case worker's hand waved dismissively. "Don't worry about it. It'll all be quick," and then she was on her phone. She cancelled her next appointment. Then there were several calls that had to do with a "possible need for a short-term placement." Jasmine's heart beat out a prayer—*let that be for someone else and not me.* Finally, there was a conversation with the police department requesting two officers. *Shit! Are they going to arrest William?* Her mind raced, and she felt as if her stomach and intestines had knit themselves together. She wished she could shrink down into something tiny—something small enough to hide away in a floorboard, insignificant enough to not be blamed.

She curled up on the bed, still clutching the pillow. Then the front door banged open and William's whistling snaked through the apartment. "What's gonna happen now?" She felt her body heat up, like it was on fire, and was gripped with a desire to run away, but where could she go? The danger was everywhere: in the police car that was surely on its way to her home, in the kitchen where William was moving pots around, in the other bedroom where Treasure would be changing into medical scrubs for her night-shift at the hospital, and even in her own gut that had so misjudged the world.

"You're just gonna stay right where you are. I'm going to fill out some paperwork in the living room and then speak with your foster parents."

"You have to do that?"

Miss Darlene cast an apologetic look in her direction and left.

Jasmine wasn't someone who prayed, even on those Sundays when Treasure dragged them to church, but today was different. She whispered, "God, please get me through this mess and out the other side. Make William stop doing what he's doing, and make Mama not blame me. Please God, make her understand."

She tried to distract herself by thinking about Drake. If he were her boyfriend, he'd come by tonight and they'd go for a walk. He'd stand with her in the alleyway and put his arms around her, he'd pledge to take care of her and always be there. He'd take a bandana from his pocket, a white one that stood for peace or something, and he'd use it to wipe her cheeks dry. Together they'd head to the poets' corner, and when it was her turn, she'd tell her tale, each word slicing the night like a sharpened blade. Windows would open, a crowd would grow, and cars would stop, their drivers drawn to her like metal to magnet. And then the world would have a sense, just the tiniest nugget of knowledge about her. And if that happened… what then?

The doorbell chimed, and she heard Miss Darlene's flat-footed steps. Jasmine moved to the bedroom door and heard the case worker tell William that they all needed to speak.

"Why are the cops here?" William sounded irritated.

Jasmine peeked into the living room and caught a glimpse of William's face. His outrage at not being the one in charge inside his own home simmered in his eyes.

"It's just a precaution, to make sure we stay safe, that's all."

Jasmine opened the door a little wider. Her confidence in Miss Darlene was fading fast. Jasmine heard William stomp through the apartment to get Treasure, and the officers questioned Miss Darlene. "Where's the girl? County shelter or you got her a placement?"

"She's right in the bedroom."

Jasmine pulled herself back into the room but left the door ajar. She didn't want the police officers seeing her and understanding that it was her who had summoned them, her who had been…what was the right word…molested?

"No shit?" the deep voice sounded annoyed.

"I'm gonna get the mom to sign a Case Plan," said Miss Darlene. "Dad will have to have no contact until we get a court order, investigate, and sort it all out. I don't think it'll be a problem. Mom seems pretty committed."

"The kid shouldn't be here."

Jasmine couldn't stop herself from taking another peek. The officer speaking was pale, and his hair was cut too short. A sea of freckles spread over his cheekbones and onto the bridge of his nose. The other was darker and spoke with a mild Spanish accent.

"Well, you take my case load and see what it's like before you…oh, here are Treasure and William, let's all sit down."

Jasmine's parents sat together on the sofa, holding hands like they always did, William fingering the carved gold ring on Treasure's left hand. His jeans were ironed, and his cotton sweater blanketed his large middle. Treasure leaned against him, a crease forming between her pretty eyes as she tried to take in the social worker's words.

Jasmine only half listened to what Miss Darlene was saying. It was so embarrassing, she felt like there were roaches crawling on her skin. She ran her hands over her arms just to make sure there was nothing there, and then began wringing her hands in a frantic effort to stay calm. Was she crazy? It had all become such a mess: feeling out of control, hating everything…even liking some of the touching. That was the worst part! "I hate myself; this was all a mistake," she muttered. She began to hit her own shoulders, chest, and head.

Treasure's voice was shrill as she posed questions to William that were punctuated with the high-pitched disbelief usually reserved for the worst offenses, like when Jasmine accidentally ran the garbage disposal with a fork in it or tossed Treasure's new clothes in the garbage because they were in a bag that looked like trash. Meanwhile Jasmine's fist pounded away, and she felt a small welt forming near her temple.

"That girl is fucking nuts!" William's voice echoed through the apartment. "We've been married for twenty years…you're gonna take her word over mine!"

"Shit!" Jasmine began using both hands against her head and cheeks. "Why did I do this? Why? Why? Why?" Each whispered word in rhythm with a punch.

It became difficult to hear what the case worker was saying because Treasure and William were shouting at each other.

"You did this? While I was at work!"

"If you were ever home at night, you'd know that I didn't do it! But you're always out!"

"Out earning a living—"

"That's what you say—"

"You think I'm not? What's wrong with you? What did you do that made her say these things? You must have done something!"

"I didn't do nothing! And anyway," he said, "she's not even really our daughter!" William's final declaration rang through the now still air. Jasmine felt like something had rammed into her gut. Her heart felt as big as a frying pan, and it pounded her ribcage.

Miss Darlene was the first to break the silence. "This is what's going to happen; there's going to be an investigation into the allegations, and we'll need William to leave the home. Treasure, you'll have to sign a legal document stating that you'll permit no contact whatsoever between them. That includes phone and text."

"What? Ain't no *way* I'm leaving my house—"

"I can watch her," Treasure interrupted. "She can sleep with me, and William can sleep in the other room. I'll work something out to get a day shift, and I'll get rid of my second job. I can make it happen."

"I know that's what you'd like, but that's not our procedure."

"That's not your *procedure*? Where am I supposed to go? That little shit—let's get her out here!"

Jasmine's body began to shake so fiercely, she couldn't even hit herself. She dropped down on the floor and curled up with her arms wrapped around her head, as if bracing for the ceiling to collapse or an enemy bomb to fall from the sky.

"Mr. Moore, I actually need to take Jasmine to the hospital now for an exam. What happens after that is up to you two. I can bring her back here—if you'll be out."

"And if I'm still here?"

"Well, then I'll have to take her somewhere else."

"Somewhere else?" Treasure's usually solid voice quivered.

"A temporary placement."

"Do that then! Go ahead and do that! What the f…is this justice?" His rage seemed to shake the walls of Jasmine's chest.

"These are the rules, Mr. Moore. I've actually already bent them a bit. I should have immediately taken her to another placement, but I didn't think…well…it's up to you both."

Jasmine pressed her whole body against the door, trying to send her embrace to Treasure, willing her to send her husband away. Jasmine now saw that she'd be punished for this—for somehow allowing it, and then for speaking about it to the case worker. She felt betrayed by her own stupidity, her own inability to see how this would all turn out.

Everything had started when William lost his job—she must have been eleven. After that something had twisted inside of him; some piece of grownup common sense had gone missing. Before William stopped working, Jasmine felt content with her life, lucky to have two parents when most of her friends only had their moms or grandmas. Now she thought the opposite was true. Perhaps she really was cursed. "Please, God, help me. I know I shouldn't have let him do it, but please...please don't let them take me. Please have Treasure put him out."

The case worker pressed the door open. "Get your jacket, sweetie. We need to get going."

Jasmine stared at her. There was no way she was going. There was no way she'd leave Treasure. This was her home too, her bedroom, her life. Her books were stacked on top of the desk; her clothes were neatly folded in the dresser and hung in the closet. Treasure had bought her a new indigo dress and matching sweater to wear to church, and they had shopped together for the stack-heeled boots that she had begged for and finally received only after promising to walk carefully in them so as not to *break her neck*. They had never even left the box.

Maybe she could just say she made it all up, that it was to get attention, that she had had a moment of insanity. Surely, she had lost her mind— someone in the apartment had!

"We have to do this to keep you safe until things are all sorted out. Come on now. Is this your jacket?" Miss Darlene grabbed a zip-up that lay on the bed and stroked Jasmine's back. "Come on, honey. We need to get going."

Jasmine took a few steps out of her room, and her eyes searched out Treasure. "Mama, please, I don't wanna go with her."

The worker gave her a gentle nudge.

"Mama, please! What did I do? You're gonna let them take me?"

William had already turned away, but not her mother. Treasure's cheeks were moist, her eyes confused. She was moving her lips like she had something to say, but no words were coming out. Miss Darlene nodded in the direction of the police officers and the two came up alongside Jasmine and guided her toward the front door.

When they reached the entryway, Jasmine tried to drop to the floor, but the officers held her aloft and carried her forward, her legs bicycling in the air. She shot out her feet and braced them against the doorframe. "Mama! Don't let them take me away! Why are you doing this?" Her voice was so gravelly that she hardly recognized it as her own. Her wild eyes latched onto her mother's, and she saw anguish and disbelief.

A moment later, the strong men at her sides maneuvered her over the threshold as she writhed and pleaded in their arms. Her mother's pitiful words, "I'm sorry, baby. I'm so sorry," hung in the dead air.

"We'll have to drive her," one of the officers snapped at Miss Darlene.

In the back seat of the police car she beat her fists into her thighs, her arms, the sides of her head. A knock on the window brought her back to her senses. It was Treasure. Jasmine raised a hopeful face.

The window was lowered a few inches and through the opening, Treasure slid Jasmine's copy of Harry Potter. "I thought you might need this," she muttered. "I'm gonna do my best to get you back." Jasmine opened her mouth to respond, but before she could form any words, the window went back up. She hugged the book to her chest as the car pulled away from the curb, taking her away from both abuse and love, and the only home she had ever known.

Tessa

Outside the leaded-glass window, a flock of starlings swirled and pulsed through the sky, landed on the giant sycamore that stood vigil over the backyard, and then looped away in a gyrating cloud. Tessa peeked out through the white wooden blinds, trying to catch a glimpse of the birds before they moved on. It was Sunday morning, Tessa's favorite time of the week, mainly because she could sleep in and not have to race off to school or gymnastics. She trotted down the staircase, and found her mother, Alice, bent over the kitchen island with sections of the *New York Times* strewn before her. From her sweaty tank top, Tessa knew that she'd already been to hot yoga. Riley, their aging Golden-Doodle, came up and pushed her silky face against Tessa's knees while Tessa reached over and gave her a rub.

Her mother looked up. "Hey Tess, how'd you sleep? I was just about to make French toast." Her mother flashed a wide smile in her direction. "Oh, wait, here's Daddy, the French Toast King! Hey, Daddy, want to make some breakfast with Tessa?"

Her father, Rob, came into the kitchen in sweat pants and a fraying plaid button down. His bright eyes glinted beneath a furrowed-graying brow. "I'll only do it if I flip and you dip."

"Ugh!"

"What's the matter? You don't like that idea?"

Tessa rolled her eyes. "Uh, I liked it when I was five."

"Thirteen...five...they're just numbers." He tickled Tessa's armpit, which made her screech. "What? I thought I saw something up there."

"Get away!" she said, though she didn't mean it. She pulled ingredients from the refrigerator and began cracking eggs into a glass bowl on the granite counter. When she leaned over to get a fork from the drawer, one of her long, honey curls touched down in the bowl. She held the lock away from her body as she moved over to rinse it in the sink.

"How many times do I have to tell you to pull your hair back when you're around food? Jesus, I find your hair everywhere!" Her mom huffed.

"Okay, okay!" Tessa twisted her mane into a bun and went back to work.

"Tessa, what do you have planned for today?" Her mother didn't wait for a response. "I was thinking we should look over the info about the Independent School Entrance Exam and you should take a sample test. Also, you'll be travelling next weekend for gymnastics, so get your long-term assignments finished up. Oh! And start working on the application essays for Newark Academy, Montclair Kimberley, and Haverford."

Tessa let her mother speak but took in none of it. She'd repeat it all again anyway, every day in fact, until Tessa finished all the things on her mother's long *have-to-do* list. Her mind was elsewhere, reviewing the new choreography from her tumbling coach. Since regionals were coming up, he said she needed to step it up, so he'd inserted a new tumbling run: connecting saltos and a twisting front layout. As the coated bread sizzled in the pan, Tessa heard the music in her head and envisioned each movement. The routine would end with her heart and palms reaching skyward. Then her eye would catch Parker Luis standing in the audience with the Eastern Champions boys' team. There he'd be, bulging biceps beating out applause. For a moment their eyes would meet, he'd nod and mouth, "Yes." Maybe he'd even speak with her after the meet.

In reality, she'd only seen Parker once, from a distance, when she had been forced by her coach to volunteer at a boys' meet. But ever since his stellar pommel-horse routine, the eleventh-grade gymnast who had a national ranking, a sculpted body, and smoldering-brown eyes had made regular appearances in her visions of gymnastics glory.

"Tessa, it's burning!"

"Oh!" She dug underneath the charring bread with a spatula, tossed in another pat of butter, and flipped it over. Then she lowered the flame and decided she better focus on the frying pan.

When breakfast was ready, Tessa and her parents slid into wooden chairs around an antique carved table that had been her grandmother's. Orange juice glasses glinted in the morning light flooding in through a picture window that faced the deep yard. Tessa had to shift her seat toward her dad to keep the sun out of her eyes.

She sprinkled cinnamon on her toast and then shook the last few drops of maple syrup out of a crusty bottle. "I'll get more."

"Try one of the top two shelves." Her mother spread raspberry jam across her own toast, while her father was scraping boysenberry blobs out of a wide-mouthed jar.

Tessa opened the pantry door and stepped inside. The shelves were packed from Alice's many shopping expeditions. Tessa moved bottles of teriyaki sauce and cans of crushed tomatoes, jars of Thai simmer sauce and outdated bottles of catsup. She lifted her palms in the air as if asking the kitchen gods where her mother had hidden the syrup. There was no way they'd run out—they never ran out of anything. Her mother's need to keep their cupboards fully stocked for the next hurricane or an unanticipated apocalypse, had become a running joke between Tessa and her older sister, Lily. Dealing with their mother's perpetual anxiety was one of the few things around which they bonded. She shifted a stack of canned tuna and discovered the three unopened bottles of syrup.

When she came back to the table, her father's eyeglasses were perched on the edge of his slender nose, and he held a pen over scrap paper. "When you're finished eating, maybe we could make a schedule for your day, Tess, just to help you stay on top of things."

"Okaaaaay, I guess." After fifteen minutes of his help—ten minutes more than she felt she needed, Tessa pushed herself away from the table. "I think I've got it Dad, really."

She managed to reach the foot of the staircase before her mother's voice trailed after her, "Don't forget to work on those high school essays! Maybe do that first."

"All right! All right! I'll write those stupid essays." That last part, mumbled under her breath. Tessa trudged up the stairs with Riley at her heels and threw herself across the wide bed that jutted into the center of her room. She flipped open her MacBook and clicked on the Haverford Academy Application. "Students and their families choose Haverford Academy for a variety of reasons. What makes Haverford the school for you, and what do you hope to gain from a Haverford education?" Tessa moaned. She grabbed a pad from the top of her desk and drew a line down the center of a blank page. On the top of one column, she wrote *Truth*, and on the other, *Lies*.

On the *Truth* side she scribbled:

Lily went to Haverford

Haverford helped get Lily into Cornell and then medical school, and I want to go to Cornell and then medical school. After a brief pause, she corrected the last sentence, so it read, *and my parents want me to go to Cornell and then medical school just like Lily and my father.*

My parents are afraid I'll get jumped if I stay in public school because my mother was mugged when she went to high school in the Bronx. Maplewood, New Jersey, isn't The Grand Concourse, but there's no arguing with my mother and her crazy worries.

My parents don't think my friends are hard workers. They want me to be surrounded by committed students, scholars, blah, blah, blah.

I'd prefer a school that would be flexible when it comes to missing classes before big meets or for team travel.

I want my parents to be happy.

In the *Lies* column she wrote:

I want to learn with other very motivated students.

I want to study with the best teachers and have the most challenging classes.

I want to have the individualized attention that is only available in a small college prep school.

I want to go to a high school that has been able to get students into top colleges. Okay, maybe that belonged in the *Truth* column.

She rolled over on her side, distracted for a few moments by the shelves packed with books. Her mother kept thinning the collection by taking stacks of children's paperbacks and picture books to the Turning Point Community Center in Irvington. The only books Tessa refused to part with were anything by Dr. Seuss, the *Pretty Little Liars* series, and everything *Harry Potter.* Reading *Harry Potter* somehow relieved her stress, so by this point in eighth grade, the series was tattered from use. She was nearing the end of the seventh book—for the fifth time. She tugged the fat volume from its place on the shelf and read a few pages, just long enough to see Harry, Ron, and Hermione achieve a momentary reprieve from *He Who Must Not Be Named.*

After an hour, she heard her mom's voice calling from the bottom of the stairs, "Tessa! Why don't you come down and we can work on those essays together?"

Tessa sighed. "Okay, coming...."

Walking into the kitchen, Tessa rubbed her hands together as if spreading gymnastics chalk before mounting the balance beam. Her mother had pulled her mud-colored hair into a ponytail, and her angular features reflected the glow of her laptop as she tapped away, finishing up what looked to be a legal brief.

Tessa sometimes felt like an outsider in her family, like she was a piece of clay that they wanted to push and prod into a specific shape, but it was a form that just wouldn't hold. She looked different from them: blonde curls versus silky brown, small-boned and compact versus long-limbed and sturdy. Away from them, her personality bubbled like a shaken soda bottle ready to burst, but with her parents and sister she seemed to go flat. She wanted to be like them, wanted to please them, wanted to want what they wanted.

When she was with her friends, Maritza or Emily or Shantel, she felt free to speak her mind, write absurd rap songs, dance hip hop, and read novels that weren't on her mother's list of *Great Books*. After discovering that list last year, her mother had decided that every month, she and Tessa would read and discuss one masterpiece. At that pace, the two would have completed the entire list before Tessa left for college. It didn't matter to Alice that Edith Wharton, Herman Melville, and Fyodor Dostoyevsky were not exactly beach reads. Tessa hoped her mother would just give up on the idea like she had with her plan to have Rob teach her all of high school biology over the summer before eighth grade.

Alice saved the document she had up on the screen.

"Want to keep working? We could do this later." It was worth a try.

"No, no, that's okay." Her mother smiled, "It's not due tomorrow."

"Um, neither are these application essays."

Her mother tossed her a critical look, and they got down to work.

A week later, Tessa entered the cavernous Atlantic Coast Gym for the regional meet. The drive had taken close to an hour, and her limbs felt stiff from sitting. Competing away from home was always uncomfortable at first, as if she were a chef being asked to reproduce her greatest recipes in someone else's kitchen. But what often unnerved her even more was the smell of a new gym. Sometimes the air would be thick with pine cleaner, a scent that made her run for the bathroom to vomit. In truth, on these high-pressure days, she often found herself praying to the porcelain gods before the first event, regardless of how the gym smelled. Today proved no different.

Once rid of her breakfast, Tessa joined her teammates and felt more relaxed. They all wore shiny royal blue leotards with tiny rhinestones sweeping in a wave from their right shoulders to the left side of their rib cages. After some warm-up and practice tumbling runs, Tessa was still nervous, but ready and hopeful even, that she might medal in floor or vault.

"God, grant me strength, grace, and courage. I'm grateful for your gifts," she whispered into the air when it was her turn on floor. She wanted all the help she could get. She knew that her parents were in the stands, and even Lily had used one of her precious days off from her dermatology residency to attend. She wasn't quite sure if Lily's presence felt encouraging or just added pressure—one more person to try to please.

As she stood near the corner of the mat, waiting for her music to begin, she heard her mom's voice, "Go, Tessa, you can do it!" and then Lily's voice echoed, "Go, Tessa!" She knew her dad was there too, sending her support.

Her first tumbling runs were smooth. She managed not to trip during any of the fast dance moves, and even finished the sequence on beat with the music. When it came time for her final tumbling series, she crossed the floor in a blur of tight flips, finishing with her connecting saltos and twisting front layout. The crowd was on its feet. Through the din of it all, she could almost make out her mom, dad, and Lily cheering. Sweat burned her eyes and applause vibrated in her chest as she floated back to her team. Coach embraced her and whispered, "Nice" in her ear. Coming from Coach, that was high praise.

The rest of the morning seemed to rocket by as Tessa moved through the rotation on balance beam, uneven bars, and vault. By lunchtime, she was in seventh place overall and leading the pack on vault. She made her obligatory jog over to her parents who stood at the corner of the stands, expectant smiles pinned to their faces.

Lily was glued to her iPhone, and only looked up from whatever she was reading when Tessa gave her arm a shove. "Sorry," she said. "I was trying to research something for a patient."

Tessa shrugged, "Whatever."

"Great job out there, though. You've gotten so much better since the last time I saw you!" Lily's perfect hair fell against her creamy cheek, irritating Tessa.

She tucked one of her stray curls back into her bun. "When was that? Three years ago?"

"Could be, but I don't think so. It was in that really big place—"

"They're all in really big places." Lily was so self-centered, as if the world revolved around her and her all-important residency.

"Right, but this one was, like…."

Her mother jumped in, "You were probably at regionals the year before last. They were held in Atlantic City. No need to argue."

Tessa's face contracted, "I'm not the one arguing."

"So, Tess," her father interjected, "when did they add that new ending to your floor routine? I really liked that. It reminded me of something that Aliya Mustafina used to do." He was trying to work his calming magic, and he was successful—sort of.

"I don't know, Dad. I have to get back now. Coach said you guys should buy raffles."

"Good luck, Sweetie! Finish strong!" Her mother shot a tense smile in her direction, and Tessa noticed she was picking nail polish off her thumb as she spoke. Walking back to the team she shook her limbs, trying to both loosen her muscles and shake off her mother's tense energy.

Tessa approached the final vault as a medal contender. It had been the meet of her season, of her year, of her life. She took several deep breaths as she approached the runway, preparing to do her most challenging vault, the Pike Yurchenko. She waited for the judge's signal. Her sprint was intense as her eyes bore into her goal: the vault itself. She did a quick round-off, landed with her feet on the center of the springboard, and then propelled her body up into a back handspring off the vault. Once airborne, she did a pike flip and landed tentatively on two feet, with just the smallest wobble. Her palms reached for the sky, her back arched, and her smile, as wide as the horizon, lit the room.

She glanced around the gym in disbelief, and caught her mother's face, her mouth gaping in jubilant shock. Her father was there too, clapping furiously as his bushy brows lifted in delight. Even Lily looked happy. Tessa took a step toward her teammates and there was Coach, lifting her off her feet in a hug. There were two more gymnasts who would compete, but she had already scored high enough to secure her place on the podium. Their performances would determine only the shade of medal she'd wear around her neck. She had done it. For the first time in her life, she had medaled at regionals! Walking past her teammates, she hugged each one, while trying to slow her breathing.

An hour later she was standing on the podium with silver hanging from her neck. Her parents were taking photos while the sea of spectators clapped politely, and her teammates' parents whooped. Tessa touched the edge of the smooth metal at her heart.

She put her arms around the other medalists and smiled for the flashing cameras.

During the drive home, Emily texted, My parents are out in the city. Come ASAP!

OK, on my way ☺, she typed back. Her parents didn't even give her much of an argument since she swore that all her school work was done. "I need a mental break," she said, without mentioning that her friend's parents weren't home.

Emily, Shantel, and Maritza all met her at the door and ushered her to the finished basement. Tessa galloped down the steps, feeling right at home. She'd played Candyland and Apples to Apples in this room, she'd built tents using folding chairs and blankets, and even watched her first R-rated movie here during a sleepover in sixth grade. But today, it looked as if there would be another first. Laid out on what used to be a Lego building table was a giant bottle of *Grey Goose Vodka*, a stack of red plastic cups, and a bag of Trader Joe's corn chips.

"We're having a party!" said Emily, and the other girls shrieked.

Tessa sat down on the tan Berber carpet with her friends and took in the spread on the table. "Em, won't your parents notice we drank some?"

Emily poured them each a generous portion of thick, clear liquid. "My parents race through these bottles, and they're always accusing each other of drinking too much. Even if they're suspicious, they'll just blame each other."

All the girls laughed, but a sadness tinged Emily's words, and Tessa's concern didn't wane until a few minutes after she'd drained her first inch of vodka. Over the course of a few hours, the girls downed several shots until they were laying on the floor convulsing in laughter, and the room was spinning. Tessa felt free, released from all the stress of her life, her mother's long lists. Why hadn't she thought of trying alcohol sooner? Sure, it burned and tasted disgusting, but then there was a warm feeling, like a blanket covering up your insides, and finally an escape.

By the time Maritza's mom showed up to drive Tessa and Maritza home, the blissful feeling seemed to have peaked, and in its place was a waving nausea that was made worse by the car's movement. The world around Tessa was turning, and not in a good way.

She managed to make it to her door and used the key hidden under the planter to let herself in. Her mother met her in the front hallway. "Hi, Tessa. Why don't you shower and then we can...." Her mother paused.

Tessa started toward the kitchen, but then made a beeline for the downstairs toilet and vomited.

Alice stood in the doorway. "Oh my God! What happened to you? You're drunk! What kind of stupid—"

"Calm down, Mom. I'm not."

"Don't you dare lie about it! You think I don't see it and smell it on you?"

Tessa rinsed out her mouth, washed her hands and assessed the damage to her clothing in the bathroom mirror, all the while trying to come up with a strategy that would keep her from being grounded. She glanced at Alice's outraged reflection, but then wondered out loud, "I thought Vodka had no smell?"

"You come home drunk out of your mind, and all you're thinking about is how I can tell? Where were Emily's parents? I'm calling them."

"No! Don't! I won't do it again!"

"Have you done this before?"

"No!"

"How do I know if you're telling the truth?"

"Mom, believe me."

"Do you know that addiction runs in your family? Of course you don't, how would you?" Alice wrung her hands, her eyes wide with worry. "This is too important."

"What are you talking about?"

Alice paced the kitchen, her brow knotted. She started mumbling to herself, and Tessa wondered if she was having some kind of breakdown. Finally, she said out loud, "I've got no choice." She took a deep breath, "You have your own family, and your family has addiction." She blurted this out, as if she could no longer contain it. "These things are hereditary, so you've got to be careful."

"What? Who in the family?"

"Your father. There's no easy way to say it. He was a drug addict."

Nothing was making any sense. Had someone dropped a pill in the Grey Goose? Had she fallen down a rabbit hole like *Alice in Wonderland*? "Dad was a drug addict?"

"Not Dad, your birth father."

"What?" Where was her father? Her mother had lost her mind. "What are you saying? Were you...sleeping around?"

"No!" Her mother circled the kitchen muttering and banging chairs. She'd never seen her like this. Where was her dad? For the first time in her life, Tessa felt afraid, both for herself and her mother. She pulled out her phone to text her father, but then her mother's words returned. "You were adopted. I wanted to wait for the right time to tell you, but now...there's no choice."

"Daddy! Where are you?" Tessa darted toward the stairway. "Mom's gone crazy!"

Alice followed her, "Tessa."

She took a step back. "I'll wait for Daddy."

Rob meandered down the steps and paused at the bottom.

"Mom says I'm adopted!" She confronted him.

Her mother defended herself, "I'm sorry, but she got drunk! I had to tell her about her biological father's addiction. What was I supposed to do?"

Rob looked hard at Alice, then turned gentle eyes toward Tessa, "Let's all take a minute and sit down." Once they were gathered at the kitchen table, he began. "We wanted to tell you before, but we were always worried about how you'd take it, so we were waiting for the right time...."

Her mother jumped in. "You see, I had trouble conceiving again after we had Lily. We went to doctors, had in vitro fertilization—do you know what that is?" She waved a hand, "It doesn't matter. Nothing worked, so we decided to adopt. Then came a long wait. We'd almost lost hope, but then we got the phone call—we got you." Her face glowed with the memory. "We were so happy—really, really happy. And we've been happy ever since."

The room felt thick with hidden toxins, things that could now contaminate their lives. "This isn't a joke, right?"

Rob shook his head.

"So, you're not my real parents." The shock of it gripped her. She felt like there was a ten-pound bell sitting on her chest. "Anything else you want to tell me? Who are my real parents, anyway?"

Alice hesitated. "Your birth mother...she had you at sixteen. The pregnancy was an accident. She was too young to care for you; she was just a child herself. She did the responsible thing and gave you up."

"What about my birth father?" she looked at her own father, hoping he'd say something positive.

"We really don't know anything—other than his drug use."

"So, you...you really aren't...?" The ground beneath her feet was shifting.

"Tessa," Her father leaned across the table and reached out a hand, as if he wanted to grab her words and toss them away. Finally, he just let his fingers fall to the table. "Tessa," his voice softened, "of course we're your parents. We always were your parents and will always be your parents. All this means is that we're not genetically your parents."

"That's why I don't look like anyone in the family, and that's why I don't feel like I fit in."

"What do you mean? You fit in perfectly with us, you've always had friends...." Her mother seemed to be searching for the right words, but Tessa wasn't listening.

"I don't get it. Why did you wait so long? I know other adopted kids, and they've known about it forever. Their parents weren't worried about how they'd take it. They just told them the truth. But now, to have to deal with it in eighth grade—what the fuck?" She looked at Alice. The heaviness in her chest was spreading throughout her body, and she wondered if she'd even be able to get up from the kitchen chair. Her heart was pounding as she slid away from the table.

"Let's talk about it; don't leave yet," said Alice.

"Unless you can remember something else about my birth parents, I'm done, just...done." Tessa managed to stand.

Her mother was on her feet, "Sweetie...."

Tessa shuffled out of the kitchen holding onto the walls for support.

In her room, she lay down, gripping the edges of the mattress. The room spun around her, making her dash again to the toilet. It all made sense now: why she wasn't good at art like Lily, why she didn't like puzzles like her parents, and why they always seemed to worry about her so much more than her sister. Did they think that at some point she was going to do some horrible thing like getting pregnant in high school? She thought about the people she knew who were adopted; there were a few girls from China in her grade, and that girl at the gym who was adopted from Ecuador. She didn't know anyone who had been born here and then put up for adoption and couldn't imagine why someone would go through an entire pregnancy and then give the baby away. She wished she could escape her anger. It was all so unfair. As she closed her eyes, Riley entered the room and lay down at the foot of her bed, offering her protection and uncomplicated love.

The next day at the gym, while standing on the balance beam, the dizziness returned. Tessa managed to steady herself by pulling in her core, but as she rose on the ball of her foot to do a 360-degree rotation, the entire gym seemed to spin with her and she fell. She hit her elbow on the smooth wood, and then landed on the mat with her arm tucked beneath her at an awkward angle.

Coach used one hand to lift her from the floor, then glanced at her arm. He shook his head, "Hmmm, looks broken, two places maybe. I'll call your mom."

Lakisha

By the time she was twenty-nine, Lakisha was sure of just a few things: her luck could change quicker than the weather, neither God nor Theo would save her, and she had to fiercely defend what she loved. Many days she'd fall into bed defeated. But there were other times when glimmers of hope slipped in through the cracks. Then she'd hear the echo of Grandma Louema's voice. Louema, having come of age on a farm near Macon, was fond of saying, "You gotta use what comes your way. After the storm, get outside and grab what's blown down. Bruised fruit bakes up into the sweetest of pies. In this here life, in the end—it's all for the good." Though at times, Aunt Dottie thought her a fool, Lakisha paid her no mind. She would use all of the bruised-up things she possessed: her body, her mind, her relationship...you name it, and create something worthy, something better than the shitty life she was born into.

She crouched over the small kitchen table with her pen poised above a black-and-white marble notebook. She had just a few minutes left to scratch out some lines.

Maizy smelled like cinnamon gum and talc, dandelions, books.
She hung with dealers and players, cheaters, crooks.
Track-marks, they marched up her wrist toward her heart,
Her leaving tore me up,

Lakisha's chest felt heavy, just like it did every time she thought about those few dream-like weeks with her mother, those tender days when she glimpsed what her life could have been. That same weight returned on sleepless nights, when she wrestled with dim memories of the infants, the daughters she'd abandoned. In those hours, sadness clung to her ribs, making it difficult to breathe. Time, that great healer of all things, seemed powerless when it came to the twins, for the older she grew, the more she understood mothering, and the more she understood, well—the worse she felt. She'd never written a poem about them, had never even spoken of them after the paperwork was signed. The reason was simple; no one but Dottie knew the truth.

"Mama?"

"What's up, TJ?" When he didn't answer, she stepped into the narrow living room. While five-year-old Devon practiced his letters at the coffee table, Theo Junior was splayed out on the lumpy sofa, his wiry arms thrown up over his head—his cheeks flushed. "What's up? You okay?"

"I don't feel good." He gave a small moan and rolled to face her. At eight-years-old, he was a clone of his father, from the subtle dimple in his chin right up to his honest eyes.

Lakisha perched next to him and touched his forehead. Her brow creased, "You have a fever. Hmm, maybe Aunt Dottie can sit with you tonight. I got my spoken-word slam."

"Don't call Aunt Dottie. She'll be huffing around. It ain't worth it."

Lakisha smiled. Dottie would be in a huff, and if by chance TJ's stomach turned and he made a mess, then Lakisha would never hear the end of it. "What should we do then?"

"Leave us home with Nikki."

Nikki emerged from her room like a raccoon that had been poked with a stick. "I'm not baby-sitting them!"

Lakisha sighed, "No one asked you, Niquela. Get back to your homework."

Nikki slammed her door and the walls shook.

Lakisha rolled her eyes but decided she hadn't the energy to argue. Instead, she got the Children's Advil from the bathroom and watched as TJ downed the gooey purple liquid.

Ten minutes later, the kids sat huddled around the kitchen table, and Lakisha was passing out plates of baked chicken with broccoli and pouring fruit punch. Then she moved to the counter, picked at a sliver of chicken and munched on a few saltines. The first trimester nausea was relentless. She stroked her middle, which pouched out where she used to have a waist. This time around she started showing even before the two lines appeared on the pregnancy test stick. She tried not to think about what would happen when Nikki learned she'd soon have to share her room.

The unsteady table rocked, the flatware clanged, and the kids talked over each other. Despite the din, Lakisha heard the front door of their basement apartment creak open. Her heart leaped into her throat. She reached for a carving knife and the room hushed. In the front hallway, things clattered to the floor and the dead-bolt slid into place. Lakisha leaned against the wall at the kitchen's entrance. Devon started to speak, but Nikki cupped his mouth. Lakisha tightened her grip on the knife and took a deep breath. Just as she rounded the corner, a familiar baritone broke the silence.

Devon raced past Lakisha. "Daddy!" He wrapped himself around Theo's middle.

"Hey, Dev! What's up? Where's your brother?"

"At the table, but I can't touch him cuz he's sick!"

Theo looked to Lakisha who now stood in the center of the living room, breathless. "Kisha, what's with the knife?"

"Jesus, I thought…why didn't you tell me you'd be home early?"

"Phone died." Theo shook his head, "Girl, you are wound *way* too tight."

Lakisha was gulping down air. She hated herself for panicking, tried to shake it off. "TJ's got a fever." Theo followed her into the kitchen and she returned the knife to the drainboard. "Your shift cancelled? Good thing, cuz it's my Slam night." Theo reached out for her, but she raised a hand to his chest. "Don't be looking for hugs now, not after scaring the life out of me."

"Sorry. I'll find a way to call next time, but you know you been afraid forever."

"No, not forever—"

"Please! I'm sorry. Okay? Now go on and get ready to slam them. I'll sit here with the kids."

Lakisha stared him down. Back in the day, he had failed her— more than he even knew. And perhaps her secrets, the ones created to spare him, were equally wrong. But the two had become so entwined in falsehood that Lakisha saw no way to tease it all apart. After tossing her notebook into a black leather bag, Lakisha grabbed her house keys and shouted goodbyes.

Out on the street, the air was ripe with cherry clouds that hung in a pale-blue sky above distant smoke stacks. She used to love these glorious sunsets before Nikki told her they were caused by pollution. *Leave it to a sixth-grade science teacher to strip away what little pleasure there was to be had in the hood.*

As she moved down Springfield Avenue, a cold wind bit at her chest and she fought against a shiver that slipped down her spine. She knew it wasn't just the breeze. Her joy in the painted sky was overshadowed by her dread of the darkening streets. On the way home, she'd try to catch a ride with one of the women who never went anywhere without their wheels. But for now, she focused on being vigilant. She passed the corner where she and Theo had first met, and her mind flashed with the memory of him leaning against a lamp post on that sizzling summer evening. Theo had been twenty-one and she had been just…she smiled inside and shook her head, just fifteen.

She reached the pillared library before dusk and pulled open the glass door.

"Kisha!" Three women, all sporting highlighted braids or long wavy locks, came over and hugged her.

Lakisha adjusted her headband and touched the gold hoops in her ears, wishing she'd had the time and money to get new extensions. After taking out her last ones, she'd grabbed up small sections of her short hair and made two-strand twists. It was a decent look. Theo always said her good bone structure and big eyes made everything else icing on the cake. But only someone who loved you could say that your hair didn't matter in Irvington. Together, the women walked to the meeting room and took their usual seats in the back row, ready to make a quick exit if some crisis arose back home.

As the seats filled, Lakisha felt a hand at her back. A man with graying temples and flirtatious eyes stood beside her. She recognized him, could even remember his poem about the night his fiancé and his girl-on-the-side joined forces against him. "Hey, how you doin?" Without waiting for her response, he leaned in. "I heard you're working at the Star Ledger. You know of any job openings right about now?"

She pursed her lips. If he wanted her to find him work, the least he could do was pretend to make some small-talk. Besides, he probably deserved the bad that came his way. She had no patience for the *players* in the neighborhood.

"I lost my job, and I got a mess of child support. Also, my sister is sick, so…." His words had an edge of desperation.

"Sorry to hear it. I don't know of anything, but I'll keep you posted." She thought back to his poem, knew there were several babies' mamas involved. His kids though, your heart had to ache for them. "I'll let you know."

"Thank you." He handed her a scrap of paper with his name and phone number on it.

The woman beside her snickered as he departed. "He probably got axed for doing his boss's girl."

Lakisha shook her head. One problem with reading your poetry out loud, was that your words followed you around like a shadow. Her phone buzzed, "Theo?"

"It's me, Mama."

"Hey, TJ, you okay?"

"Can you come home? Nikki won't stop yelling, and I feel like something is sitting on my chest."

"You got your inhaler?"

"Um, is it in the medicine cabinet?"

"There's not one in your backpack? You're supposed to always have one with you!"

"It kinda...went missing."

Lakisha pressed her lips together and closed her eyes. "Where's Daddy?"

"He fell asleep on the couch."

"Shhhh...find your inhaler and wake up Daddy! I'm on my way."

Jasmine

The rest of the evening consisted mostly of sitting in a crowded emergency room. Jasmine was eventually examined by a soft-spoken nurse who apologized several times for having to "poke around down there." She was a sad-looking, middle-aged white lady who took some close-up photos of her privates and then began snapping pictures of the swelling on her forehead and cheekbone.

"He didn't hit me. I did that to myself."

"Oh, okay, I'll make a note of it." The nurse put the camera down, reached into a cabinet and extracted an ice-pack which she shook and then twisted until it made a popping sound. This she placed on the welt at Jasmine's temple.

At the end of it all, Miss Darleen hustled her out of the hospital and into her minivan, which was littered with the backs of preschool-stickers. "I had to drive these triplets around yesterday, and I gave them some things to keep busy. Sorry, I didn't have time to tidy up."

Jasmine, now overcome with exhaustion, didn't even bother to respond, and when she was dropped off at a temporary placement, she left Miss Darlene without an argument. A woman in her late fifties with salt-and-pepper hair and sympathetic eyes welcomed her and ushered her to a seat at her cozy kitchen table. She cut Jasmine a thick slice of chocolate cake that she said was home baked and placed a steaming mug of peppermint tea next to the plate. Jasmine picked at the cake and let her tears fall into the yellowish brew.

The older woman's gentle fingers stroked Jasmine's shoulder blades. "Sugar, it probably seems like there's no way through this, but that feeling? It's gonna pass. Eventually, that is. This here is the worst part, the absolute bottom. Nowhere to go but up from here. You may not wanna be here with me, and I wouldn't think you wrong, but you need to know—you're safe here. The world could go to hell in a handbasket on the street, but inside my house, no one'll hurt you."

Rising from the table, the kind woman returned with ice-packs that she held against Jasmine's bruising head. "I'm sorry someone did this to you."

"I did it," Jasmine whispered without lifting her face.

"Then I'm even more sorry." She cleared her throat, as if her next words were stuck there. "Some kids, they come in here and for some reason they think they caused the problem. They blame themselves for the bad stuff adults do—as if a child could make it happen. But that there is just not how life is. Uh-uh. It's adults that make life ugly. There's not a thing you did, that made Social Services take you away." She moved in closer so that the back of Jasmine's head could rest against her soft middle. When the ice-pack was no longer cold, she showed Jasmine to a side room on the first floor of the house. "Towels are in the hall closet next to the bathroom upstairs. It's just me here with you, so you don't have to worry about anyone else coming in. I always bolt and alarm the house, meaning I'll know if you leave, so please don't. I'm too old to chase you." Her eyes smiled.

"I'm not gonna run."

"Glad to hear it. So, have a good night then. I'm right up the stairs, first room on the left, if you need me."

An automatic "thank you" slid from Jasmine's lips, for Treasure had drilled in good manners.

All night she lay in bed tossing about, wrestling the blankets and tussling with imaginary police officers. When sleep finally arrived, she dreamt about William locking her inside a cupboard beneath a newly formed staircase and throwing the key down the kitchen garbage disposal. Though she banged on the door and screamed, Treasure went about her business, cooking up breakfast. In her dream, Jasmine felt moisture gathering around her shoulders and stomach. She touched her damp shirt and brought her fingers to the crack beneath the door that allowed a sliver of light to enter. It was blood! Frantic, she pounded on the small door, pleading for help, but William just started whistling, and Treasure told him that breakfast was ready.

Jasmine awoke in the strange bed and tried to shake off the dream. She felt a dull ache above her jaw. Sunlight was streaming in through the slotted blinds next to the bed. She was now able to take in the dark-stained wood around the door and window, and the aging wallpaper with buttercups and yellow birds in cages. She spotted a round mirror perched on top of a dresser and went to inspect her face. "Damn," her right temple was black and blue, and her eye was swollen. "I guess I look as bad as I feel."

There was a soft knock at the door. "Jasmine? Jasmine, you awake?"

"Yes, I'm up."

"Good, come on out and eat breakfast. Miss Darlene will be here soon to pick you up."

"Am I going home?" Jasmine opened the door.

"You'll have to speak with her about that. Hmm, I wonder if we should try and ice your face some more."

"Naw, I'm already all puffed up. I'd just as soon not. Maybe I won't have to worry about getting jumped today, since I look gangsta."

The woman's lips curled into a smile. "You got your sense of humor still. That's good. Come on and eat some breakfast."

After pushing scrambled eggs around on her plate for a while, Jasmine was relieved to hear the doorbell ring. Maybe Miss Darlene would be taking her home.

"Where are we going?" Jasmine accosted her before she had even crossed the threshold.

"First, we'll pay a visit to the county prosecutor's office, and they're gonna ask you a few more questions. It'll be recorded on video, so you won't ever have to talk about it again. After that, we'll head on over to speak with a social worker."

"Isn't that what you are?"

"Yes, but we're going to speak with a clinical social worker, a therapist."

"What for? You think I'm crazy? I'm not the one that's crazy. You should send *them.*"

Miss Darlene paused. "No one thinks you're crazy. You've been through a lot, and it helps to talk. We want you to share or vent or play or do whatever it is you need to do to feel better after...this...."

"Nightmare?"

"Yeah, I'd say so."

At the Prosecutor's office, Jasmine was seen right away. A female attorney with red lipstick and a coffee stain on her egg-shell blouse sat across from her at a fake-wood table and posed a series of questions. Her voice was unemotional, and Jasmine tried to respond in kind. This was true right up until the end, when she couldn't help but ask, "Will I go back home?"

"We'll try our best to make that happen, but I can't promise. We'll just have to wait and see." As the tears that had been pooling in Jasmine's eyes dripped down her face, the attorney reached for a box of tissues that was on a bookshelf behind her and slid it across the table. Then she knocked on the outer door.

Miss Darlene entered. "Let's get out of here."

They drove to their next appointment in silence. Soon, they arrived at a 1930s firehouse. "What are we doing here?" Jasmine asked.

"The clinic is on the second floor."

Jasmine followed the case worker up the steep steps. "What's gonna happen? Are they supposed to put out this fire I got burning up my insides now?"

"Maybe, Jasmine, they just may try."

As she sat in the sparsely decorated waiting room that smelled faintly of chlorine bleach, Jasmine thumbed through *Highlights for Children* magazines, and tried to keep from staring at the adults around her. One old woman, who had a tongue that looked too big to fit inside her mouth, was licking and chewing her lips, while a dude in his twenties, who sat low down in his seat with his legs spread wide, was shaking his heel like he couldn't wait to escape. When he glanced at her and caught her eyeing him, he raised his black hoodie, so that all she could see was the tip of his nose and the trail of a tattoo that curled onto the back of his hand. She wondered what brought them to this pitiful place. At one point the room seemed to fill with patients, but then a woman came out of an office and announced that *anger management* was about to begin, and most everyone strolled into a conference room and the door slammed shut. The members of that group seemed to be loud talkers, for despite the white noise machines that purred outside every doorway, Jasmine could still make out much of their discussion about *taking space* and *cooling off.* From time to time they'd erupt in laughter. What could they could possibly find funny about their situation? Fifteen minutes into the session they became so rowdy, she thought that the firemen were going to have to climb those steep steps and use a hose on them to calm things. She glanced over at Miss Darlene, who had her nose in *Ebony* magazine. Jasmine wanted to read *Ebony* too, but Miss Darlene had snatched up the only copy.

By the time the young, perky therapist came out to get her, Jasmine's stomach was growling, and her mouth tasted like ash. She entered a tiny office and sat in a narrow padded chair next to her desk. Paint was peeling off the iron radiator and a dented metal file cabinet was stacked with charts. A framed diploma from NYU was the only thing hanging from the white-washed plaster walls, and it was tilted at an angle, as if someone had brushed up against it and no one had straightened it. Treasure would not have approved.

The therapist was a white lady with a crooked smile and a blonde ponytail, who said her name was Maggie. "First off, everything you say in here is confidential. That means I can't tell anyone anything you say without your written permission. The only exceptions to that are if you tell me you plan to hurt yourself or someone else, or if you are involved in any dangerous activities. Then I'd have to share that information to keep everyone safe. I am also a mandatory reporter of child abuse, so if you tell me about any kind of abuse, physical, sexual, any kind…I have to report it to the authorities."

"You're a little late for that," Jasmine quipped, but Maggie just tilted her head and got right down to business. She asked Jasmine a slew of questions about her life with her foster parents and then let her play with Lego figures of a family. Jasmine felt way too old to be playing with plastic blocks, but something about it felt good, like she didn't have to act grown up and pretend that everything was all right, when clearly, it wasn't.

A few days later, when Miss Darlene told Jasmine that the medical report included mild vaginal trauma, Jasmine discussed it with Miss Maggie. And when Jasmine was told that there was a settlement in her case which included her being moved from the peppermint-tea lady's house to another foster home, she had an emergency session with the therapist that included beating a drawing of William with a plastic inflatable bat and going through half a box of Miss Maggie's soft blue tissues.

At the next session, on the floor above the fire station, Jasmine squeezed a yellow smiley-faced stress ball into a tight knot and then slammed it down on the seat cushion, "How could Treasure have done this to me? How could she let them take me away?"

Miss Maggie bounced her foot up and down as she considered these questions. It was a nervous habit that irritated Jasmine, primarily because she wanted answers, and nice as Miss Maggie was, she didn't seem to have many. "We can't really know why she did what she did, but what I do know is that you didn't cause it. Probably it's her own stuff. We don't know what shit *she's* been through! Excuse my language, but it's true. Maybe her parents threw her out or left her when she was little, or maybe she's just so afraid of being alone, she thought she couldn't survive his leaving. Maybe she knew the truth: that the courts would never let him back in the house because she knew what he was doing to you."

"No. She couldn't have known."

Miss Maggie paused, like she was weighing her response. "Either way, it's not your fault, Jasmine. That's all I'm saying. People can seem like they have their lives together in one way, but then totally lose it when things begin to fall apart. You said she cried when they took you away, right?"

In that moment, Jasmine was back there: the grip of the officers' hands on her upper-arms, William staring at the floor as she passed, the desperate look on Treasure's face, her hand covering her mouth. Yes, there were tears on her face, but when she came to the police car—it wasn't to take her back.

"Jasmine?"

"Yeah, Miss Maggie. Yeah, she was crying, but tears don't mean much to me anymore."

Miss Maggie was quiet, and Jasmine could practically hear the wheels turning in her head, trying to find some way to lift her spirits, some words that would make it all bearable. Finally, she offered, "I know this may not help much now, but this horrible hurt feeling you have inside you—it's not going to last forever. It's gonna get better. We'll just have to help you hang in there until...well, until that happens. Okay?"

Jasmine raised despairing eyes. "Is there a choice?"

Before another week had passed, Jasmine was moved to her new placement with a nervous woman named Carlina and her four-year-old son, Jackson. "I've never had any foster kids before," Carlina stated as she ushered Jasmine from the front porch of the two-family wood-frame house into her apartment. Months later, Jasmine would wonder if she was motivated to take her in by the government money or free babysitting, but on that first day, she tried to be open-minded. Carlina made a big show of waving goodbye to Miss Darlene and then hustled the girl back inside. "Sit yourself down," she said waving her plump hand toward the living room sofa.

Crossing her arms at her center and hugging her sides, Jasmine did as she was told, slouching forward as she sank into the brown, fake-leather sectional. Her jaw clenched rhythmically as she watched Carlina pacing the length of the beige area rug. Jasmine scanned the framed posters on the wall behind her new foster mother. One had the logo from the *Hard Rock Café* and a picture of a guitar, another was a photo of a Georgia O'Keeffe painting that hung in The Newark Museum, and a third had something called *The Serenity Prayer*, which made Jasmine wonder if she'd have to go to church on Sundays.

"In this house, we got some definite rules that we need to get out there on the table. First off, there are chores. Did you have chores at your last placement?"

"Yeah, sort of...." If making her bed and emptying the dishwasher when asked were considered chores.

"Well, here you need to keep everything nice 'n neat. That means your clothes put away, your books and shoes and jackets and such put where they belong, and not tossed all over the house. You'll do your own laundry and maybe ours too if you don't mess it up. Then once a week we'll be house cleaning. I'll take care of the kitchen and you'll do the bathroom and vacuuming. Cleaning day for you will be Saturday. Nothing happens on Saturday before cleaning: no friends, no parties, not even homework. Got it?"

Jasmine nodded her agreement. Carlina tapped at the side of her head, readjusted her chin-length hair piece, and then pulled a stray dot of glue away from her temple. She should get a better wig, Jasmine thought, recalling the human hair one that Treasure had kept under plastic in her closet, for use only on special occasions. Her eyes clouded with the memory.

"Next, we need to discuss your behavior. You seem like a nice enough girl, and Miss Darlene didn't say boo about you getting into trouble, but at this age, trouble—it's gonna come looking for you. That means *you* got to avoid *it.* So...no one is allowed in this house when I'm not home—except for you a course, but no friends, and especially no boys! You are not to go into anyone else's house unless I know who they are and give you permission."

"What if a friend invites me, and I can't reach you?"

Carlina's thick arms shot up into the air and started to wobble around as she waved them. "I said, unless I give you permission, the answer is no! That's why I'm telling you right now! No means no! No kids here and no you going to anyone else's house unless I say so. Also, no hanging out on the streets with them scrubs—especially not with them boys who are always posted in front of that garage on the corner. You'll know 'em when you see 'em. They got wads a cash in their pockets, and they're wearing their bling and their colors. I can just tell, when I pass them on my bus, they're all packing something."

"You drive a bus?"

"A school bus—so me and Jackson are gone early. You'll have to get yourself out the door and to school on time." Just then, Jasmine heard Jackson screeching and turned toward the bedrooms. Carlina kept right on talking. "So, you got that? Stay away from those boys at the garage, and any other ones for that matter. Boys your age and older, if they're out on the streets, they're up to no good." Jackson's screeching increased in pitch.

"Ok, I hear you, but…." Jasmine glanced in the direction of the noise. "Do you want me to check on him or something?"

"What, Jackson? Hey, Jackson! Come here, right now!"

The boy raced over in stocking feet, slipping to a halt just as his forehead banged into Carlina's rounded middle. He looked up at her and squawked like a bird.

"What is going on now? Why are you making that racket?"

"Skwaaa! Skwaaa! My dinosaur is stuck behind the leg of my bed. I can't get it."

"Jasmine, maybe you can help him." She looked at her son, "What do you think you should've done? Made all that screeching or come ask for help, hmm?"

"Skwaaa?" He bounced his face against her middle, and then nuzzled in.

Carlina rubbed his head, and glanced up at Jasmine, "He's going through this dinosaur thing: obsessed with Pterodactyls."

Jasmine followed the boy back to his room, while weighing the unfairness of the situation. This boy could run around the house like a crazy kid, but if she was somehow able to make a new friend, they'd probably never get to hang out after school, for what were the odds of Carlina granting her permission? Crawling past the dust bunnies that gathered under his bed, she easily retrieved Jackson's toy, pushed it out into the center of the room and stood up, waiting for his response. When there was none, she prodded, "Thank you?"

"Skwaaa?"

Later that night, after unpacking her clothing into a narrow, musty smelling chest of drawers, Jasmine lay down on the lame Disney quilt that stretched across her new bed. Everything in the room looked like it had been purchased at some garage sale—the rickety side table still had a sticker on it marked $10. She would have cried then, but instead, she felt a weighty acceptance. Carlina would not be easy to live with, that much seemed clear. Since the night Treasure had slipped her book into the police car, her escape through Harry Potter's adventures was ruined. She tried other book series, but found it hard to concentrate, for her thoughts kept circling back to Treasure and William and all that she'd lost. She opened her poetry notebook and put pen to paper:

> *Case worker says can't stay, no way*
> *Dad's story's shit – dude lies all day*
> *Mom cries tears, like crocodile play*
> *Foster walks in, lays rules*
> *Choose your fool:*
> *The fucking police*
> *Or Carlina the Tool.*

She drew a small cartoon of Carlina as an angry hippopotamus in a bad wig, shaking her arms in the air. Maybe she'd be able to sleep now. She buried her notebook beneath underwear in her laundry basket. Since Carlina made it clear that Jasmine would be doing all her own wash, it made for a safe hiding place. Jasmine grabbed her toothbrush and got ready for bed.

Walking through the wide halls of University Middle School for the first time, Jasmine was overwhelmed by the noise and tumult around her: kids grabbing each other, throwing books, joking, shoving, whispering, taunting. It wasn't much different in her old school, but back there, she knew the lay of the land, knew who to avoid and who to ignore, who could be trusted and who'd have her back. Now everything was uncertain, and everyone seemed menacing. She was swept down the hallway in a crowd that smelled like piña colada hair cream and Victoria's Secret colognes, and passed classrooms scented with rubber cement and construction paper.

When the bell rang, the commotion briefly intensified, and once most of the students had cleared out, she made her way to the school office. She was annoyed that Carlina wasn't able to take off one morning from work to take her to school for the first time. Instead, Carlina had handed her an envelope and drawn a small map on scrap paper that showed the walking route. "Sorry, I've got my bus kids," she'd said. "Just hand that letter in to the office, and they'll get you all situated."

Her first class was math, and since University hadn't received her school records yet, she was sent to a low-level section. When she entered the class carrying a note and a late pass, she felt the gaze of the other students. Some boys, who looked like they'd been left back a year or two, seemed to be eyeing her curves. A few of the girls cast jealous glances, and Jasmine wondered what they could possibly be coveting. William had told her that her eyes were beautiful and that her lips were bow-shaped, but she hated every memory of him now. No, she was not, and could not, be pretty or hot or any of the other things he had said. *I've wrecked everything in my life. I'm nothing now.* She blinked, trying to refocus on the present.

No one greeted her except for a girl named Amani, who offered to share her textbook and help her catch up. Jasmine didn't want to tell her that she'd already learned all the material they were covering back in fifth grade, so she just muttered, "Thank you."

Fourth period was lunch, and Jasmine was relieved when Amani waved her over and began whispering in a conspiratorial way about the boys who were checking her out. "I seen DeShawn and Ray staring, they even gotchu in range now. They think they all that, but I'd steer clear. They been up under so many skirts, ain't no way a knowing what they got. DeShawn's brother is a banger—Crips I think."

"I'm gonna wait a minute on all a that, but thanks, I'll bank it."

"Whatever, I'm just saying. Where you go to school before?"

"Union Avenue."

"Huh, so you went from the pot to the frying pan." Amani was rolling khaki colored peas off her plate, leaving only the mounded mashed potatoes and cold fish sticks. "I used to go there too."

Jasmine was busy checking out the other students in the room, trying to get a feel for who she needed to avoid. She wasn't at all sure that an alliance with Amani was a good idea, but hers was the only offer of friendship. "Say what? You went to Union Ave?"

"Yeah, when I was at my last placement."

"You're in foster?"

"Um-hmm, third year. I got my brother with me, and I see my aunt sometimes, she just couldn't take us in. So…is what it is."

Jasmine searched Amani's deep-set eyes wondering why she was in foster care. Before she had a chance to even consider sharing her own foster-care status, Amani was on her feet bussing her tray, her round hips catching the attention of several students as she swayed down the aisle to the garbage can. Jasmine shoved a few fish sticks in her mouth and caught up to her.

"We can go out for a few. I'm gonna look for Edwyn."

"Edwyn?"

"He's my boyfriend. He's in high school, but some days he comes by, and I…see him."

Treasure's voice sounded in her mind, warning her away from this girl, but Jasmine ignored it. There wasn't anyone else offering her a drop of kindness, and besides, Treasure's opinions were meaningless now. "You're allowed out the gate?"

"No, but I'm not one for the rules." Her mouth curled into a Cheshire cat grin.

The door from the cafeteria to the yard swung open, and a few other eighth graders brushed past them. Amani strolled ahead, and Jasmine fell into step behind her, then struck a pose next to Amani who leaned against the metal gate, eyeing the street.

"Hey, Mani," A boy from the lunchroom was fingering the back pockets of Amani's skin-tight jeans.

"Hands," she said, lifting her eyebrows and pursing her glossy mouth, and the boy's palms shot up like he had just touched something hot.

"Who's your friend?"

"Someone too good for you," she quipped and shoved him backwards with two fingers.

Jasmine tried to suppress her smile as the other girl stared him down. Finally, Amani pointed to Jasmine, "All right, this here is my new girl, Jasmine. She's from Union Ave."

"Hey, what up?" Jasmine offered as she cast a sideways glance in his direction. He was tall and lanky with a large cross hanging against his sunken chest. Were his sharp features similar to William's in those pictures Treasure kept on top of her dresser—the ones where William was young and thin and happy? She felt drawn to him, but disturbed by it. Maybe it meant that William was right. Perhaps what happened really was all her fault. She was adrift on a sea of self-hatred and tapped the side of her head with her palm.

"Hey, what up to you too. I'm Peirce." When Jasmine didn't respond, he filled in, "I know some guys at Union, they play in my baseball league at the Y. Um…let me think a minute…Marcus and Damien or something? We used to call him Damn."

Jasmine shook her head.

"A'right. So why you move to University?"

Jasmine thought for a moment and then decided on the truth, the *is what it is, no big deal,* truth. If Amani could just blurt it out.… "New foster placement," she said, cocking her head to one side.

"Mom sent away?"

Shit, this boy was nosey. "Naw…but dad should be."

His eyes caught hers and held them. "Got it." There was a long pause, as if there was nothing else that could be said in response. Then Peirce pushed forward, "Let's take a walk. Mani, you're gonna stay and look for your man, right? I'm gonna cop Jasmine for a minute."

Jasmine's mind shot through with indecision. In her old school she'd never go on lunch time *walks* with guys like Peirce, but back then she had honors classes and Treasure, nice friends and self-confidence.

"Whatever." Amani waved him off like she was shooing a fly.

Peirce put his fingers on the back pocket of Jasmine's jeans, but unlike Amani, Jasmine let them stay there. It didn't matter whether or not she did something with this boy. Her life was already in the toilet, and it felt good to be wanted by someone. He led her to a deserted corner of chain-link fence and pressed his body against hers. His lips were warm and salty and tasted like tater-tots. She let his hands explore her hips but shoved him away when they travelled to her small breasts. She was going to make the rules now: not Treasure, not William, and not some boy with a lunchtime hard-on.

The rest of her day was uneventful, as she went through the motions of sitting in classes and listening to teachers talk about things she had already learned. During her walk home from school, a voice called out to her from the garage at the corner, the very place Carlina had cautioned her to avoid. She didn't respond—not on that first day at least. But after several more trysts with Peirce in the school parking lot, and a few outings with Amani that included hookups with some Crips in exchange for two blunts of weed, she saw no reason to avoid them.

Tessa

Tessa had seen other injured gymnasts hobble through the conditioning exercises, doing whatever movements their orthopedists permitted before departing, leaving the rest of the team to practice on the apparatus and learn the new challenging tricks. But now it was her sitting on the sidelines, and she felt as if she'd been tossed onto the sidelines of life itself. As much as they were a team and always rooted for each other, watching several others squeak past her in their skill level gnawed at her insides. She felt her muscles twitch with envy as she watched them perfect their uneven bar dismounts and participate in a special Sunday workshop offered by a dancer from the New York City Ballet.

"Tessa, don't look so down; no one died." Coach's eyes flashed amusement but then turned serious. "You'll get back to yourself. Injuries are part of gymnastics. Everyone has them."

He stood over her, waiting for Tessa to show something—resilience? Her father kept using that word. Everyone wanted her to bounce back, everyone thought it should be so easy—no, not exactly easy, but definitely doable. Perhaps it would be doable on another day, but that wasn't the case today, and it didn't look like it would be the case tomorrow either. She looked away, not able to give Coach whatever it was he wanted. After a beat, he let out a grunt tinged with disappointment and walked on.

Back at home, things were no better. She tried to let go of the anger she felt toward her parents for keeping her adoption a secret. The rage had morphed into a slow-spreading misery that seemed to sneak in beneath the blanket of stillness, the immobility while studying, and the hours spent observing rather than practicing at the gym. And once the cast was removed from her arm, it only worsened. The healing limb was spindly and weak. She couldn't even do a bicep curl! For Tessa, it came to symbolize the degeneration of everything she had been, the crumbling of her identity. Who was she now? Someone who had been tossed aside both at the gym and by her birth mother: a teenage accident. Maybe her entire life was one big mistake.

Worse still, her fall had awakened in her a certain newfound fear. Prior to her parents' revelation and her subsequent injury, Tessa had lived as if she were inside a protective bubble, invincible, unshakable. But now she knew the truth; life was dangerous, horrible mistakes happened, and no one, not even the person she viewed in the mirror, was exactly who they appeared to be. The uncertainty of it all made her stomach turn.

It was during her seemingly endless hours of physical therapy, that Tessa embarked on a search for her birth mother. It happened almost by chance, as she surfed through internet sites on her phone and her mind wandered from the icepacks on her arm to a fellow patient, a young pregnant woman who sat on the padded table to her right. Tessa's thoughts drifted to the woman's rounded belly, and then...to her birth mother.

How difficult it must have been to be pregnant in tenth grade, and then why not abort, or more to the point—why didn't she use birth control? Tessa had learned in health class about condoms and how they don't always work, but then there were other ways to prevent pregnancy, and if not pregnancy, then birth. There was the morning after pill; she'd learned about that somewhere on social media, and then there was also abortion. Her mother had talked to her about that after they'd heard abortion rights discussed on an NPR radio program. *It's a last resort,* her mother had said, *but must* *be kept legal to protect women from having unsafe abortions, blah, blah, blah…*so why didn't her birth mom abort? Then again, if she had aborted, Tessa wouldn't even exist. So even if it was by accident, Tessa reasoned, the pregnancy was a good thing, at least for her. Perhaps if she knew the circumstances, then she could understand her birth mom's decision, and if she could do that, then maybe she could understand her place in the world.

Tessa googled *how to find my birth mother* and got a string of hits. There were paid sites, advice columns, and then several other free sites that had listings of kids looking for their moms and vice versa. Tessa began scrolling through the listings, filtering for her date and city of birth. Nothing came up. Back in her bedroom that night, she searched through two more websites. As she swiped through post after post, it dawned on her that finding her birth mother might leave her feeling even worse about herself. What if she discovered that her birth mom was a drug dealer or prostitute or something else awful? Tessa turned off her phone, unsure if she was ready for the truth.

After a summer spent doing strength training and trying to fight her way back to her former self, Tessa was looking forward to high school. On opening day, she rode with Alice down the tree-lined drive that led to Haverford Academy—the school Alice and Rob had chosen for her during her "lost days." The building itself had once housed an order of Franciscan monks, and so it was constructed from stone and brick, with high arches and soaring windows. Tessa left her mom at the curb and made her way inside, following signs that pointed toward the ninth-grade wing. The halls were thick with the sound of laughter, shrieks of reunion, and the squeaky soles of Adidas, Converse, Nike, and Sperry footwear hitting smooth tile floors. Tessa was surprised at how similar the kids looked. It wasn't that they were all white like her, in fact the group seemed more diverse than at her old school because there were a lot of Chinese and South Asians in addition to the whites and blacks. But they all appeared to be members of the same tribe. No one had more than a few visible body piercings, there was no pink hair, no tattoos, no boys with boxer shorts showing above low-slung pants, no four-inch fake fingernails or bling. No one here reeked of hair pomade or wore plaid short-sleeved button-downs with mechanical pencils in the pockets.

"Hi," a girl with a silky braid and wide-rimmed glasses greeted her. She had the locker next to Tessa's. "What do you have first period?"

Tessa glanced at her schedule, which was slipped into the cover of her binder. "Honors Bio and then…Spanish."

"Cool, me too! Bio is in 108. Go down this hall, make a left and a then two rights."

Tessa stared at the girl, "How do you—"

"Know my way around so well?" Her eyes glistened, "My brother went here. He just graduated. I've been in the building to watch his basketball games, and they have all kinds of visiting days for siblings; you know, rah, rah, we're so great. Come on, Dr. Beckerman gets pissed if you're late. Señora Muniz doesn't really care, though. She's pretty cool, which is great because those classes are far apart."

As they walked, Tessa glanced down at her schedule to check the second class's location, then raised her eyebrows toward the girl at her side.

"Oh, I memorized the schedule. It's just a thing. I like to be prepared. I'm Kate."

And that was how Tessa met her soon-to-be best friend. When they arrived at class, Tessa headed toward the back of the room, but Kate grabbed her sleeve and motioned her to the front. Once Tessa was seated in the second row, Kate leaned over and whispered, "Beckerman hates the kids in the back. He thinks they're lazy."

"What?"

"You'll see. Give it a week." Kate opened her brand-new MacBook Air, and began clicking open applications.

Tessa glanced at the student sitting on the other side of her, an Asian boy with braces and a cast on his wrist. He was also opening his MacBook. When he caught her eye, he grunted, "Pre-season Lacrosse injury."

"Oh, sorry." She opened her loose-leaf binder and pulled out a purple mechanical pencil, feeling stupid for leaving her laptop in her locker.

By lunch-time, Tessa's head was jumbled and aching. She sat down at a long table beneath florescent candelabras and trained her brain on the giddy conversation between Kate and two girls she knew from the Y, Haley and Cassandra.

"Do any of you have Sabin for history?" Haley asked as she shoveled over-dressed salad into her mouth. "If he were any more stooped over, he could eat his lunch off his tie."

"Maybe he does, and that's why it has so many stains on it." Tessa quipped as she picked raisins out of a yogurt and granola mixture that she'd brought in a Tupperware container.

"Poor thing…you guys are so mean." Cassandra tossed wisps of blonde hair off her shoulder. She glanced behind her and then grabbed the forearm of a passing boy, whom Tessa recognized from her Spanish class. "Hey, Eric!"

He leaned down and pressed his royal blue polo against her beige lace. The two spoke for a few minutes while Kate and Haley traded stories that had been passed down from their older siblings. If only Lily had been closer in age, less obsessed with medical school, or someone who called her sister—even occasionally, then Tessa might have had something to add to the conversation. Instead, she tried to laugh at all the right moments and did her best to be witty. Near the end of the period, her stomach began to churn, and she moved with urgency toward the bathroom at the side of the cavernous room, elbowing past sports arguments, dance moves, an acapella group, and an impromptu discussion of algebraic equations at a chalkboard.

Inside the girls' bathroom, Tessa began to jog. She banged into the last stall, and back-kicked the door shut as the contents of her stomach shot out of her mouth and into the bowl. *Shit,* that was one disaster narrowly avoided. At the sink, she rinsed her mouth and pressed cold hands against her cheeks, trying to calm herself.

The rest of her first day was thankfully non-eventful, and when she slid into a seat next to Kate on a school bus that would wind its way through three towns, she felt relieved. She'd survived the first day and made some friends. Kate was obsessed with school, but she could also be funny without knowing it. And she seemed to have adopted Tessa as one of her pet projects, like the shelter beagle-hound she told Tessa about, or the disabled children she said she worked with on Sunday afternoons.

Later that night, the gym, which had always been her second home and refuge, began its transformation into something else—something closer to one more thing on her *have to do* list. This subtle shift seemed to parallel her descent in the rankings, as if the apparatus was moving in concert with her feelings or vice versa. Coach was yelling commands at her just like he always did, but now there was something added, some unspoken edge of disappointment.

"Tessa! You're not moving on to bars until you stick at least one landing! Focus! You keep over rotating!" His arms were folded, wall-like and unforgiving. When her mother had once complained in fourth grade about his harsh attitude, Tessa had overheard his response, "This is how champions are made. You want her to be coddled? Try one of our recreational classes. I think those ten-year-olds are almost done polishing their cartwheels." Alice had been incensed but never questioned Coach again.

After another handful of runs, Tessa finally stuck the landing. While strapping on hand grips and chalking up, she looked toward the glass enclosed spectators' lounge and saw that her mom had arrived half-an-hour early for pickup. She had a habit of doing this so that she could catch the tail-end of practice. She kept *forgetting* that this annoyed Tessa.

Tessa hustled over to the uneven bars and slogged through her routine while trying to ignore Alice's presence. Of course, she was used to being watched and judged, but when it was her mom, it felt different—like the achievement bar was set up in the sky somewhere, and there was no way to reach it—not in the classroom, not at home, and lately not at the gym either.

Before releasing them for the evening, Coach called the team together. "Our first meet is in three weeks, so we have a lot of work to do. Here are your levels for this competition season. Cara, Laurel, and Kim have moved up. The rest of you will start where you finished last year. Tessa, we'll talk when it gets closer. Hopefully you can stay where you are. That's it. Have a good night."

Tessa walked ahead of everyone else into the room where her mother waited, grabbed her bag from a cubby, and darted out into the parking lot. Inside the car, her mom turned to her, "What's wrong, Sweetie?"

Tessa looked away, "Can you please drive? I wanna get out of here."

Alice started the car and they were on their way. "Tessa?"

"Why did you have to come early?"

"Why did I—"

"I told you I don't like when you watch. It makes me nervous."

"I know, but this was just a practice, not a meet. I didn't know that was a problem too. What's wrong?"

"What's wrong is that you're always nervous, and then when you come early…I don't know. It messes with my head!"

"Really? I was just trying to be there for you."

"I don't want you to be there for me! It's like your crazy worry creeps into my head, and I can't get it out."

"This is my fault? I wasn't there the day you broke your arm. I was the one that took you to the hospital!"

There was so much Tessa wanted to say. She wanted to shout that it was her mother who kept her adoption a secret for thirteen years, her mother who made her believe that she had to be perfect, her mother who wanted her to go to that prep school, hang with those rich kids from Short Hills and Livingston, and expected her to somehow get into an Ivy League college. It was her mother who wanted her to be just like Lily; Lily, the golden child, the one they wanted to clone but couldn't, so they got stuck with her instead. But now she knew why she was not like Lily, could never be like her. They shared nothing: no interests, no talents, no gene pool, nothing. The only thing they had in common was their parents. Those were the things she wrestled with. She let them tumble through her, and then tried to let them go. They'd change nothing, and allowing them a voice would only cause hurt. Anger bubbled in her veins. She couldn't avoid the thought—*I hate her.*

Lakisha

Dottie strutted into Lakisha and Theo's ground-floor apartment, looked around the center room which served as both communal living space and bedroom for Lakisha's two boys, and gave a critical sniff. "Still having trouble with that stench?"

When Dottie had phoned the day before and said she needed to come by and talk, Lakisha had felt a migraine begin to blossom. Now she stood in the heart of Lakisha's home, finding fault right from the get-go. "It's only on garbage days, when they put all the cans up close to our window. I spoke to the landlord. Nothing he can do." Lakisha glanced at her aunt's fingernails, filed perfectly and painted to look like tiny dollar bills. She always seemed to get her nails done right before she visited Lakisha, like she was trying to rub it in or something. Lakisha stuck her unadorned hands into the pockets of her cardigan.

"Where your kids at?"

"Theo took Nikki and the boys to the library. They should be home soon. Come on and have a seat." She pointed to the midnight-blue couch that had seen better days. Her apartment never bothered her until she saw it through her aunt's eyes. "Want a drink?"

"I really shouldn't…oh, hell, your man still like his rum?"

Lakisha shot her a half smile, "Now and again. Why? You want some?"

"If you got something to put with it, soda maybe?"

Lakisha headed into the kitchen.

"Pour one for yourself while you're at it. You're gonna need it."

Lakisha returned carrying two tall glasses with dark bubbling liquid and ice and took a seat next to her aunt. "What's up?"

Dottie straightened her freshly ironed slacks and then took a few gulps of her drink. "There ain't no way to make it sound pretty, so here it is: Maizy, your mama, that is…well, she passed. She passed last week. It took them some time to track me down since she wasn't exactly in touch, and once she died, whatever fools she had around her made themselves scarce."

"What fools? How did she die?" Lakisha's fingers covered her mouth.

"Heart attack is the official reason, but it was the drugs." Dottie lifted defeated eyes. "You know it was the drugs. I told em to just bury her wherever. It don't make no difference where. It's not like she's gonna care, and ain't no one gonna visit her either."

"Lord! How old was she? Was she even fifty?"

"Forty-nine."

Lakisha wrapped her arms around her center. "I can't believe she never came back—not ever. I really thought…."

"We all thought she'd resurface, at least come back for some money or something. I thought for sure she would've come for your grandma's funeral or any time in the past twenty-odd years."

"And if she did come back?"

Dottie bobbed her head. "Are we playing make believe now?"

"I thought about it *a lot*. I would have given her a real hard talking to first. I'd scream at her and curse her. Then, when she was just about to give up and leave—that's when I'd take her back. I hate that I didn't even get the chance."

"The chance to what? Hurt her? Love her?" Dottie pursed her mouth. "She was trouble, trouble right from the start. Wishing on Maizy was a mission of fools. Forget her. You got a good little life going here." She glanced around the narrow room and took in the shabby furnishings: nicked-up oak tables, floral Bed Bath & Beyond curtains, and particle board shelves with discarded library books and plastic trophies from the YMCA. "It's a fine life. When the kids are out, maybe you'll spruce up, but you're a'right, Kisha. Maizy is dead and buried. Let's just leave it right there." Dottie sighed like she'd had a long day and then stood.

Lakisha lifted a hand. "Hold up. Did she leave…anything at all?"

"Oh, I almost forgot." She opened her Coach bag, tugged out a small manila envelope and handed it over. "This is the only thing she owned that was worth passing on."

Lakisha peered inside the envelope and her jaw dropped. "Her ruby ring!" She remembered playing with it, moving it around on Maizy's spindly ring finger.

Lakisha heard the jostling against the front door and the key in the lock. It was Theo returning home with Nikki, TJ, and Devon. In a minute, the room was a storm of activity with jackets and sneakers being tossed in a pile next to the door and children talking loud on top of each other. Library books sailed onto furniture, and Nikki went into her bedroom and slammed the door.

"What's up with Nikki?" Lakisha glanced at Theo while straightening the books on the sofa.

"It's nothing. She met some of them other little sixth grade girls at the library and I told her it was too late to stay. Hey, Dottie." Theo's body seemed to stiffen.

"Theo! Nice you came home in time to help out."

"Yeah, well, I ain't like a lot of other men you might know. I come home."

"Pfff! Look at you all self-righteous!" Dottie had a hand on her hip.

Theo brushed passed her into the kitchen.

TJ sat on the living room floor next to the coffee table, flipping pages in an astronomy book. He began coughing in what seemed like a fruitless effort to clear his throat. Still, he glanced up at Lakisha, and she sensed his mind chewing on the situation, weighing the impact Dottie's visit was having on her. Later, he'd catch her alone in the kitchen and ask what's up. She'd probably share more than she should. Then he'd nod like he got it and wrap those bony arms around her.

Dottie raised a brow, "He's about ready to cough up a lung."

"I'm okay, Auntie," TJ said, but kept right on hacking.

"Doctor says it's just viral, and he's unusually susceptible."

"Well cover your mouth! Jesus, it's a miracle you're not all sick."

TJ covered his mouth and Lakisha grimaced. The only thing worse than Dottie's critique of her, was when she did it to her kids, especially TJ.

"I was just leaving," Dottie called to Theo, like she was trying to get a rise out of him.

"Thanks for bringing the ring." Lakisha walked her to the door.

Dottie placed her hand on Lakisha's mounded belly. "Take care of you and whoever you got riding along in there. How many more of these kids you gonna have?"

Lakisha leaned in and cocked her head. "Take a look at my kids here. Go ahead, take your time. Now which one a them do you think I shouldn't of had?"

"That's your answer?"

"Way I see it, there's not a whole lot of fabulous shit going on in this life. I figure I might as well do something worthwhile. Raising these kids will most likely be the best thing I ever do before they toss dirt on me." Unwanted emotion rose in her eyes and she blinked it away.

"Kisha…."

Lakisha pasted a smile on her face and held open the front door. "Goodnight, Auntie. Thanks for bringing by the ring."

"Birth control is cheap...I'm just saying." Dottie leaned forward and gave Lakisha's cheek a kiss.

Throughout the rest of the evening, Lakisha thought of Maizy. She felt her presence as she spread peanut butter and apricot jam on bread for the next day's lunches, and smiled absently as she rinsed apples, remembering the one sweet fruit pie she and Maizy had baked together. But as she tucked her kids in, even cajoling Nikki into a reluctant good night hug, Lakisha couldn't help but wonder how Maizy was able to just walk away. How could she have left her when she was so small, her arms barely long enough to reach around her mother's middle, her hands smaller than Devon's? What kind of a person does that? "Maybe I just wasn't loveable," she muttered, before realizing she'd spoken out loud.

Nikki looked up, "Huh?"

Lakisha shooed away the thought with her hand. "All good. Lights out now." Before leaving, she peeked in the closet, caught sight of the topsy-turvy doll half buried beneath a pile of out-grown clothing, and tugged her free. Nikki had banished her dolls more than a year ago, but tonight, Lakisha needed this one.

While the apartment filled with the heavy breath of sleep, Lakisha settled into a kitchen chair and brought the rag doll to her cheeks, her neck, her forehead, trying to connect with her younger self. She placed the doll on her lap, fingered the black hair and polka-dot dress, and then glanced underneath it at the white face. Had this gift from her mother been a clairvoyant message? Was it meant to bring solace or serve as a reminder of her mistakes? Her mind drifted to the twins. They'd be fourteen by now. *Wherever you girls are, I hope you're happy.*

A short time later, Lakisha lay down beside Theo. Her awkward size made sleeping difficult on most nights, but tonight was even worse. Her mind was caught up in a web of memories, and she twisted the three-stoned ruby ring that now graced her right hand.

On the first night of Maizy's one and only trip back home, she cooked up a large pan of fried fish and a pot full of potato salad that she said was prepared in the special Macon, Georgia, style. Grandma Louema entered the kitchen with a cross look on her face, an expression that only seemed to soften when she peered into the battered pots and pans on the stove top and sniffed. The three of them pulled up chairs around a black Formica table in the small kitchen and began to chatter beneath the thick cloud of grease that hung in the air. Over dinner, Lakisha asked question after question about her mother's life down south.

"The weather? Well, it's much nicer than here—warmer and sunnier. The sky is clear and blue, and the air smells like magnolias and cornbread. The summer seems to last right on into November."

"And where you lived at? With who?"

"I lived with a friend. We do have some family there, but I lived with a friend. Everyone is real warm and cordial in the South, real polite like. No one would dare cuss in public...least not when a lady is present."

Louema sneered. "And who that lady be? Cause she sure as hell ain't you."

Lakisha ignored her grandmother. She touched her mother's arm as she spoke, wanting to confirm that she was real, and turned the red and gold ring that weighed down her mother's right hand. Then her eyes glimpsed a trail of scars on Maizy's arm that marched like tiny footprints from her wrist toward her heart. She fingered one and felt the rubbery bounce of the wound before Maizy shifted herself out of reach, signaling that the scars were off limits. Lakisha plowed forward, "And what was your house like?"

"The house? It was small, but pretty, with flowered curtains and a dining room with a big window that let you look out at a few old apple trees we had growing in the yard. Georgia is known for the peach, you know. But we had those apples instead. They didn't look that beautiful, but they were sweet and tart all at the same time. There was a little piece a heaven in each bite."

"Oh, I ain't a big fan of regular old apples, but did you bring any?" Lakisha's fingers were now on her mother's back. Moving her hair from side to side, she wondered when she'd be old enough to get long braids like that.

"Well, they'd a gone bad on the trip—got banged up and such. But what I liked most to do with them was bake em into pies. They made the best apple pie you ever tasted!"

Lakisha's grandmother dropped her plate into the sink and leaned against the counter, observing the two and shaking her head. "You bake them pies? With your own two hands?" When no one in the kitchen responded, she whipped the dishtowel down on the counter, "Maizy, when you're done with your fairytales, clean up the kitchen. I'm going to watch TV."

Later, after her bath, Lakisha pulled Maizy into her bedroom, hoping she would read her a story.

"These all the books you got?" asked her mother, holding a small pile in her hands.

"Yeah, that's it. I'm kind of tired of them."

"I bet. They were here back when this room was mine." Lakisha's mother sat down on the bed and began flipping through pages.

The young girl climbed up next to her and pressed her shoulder against her mother's side as if Maizy's body were a magnet. Her mind was buzzing with more questions. Chief among them were: "Why did you leave me? And if you leave again, will you take me with you?" But these were things she dared not ask, at least not yet.

After Maizy read her a picture book about a grandma rabbit who was saying goodnight to everything, Lakisha wondered out loud, "Where are you sleeping?"

"Right here with you, baby. I just have to brush my teeth. You go to sleep. I'll be right back." She stood and ran her palm over

Lakisha's short puffy braids and along her cheek to her jaw line. Maizy cradled her chin for a moment, before planting a kiss on her forehead.

"Uh-uh, I'll wait for you." Lakisha pressed her head against her mother's belly.

For thirteen dream-like days, Lakisha moved through life at her mother's side. She discovered an old bottle of nail polish in Maizy's striped bag, and the two took turns as manicurist and client. Her mother didn't even complain when Lakisha painted her cuticles or got spots on her knuckle. In response to her worried look, Maizy simply wiped the polish away with a paper napkin and gave her a sideways smile. "See, no big deal."

Lakisha and Maizy breathed in the mid-day air scented with automobile exhaust and Caribbean shea butter as they strolled to the library. When they arrived, sticky and overheated, the two had no trouble fitting into a well-worn plaid upholstered chair meant for one. Maizy read to her from Hans Christian Anderson's Little Mermaid: *the one where the young mermaid doesn't get the prince, but instead sacrifices herself, turning into sea foam to save the prince's life.*

On the way home Lakisha picked a bouquet of dandelions from the weed-infested grass that passed for a lawn in front of the local elementary school, and her mother accepted the gift with the gratitude of roses. Maizy tugged a package of cinnamon gum from her skirt pocket, offered Lakisha a stick, and they both chewed, Lakisha's mouth tingling with the sweet and spicy flavor that was her mother's.

Lakisha was settling into the rhythm of life with Maizy when the phone call came. She had been standing on a kitchen chair, helping with the dishes, but shut the tap so she could hear the conversation. The voice on the other end of the line was deep and sad. Leaning against Maizy's arm, she heard the man say that Levon had died, and watched as her mother crumpled onto the floor, her floral skirt spreading wide against the speckled linoleum.

Jumping off the chair and shoving it away, Lakisha knelt down to be close to Maizy. The man said that Levon had come out of the coma for a short while before having a massive stroke and passing. "I'm sorry, Maizy, but maybe it's for the best. Least now he won't be beatin' on you no more."

"Hollis," Maizy whispered into the phone, "I think I might a killed him."

"Baby, heroin don killed him."

"But what I gave him…it was too much…I—"

"Maizy, don't be sayin that, and don't think it neither. He went out like he lived, and now you're free, so go figure. It's the Lord's will. Don't be sayin that shit to no one. I mean it. Just let it be. You'll figure out what to do with your place. Funeral is on Thursday."

She released a high pitched, "I gotta go," before turning off the phone. Sobs shook Maizy's shoulders, and her tank top and cotton skirt became moist with tears. She hugged her knees to her chest and rocked back and forth.

Lakisha slipped her arms around her mother's center. "It's okay Mama, you're okay."

Maizy kissed the top of her daughter's head, held her for a few moments, and then stood up. She blew her nose on a paper towel and gave Lakisha a weak smile. "Thank you, baby. I just got some bad news about a friend. But don't worry."

"Levon, he died?"

"Yes, sugar, he did."

"Who was he?"

"Just someone I used to care about…back in the day." She left the room and climbed into Lakisha's bed, pulling the covers up over her head.

As soon as Lakisha's grandmother returned from work, Maizy got up and announced, "I think I'll take a walk."

Lakisha felt something cold ripple up her spine. "Can I go with you?"

"No, Kisha, not this time. I'll see you later." Maizy was almost out the door when she tossed back, "Don't wait up."

Lakisha awoke with a start to the sound of angry shouts, not long before dawn. "I knew you'd never change! Why the hell did you come back? You think being a mama is some game you can play at?" Her grandmother's voice was bitter. "You think you can just stroll in here, sit your scrawny bottom back down in our lives, and then sneak out the streets chasing a good time!"

Lakisha, sitting up in her bed, began chewing on the bottom corner of her cotton undershirt. There was a long pause. The piece of fabric dropped from her mouth. "Answer her, answer her," she whispered into the night. "Tell her it ain't no game. Tell her…" the rest of the sentence, "you love me," was left to silence.

After several beats, Maizy spoke. "Chasing a good time. You think that's what I do? Why don't you ever ask me instead of just assuming the worst?"

"What good would that do? I've heard enough of your lies over the years to last me a lifetime! Why don't I just ask you? You must think I'm a fucking fool!"

"Mama, I never said—"

"You're right; I must have been, to let you back in through the door!"

"Please, listen to me a minute…." Her mother's voice trailed off, and Lakisha jumped from the mattress onto the wood floor and moved toward the door, pressing her ear against the dark wood trying not to miss anything.

"What did you do to get it? What did you do?" Louema's voice rasped into a guttural cry, releasing a pain so deep, it seemed to shake the house.

"Answer her, answer her," Lakisha whispered, hoping her mother might receive her message. She had never heard her grandmother cry, had never seen her show weakness or despair. She was afraid to move, afraid that anything she did might bring the ceiling crashing down or, something worse, her mother running for the front door.

Then came a horrible sickening sound: leather meeting flesh, whipping the air and then meeting its target. Primal groans were followed by the sound of kitchen chairs scraping against the floor and then toppling. Over it all was her grandmother's chorus of "Out! Out! Out!"

Running back to her bed for safety, Lakisha huddled beneath her wrinkled pink sheet and spoke a rhythmic answer to her grandmother. "No, no, no," she muttered, as if they were in church and the two were doing a responsive reading.

Then everything was still. Lakisha's bedroom door creaked open, and her mother entered the room pressing her palms to the wall for balance. Lakisha lowered the sheet from her head.

"Hey," said Maizy, not looking at her. Instead, her eyes were scanning the floor. When she found the blue-and-white striped bag, she took her few belongings that had been piled on top of the dresser and placed them inside the vinyl case.

Lakisha now realized her mother had never even unpacked. As she teetered around the room, the hallway light danced across her long graceful arms and the fresh track mark—red and wounding. Even at five, Lakisha knew this was not good. "The sign of the devil," her grandmother had said as they maneuvered around a junkie passed out in the lobby of her aunt's apartment building.

When Maizy had returned her clothing to her traveling bag, she sat down on the edge of the bed. She lifted Lakisha's smooth chin with one hand and stroked her short pink and white clipped braids with the other. "Be good," she said.

"Where you going?"

"Be good, baby."

"Where you going—Mama?" Lakisha tried to draw her closer, but her mother had already slid off the bed.

"Shit," she murmured, struggled to her knee and then used the dresser handle to pull herself back onto her feet.

"Mama!" Standing on her bed, Lakisha's hands reached toward her mother's shoulders. "When you be back?"

Her mother's drugged eyes lifted, and as her lips began to form a response, the bedroom door swung open.

Her grandmother's silhouette filled the entryway, eclipsing the hallway light and swallowing her mother in the darkness. "Get the fuck out! Get the fuck out my house and don't come back! You ain't never gonna change! I must a been a fool to think you could. Garbage—that don't change. You can dress it up and make it smell good, but when you open the bag, you just got garbage. I ain't got time for your lies, and this child don't neither!"

Lakisha's mouth fell open, ready to shout, "I got time! I got time for you! Take me with you!" But fear made the words evaporate, as if she knew, without knowing why, that Maizy would not be able to care for her. Instead, she placed the corner of her undershirt in her mouth and began chewing, and her hands groped through the knot of pink sheet and frayed yellow blanket for her doll. She brought it to her nose and breathed in the sweet scent— the scent of her mother. Lakisha watched Maizy shuffle across the living room. After more declarations of sorrow and rejection, the steel front door clicked open and shut. Leaping off the mattress and running to her bedroom window, Lakisha caught a glimpse of her mother's narrow back and the blue-and-white striped bag, before both disappeared into the shadows of the early morning.

Jasmine

By the time she reached her one-year anniversary with Carlina, Jasmine had settled into a comfortable routine. Every day after school she'd hang with Amani at Irvington Park or around the corner at her friend's place. Since Amani's foster parents both worked, and her brother was always out on the streets, the girls had free rein of the apartment. Once she left her friend's house, Jasmine would stop in at the corner garage and check out what was going on. Some days the guys would be dealing, but other days they'd just be *chillin* or working on autos. If the garage door was down, she knew they were probably taking apart a stolen car, and she'd keep her distance. Hot cars seemed to put everyone on edge, but after the door was raised, the brothers were happy to have her help celebrate the heist.

Jasmine would sometimes still take out a small spiral notebook and commit her feelings to paper before burying her confessions at the bottom of her laundry basket. Along with laundry duty, Jasmine was charged with returning Jackson's picture books to the library, but that at least was an assignment she liked. It gave her a reason to leave the house in the evening.

On one such library trip, a smoking-hot boy from school held open the door as she entered the building. "You headed to the teen spoken-word slam?" he asked.

Treasure taught her to appreciate good manners, but it was his playful smile that caught her attention. "It's happening now?"

He nodded, "Come on. You'll like it."

She followed him downstairs and into a stark meeting room set up with rows of folding chairs. She took a seat in the back row, while he took his place with friends near the front. The room filled quickly, and kids began to line the walls. A middle-aged white woman with an auburn halo of hair and the most powerful green eyes Jasmine had ever seen, walked to the front. She cleared her throat and the room quieted. "I'm Mrs. Morrison, the Irvington child-and-young-adult librarian. Thank you all for coming. I'd like to reiterate the rules of this place, so listen up. This is communal space. This room is about to house our words, thoughts, and emotions—the stark and beautiful, the raw and painful pieces of our lives. Rule number one: What is shared in this room, remains in this room unless you receive permission from the speaker to do otherwise. Rule number two: This is a respectful and caring place where everyone is accepted, and no one is judged. To that end, there should be no visible signs of things that divide us. By that I mean, no gang colors or symbols, no dealing, no heckling, no talk backs…unless you're calling out encouragement. You all got that? If you agree, let me hear you say, yes!" The room erupted in affirmation.

It took a few more meetings before Jasmine felt comfortable enough to stand up and share her own words. On the first night that she gathered her courage and her best poem clutched in trembling hands, she felt the wild rush of power and freedom that comes from tearing off your mask and baring the naked truth of just one moment in life. When she finished, there was a crash of applause and cheers. As she stepped back through the group camped out on the stained carpet and sandwiched into metal chairs, a rapper named Ace, who was a minor celebrity, caught her wrist and then her eye. "You did good," he said simply, and then released her. She half tripped over the next person on the floor and somehow managed to return to her place, her heart beating to a rhythm of hope, as elation rushed through shaking limbs. Poetry was transformational—for a few hours a month anyway.

The next day, Amani grabbed her elbow as they walked home from school. "You're coming over right? I got a cool new pair of leather to show you."

"Your foster folks popped open a wallet for them?" Jasmine had learned about Amani's tendency to exaggerate.

"No, my brother got them from this guy he knows who works at Van's at the mall."

"Shit, Amani, you know he didn't buy them."

"Who the hell said that? They're in my closet, ain't they? I can ask him to snag you a pair too if you like. You'll try them on and see. Also, I want to show you a website."

"What is it? A place to buy stolen shit?"

Amani shoved her arm and swung her hips around, so they were standing face to face. "Jesus Christ, you for real? It ain't.... I'll show you at home. My case worker is coming today, so you can't stay long."

When they arrived at the apartment, the two girls tossed their backpacks on the linoleum floor and sank down on the wide sofa that filled most of the living room. Amani flipped open a laptop that sat on the side table. "Look at this," said Amani as she clicked through listings on a website.

"Birthparents locator dot net? Huh, any luck yet?"

"Uh-uh, but new listings come up on the daily. It also says legal stuff, like if there are new laws and shit about opening the records."

"Hold up, I thought you know who your mom is." Jasmine took the laptop out of Amani's hands and began scrolling through the listings herself. When she didn't answer, Jasmine put down the computer and looked at her friend. "Mani?" Amani brought her knees to her chest and looked up at the corner of the ceiling. It was the first time Jasmine had ever seen her look vulnerable. Jasmine's voice softened, "Hey, Mani," she reached out to touch her friend's leg.

Amani's hand shot out, warning her to back off. She spoke to the ceiling, "The lady that I lived with, who raised me and my brother, that was my Godmother. My mom, she disappeared when I was a baby. Don't no one know what happened to her."

"But you got her name, right? You're gonna look for her?"

"I done that, for months already!" Her charcoal eyes sizzled. "Whatchu think? Besides, I'm not sure I got her real name. They called her Hattie, and thought it was short for Hortense, like a real southern name, but it could a been Patience or Hatika or Hatima or something else."

"Damn."

"Don't be feeling sorry for me!" she got up and brushed herself off like she was getting rid of something unpleasant that had settled on her skin.

Jasmine stood too, then touched her shoulder. When she met no resistance, she pulled her in close and wrapped her arm around Amani's thick shoulders. In that moment, she thought of Treasure and felt a pang of loss, still ripe. After a few seconds, Amani shoved her away.

"Don't be thinking you're my sister from another mister now." That's what Amani said, but still, she wiped the corner of her eye. "Okay, maybe you can think that." She sighed and dropped back on the couch. "So, if you want, you can search too. We could do it together."

Jasmine had never thought much about her birth mother. With Treasure around, there was no need. Logic said a mother who didn't want her as an infant wouldn't be much use now, and she could do without more rejection. Still, the thought of finding her *real mother*, made her heart dance. It was like hope was determined to take up residence and refused to be banished. She hated herself for hoping but hated her pitiful existence more. "I guess I could look. There's no internet at Carlina's, so I'll do it here."

Amani's round cheeks lifted into a rare full-blossomed smile. "All right."

Going to Amani's and looking for their mothers became routine. Each day's search carried them on a rollercoaster from optimism to despair. The sting of it needed to be fixed somehow and Amani gave her the tools. There was weed, whiskey, pills. And the boys? They were part of the process. Jasmine had been well trained in the art of satisfying a man between his legs. William had seen to that. With William it had been forced upon her, but now—she was choosing. It was her decision to crouch down in the high-school parking lot, while a grateful 11th grader thrust himself in and out of her mouth, holding the back of his pants in one hand and the base of her head in the other. Unlike William, these boys finished with lightning speed, and afterwards they'd place a blue pill or blunt in her palm. They made her feel valued—for about ten minutes. By the time she saw the truth, she was too high to care. Hooking up brought her close to someone without really being close. It made her feel worthy, but worthless at the same time.

When Jasmine lay in bed at night, her mind often drifted back to Treasure and William. The thoughts of all she'd lost would roll in like a wave, and she'd be overcome, her emotions like a riptide threatening to drag her out to sea. She hated those memories but couldn't fight them. And so, she surrendered, doing whatever made it possible to survive each day without looking longingly at the pocket knife she kept stored in her sock drawer; a tool that could so easily be drawn across the tender skin at her wrist, allowing her to be pain free...forever.

"Jasmine! You get your report card yet? My friend said her girl got it two days ago." Carlina peered into Jasmine's bedroom, scanning with sharp eyes, as if expecting to find something amiss. Then she entered and fingered a few Algebra worksheets that were scattered on top of the dresser.

"Um, yeah, I got it."

"Why didn't you show it to me? I told you I always want to see it. Grades are important." She gave her latest shoulder-length pageboy a scratch. "You got something to hide?"

"No! It's...okay. I don't know, I just forgot."

"It was addressed to me, wasn't it?" She held out her palm, "Hand it over." As Jasmine tugged it from her backpack, Carlina snatched the white page and shook it. She shifted her considerable weight back and forth over tree-trunk legs. Her eyes squinted like she couldn't quite make something out, but then she nodded. "Not terrible. But you could do better."

"It's mostly As and Bs."

"You got a C in History, and a D is Spanish. And why do you have a C in Phys Ed? That should be an easy A. You just have to remember your gym clothes and chase around a ball!" She pressed the paper back against Jasmine's chest. "Bring these grades up. If you really had all As and Bs, you'd have a chance to get a scholarship to a state university. Keep going like this and you'll be stuck living here and taking the bus to Essex County College."

"What? That's not true...."

"Just wait and see. It's your grade point average that matters. It should be up near 4. Yours is less than 3. You see?" She shook her head and her nose scrunched up like she was smelling cauliflower cooking. "Also, your laundry is about ripe. Get it done tonight."

Once the door closed behind Carlina's square behind, Jasmine flung open her closest notebook, grabbed a pen in her fist, and drew deep-angry gashes down the page. Then she dumped her laundry out on the floor, searched for her gym socks, and stuffed them into the crevice beneath the door. "Have a good whiff," she whispered. "Girls keep swiping my gym shirts, and you said you'd only buy two, but don't you worry. I'll get into college, because I'm sure as hell not living with you for a minute more than I have to!"

When the next report card arrived, Jasmine opened it and then stuck it on the refrigerator with a magnet. But when she received the ninth-grade Biology Award at the end-of-year assembly, she took the gold-embossed certificate and hid it in her desk. And when she earned the tenth-grade Chemistry Prize, she did the same. She'd done it herself and had no desire to share her pride with Carlina, who'd likely taint it. In defeated moments she'd hold the textured papers and caress their gold seals, trying to convince herself that she had potential, that her life might someday change.

Had it not been for an incident early in her junior year, Jasmine might have coasted through the rest of high school and graduated from Carlina's home into adulthood. But that was not to be. For one balmy evening, Jasmine found herself opening the belt buckle of a brother who had introduced himself as Jayz and made it clear that he had a few lose joints that he'd be happy to share. They stood behind a line of empty oil drums at the back of a garage around the corner from Amani's apartment, and were serenaded by Tupac blasting from a boom box secured to the sidewall. The sweet, toxic scent of gasoline wafted into Jasmine's nostrils, and she crouched down on her haunches, not wanting to soil her jeans. Just as she lowered the zipper of his jeans, she heard Amani shriek behind her. She jumped upright, sending the stacked metal drums cascading like so many pins being dispersed by a bowling ball.

"What the fuck is going on here? You mother fuckers!" Amani flew at them, and they both pulled away, dodging her between the metal canisters as she spat obscenities.

"Amani, hold up a minute! You got something with Jayz?"

"Do I got something with him? You fucking nuts? He's my boyfriend! You know that, you piece a shit ho!" Amani lunged at her, but Jayz grabbed her arm and held her.

"Let go a me, you cheatin' son of a bitch! Mother Fucker!" She wrestled against him.

"Amani, believe me! I didn't know! You said your boyfriend was Jamar."

"It is! They call him Jayz!"

"Oh…I'm sorry… really, I…but anyway, nothing happened." Jasmine back-pedaled.

"You skank! Nothing happened cuz you got caught!" She squirmed against her boyfriend, managing to leave a deep scratch on his cheek with one of her long fingernails.

Amani's new bouffant hair piece knocked into his mouth and got caught in his teeth. He craned his head backward, "Jasmine, you best be gone; you feel me?"

Jasmine searched Amani's face for some semblance of the best friend she had known.

"Fuckin whore! Go sell yourself someplace else!" Amani's words filled the space between them.

Jasmine glanced behind her and found Jayz's friends milling around at the mouth of the garage, ready to step in if necessary. "Okay, I'm out," she announced and walked past the brothers and into the late afternoon light. Once on the sidewalk, she quickened her step, trying to put as much distance as possible between her and Amani's rage.

Amani showed up at Carlina's house at dinner-time, screaming and cursing on the front porch.

Jasmine banged open the screen door. "I already told you I'm sorry! I didn't know he was yours…or maybe I…I…I fucked up!"

"Damn right you fucked up. You are one big fuck up!" Amani was leaning forward, her hands gesticulating through the muggy air, "How many times I tell you! Huh? How many times? You even met him two weeks back at the school dance!"

"He wasn't at the dance."

"No, stupid…before, outside, we were getting high." Her eyes hardened, and her mouth was pulled in so tight, it looked like it would soon disappear from her face.

Jasmine searched her mind, "Okay, okay, I sort of remember that, but I thought you were cozy just to get a few blues. I had no idea who he was!"

"So, you'll just put your filthy mouth on anyone?"

Jasmine considered this and then snorted, "Anyone with blunts or a blue…yeah, I guess."

Amani picked up one of Carlina's small flower pots that sat next to the porch railing and held it like an outfielder preparing to toss a ball to first base. "You skank!"

Jasmine's body tensed, "I don't get it! Why aren't you standing on his doorstep? He's the one that opened his pants!" The bright-pink geraniums flew toward her head and she ducked left, narrowly avoiding them. The pot crashed against the side railing and cracked apart on the floor, splattering dirt and petals in front of the door. Jasmine felt the vibration of Carlina's heavy footsteps before the door opened.

"What the hell happened here? Jasmine, you did this?" Carlina's index-finger shook toward the mess of flowers and soil.

Jasmine tilted her head toward Amani.

Carlina's eyes scanned the porch and then she grabbed the broom that leaned against the doorpost. She went after Amani. "Get out a here! Go home, and don't you ever come back here again! Go, go, go!" She swatted at the girl as if she were just a clod of dried mud that needed to be swept. Amani had no choice but to back up, tripping down the few porch steps and landing hard on the curb.

"What the fuck? You lunatic, cunt! You're gonna be sorry for that! Shit, yeah!" Amani rose to her feet and hobbled away.

Handing the broom to Jasmine, Carlina spat, "What the fuck? She got that part right. See, that's why I don't want none of the neighborhood trash over here." Jasmine opened her mouth to speak, but Carlina's hands were raised, her arms jiggling side to side. "Don't be telling me that it wasn't your fault. You made friends with that!" She shook an angry finger in Amani's direction. "So much for your judgment. Now clean this mess up and get washed for supper. You're grounded for two weeks!" Carlina stepped into the house and allowed the slap of the flimsy screen door to be her last comment on the matter.

Amani's final revenge came just as Jasmine was clearing the supper table. Jackson entered the narrow kitchen at the back of the house sucking in hard through his nose. "I smell something funny," he said. "It's like that trash can fire that we passed underneath the highway."

At the mention of fire, Carlina rushed through their apartment sniffing the air and searching for the stench's source. Finding nothing in the interior, she banged opened the front door. There it was, right in the center of the porch, a blaze that threatened to consume the entire house. "Call 911!" she screeched to Jasmine, who grabbed the house phone and dialed.

Carlina pounded through the apartment, her palms waving in the air, her utterances a shrill word salad of curses. She was making so much noise that it was hard for Jasmine to hear what the emergency operator was saying. While still holding the cordless phone to her ear, Jasmine ran back to the kitchen and grabbed a pitcher of water sitting on the counter. She maneuvered around her hysterical foster mother, and then hustled out to the porch. After hearing that help was on the way, Jasmine let the phone clatter to the floor, took aim, and tossed the pitcher's contents.

The result was immediate. The flames that were licking the wooden banister vanished, and a plume of smoke rose in their place. By the time the firemen arrived, only a smattering of embers smoldered, and in a few moments, the firefighters were able to douse the rest with a hand–held extinguisher.

Once assured that there was no further danger, Jasmine followed her foster mother back into the house and watched her disappear into her bedroom. Jasmine released the breath she'd been holding and let her body fold into the living room sectional. Almost without forethought, her right hand clenched and began pounding her face. She might have actually hurt herself had Carlina not reemerged carrying two small white pills in her palm that Jasmine recognized from the streets. She trailed her foster mother into the kitchen and watched as Carlina downed the medication with an inch of whiskey, poured from a dusty bottle.

"Carlina, I'm so, so sorry. I don't know why she did that. I had no idea she was mad crazy like that. I—"

"Go wait at the curb." Carlina was looking at the sink, still stacked with dishes.

"Huh?"

"You heard me. Go wait at the curb."

Jackson entered the room and grabbed onto his mother's free arm, as if he wanted to be sure that he at least would be staying put.

"What's going on? That's it? She sets a fire, and so now I'm out on the street?" Panic raced through Jasmine and she felt light-headed. She reached for the refrigerator handle to steady herself.

Carlina gulped down the last of her whiskey and banged the glass onto the counter. Her eyes bore into Jasmine's. "I told you the rules the first day you were here, and I thought I made myself pretty clear all along. I put up with your going around the neighborhood and messing with them boys—don't think I didn't know about that. And I didn't say boo about that burnt smell that sometimes snakes in behind you—and yeah, I do know what that's from. But this here?" She paused and shook her head, "Uh-uh. This I cannot live with. And Lord knows what you're gonna get into later on if this is what you're doing now! I'm done…just done. Like I said, go wait at the curb." She tilted her head toward the front door.

A shudder travelled through Jasmine and then seemed to take root. Soon her whole body was trembling, her mind muddled. "Carlina, come on…I wasn't the one who set the fire…I…I'll never talk to her again. I'll never even look at her! Please! Just take a minute and think about it. Will you? I thought things were okay with us, with me living here an all. Jackson and I, we get along. I take care of him when you go out, I clean, I…I…." Where were her words? Where was her breath? There wasn't enough air in the room. She felt her throat constricting. "Really? Just like that, I'm out? Think on it a minute, okay?"

Carlina lifted her hands up into the air one last time and motioned toward the door, like a policeman directing traffic.

There was no choice. Jasmine moved in slow-motion, as if walking through mud. Once outside the front door, she heard the dead bolt slide into place, locking her out.

She could hear Carlina moving around the apartment, cursing as she slammed drawers, banged boots, and clattered closet hangers. Then the house went quiet and Jasmine held her breath, praying that Carlina had changed her mind. The front-door lock clicked open and Jasmine scrambled off the porch, wanting to at least appear to be following Carlina's directions.

While standing at the threshold, Carlina began tossing black garbage bags overflowing with Jasmine's belongings, out onto the charred porch. Once the plastic pile had grown sizable, Carlina let the screen bang shut and re-locked the inner door.

Jasmine stared at the entrance wishing for Carlina to reappear and talk through the situation. She believed there had to be a way to fix things. Hey, Carlina, can we talk about what happened? she texted. I think we can work something out. When there was no response, she added, I can change. I can do more. I can do whatever it is you need me to do. Can we speak a minute? When there was still no response, she closed with, Jackson is gonna miss me. I didn't set the fire. Please, think on it.

With no other option, Jasmine grabbed her bags out of the puddles on the porch and parked herself at the curb, feeling one with the street trash which, like her, would soon be hauled away.

PART TWO
The Color of Promise

Lakisha

Writing classified ads and occasional obituaries for the *Newark StarLedger* was not Lakisha's dream job. The plumbers and dog walkers, the deck specialists and psychics, they were all nice enough and they surely needed assistance in writing their copy, but it was a job she could do with her eyes closed. Some days, if her 3-year-old, Shonda, had been up during the night, she walked through her day in a sleep-like trance. It wasn't just the repetitiveness of writing short ads that she found irritating, but also having to mindlessly repeat the pricing structure to the stream of new customers. Still, she was grateful for a steady paycheck. Also, she'd talked her way into writing a bi-monthly poetry column about inner-city life. While it paid next to nothing, Lakisha was thrilled. She'd have done it for free!

She sat in her work cubicle and scribbled *Street Corner Love* on a legal pad. The poem had been bubbling up all week, perhaps because she and Theo were coming up on their eighteenth anniversary—eighteen years together, that is. They had never married. When she was young, Lakisha had longed for marriage, but there never seemed to be enough money for a proper church wedding and reception, and Theo said, "I'm not about to marry you with no dime-store ring and city-hall judge." Theo was good about a lot of things, but sometimes he could be as stubborn as a mule. Dottie too had never married, and she chided Lakisha for not doing better. The stupid woman couldn't see that she'd already done light-years better just by being with someone who came home every night without the scent of alcohol or other women trailing him.

Her cell phone began playing Chaka Khan, and she knew it was one of the kids' schools. *Let it not be too bad.*

"Ms. White? It's Mrs. Lawrence, the—"

"Yes, what's wrong with TJ?"

"He's got a fever."

"Again?"

"And some lymph nodes in his neck seem a little swollen. I think he should go to the doctor—today."

There was something about that last word that felt patronizing. "Just so you know, Mrs. Lawrence, I've done that, again and again as a matter of fact."

"I didn't mean to imply…I'm just concerned."

"I got you. I'll be there as soon as I can make it through the traffic, a half hour at most."

On her way out, Lakisha stopped into her manager's office. "TJ's sick again. I'll write all the copy soon as I get home and return calls too. I'm really sorry."

Her manager looked up distracted, then his eyes narrowed. "Next week's "Life Out Loud" column…is it ready? We've gotten some great feedback."

Lakisha couldn't suppress her smile.

"The last few were damn good, I have to say."

Heat rose in her face. "I've got a handle on next week's column. It's called *Street Corner Love*, about Theo and me meeting at a street-corner poetry slam."

"A love story—nice! Hope your boy feels better."

Lakisha found TJ lying in the nurse's office, with limp hands at his sides, like they were too weak to lift. "Hey, TJ," she rallied her spirits to rally his, and smiled.

"Make sure they run all the tests," said Mrs. Lawrence. "Tell them this has been going on for months; these fevers and weakness, and also the lymph nodes—make sure they feel them. Sometimes the clinics let things fall through the cracks."

Lakisha tilted her head. "We're not on Medicaid, so we won't be at any clinic."

"Oh, I…I didn't mean…." Her pale skin blushed over a band of freckles. "It's all insurance; doctors are so rushed."

"Uh, huh." Lakisha took in the nurse's puffy caramel braid and wrinkled jumper. Was there some rule that white women who worked in their schools couldn't take time to make themselves presentable? Ten minutes with an iron and five with a good brush and pomade would do it. She'd heard enough. "Let's get going TJ. Need help getting up?"

"Nah, I'm good." That's what he said, but his body teetered as he stood. She steadied him, and they made their way to the parking lot.

"Sorry you had to miss work to come get me."

He was so good, it made her chest ache. "Don't you worry. I got my boss tied around my finger. I bet he's wishing for an award, *most innovative newspaper column,* or some such nonsense." She watched TJ's face light for a moment and then go dark.

At the pediatrician's office, the waiting room was bustling with children and caregivers. TJ curled up on a chair and rested his head against the textured wall paper, and Lakisha took a seat at his side. She thought of the school nurse, and she felt bad about giving her a hard time. She was only trying to help, but there seemed to be some implicit blame if your kid kept getting sick, like you must not be parenting well. But she was taking good care of him…wasn't she? Lakisha reached over and stroked his forehead. Despite the tumult around them, TJ's eyes drifted shut.

Judging from the number of sick kids crowded into the vinyl-coated chairs, it looked like they'd be waiting awhile. Lakisha pulled a pad from her work bag. *Street Corner Love,* she read to herself and allowed her mind to drift.

"That was one bad-ass poem," he said simply, leaning his upper arm against a light pole so that her eyes were drawn to the size of the muscles in his arms and his strong chest that stretched the fabric of his turquoise T-shirt. "I write too." His wide forehead glistened with perspiration. He tugged a handkerchief from his back pocket and wiped down his face.

Lakisha wondered if he was really speaking to her, but she looked around and noticed that no one else was listening. She decided to respond with a nod and shoved her fingertips into the back pockets of her jeans in an effort to display the subtle curve of her hips and size 34B breasts that had blossomed over the last year.

Aunt Dottie had warned her about the devil between a man's legs. Still, many of her classmates already had sex. A few even sported baby bellies or had gone to the clinic in East Orange for abortions.

Theo looked at Lakisha expectantly, as if he had passed her the basketball and was waiting to see where she'd take it, but her eyes remained fixed on the cracked pavement, examining a piece of chewing gum that had turned black and hardened into the shape of an elephant's head.

He made another attempt, "So what else you got?"

"Say what?" She looked at him now, his eyes warm brown, his hair shaved close to his head, his dimpled chin.

"Poems. What else you got?"

"Oh," the fingers of her right hand brushed her mouth. "Well, what do you have?" she shot back. "You say you write; let's hear it."

"A'right, I'll do it for you, but I ain't got all the words memorized, and I ain't got it on me. Walk with me to my brother's house. That's where I'm staying."

"How far does your brother live?"

"Just a few blocks away."

"Is it worth the walk?" She tried not to smile.

He chuckled, *"You'll let me know."* He placed the palm of his hand at the small of her back and urged her forward, as if he had taken ownership of her—which for all intents and purposes, he had.

Theo directed her down Springfield Avenue to Clinton, where they turned toward Newark. She was so wrapped up in the hand that had come to rest on her hip, and the musky scent of his aftershave, that she was unaware of what was going on around her until a blaring car horn and Theo's strong arm around her waist pulled her out of the path of an oncoming car. Only then did she take in the sound of a mother shouting at her son from the second-floor window and the strong stench of rotting vegetables coming from a dumpster behind the corner grocery.

Theo's brother lived in a basement apartment, and when trucks came speeding down the avenue, the foundation of the building seemed to shake. The place smelled of mildew and old Chinese food, and Theo hustled around picking up empty soda bottles.

"It's my brother; he's a slob."

"Uh-huh." Lakisha began to chew her lip. The last time she'd been alone with a boy he was just that—a boy, an eighth grader named Jihad who tried to stick his tongue down her throat and get his shaking hand inside her winter jacket.

"Where's your poetry?"

"You got someplace to be?" His eyebrows lifted.

Her charade of toughness dissolved. *"No,"* she muttered.

"Then sit down and take a load off." He pointed to a fraying rust-colored sectional with coordinated pillows. *"Where are you in school?"*

"Irvington High."

"Yeah? Is old Mr. Harris still principal?"

"Uh-huh."

Theo shook his head smiling, *"Man, I spent lots of time in his office. That was back when they used to do a whole mess a that lecture punishment. Now, whatever you do, you get suspended. It's hard to get an education unless you're a saint."*

"I manage."

"I bet you do." His stunning smile lit the room.

As they spoke Theo maneuvered around the small apartment retrieving glasses and Coca-Cola from the kitchen, and a large bottle of rum that was three quarters empty from a cabinet next to the television. Lakisha followed him with her eyes, marveling at his form. He was a grown man and she knew that despite her budding curves, she was not yet a woman. She still slept with a doll, laughed with her girlfriends in the school cafeteria, and idolized rappers on the radio.

He handed her a glass that tinkled with ice and alcohol and sweetness. Lakisha took a tentative taste. In movies novice drinkers often choked, but this went down smoothly, the rum disguised in familiar brown bubbles.

"Where you live?"

"On Wagner, off of Stuyvesant."

She watched him as he mulled this over, and she wondered if he was thinking about how long it would take him to walk from here to there, already considering when he'd see her next, already planning—

"Where's your head at?"

She gave him a nervous smile. *"Sorry. So, you live here with your brother and his girlfriend. Where are they now?"*

"They're at work!"

The question was somehow offensive, but she wasn't sure why. The alcohol began swimming through her veins, and she lost some inhibition. "And you?"

"Me? I was just laid off. I was working in shipping for a company in Newark, but they got into some trouble and 'last one hired, first fired,' so it was me. But I'm on unemployment, so it's cool. And I got a little night job—off the books, covering a security-guard shift for my cousin."

He was wonderful. The more she drank, the more she allowed herself to know it. "I'd love to hear a good poem right now."

"You would? Well I don't know that I got a good poem, but I got a poem anyways."

"Modesty, humbleness; my pastor says those are noble things."

He laughed. "Well, your pastor gonna love me." Theo escaped into a bedroom and returned with a black and white marble notebook in hand. He began to read aloud with conviction, putting emphasis on the power syllables.

My brother was the moon, he was king a the streets,

Others tried to play him, slay him, but he had them all beat.

Guns packin, ladies sackin, he was hackin em up.

Bags a blunts, cunts, chumps, he was stackin em up.

Mama warned him, "Baby it's comin, ain't but time—and yours is gone."

That bullet snagged him, police they bagged him, Left blood puddlin on the lawn.

That empty-eyed chick, wantin to buy shit, still comes round and starts to cry.

I shout, "He's dead now! Clear your head now!

This shit gon kill, like my brother done die."

Lakisha felt the beat of his words resonate inside her. He was describing her streets, her neighborhood, those men in her world—

the ones admired by the young, scorned by the old, and avoided by anyone in between. These were the ones who had captured the heart and veins of her mother, had stolen her away. She knew his message, his loss so much like her own. He got it. He'd understand what she'd been through, the tragedy of her life.

Emotion rose in her throat and she pushed it back down. She wouldn't cry. He'd think her crazy. When he finished, and the room hung in silent expectation, she lifted moist eyes to him and began to applaud. "All right, that's all right, yes." She continued clapping until her hands hurt and fell into her lap.

Theo looked shocked. He sat down next to her, lifted her hands into his own and kissed each palm before whispering, "Thank you."

"When did you lose him...your brother?"

"It'll be two years in September. He was only eighteen but caught up in the gangs. We tried to get him out, begged him to leave town. That was the only way to do it. We were gonna send him to family in Virginia, but the streets took him first."

"I'm sorry. Pastor says the dead are at peace and with God and all. Hard to know."

"I wish I could believe." His face tightened.

Palms still tingling from his lips, Lakisha drained her glass and leaned back against the soft cushions feeling herself float in a pool of drunken bliss. She was relieved to have her guard lowered for her, and her body relaxed. When Theo brought his hand to her cheek and placed his soft mouth against hers, she didn't even flinch. It felt good and right. It felt magical.

His hands circled in slow motion over her body, measuring her readiness, her response. When he removed her clothing, it was in small half movements, exposing her smooth stomach, and then waiting; a breast, and a long pause; the button of her jeans; and what felt like an eternity to Lakisha who had psychologically surrendered her girlhood long before he discarded her panties and entered her.

*When he had finished, he shoved himself up from the couch.
"I work nights." He looked at the wall clock, "Shit, its six-thirty and
my work shift starts at seven, I gotts to go, princess."*

*Her head swimming with rum and her stomach queasy, Lakisha
felt around for her clothes. There was a wet spot beneath her, and
when she rose to shimmy into her jeans, she saw that it was tinged
with blood. Her cheeks flushed. She imagined how much a new
couch might cost, how she could ever explain the expense to Aunt
Dottie, how severe the beating might be. When Theo ducked into
the bathroom, she pulled the square cushion from its spot and flipped
it, revealing a faded coffee stain. Coffee is better than blood, she
thought and pressed it into place.*

*Theo was at her side, "Let's bounce." Racing out the door with
her trailing behind, he said, "How's Friday night?"*

"Friday?"

"Meet me here at five. I'm off that night."

"Okay."

*On the street, he pressed his lips to hers and ran toward the 94
bus that was pulling to the curb. Lakisha watched as he boarded,
flashed the driver his transit card, and was swallowed in the rush-
hour crowd. The bowels of the vehicle heaved and grunted, blowing
black exhaust into her face, and then he was gone. She was left
standing on the corner, breathing fumes and feeling wetness gather
in her panties.*

Lakisha lifted her pen; looping black ink across white paper, memory
across years, weaving with words the hopes and losses that brought
them together—those tragedies that bound them still. TJ's head fell
against her shoulder, and he started, but then relaxed, accepting his
fatigue and his need of her sturdy support.

Jasmine

Jasmine was sent back to the peppermint-tea lady. While she waited for a new placement, she had an emergency session with Miss Maggie, and tried unsuccessfully to concentrate on the schoolwork brought by her case worker. Since her temporary placement was in a different school district, Jasmine could either take two public buses to her old school or try to keep up with a twice-a-week tutor. Not wanting to ever see Amani again, she chose the latter. Alone with her schoolbooks, Jasmine had plenty of time to ruminate on her many mistakes and their consequences. She didn't really miss Carlina or Jackson, but she'd grown comfortable with them, and in her experience, change was never good. Nothing positive had come from leaving Treasure and William, and she feared that this next placement could be even worse.

Miss Maggie suggested she try journaling, but that seemed lame—especially when she had poetry. In her bedroom, Jasmine dug through the black garbage bags until she found it: her old spiral notebook. She leafed through the pages to her last poem, written three months earlier. How had she stopped writing? The book felt weighty yet fragile, much like the emotions it held, much like the person she used to be or—perhaps still was.

She fished out her favorite writing pen and fingered it. *Atlantis* was engraved in silver and it had a black rubbery band near the point. It was Treasure's pen, stolen from her purse back when…no. She would not relive it again. *Fuck Treasure, Fuck William, Fuck*

Amani, Fuck Carlina, Fuck them all! Anger was good. Anger had a taste like salty blood, a hot smell like charcoals waiting for burgers, a feel like steel nails sprouted from her knuckles, ready and waiting. Anger was power, while the sadness beneath it was a mound of helpless ash. She was done with ashes.

Jasmine crossed her legs on the bed and settled back against the birdcage wallpaper. The late afternoon light angled in through the black-iron grating. She turned to a fresh sheet of paper; white, clean, ready. Jasmine often wrestled with her words, but today she coughed them up like a single cathartic retch across the page.

Sister says we gotta go
Sun's too strong, and she aught a know.
Brothers they pull at my jeans, at my mouth
Saying light burns, I must shut it out.
But my heart it tears open, it's drawn to what's bright.
It begs the grave off,
Screams:
Put up a fight!
Me, I'm blind in the darkness,
No exit, no sight,
No way to undo what's been done—what ain't right.
Ain't no God up above in this place that I'm in
Ain't no hope, and no fixing
I'm way beyond sin.
Still, my heart beats a war drum
Commanding me, go!
Toward daylight, toward something, toward where?
I don't know.

A few days into her exile, the texts began to ping on her phone. The messages were short and noncommittal at first. When Jasmine didn't reply, Amani started texting more frequently, creating an insistence that filled the room until Jasmine silenced it, and shoved the phone into her back pocket. There was no reason to read about Amani's desperate need.

They had bonded together, had felt so much alike, but Jasmine now understood that it was their similarity that had sent a wrecking ball through everything. They were promiscuous, brazen, and thoughtless in that way that people are who've already lost just about everything, and don't much care about losing more. Thank God she hadn't joined a gang. She and Amani preferred to avoid that drama, along with everything that came along with initiation. She may have hooked up for drugs or kicks or out of complete loneliness, but it was always her choice, on her terms—sort of. She wasn't about to let a whole room full of Crips pound into her or beat on her, just so she could be a member of a stupid club. They'd protect her if she needed it, at least that's what she'd hoped. It never came to that though, and now it never would, not with that gang anyway, for she was in another neighborhood now, the equivalent of another planet.

Amani had taken a match to the only solid things Jasmine had: her lousy home, her street family, her poetry group, and the school where she had somehow managed to quietly succeed. Now she lay alone and bleeding on the asphalt of her life, unsure if she'd be able to survive whatever came next.

Sometimes, after begging a few bucks from the peppermint-tea lady, she'd board a local bus and take it in a loop through the streets of Newark. She found the steady sound of the engine, and the rocking motion of the bus, comforting. No one knew her there, and no one would be questioning her about her thoughts or the reason she stared off blankly.

One day as the bus heaved exhaust into the city streets, Jasmine recalled Miss Maggie asking her to imagine that she held a magic wand capable of changing her future. If Jasmine could cast a spell, she'd conjure up a foster mom who cared about her and would help her get into college. Also, she'd vanish all the partiers and crazies from her life. She and Amani had laughed at the charter school kids with their neat uniforms and backpacks full of hope, but now she wanted that. The bus hit a pothole, jostling her thoughts. Her birth mom—she needed to find her too. Maybe her next house would have internet access, so she could keep searching.

When Jasmine's new case worker, Miss Raymelle, asked for her phone so that it could be returned to Carlina, Jasmine felt mostly relieved. Some of the boys from the garage had also been texting, asking when she'd be coming by. *Never*, Jasmine thought. They'd helped trash her life. Still, perhaps she deserved nothing better.

During those weeks of waiting, she cursed herself as she scribbled poems. The anger was slowly burning off, leaving her charred in a silent reverie of regret. One afternoon she fingered through her jacket pocket and pulled out a small blade. It was a pocket-knife that Amani had convinced her to carry. She pressed the black button on the casing and the blade jumped out, sharp and threatening. Jasmine contemplated the steel edge, catching glints of light in the dying afternoon sun. She didn't want to end her life; in fact, she wanted to begin it. Yet her misery was so deep and visceral, she often felt lost, unhinged. It was only when she ran the sharpened metal over her exposed belly, that she found relief. As the thin line of blood emerged, she calmed; her injury now visible—if only to herself. Would anyone else ever see these cuts or the wounds that lay deeper still, the ones far below her skin?

Before deciding on Jasmine's next placement, Miss Raymelle took her out to Dunkin Donuts for a talk. There she sat across from Jasmine on an orange seat that was bolted to the floor, a deep crease in her brow, making her thirty-year-old face look much older. Jasmine appraised her and decided that aside from her slightly crooked teeth and the sadness that lived in her eyes, she looked a little like a young Michelle Obama. Something about the way she leaned forward to catch every word, and her kind head nodded, put Jasmine at ease.

Over hot chocolate and doughnut holes, Jasmine shared her story; William touching her, Treasure abandoning her, the crazy things she did with Amani, Carlina's hysterics and lousy parenting, all leading up to the porch fire and being tossed out to the curb. At the end of the telling, Jasmine made a simple request, "I'm gonna do my part, Miss Raymelle. I've learned my lesson, I promise. But I need help to…to make a fresh start. I know I messed up, but to throw me into the gutter? That was just wrong. Please, I need a solid place with someone who can just get me through the next few years." She took a sip of her now cold drink. "Treasure always talked about school. I know that's the way out, but I won't be able to do it if I'm living with someone who doesn't give a shit about me. I don't mean to curse, but it's the truth. Please, the next place…it has to be my last." Her despair seemed to fill the air, sucking the sweetness from the baked goods, the energy from the coffee percolating behind the counter.

Miss Raymelle then broke the rules. She slid out from her chair and went to the other side of the table, opened her arms and allowed Jasmine to fall into them. She held Jasmine against her sturdy frame and spoke hushed words of comfort as Jasmine let go, her silent tears falling on Miss Raymelle's print paisley blouse.

When her sadness was spent, Miss Raymelle cupped her cheek and whispered, "We are going to find you a good place, all right?"

After Jasmine nodded her agreement, Miss Raymelle dropped back into her seat. Jasmine felt her body tingling with the memory of the hug. How long had it been since anyone had held her—not a boy using her for his own pleasure, but an actual caring person? How much longer could she go on without hugs, without love, without feeling she had some place to call home?

After five more nights of chocolate cake and tears, Miss Raymelle brought Jasmine to her new residence in Newark. It was a cheerful-looking brick two-family house with flower boxes that overflowed with fuchsia petunias.

Champaine, a woman in her late fifties, with a too-big smile that offset a permanently furrowed forehead, met them at the door. "Come in, we've been waiting on you." As they entered, Miss Raymelle started to say something, then was cut off by Champaine's powerful index finger. "Kids!" she shouted, "Come on down! Jasmine is here!" Jasmine saw three grade school boys of various ages practically fall out of a stairwell and elbow against each other to get a glimpse of her. They had lots of energy like Jackson, and she hoped they weren't as spoiled. Then a girl a few years younger than her appeared, looking skeptical. "Here, come make yourself at home." Champaine ushered Jasmine onto a brown living-room sofa, and Miss Raymelle took her place on a beige club chair.

The other children stood staring until Miss Raymelle said, "Let's begin the introductions...."

Champaine was holding up that index finger again and marching to the stairs. "Karah! Get down here now! Jasmine's here, so don't make me give you a consequence. I'm waiting 30 seconds more and then taking your phone."

A few moments later, a girl close to Jasmine's age slid into the room wearing a scowl and an attitude. Champaine ignored both. "Thank you for joining us." She looked at the group, "Jasmine, this here is Karah and LaShaunna." LaShaunna gave her a subtle nod. "Pete, Lamar, and Danny." The two older boys waved, and the youngest, Danny, jumped up and down like either he had to go to the bathroom or the floor was too hot for his feet. "You'll get to speak with them when we have dinner together, but I just wanted you to begin to put faces with names and know that we're all happy to have you here."

Jasmine saw that the boys were excited, but the girls with whom she'd be sharing a room, were wary at best.

Champaine scanned her kids, "Okay, Jasmine, Miss Raymelle, and I are going to have a little talk. Y'all can go back upstairs."

Before Danny left the room, he went to Jasmine and gave her a hug, "Glad you're moving in. You look nice."

Looks can be deceiving, that's what she wanted to say, but instead she went with, "Thanks, Danny. Me too."

"She remembered my name! Cool!"

"Upstairs, Danny," said Champaine.

Miss Raymelle graced her with a warm smile. "Thank you, Champaine, for arranging to have everyone home today. You know sometimes it just feels like a good fit, and I think this is one of those times. As I mentioned when we spoke, Jasmine here is committed to turning her life around. In all the years I've been doing this, I don't know that I've met a kid so committed to making a fresh start."

"Oh, I'm all for fresh starts!" Champaine looked animated.

"And I've told her about your track record for turning teens around and successfully launching them."

"Well, Lord, I do try. Of course, it's mostly up to you, honey." Her eyes caught Jasmine's and held them firm. "I'll have your back. If you stay out of trouble, I'll be in your corner. If you want to make something of yourself, I'll do everything I can to see that it happens. If you got a problem, come to me. If the other girls give you a hard time, a definite possibility, you come to me. Same goes for messes you get into at school or in the streets. Don't go trying to fix it by getting even or threatening or whatever else you might've done in the past. I keep the order. You just behave, and I'll take care of the rest. Deal?"

Jasmine stared right back at her, hoping to God that this bossy woman would be able to deliver. "Will you help me when it's time to apply to college?"

Champaine beamed, "I'll be happy to help you, but last I heard, it was the student's job to do most of the heavy lifting with that. Don't worry though, I'll do my part. Like I said, you just have to do your job at school and applying and such. Also, I should mention that we all have a few chores we do here in the house. If you're okay with it, I could use some help in the kitchen with the cooking and sometimes with clean up. I don't trust the boys in the kitchen, and the other girls…you'll see for yourself. That is what it is. Can't change a person's nature, though I've done my share a trying, believe you me." Champaine's face erupted into another huge smile that felt contagious, and before she knew it, Jasmine's cheeks were lifting, as if a small seed had just started to burst through its hard shell.

Saying goodbye to Miss Raymelle at the door, Jasmine found herself falling into the caseworker's arms.

"You'll be okay. Champaine will be here for you. Stay out of the streets, and it'll all work out. You got me?"

Jasmine released her and took a step back. "Yeah, Miss Raymelle, I definitely got you."

On some Wednesday evenings, Miss Raymelle would come and visit to check on her progress. Jasmine tried not to get her hopes up, yet as she walked home on a chilly Wednesday in November, she felt her chest lighten with the possibility of seeing her. Once she reached Champaine's house, she went right to the bedroom she shared with her two foster sisters, pulled out her books and began studying. The best time for homework was always before the other kids came home and the house erupted with sound and motion.

A half hour later, the door banged open and the other girls entered, already engaged in a heated argument. They didn't acknowledge Jasmine's presence, and one even knocked into her arm as she moved toward their shared closet. Karah, the older of the two, had a sturdy athletic body, full breasts, and smooth brown skin.

She would have been pretty if her face wasn't always contracted as if she had just tasted curdled milk. LaShaunna had a somewhat thicker build and eyes that looked forever bored. The two seemed committed to sparring over just about everything, each one considering herself perpetually *disrespected* by the other.

Slamming her hand down on her text, Jasmine glared at the two of them. "Can't you fight someplace else? I have a test!"

Karah shot a sideways glance, "Why don't you take your book outside?" Then under her breath she muttered, "Geek."

Though Jasmine tried not to take the bait, she couldn't resist. "Yeah, well I'd rather be a geek than a ho. Does DeMarco know that baby isn't his, or is he just gonna buy you an abortion?"

Before she had finished the sentence, Karah was upon her, swinging her fists, trying to inflict as much damage as possible before Champaine entered the room and pried the two apart with strong hands.

Champaine smoothed her graying hair back into place and turned to the aggressor. "You stay here and think about how the hell you're gonna get along in life with that kind of behavior!" She then fixed her eyes on Jasmine who now sat straightening the bent pages of her textbook. "You are supposed to be the mature one. You're the oldest. You're not innocent here." She sighed and turned away, "Come on, Jasmine, let's make some dinner. Miss Raymelle is coming by soon, and I want us to eat before she gets here."

Jasmine followed her foster mother down the steps and into the large aging kitchen at the back of the house. "When did she call and say she's coming?"

"I don't know—yesterday, day before." Champaine was tying an apron on her rounded hips.

"Next time, when you find out she's coming, could you just let me know?"

Champaine was bent over a low kitchen cabinet extracting pans. "I'm letting you know right now!"

"No, I mean in advance, when you find out."

"Why? You gotta look pretty or something?"

Jasmine considered her response. She didn't want anyone to know she'd grown attached to her caseworker, that Miss Raymelle had become the closest thing she had to a mother, and that her visits held a certain importance. Instead of the truth she offered, "I like to plan my study schedule. These grades count for college and...I have to show the colleges I'm smart. That's all."

"Be plenty a time to study after she leaves. Can you season some flour? I'm gonna bake up a batch a pork chops real quick." She took a step over to Jasmine and ran her palm over the girl's shoulder. "It's okay, you worrier. You'll get your time with Miss Raymelle and study too. Just get the flour ready and you can go."

Once the chops were cooked and placed on the dining room table next to a huge tub of Costco kale salad and a bowl of wild rice, they all gathered. Champaine's crew used disposable plates and cutlery to cut down on cleaning but rotated washing the pots and pans every day.

Danny, the five-year-old, posed the question he asked each night, "Can we have soda?"

Champaine sighed. "How many times I have to tell you? There is no soda during the week. It's only on Sunday. Too much sugar is gonna rot out your teeth and make you crazy."

"Okay to be crazy on Sunday though." He flashed a mischievous smile.

"Sunday is the Lord's day. Up to him to calm you down."

"Pastor Blackwell does that for me," LaShaunna chimed in. "He puts me right to sleep."

The room erupted in laughter, and even Champaine offered a reluctant smirk. "Miss Raymelle is coming by after dinner, so...."

Before she could finish her sentence, the rest at the table exclaimed, "Best behavior!"

"Yes, that's right, best behavior. That means you too," she said glaring at Karah.

"Uh-huh," responded the teen without looking up from her plate.

A few minutes later the doorbell rang, and Danny opened it as he offered a belated, "Who's there?"

Champaine rushed to his side as Miss Raymelle stepped across the threshold. "What did I tell you about answering the door? You have to ask who's there!"

"I did!"

"Yes, but you have to ask it *before* you open the door!"

"You said Miss Raymelle was coming, so I knew who it was."

"But that don't mean it's her at the door!" replied Champaine, clearly frustrated. "Come on in Miss Raymelle. We were just finishing up dinner," she added as the case worker trailed after her into the kitchen. Jasmine was bussing plates, and Champaine bustled about like a nervous hen. "Everything in the garbage! Karah, you wash the pans!"

Miss Raymelle bit back a wry smile at the show of over-involved parenting. She walked into the living room and took her usual seat on the single club chair and Jasmine followed close behind. As the case worker extracted a notebook and calendar from her bag, Jasmine took her place on the right side of the sofa and Champaine brought her wide bottom down on the other end of the long cushion.

Miss Raymelle began, "Okay, so how..."

Before she could finish her sentence, Champaine raised her finger and shouted, "It's homework time! You all go to your rooms! If everyone in your room is done, then you can turn on the TV— but only if *everyone* is done. Got it?"

A chorus of mumbled yeses echoed through the house.

She turned to face the case worker, "All right, you go ahead now."

Miss Raymelle raised her eyebrows and addressed her question to Jasmine. "How are things going for you?"

"Okay, I mean good, they're good." Her eyes scanned the Berber carpet and she began chewing on a fingernail. She much preferred the visits where Miss Raymelle took her out alone instead of asking her questions in front of Champaine.

"Good how?"

"The school is okay. I like the teachers; that's the most important thing." She hesitated before adding, "The kids aren't the greatest."

"Just takes some getting used to, that's what I tell her," interjected Champaine.

"Yeah, its reputation isn't the best, but not really worse than Irvington High where she went last."

"No, it's not worse, just different kids is all."

"How are you getting along with them?"

"Okay. I don't get into any trouble or anything."

Champaine added, "I haven't heard anything from the school, and so far, her grades are terrific."

"Friends? You have some friends yet?"

She thought for a few moments. "I'd say I have acquaintances, not really friends."

Miss Raymelle shifted in her chair. "No? Still no one? How come?"

"I don't know, I just don't...I don't want people to be able to use anything against me. I don't want to give them ammunition." She looked down at the sofa cushion and began fingering a fraying edge of fabric.

"Ammunition to...."

Jasmine hesitated. It was always difficult to decide what to say in front of Champaine and what to withhold. Still, she needed to share with someone. "Ammunition to hurt me...if I tell them...

personal stuff. They might run their mouths. Especially if I tell them anything about my past or my living situation or whatever."

"I know you don't want to share too much too soon, but I was hoping that you'd make a few friends here. Talk about neutral stuff: school, TV shows, or movies—"

"That's what I been telling her," said Champaine.

"Y'all are talking like the kids round here can be trusted, like they're not all out for themselves and looking to screw me over. Well maybe you're right, but I'm not taking any chances. You know I've been burned before."

"You think a lot about what happened at your last placement?" Miss Raymelle's voice was gentle.

"Well that wasn't my fault!" she was incredulous. "I don't know why she blamed me!"

"Arson is serious, Jasmine. The house could have burned down, and it was your friend that set it."

Jasmine was on her feet now. "She wasn't my friend! Once she started harassing me, she wasn't my friend anymore! She did that to hurt me. and then I get thrown out of my house! Is that what you call a friend? You can keep em all!"

"Jasmine, you gotta calm down." Champaine scolded.

"Baby—come and sit down." Miss Raymelle's fingers reached over and touched the sofa cushion. "No one is saying it was your fault. I know it's been hard moving from place to place. But this is it. You're staying here with Champaine."

"I really can't take any more drama. I'll make acquaintances maybe, but no friends."

A scream came from the boys' bedroom upstairs, and Champaine excused herself. Her loud reprimands were soon heard, followed by high-pitched responses.

"Miss Raymelle, I'm fine this way—really."

"All right, we'll drop it for now."

Champaine returned with her lips pressed tight and her eyes still angry.

"So, if there's nothing else, we'll just sign our paperwork, and I'll get going." She shuffled a few papers on her lap and passed a clipboard and pen to Champaine.

Walking Miss Raymelle out, Jasmine felt emotional. She remained in the doorway until the last glimpse of Miss Raymelle's red-wool pea coat disappeared.

Tessa

Tessa sat on her lavender duvet with her MacBook resting on one knee and her advanced placement physics text book lying across the other. Kate's voice sounded from her cell phone on the bed and Tessa's brow creased as she tried to make sense of a complex formula. "I'm gonna fail tomorrow," Tessa declared.

"You know it! Explain it back to me."

"Okay, but...no, I've got practice."

"Ugh, so when should we work on this week's editorial for the newspaper? Oh, yeah, we have that psych project."

"Hmm...just chill, and we'll figure it out. We don't have anything else big coming up do we?"

"Naw, nothing much. Unless of course you count the physics test Monday and calculus this Friday."

"Shit. Okay, we'll also study calc tonight and start physics tomorrow. Do you have any more Red Bull?"

"My mom banned them, but I have a few stashed in my camp trunk."

"Bring them tonight and get here at 8:30." Tessa tossed aside her schoolbooks and went in search of a clean leotard. Finding none, she headed over to her laundry hamper and began picking through the clothes.

"You never get home before nine," Kate's voice chided.

"I'll leave early!"

"Yeah, right. States are coming up."

Finding a leotard in the bin, she brought it to her nose and gave it a sniff. "All right, nine then, but tell your mom you're sleeping over, otherwise she'll start bitching at eleven."

She wriggled out of the long layers of shirts and tight jeans that clung to her body and stepped into a shiny gold leotard. She glanced at her phone and saw that she still had a few minutes. Instinctively Tessa went to the three websites she always had open on her phone and checked the latest listings of birth mothers looking for their children. The search had become a habit since the start of 10th grade. At that point, Alice had become panicked about getting Tessa into college and began micromanaging her life. After one particularly irritating discussion with her mother, Tessa went up to her room and began scouring the internet in search of her birth mom. It was a passive-aggressive move; a fuck you of sorts that remained her own private secret. Over time it also became a way to escape her pressure-cooker life and imagine herself as a different person—someone rooted to the ground, someone who knew about her past—all of it. She scrolled through the dozen or so new profiles and broke from her research only when her mother called from downstairs, "Tessa! You've gotta go!"

The next morning Tessa woke at 5 am. Her one thought was of coffee. She grabbed her computer, shoved her feet into furry blue slippers with yellow moons and stars sewn onto the top, and pulled her long tangle of honey curls back into a bun. Riley met her at the door and the two padded down the steps to the first floor.

In the kitchen, Tessa made instant coffee, and then got to work proofreading her English essay already edited by her mother. "I don't even remember writing this," she mumbled to the empty room. "Oh, Mom, what did you…that wasn't…we discussed that in class."

At 5:30 a.m., satisfied that her English essay was decent, *sorry mom, it's not perfect,* she began downloading articles for the school newspaper. As editor, she was the only staff member with complete access to all the stories. It gave her final say on every piece, but also meant that she had to at least peruse everything submitted. She sifted through her inbox and sent several files to others for editing, while keeping for herself the op-ed piece about a fight at a boys' varsity soccer game involving two parents, a referee, and a questionable out-of-bounds call.

Tessa did aim for perfection, but knew she fell far short. She was in the top ten percent of her high school class but would never be valedictorian. She'd received a few gymnastics medals but had fallen in the rankings. She was well-liked within her clique of friends, but they weren't the most popular. Fortunately, she also had romantic options if she wanted a hook up. Her thoughts travelled briefly to Eric Leaderman, and the way his soccer thighs had glistened after last week's game, right before he pressed them up against her own in a deserted stairwell. *Sorry, Mom, that part of me isn't perfect either.*

On a rainy Saturday morning, Tessa entered the Wildwood Convention Center and joined her teammates who were warming up for the state competition. As the meet progressed, Tessa felt happy. It turned out to be one of those rare days when everything seemed to be going her way. On the balance beam she only had two small bobbles and no falls, her vaults were solid, and her uneven bars routine stellar. Once the first round was finished, she and her crew pulled out their lunches and Coach called her over for what he now called the *mid-mortem.*

Coach stood while talking to her. Tessa had almost never seen him seated. It was as if his steel legs were opposed to repose, and he didn't seem to like it much in his athletes either. He leaned forward as he spoke, his face close to hers, so as not to be overheard by any of their opponents. "You're doing well. Solid so far. Don't be distracted by the North Star girls. You're here to do your personal best—the marks will take care of themselves."

"I'm nervous about the bars dismount."

"In the moment, you'll know. You'll know if you've got it in you to do the double. It doesn't have to be flawless, just solid. Stay focused, and it'll happen." He gripped her shoulder and nudged her back toward the other girls. "Send Caitlin over."

When the break ended, Tessa packed up her things and moved through the cavernous space along with the other girls wearing shimmering scarlet long-sleeved leotards with white diagonal swirls. Fatigue was setting in, but her efforts proved productive; she received respectable scores on both vault and balance beam.

The uneven bars were next, and Tessa found her doubts resurfacing. She glanced at the scribbled score chart in her bag. She might take home bronze or even silver if only she could have a smooth routine and stick the landing. It would be a fabulous way to end her high school career. Even better, it would prove her mother wrong; she could succeed in her own way. She didn't have to be like Lily. Before beginning, she rubbed chalk on her hands, looked up at the high ceiling, and offered a silent prayer.

Right from the start, Tessa's grip was firm, her limbs rope-like and tight, her toes exquisitely pointed. She mounted the high bar and began her long-armed circles. She was in the zone; in that ideal place where strength, art, and determination combine to create something that feels at once ecstatic and terrifying. She had seen other girls achieve this, but now it was her—she was the one whose lines were seamless, whose body moved with perfect grace.

All that remained was the dismount. During her final loop around the high bar, she'd release her grip at precisely the right moment, contract herself into a ball, and do two somersaults as she flew down towards the mat. This was the double salto backwards tucked dismount that she'd been practicing for over a year. She'd mastered the simpler salto backwards tucked and salto backwards straight. But she'd struggled in recent weeks with finishing the second rotation. Though she was feeling drained and wasn't completely confident in this final skill, it would earn her an extra 0.1 point. She gathered her last bit of strength and went for it.

It was all perfect; she was perfect, right up until the moment that a toe on her left foot caught on the high bar during the dismount. She felt her tight body unravel. She needed to get her feet below the rest of her, but there was too much momentum, and her head was coming down first, while her legs were poised up above, her entire body arched backwards. She landed on her cheek and neck, and then her chest and abs slammed into the mat.

Tessa heard her mom saying, "It's okay, Sweetheart. You're gonna be okay," even before she opened her eyes and saw her mom's long face and her dad's distressed eyes next to her. She tried to get up, but Coach told her no. Methodically, he went through every part of her body asking about pain. At some point during this process, she glanced up at the stands and realized that she had become the main event. The parents and family members of the other gymnasts were all on their feet trying to get a glimpse, like rubberneckers passing a highway crash. Would the paramedics be called? She willed away her tears. When she was permitted to slowly rise and walk across the mat to her teammates, the entire audience cheered.

Through the din, she heard her mother telling Coach that she should be brought to the hospital. Coach ignored Alice and had Tessa lay face down with giant ice packs on her neck and back. The girl next to her rose for her turn on the bars, and Tessa noticed her trembling. *It must have looked horrific, and now they're all shaken.*

Despite Tessa's setback, her team proved resilient. They finished surprisingly well on the uneven bars and then moved on to their final event. Tessa tried to watch the other girls on the team and even managed to cast a smile here and there when one of them had a particularly good routine, but inside she was wrecked. It wasn't just that that her back ached and that she'd quashed any chance she had of medaling. It was more the humiliation of having sailed off the high bar in such a spectacular way. Her greatest applause came not for her performances, but for her ability to still stand up and walk.

Once all the medals were awarded, Coach came over to Tessa and her parents. "You feel a little better now?"

Tessa lowered her eyes and nodded.

"Good. If she's in pain overnight, you can take her to be checked out, but probably it's just muscle. Rest tomorrow and ice it."

Tessa maneuvered as fast as she could through the crowd, and once their car left the parking lot, her face contracted, tears trailed down her cheeks, and a sob escaped her throat.

"Are you hurting?" her mother turned around and touched her knee.

"No, not much."

"Oh, Tessa, sweetheart, it's gonna be okay. We're going to the ER to get you checked out. Coach...this isn't the 1970s Soviet Union. I don't know what he was thinking."

Tessa wiped her face with the sleeve of her warm-up jacket. "He was thinking I'm a fuck up."

"Tessa!" both her parents said in unison.

"He wasn't thinking that!" Her mom's eyes widened. "How do you think he knew right away what to do when someone has a fall from the high bar? He's probably seen it a hundred times! You think you're the first one to snag a toe during a dismount?"

"Mommy is right." Her father chimed in. "As a matter of fact, once at your gym last year, I saw a younger girl make the exact same mistake. But because she was small and not as well trained, she didn't have much momentum."

"Exactly, that's what I'm saying; it was a mistake that someone inexperienced would make."

"Don't be so hard on yourself." Her father caught her eye in the rear-view mirror.

They don't have a clue. "I'm gonna listen to some music and try to calm down." She put earbuds in and scrolled through her playlist. "I hate myself," she whispered under her breath and tapped on a Rihanna song.

After waiting hours in the emergency room, Tessa was finally examined and x-rayed. She lay on her stomach, the ice on her back doing little to numb the pain or her hot nest of emotions. When her mom tried to speak to her, she grunted out answers. She was not ready to be cheered-up, not even close.

At a quarter past midnight, a physician who reminded her of Michelangelo's David with clothing and less pasty skin, entered the curtained cubicle. "Fortunately, it looks like it's a soft tissue injury," pronounced the doctor who held an x-ray in his hand. "Ice it; twenty minutes on/twenty minutes off while you're awake for the next day or two. You can take ibuprofen for the pain, and definitely rest."

"How long should she rest?" asked Alice.

"Coach said—"

"Tessa, let's hear the doctor!" Her mom stared her down.

The physician lifted his shoulders, "It all depends on how she feels." He turned to Tessa, "Your back is going to be tender for a while. You really don't want to do strenuous activity until the pain is gone. Otherwise, it might not fully heal, and the pain could become chronic. Okay?"

Tessa stayed away from the gym for a full two weeks, all the while arguing with her mother, until her mother shouted, "Go ahead! Do a back walkover right now and see how you feel!"

It was a simple request but a scary one. Tessa moved into the wide-open entry hall and planted her bare feet on the wooden floor. She hesitated and lifted her arms up over her head a few times, gathering courage. Then she arched and brought her hands to the floor. "Owww!" as her feet became airborne, the sound escaped her throat.

"There's your answer. You're not going back."

Tessa stood massaging her back. "What, not ever? Of course I'm going back!"

"Why? It's your senior year, there are less than a hundred colleges that have gymnastics teams, and you're injured."

"But I'll get better!"

"What if you don't get better? What if going back to the gym makes it worse, or you get hurt again and this time it *is* serious? What if you permanently injure yourself? Next time you could really break your neck. Is it worth it?"

"That won't happen!"

Something seemed to tighten inside Alice. She pressed her hands against the sides of her face and shook her head as if to rid herself of a disturbing thought. "You didn't see it! You didn't see your daughter go flying head first toward the mat. You landed on your neck with your body in a backwards arch; your toes were practically on your forehead! Then you didn't move! You didn't move...you just laid there and the whole gym went silent. They didn't even start the floor music. It was like we were all waiting to see...waiting to see if you'd...ever move again." Her mom was quiet for a few moments, then her face hardened. "Don't tell me what Coach said, or what you think you have to do. Put yourself in my shoes. I spend my whole life protecting you and then I see...that!" Her flaming eyes wouldn't let her go.

Tessa's voice was soft. "I'm sorry I scared you. But, please... don't punish me."

"It's not up to me. We'll discuss it again when you have no more pain."

"But by then I'll be completely out of shape. It'll be too hard to come back."

Her mom shrugged, and after a long sigh walked away.

Being banned from the gym eased Tessa's tight schedule. She began speaking with kids at colleges where she'd already been accepted and considering possible majors. Her parents had pushed her to apply to schools even if they didn't have her sport, and now she researched their programs carefully.

She also now had time to intensify her birth-mother search. She learned how to appeal to the courts to unseal her adoption records, and even composed a letter for her parents to co-sign, but then thought better of it. She'd wait until she turned eighteen and could handle it on her own. Alice was sensitive, and whenever Tessa tried to speak about her search, her mother became quiet, practically catatonic. Perhaps Alice worried that Tessa might come to prefer her biological mother, but whatever the reason, the topic felt completely taboo. Tessa's only option was to continue her secret search for that one elusive listing, and the mother who could explain her past.

She wondered what her birth mother looked like and what things she enjoyed. Did she have curly-blonde hair or amber eyes? Thick lips or a small, tight frame? Did she like rhythm and blues or fantasy fiction? Lyrical dance or story slams? Was she smart and driven? Was she living a good life? And most importantly, why did she give her away? She joined a Facebook group, and got to know others who'd spent years looking for their birth parents, and even joined an online support group called *In Search of Mom.*

"What are you always looking at on your phone?" Alice asked one day as Tessa sat at the kitchen table tapping on the screen.

"Huh?" she clicked her phone off. "Nothing, just surfing."

"You do an awful lot of that."

Tessa tossed her curls back, feeling defiance kindle in her chest. She tucked her phone in the waistband of her leggings and ran upstairs.

Tessa's senior year seemed interminable. Coach phoned twice to ask when she'd be back. After that, she never heard from him. Occasionally, she'd still argue with her mom about going back to the gym, but she knew it was futile. As if admitting defeat, she'd return to her screens and her search for answers.

Then on one fated day in March, two envelopes arrived. One was from Cornell and the other from Barnard. Tessa held them both in her palms as if weighing them, one against the other. Perhaps a heavier envelope meant an acceptance and a lighter one contained rejection. Which one should she open first? Her chances with Barnard were better, so should she open that one first? Or maybe it'd be better to open Cornell first, so that if she was rejected there, an acceptance to Barnard would lift her spirits. She put them both down on the kitchen counter. Without further thought, she grabbed the one from Cornell, ripped it open, and tugged out a crisp piece of stationery. She scanned it and then slammed it on the counter. "Shit!"

"What's the matter?" Her mother's voice echoed from the front hall.

She felt humiliated. It was true that getting into Cornell was now much more difficult than it was twelve years ago when Lily had applied, but that meant little to her parents. If only she had been accepted, she might have felt good enough and accomplished enough to fit in with the rest of her family. Without waiting for her mother to enter the room, she tore into the envelope from Barnard. "Yes!"

Her mother was beside her, "What's up? Did you get in somewhere?"

"Yes, I got into Barnard!"

"Hey! Congratulations!" She gave Tessa a hug. "Nothing yet from Cornell?"

Tessa motioned to the bent letter sitting on the counter. "Go ahead, take a look."

Alice lifted the letter printed on formal stationary. "Oh, you were waitlisted. Okay, that's not so bad, really."

"No?"

"There's still a chance…"

"Not likely."

"Still, you can call and write to them. I've heard that helps."

"Pfff, I've read the statistics. They don't accept many from the wait list. I think it'll be Barnard." Why get her hopes up. Kate was going to Columbia for Engineering, so Barnard would be just fine.

Even after she'd been accepted to college, the academic pressure continued. Finals and Advanced Placement exams loomed large. Alice continued hovering over Tessa, as if she was one of her mother's rose bushes that needed constant attention. Tessa came home late one Tuesday, and her mother and Riley met her at the door. "Hey Tess, how's it going?"

"So, so." She bent down and stroked Riley's side. "I still have more work, but I got a lot done at Kate's. I keep waiting for these teachers to wake up and realize that this is the very end of senior year and we are just done—toasted, stick a fork in me I'm ready, and stop assigning more work."

"I guess they're trying to prepare you for the AP tests, so you can get your college credit."

"Ugh! No college is going to accept all the credits we have. It's just a waste of time."

Her mom was behind her, giving her a backwards hug, and Tessa tried to keep from tensing or pulling away. Her lips pressed against the side of Tessa's head instead of against the top of it like they used to before Tessa hit her late growth spurt in ninth grade.

With her mother so relaxed, Tessa thought the timing might be right, "Hey, Mom? You know we had to bring in those baby pictures to school for the senior send-off."

"Uh huh, I saw you pick them last week."

Tessa turned to face her and began twisting a stray curl at the nape of her neck. "So, Kate and I were over at Haley's, and we were looking at pictures of her mom on the day she gave birth and these pictures of Haley with the umbilical cord hanging off her belly. And I suddenly realized, I'd never seen pictures of me on the day I was born. Also, I don't have a clue what my birth mother looks like. I could pass her on the street without knowing it. Do you have pictures anywhere? Did you ever meet her? You did, didn't you?" Tessa tried to keep the desperation from her voice.

Her mom paused and appeared lost in thought. She blinked hard and said, "We never met your birth mother. I wish we had. It was all done through an agency. We met you when you were five days old." A smile blossomed on her face and her eyes looked distant. "God, you were so adorable. We were in shock—thrilled, but in shock." Her hand reached out and stroked Tessa's back, "No, unfortunately, we don't have pictures—of you or…her."

"You know there's another kid in my class who's adopted, and he sees his birth mom on holidays. They kind of treat her like an aunt or a cousin." Her feet felt like they were shoved into ice-buckets. "You really don't know anything about her?"

Alice pressed her lips together and withdrew her hand. "She was sixteen."

Tessa waited for something else, but there was nothing. "So, she was sixteen…that's it? That's all you know?"

Her mom's eyes grew wide. "Tessa, don't have such an attitude. If you tell me what you want to know, I can try and do research, but other than learning that she never had any major illnesses and wasn't drinking or on drugs during the pregnancy, that's all I remember. We got you, and that was what mattered to us! Why are you asking?" Her mom started picking invisible lint off her black yoga pants.

Tessa raised her palms. "All right, Mom, just chill! Just forget I ever asked."

Alice walked away, and Tessa was left in a vacuum, wondering if there might be something important that her mom was hiding—some piece of information about her birth mother that was upsetting. It might take time, but she was resolute. Someday, she'd learn the truth.

Jasmine

The letter from Rutgers arrived in a large envelope. *Was that a good thing?* The word "Rutgers" was printed in scarlet ink on the corner. Jasmine had done everything she was supposed to do: kept her grades up, gotten involved in the student newspaper, and joined the tutoring club. She had also dragged Champaine down to the Rutgers campus in Newark so that she could apply online using one of their computers, and even convinced her to take two hours off work and join her on the campus tour. She had solicited recommendations from her physics and English teachers and had applied to the special low income program that would give her a virtual free ride if accepted. Still, she wondered if all her efforts had been enough. The state paid for her to take the entrance exam only once, and she had no money to take it again or even pay for the six session Kaplan course that was offered at the Baptist Church.

Now she was holding it in her hands, the letter that would let her know whether she would be a Rutgers student living in a college dormitory, or a student at Essex County College forced to live in a transitional group home with other damaged young women, people she imagined would be brimming with anger about their lousy lives. They would laugh at her studiousness. Poke holes in her fledgling self-esteem. She just wanted a quiet life away from the drama of those who came into this world unwanted or were abandoned by those they loved, a life where she could help others instead of always being helped, a life free from the therapists, case workers, and foster parents who populated her life up until now. Jasmine craved privacy. Two of the boys were sitting at the dining room table doing homework, and one was at the living room coffee table coloring in a picture for school. His backpack and school papers were strewn across the floor. On any other day, she'd be annoyed, but today she stepped through his mess without noting the crunch of paper beneath her feet.

"Hey! Get off my stuff!" he protested.

She found her bedroom empty. "Thank the Lord," she whispered and sat down on her bed cross-legged, the letter resting on one knee. "Here goes," and with that she tore open the envelope and pulled out the contents. She held a shiny red folder with a crisp white letter on the top.

There was no mistaking the first word on the page, for it was written in all capital letters and bold print, and it was followed by an exclamation point. "*CONGRATULATIONS!*" it read. "The Committee on Admissions at Rutgers University Newark, is pleased to offer you admission...."

A high pitched, "YES!" filled the air. Her mouth fell open and she shook with happiness. She read through the rest of the letter without taking much in. A second letter let her know that she was also admitted into the low-income program which meant that if she did well academically, she'd go tuition-free for all four years. Another letter from the financial aid office explained the work-study program and federal loans that would cover her housing and expenses.

After placing the letters back in the folder, she hugged it to her chest. "Lord, if you're up there and you had anything to do with this, then thank you." She pulled out her cell phone and was grateful that she had some minutes left. She'd wait to tell Champaine when she returned from work, but Miss Raymelle—she needed to know. She dialed her number and was surprised when she answered after the third ring.

"Miss Raymelle, it's Jasmine. I just opened the letter—I got into Rutgers!"

"Baby, that is the best news I have heard in a long time! I am so, so, proud of you! And you should be proud of yourself!"

"I am. I mean, I guess I am. I just can't believe it."

"Well you believe it, baby. You worked so hard for this and you deserve it. Did the letter talk about the scholarship?"

"Yeah! I got into the program—the free one! I don't even know what to do with myself."

"What did Champaine say?"

"She's not home yet. I phoned you first."

"Aww, y'all have some celebrating to do! She'll be thrilled! I'm scheduled to come by tomorrow—so we'll talk all about it, okay?"

"Okay, Miss Raymelle."

"Thank you for calling me. Tell Champaine I said congratulations to her too."

"I will."

"Bye-bye, college girl!"

Jasmine pulled the phone to her heart and laid back on her bed. Her fists punched the air as she shouted, "Yes! Yes! Yes!" Then she was on her feet arching backward as she punched out a celebratory dance. She opened the door of her bedroom, trotted down the steps, and looked at the boys who played the role of her brothers. "I'm into Rutgers!"

It just took a moment for them to jump on the furniture and start whooping it up. Into this jubilant mayhem came LaShaunna and Karah. They both wore school backpacks, and Karah balanced her one-year-old son, Georgy, on her hip. He was a chubby, docile baby with a crop of soft curls. Champaine had agreed to let him stay with Karah in the tiny room that used to be her office, so that Karah wouldn't have to move away.

"What the fuck is going on here?" Karah dumped her baby on the couch with her backpack.

It was Danny who ran to her and gave her an unwanted hug before sharing the news as he bounced on his heels, "Jasmine got into Rutgers! She's going to college!"

"Huh, so being a freakin' geek paid off! Congratulations Brainiac."

"Uh, thanks—I think."

"Way to go Jas!" LaShaunna lifted a fist and bumped it against Jasmine's. "You just heard?"

"Got a letter."

"That is mad cool. Where is the school?"

"I'm gonna go to the Newark campus."

Karah smirked, "College in Newark? That don't sound like nothing special."

"There's actually a nice campus with dormitories, grass, and trees. Maybe you'll come visit."

"Yeah, well, I wouldn't hold my breath. I'm not even interested in going to high school, so why would I go to see you at college? You want a visit, you come on back home." Just then her son, who had climbed down from the sofa, latched onto her leg and started to use it as an anchor to pull himself up to a standing position. "Whatchu want, Georgy!"

The baby looked up at her with large empty eyes, and a strand of drool that was hanging from his mouth broke free and dropped onto the leg of her jeggings.

"Shit, Georgy, when you gonna get all them teeth and stop your drooling!" She grabbed him under his arms and tossed him back on the couch. "Sit yourself down and you won't be drooling all over me."

Danny tapped her arm. "You shouldn't curse in front of him. That'll teach him to curse."

She bobbed her neck, "Oh, you the expert?"

"And if you keep telling him to sit, he's not gonna learn to walk, so you'll have to keep carrying him."

The room erupted with laughter. "Okay, you got a point there. He is fucking heavy."

Danny shot her a reprimanding look.

"I don't give a fuck if he curses!"

"Yea, but his teachers will care—trust me."

Karah reached across the coffee table and tugged her son off the sofa and onto his feet. "There you go little man. Mama is tired of lugging you around, so go ahead and walk." She gave him a gentle shove and he fell forward onto the carpet, his head just missing the rectangular coffee table. He gave a few grunts while pulling himself up again, this time holding onto the table for balance.

"There you go, Georgy!" Danny was bending down next to him.

"You can do it!" The other boys joined in.

LaShaunna suggested, "Let's try holding one hand and see if it helps."

Soon Georgy was in the middle of the living room with an encouraging audience. Karah let him use her leg to pull himself upright, and then grabbed onto one chubby hand. "Come on baby, we're going for a walk now."

"You can do it! Come on, Georgy!" The room echoed with their cheers.

Georgy gave a grunt or two before taking one tentative step forward on his toes, grabbing onto his mother's hand with both of his own, and collapsing his bottom to the carpet.

Karah righted him, and again came the words of support—even from his mother. This time he grunted his way through a few steps before falling, and the group began the process all over. After several attempts, he managed to walk across most of the long narrow room and the boys and girls hooted like their team had won the Super

Bowl. Karah lifted him up and danced around with him, shouting, "Good boy, Georgy! You're the man! My little walker!" and Georgy's round cheeks lifted.

Danny rubbed his hand against the baby's belly, and Georgy giggled. Soon everyone was taking a turn and the baby's laughter filled the room.

Into this tumult came Champaine. "What's going on here?" she was chuckling. Her children's delight was contagious. Danny grabbed her around her thick middle and began recounting the events of the afternoon with breathless enthusiasm.

"So, Georgy is walking, and Jasmine is going to college?"

Danny nodded his head, "Uh-huh!"

"Well that news just made my day...my week...maybe my year." Georgy was right in front of her, still smiling in Karah's arms. Pressing both of his chubby cheeks between her palms, Champaine brought her nose to his and then kissed his forehead. "Georgy, you are such a big boy now—walking all over the living room! Good for you, big boy!"

She released the baby and looked around the room for Jasmine. Finding her receding into the back of the group, Champaine caught her up in a hug. "I am so proud of you—I can't even tell you. Rutgers University, my-oh-my!" She took a step back and held Jasmine at arm's length. "If you want, you can still live here. You know that, don't you? You don't have to pay money for a dorm or go to one of those transitional homes or whatever."

Jasmine could feel color rise in her face as her eyes met Champaine's and then darted away. She fumbled for words, words that might express her appreciation, but at the same time.... "Thank you—I'm grateful, really. I'm just not sure yet...."

Champaine cut her off. "No need to decide yet. Right now, we got some celebrating to do!" She gave Jasmine another squeeze and looked around the room. "How about we get our homework done real quick and head over to Red Lobster?"

The room erupted into more cheers. "Go try and get it all done so that we can watch a fun movie together when we get back!"

The boys began scrambling to their books and Danny sang a song of celebration that he'd made up for the occasion. He kept singing it right up until Karah gave him a slap on the back of the head and muttered, "Enough."

But that night nothing was enough. The children toasted Jasmine and Georgy over forbidden night-time Coca-Colas, consumed giant plates of shrimp and crab sautéed in butter, mounded their plates with over-dressed salads, and ordered every dessert on the menu. When the check came, Champaine just smiled and said, "That's why God created credit cards."

Once the waiter had collected the payment and the children around the table were all talked out, Champaine looked hard at them and announced, "I got something to say." Since her audience was in the unusual state of being over indulged, they all gave her their attention. "Life—it ain't easy, and Lord knows it takes a whole lotta work, but," her eyes lingered over the children, "if you do work hard, and you set goals for yourself, each and every one of you can make something of yourself." As she said these words, Jasmine felt her caring reach out and take hold. "You've all had tough times, and all that you been through makes it that much more difficult, but it doesn't make it impossible." She shook her head, "It don't make it impossible. Each of you can finish school, have a profession, have good relationships with people that treat you right—all that." She paused, her eyes hopeful, "Just look at Jasmine going to college, look at Karah finishing high school despite having her little man there, and look at Georgy, who with some encouragement, was able to walk today." Champaine appeared filled with certainty. "Family is what you make it. Everyone around this table is your family. You may not think it all the time, but you see that when we help each other, we can do great things—and here is the proof." She raised her strong hands as if she was presenting them with a gift. "Here is the proof. You all remember this night and what I'm saying."

The other children seemed to bask in her warm words, but by the end of her speech, Jasmine's chest felt tight. She was with Champaine when the lecture was about making something of yourself, but she couldn't think of these kids, whom she'd known for less than two years, as siblings. The other kids had had families of their own. But she had only known foster care. There was no one in the world who was her mother, her father, her sister or brother, her grandmother or aunt—no one. While Champaine was nice enough, she was hardly a mother. Then there was Miss Raymelle—but she was paid to be there. No, she could not join Champaine in believing that the people around that table were her family. She accepted this with stoicism. This was her lot in life, and she could not, would not, sugar-coat the truth of it. One celebration at Red Lobster would not alter the reality: she was alone in the world, and perhaps always would be.

Lakisha

Stepping into the public library, Lakisha inhaled the musty smell of aging paper and felt the pang of memory; her mother's hand clutching her own small one and leading her to a cozy corner in the children's section. While she'd sat in the same aging upholstered chair and snuggled every one of her five children, when she crossed the threshold, she was always met with those fleeting thoughts of Maizy.

The poetry slam was already in progress. She stood in the back until the current reader finished, and then tip-toed through the crowd of people to the front of the room and penned her name on the readers' list. Finding a chair at the rear of the group, Lakisha closed her eyes and took a slow, deep breath. It was difficult to leave her kids after a long workday, and the two youngest had whined when she'd put on her coat, but Theo said he'd handle it. She knew that he occasionally wrote poetry too; that was how they'd met, after all. Yet she was the one who had made it a hobby—no, it was more than that. It was not exactly a calling, but perhaps her chosen art form. Her poems were rarely good, but most were cathartic, a purging of bitter memories, emotions. Those buried feelings reached the light of day through letters, phrases…and then finally—sound. Once they were spoken, she could tolerate what was left in their wake: her exceptionally difficult, and in moments, beautiful, life.

She listened to other people's words, sometimes feeling the truth in their work, sometimes feeling bored, and sometimes feeling nothing at all. When the applause sounded, Lakisha always looked to see that sweet moment of triumph as it spread across the reader's face. Their words had been set free. If they had done little else in their lives, at least they had done this.

When it seemed like the event was about to end, the facilitator came to the microphone and said, "We'll squeeze in one more, Lakisha White."

Lakisha stood and picked her way back through the people to the front of the crowd.

"A'right, Kisha!" called a voice near the rear.

A smile flitted across Lakisha's face and then disappeared. She cleared her throat.

She smelled like cinnamon gum and talc, dandelions, books.
She hung with dealers and players, cheaters, crooks.
Track-marks, they marched up her wrist toward her heart,
Her leavin' tore me up,
Ripped my insides apart.
She left nothin' but a doll, with two sides that could change,
But her life—she never could rearrange
So that she'd have a place, a space,
A chase; she made haste—so far away.

Writing ads and obits for cash, when lives smash, cars bash, I hash
Out words saying what survives, belies justice—
Is life fair?
Not for me or Mama,
Or even a changeable doll, who can shift,
While we're stuck,
and the heavens—
They fall.

The room erupted with sound and Lakisha felt the relief of granting wings to one more hurt that echoed in her bones. Once she returned to her place in the crowd, she looked down at her phone and saw that she'd missed a call from Theo and a text that read, "Phone me ASAP. TJ sick again."

Lakisha exhaled her frustration. *Why couldn't she ever catch a break?* She made her way to a deserted hallway and Theo picked up on the first ring. "Kisha, I'm on my way to Newark Beth Israel with TJ."

"What? What happened?"

"He couldn't even stand up. He was freakin. To be honest, we all were."

"Was he breathing okay? Did he use his inhaler?"

"It wasn't the breathing this time. He said his head felt like it was ready to explode, and his fever shot way up. I went to get Advil and when I got back, I couldn't hardly wake him."

"The others…."

"I left Nikki home with them and called Dottie. They're taking him to Newark Beth on Lyons Ave."

"What about Saint Michael's?"

"They said Beth Israel's the best. We'll be there soon."

During the frantic drive, Lakisha's mind flashed with stories she'd heard about children getting sick suddenly with terrible things: aneurisms, cancer, organ failure, even heart attacks. These fears filled her thoughts until she entered the Beth Israel emergency room and met with older ones. She had avoided returning there ever since that horrific night in high school. Other hospitals were just as good. That was what she'd told herself, so that she'd never confront these memories again. Yet here she was, back where they'd treated her after the blonde-haired monster had finished his work.

When Lakisha reached her son's bedside, she tried not to gasp. His lips were pale, and he had packing collecting blood that must have been dripping from his nose. Why hadn't Theo mentioned the nose bleed? TJ was barely thirteen, he'd just started to shoot up in height, making his limbs look too long and thin, and his torso appear narrow compared to his head. He'd been fighting infections, had been on and off antibiotics for the past two months, but it wasn't anything that seemed out of the ordinary—at least for him. A nurse came in and connected an IV tube to the catheter in his arm.

"What's in that?" Lakisha wanted to ask the right questions, was committed to getting him proper treatment.

"It's just hydration. We'll wait until he's seen by the doctor before adding anything else." The nurse looked like she was just out of school.

Theo touched Lakisha's arm. "I only left for a minute to fill out paperwork."

The nurse began peppering Lakisha and Theo with questions about TJ's health. Why couldn't she remember everything? It wasn't a lack of caring—TJ was her oldest son after all, but there was just too much to keep in her brain. Something had to give. Did he finish the last round of Amoxicillin over the weekend or was it last week? Was that the third respiratory infection this year or the fourth or fifth? He definitely had a chest x-ray at some point. She thought there was one at the Urgent Care last month, but where were those records? She was relieved when the nurse got to the bottom of her questionnaire and left the three of them alone. Their pediatrician's office was closed for the day, so there was no way to quickly access his records.

Lakisha pulled up an orange plastic chair next to her son and dropped down into it. TJ opened his eyes. "You look tired, baby." She stroked his brow.

"Yeah, I didn't sleep well last night."

"Why didn't you tell me?"

He shrugged, "I thought I was okay." The marble in his neck bobbed, and his face scrunched, like there was something caught in his throat. Lakisha handed him a cup of water. TJ took a few pulls on the straw and seemed more comfortable. "So, did you slam em?" His heavy eyes lifted.

"Huh?" She reached for him, letting her hand rest on his blanketed leg, wanting to keep hold of him—as if that might prevent some further calamity.

"At the library…the slam…how was it?"

Lakisha chuckled, "You trying to distract me, like I taught you?"

"It works for Shonda."

Yes, well I'm not a five-year-old."

He responded with a shrug and then closed his eyes. He was kinder than any boy she knew. Maybe being too ill to run the streets had protected him, or perhaps the sickness softened him. His sensitivity would make his life rich but his path difficult. It would be easy for people to take advantage, and his heart would be right there for the breaking. Lakisha brushed her hands over his soft cheeks, then noticed a few small lumps that were under the tender skin of his neck. *Lord, please let this be nothing.* Theo stood next to her, his hand on her shoulder. She wasn't sure if he was trying to steady himself or her but decided it didn't much matter.

Theo leaned down, "I know you don't like all the kids left with Nikki, but she's sixteen now—"

"I don't care about that. It's fine."

"And I know you don't like this hospital, not since way back… when…."

"When you got high and abandoned me."

"I'm not gonna fight you tonight. One of these days, you're gonna find forgiveness."

"Yeah, well, today is not the day." She stared him down.

"I only brought it up to say I'm sorry we're here."

"Whatever, it doesn't matter. Nothing matters—except him." An hour later, Aunt Dottie phoned and said she was camped out with the kids at home, and she was microwaving popcorn and getting ready to watch a movie with them. "On a school night?" asked Lakisha but knew better than to argue with Dottie. She'd do what she wanted anyway.

Struggling to her feet, Lakisha, pushed open the curtain around TJ's bed and stepped into the corridor. A woman in purple scrubs was tapping at a computer behind a large circular nursing station. Lakisha smoothed back her chemically relaxed hair and redid her ponytail. "Excuse me. My son, Theo Michaelson Jr., has been waiting to see a doctor. He's only thirteen and we've been waiting for a while. Any idea when someone will be over?"

The woman glanced up, and then returned to her screen. "The doctors see patients based on severity of symptoms. Someone should be by soon. Does your son want some ginger ale or a snack? I could bring that over."

"Yes, that would be great, thank you." Lakisha started back toward TJ and Theo, but couldn't keep from wondering about why TJ was taken to *this* hospital? Did God want her to remember? Lakisha felt a chill and squeezed her eyes shut.

When she drew back the curtain, she found Theo dozing, his forearms and face resting on the hospital gurney. She gave him a nudge, "The nurse doesn't have any idea when he'll be seen. Why don't you go on home and get some rest? We'll need to take shifts."

"You sure about that? I'm happy to stay with you until we know what's wrong with him."

"One of us should go home and make sure the kids are asleep. The baby doesn't like Dottie—"

"Don't none of the kids like her!" They both smiled. Theo looked from her to TJ and then stood. "Text me as soon as you know something; it don't matter the time."

Once he was gone, Lakisha took his place and leaned back so that her head rested against the wall. Soon her eyes fluttered shut. She surrendered to the memories.

Whatever magic Lakisha felt between them seemed to vanish as she and Theo entered the smoke-filled second floor walk-up apartment. Lakisha had just turned sixteen and was still in awe of Theo's older and more worldly friends. She felt like a child at an adult party. She tried to pull herself up to her full five-foot-two inches and set her face in an adult-like mask. Theo was engulfed by a crowd of strong black hands that shook his, and then passed him a can of beer and a blunt that looked the size of a small baseball bat. He made a lame attempt to include her in the festivities by handing her the long burning baton, but she shook her head and looked away. She was already beginning to feel light headed from breathing the drug-infused air and taking a few sips from her beer can. She gazed with envy at the girls in the room who were heavier and could handle the alcohol. "You need more meat on your bones," Aunt Dottie had said, and in that moment, she felt it was true—she was a light-weight.

Squeezing her way past Theo and the men, she moved through a narrow hallway where a guy and girl stood kissing—their arms wrapped around each other, his right hand halfway submerged in the back of her jeans. Lakisha slid by.

In the cramped kitchen, she found a group of girls huddled together. A curvy woman with a fan of black lashes and a kind smile greeted her. Lakisha recognized her as the girlfriend of Theo's cousin. The name came to her—Amanda. "Hey, it's a chimney in there."

"They like children in men's bodies. Whatcha expect? Kisha, these are my girls: Nyasia and Mattie." The two lifted their bored eyes in her direction and scanned her outfit.

"Nice pumps," said the one with braided hair extensions that reached half way down her back. *"Where'd you get them?"*

"Um…my friend's closet?"

The small group erupted with laughter.

"Here sisters, from the cooler." A man with pock-marked skin and a red bandana hanging from a pocket was pushing through the klatch of women carrying two six packs of beer. He placed them on the counter and Amanda began pulling out cans and handing them around.

"You're behind," she said, pressing a cold one into Lakisha's free hand. *"Drink up."*

Four beers later, Lakisha no longer felt grown up and appealing—she felt sick. Making her way back to the living room, she found Theo seated on the couch, his eyes bloodshot, and his hands clutching a fresh drink.

"Theo," she said, searching for some semblance of the man she had arrived with. He seemed not to hear, so she stepped on his foot. *"Theo, I need to talk to you."*

"Go ahead baby, my boys and I is listen'n." Peals of laughter rose up all around him and Lakisha felt each one as a slap.

"I need to go."

"Is you turning into a pumpkin, Cinderella?"

More laughter assaulted her until she stepped back away from them, catching her heel on the carpet, and wobbling for a moment before falling.

She knocked into people who glared, and then laughed at her splayed position on the floor. The bellowing sound of amusement filled the room and drowned out the music and loud conversation.

An unexpected large hand reached beneath her armpits and lifted her to her feet. She felt a dull throbbing in her hip and winced, trying still to move herself away from the laughter, the embarrassment—Theo.

"Hey there," said the baritone voice of the man who supported her, "if you want, I'll see you home."

The man who picked her up like a fallen petal could have had the best of intentions. He could have had a younger sister at home whom he cared about and wouldn't want to see drunk, bruised, and abandoned at a party. He could have been raised by a fine woman who taught him to take care of others in need, to help the injured, the vulnerable. He could have just been a good soul trying to help out a sister. On the other hand, he could be dangerous.

Lakisha didn't wait to find out. As soon as she was back on her feet, she turned away from Theo, extracted her arm from the grasp of the stranger, and pushed her way through the crowd to the front door. She walked down the two flights of stairs clutching the banister and moving hand over fist sideways in the hopes of avoiding another spill in the spiked heels. At the outside door, the cool night air met her face, shocking her with the relief of freedom. At that moment, what was left of the burger and fries she'd eaten for lunch rose into her throat. She grasped the metal handrail and leaned over, sending a cascade of partially digested food and drink down onto the walkway of the basement apartment. Her body shook several more times before the gagging transformed into dry heaves and finally ceased.

Peeling herself from the railing, Lakisha assessed the damage to her shoes. "Praise the Lord," she whispered to herself. Nothing was on them.

With each step down the final brick staircase to the sidewalk, she felt pain, both in her feet, which were not used to being squeezed into high-heeled shoes for an extended period of time, and in her right hip, still aching from the fall. But the only thought she had was of home. She needed to get there. She had never been in this neighborhood before and had only a vague idea of where she was in relation to her aunt's apartment. She knew that if she could reach one of the major avenues, she'd be able to find her way on foot or beg her way onto a bus that would bring her to a familiar street.

Though it was just past dinnertime, the streets were mostly deserted. A few brothers sporting tilted red baseball caps gathered on a corner in front of a bodega. Lakisha recognized them as gang members and crossed the street. She hustled forward, glancing back frequently to make sure that the Bloods were keeping their distance.

"Hey, yo!"

Lakisha's face bumped against a man's chest. Startled, she looked up at him. His mop of blonde hair fell forward, partially hiding the redness that stained the milky white of his blue eyes.

"Sorry," she said, pulling back from him, her eyes darting, trying to assess the lesser of two evils: this white drug addict or the Bloods.

For the second time that evening she found a stranger's hand grasping her arm. "Where you headed?"

"Home," her pulse quickened. "I'm going home," she repeated and tried to back away.

He held on, "This is a rough neighborhood. Shit, look around you. I'll get you home."

Panic gripped her. "That's okay, I know my way."

"No, it wouldn't be right. It wouldn't be right to send you on alone." His hands gripped both of her arms now, and he was backing her toward the corner of the building.

"I'll be just fine! This is my neighborhood," she lied. "I walk here all the time. All the time—really! As a matter of fact, my boyfriend just sent me out to get him some snacks. He's right up in that house over there." She tried to lift her arm to point, and he released her. Lakisha's heart was now like a basketball banging against her ribs, shaking her narrow frame. She glanced toward the man's companion, a stocky, dark-haired, collegiate-looking guy. Would he help her?

She tried to slip away, but he clutched her upper arms. "Hey, don't go yet."

Lakisha didn't want to meet his gaze, didn't want to know his face—that would make it real. But what choice did she have? "Look, I gotta go." Her eyes confronted his, "Like I said, I got people waiting."

The grip on her arms tightened, and he shoved her toward a narrow alleyway that divided a brick apartment building from a neighboring row house.

Teetering backwards on stilettos, Lakisha twisted and turned her body trying to wrench her arms free. She knew better than to scream for help. "No one ever wants to help," her aunt had told her, "It's best to scream fire."

"Fire!" she began to shout, but he slapped her faced and shoved her harder.

"You're losing it man. Come on, let's get out of here." The voice of reason came from the other fair-skinned man who wore a New Jersey Devil's baseball cap and a worried expression.

"Your friend says you have to go." Lakisha tried not to sound desperate. The blonde man paused and seemed to consider her words while surveying her breasts beneath her tight tangerine blouse, her hips hidden in palazzo pants. For a moment Lakisha felt saved. He'd let her go and she'd walk the two blocks back to the party. She'd find Theo, wrap herself in his protective arms, and never leave his side again.

A wry smile spread across the attacker's ruddy face. Lakisha couldn't read it. Finally, he said, "He'll wait," and pushed her further into the alley.

She turned to see if there was an escape route behind her, but all she saw were brick walls covered in graffiti and a locked gate topped with barbed wire. The sky above was indigo, smudged with black clouds. Jesus, help me! Her mind raced. The only way out was to get by him. Lakisha threw her body down to the ground and rolled right, freeing her arms from his grasp. As she rose to her feet, set on charging away, she felt his wide palm pull at her navel, and she was propelled down to the pavement.

"Bitch, we're done when I say so."

His long legs straddled hers; he rolled her over, his hands pressing on her ribs with such force, she felt them cracking. She could barely breathe and could think of nothing more than living through each moment—taking in and releasing air from her lungs.

"And we are not done yet."

With his hips poised in the air, and adrenaline pumping through her veins, Lakisha seized what she feared was her last chance. A guttural cry shot from her throat as she jerked her right knee up to his groin.

The result was immediate. The man let out a deep animal-like groan and pulled away. Lakisha shifted beneath him and rose to all fours before her waist was encircled one final time. Her back and head met the concrete, her loose pants were ripped, and her legs were pried apart. Then his angry organ pounded into her with vengeance until he lay on top of her—spent.

Through a veiled twilight, Lakisha felt him being pulled from her, and she was once again able to take in air; each breath bringing a searing pain. Then she saw him pressed up against the brick wall. There was a flash of metal and screams—and then more metal, more screams. There was a red bandana waving from a back pocket like a flag and sets of high-tops kicking him to the ground. She listened to the moaning and curses, and then she watched the sneakers run away, leaving behind a scarlet mark on the rapist's torso. Was it the letter B? Her mind was jumbled.

Lakisha heard the siren long before the vehicle arrived—and so did he. He clawed his way up the wall, pressing his palm over his now shredded t-shirt. Though crimson flowers bloomed where the box cutter had met flesh; he still stumbled out into the night, leaving Lakisha alone and broken on the Newark street.

By noon the next day, TJ was on the Pediatric Unit, and Lakisha was doing everything she could to keep her world from coming apart at the seams. Aunt Dottie had reluctantly moved into Lakisha's apartment, although according to Nikki, it was mostly the kids who were taking care of Dottie and not the other way around, but that was to be expected. It was Dottie after all.

At the hospital, time seemed to inch forward. Doctors, nurses, and aides came and went, but no one seemed to know what was wrong with TJ—or if they had a suspicion, they weren't sharing. Lakisha knew that TJ was miserable, could see it in the hard set of his eyes and hear it in the constant grinding of his teeth as he slept. There were moments when tears tracked down his face, and though it was difficult to find words of consolation, she actually preferred that to the silence of his stoic resignation when he seemed so withdrawn into himself, she wondered if he'd ever return. She didn't want to think of the horrible things that could be wrong and jumped to her feet when the chief resident summoned her into the hallway. The doctor had a crease between her hazel eyes. "The routine blood tests returned an abnormal white blood cell count. We've called in specialists for consults, and once they've been in, we'll move forward with a bone biopsy."

Lakisha took a deep breath, "so you're looking for...."

The physician hesitated and then the fold in her brow deepened. "We want to rule out any form of cancer."

Tessa

Tessa followed Kate through the vestibule of the Saint James Club into a lofty atrium with a marble staircase. A huge tapestry bearing the club's insignia hung from above, appearing to defy gravity. The insignia, a bare-breasted woman holding a book and a sword, was embossed on a medieval-style shield in muted tones of ochre and steel gray.

Kate had visited Saint James repeatedly during high school when her brother was a member, and warned Tessa, *the club can come off a bit pretentious, especially before you get to know people.* Saint James attracted young men who considered themselves too sophisticated for fraternities, but who still wanted the fun and social connections. Many of the members had family jets or owned small islands. Several even had their last names on Columbia University buildings. Kate's brother had fallen into this elite crowd as a member of the crew team.

Unlike the fraternities, the majority of which huddled together in congested rows along 113th and 114th Streets, Saint James occupied a wide limestone building on Claremont Avenue. It bore neither the aroma of keg parties past, nor the ancient sticky floors and wooden beams carved with lovers' initials. Saint James was a place where the well-heeled made the connections that would enable them to become even wealthier.

The girls were thoughtful in choosing their cocktail-party attire. Each wore a fitted dress, narrow gold chains, and high-heeled designer shoes made from supple leathers. Ignoring Kate's advice against standing out, Tessa chose a red dress that she felt complimented her amber eyes. Their eyelids and lips shimmered, and their manes were well-conditioned and glossy. Kate wore her hair down and styled with a gentle wave at her cheekbones. Tessa allowed her long sun-kissed locks to fall in soft curls, and she had pinned them back in several places near the front so that a few tendrils framed her face. While Kate's thin torso curved forward in a model-like slouch, Tessa, having spent years learning to straighten her spine while in pursuit of medals, always stood erect when nervous—and she was beyond nervous. She would have much preferred being jean clad at a frat party and gulping down beer while checking out the crowd of young men, in search of that special someone with a wicked sense of humor, killer body, brilliant mind, caring heart, and sense of social justice. By the end of the night, she'd settle for someone who was a good kisser, but that was another story. For now, her only concern was not embarrassing herself.

As she walked through the double doors leading to the club's party room on that September evening, Tessa felt her body lengthen. Several young men in dinner jackets caught sight of her and seemed to stand transfixed. A few women cast subtle glances toward the door. Conversations continued while eyes darted, averted, but then returned.

"Tessa, maybe you should have worn black." Kate mouthed in her ear.

"Why?" Tessa's heart quickened.

"They can't keep their eyes off you."

"Huh?"

Kate flashed a wry smile. "Because, Cinderella—you're stunning." She touched Tessa's elbow and led her across the room. "Come on, your fairy godmother needs a drink."

A bartender wearing a white shirt and black bow tie lifted his brow as they approached. "Ladies? What can I get for you?"

Tessa's face lit. "Sam!"

"Tessa, what would you like?" He tossed back a wayward crop of dark hair that immediately fell back into his eyes.

"Sam—wow, I didn't know you worked here. Were you able to finish that lab after we left? I felt bad leaving since your partner was a no show."

"Yes, thanks, I got it done." His jaw clenched as he scanned the room and adjusted his cuffs.

Tessa fingered one of her curls. "So how long have you been working here?"

"Just since the beginning of the semester…but not much longer if you keep chatting me up." His sharp eyes glanced around the room and then back to Tessa, opening wide with the expectation of her order.

"Oh, I'm sorry." Her lips pressed together.

"Chardonnay, we'll both have Chardonnay," Kate interjected.

Sam wrapped the neck of the wine bottle with a linen napkin and poured their drinks into long-stemmed glasses.

Tessa gave him a small wave goodbye and stepped over to where Kate waited next to a carved bust of Sir Isaac Newton.

"Rule number one: don't hit on the staff," Kate spoke through tight lips.

"I wasn't…we're in the same lab—"

"This isn't about school. Even though it's an all-male club, the parties are by invitation only. We want to be on the permanent guest list. Come on, I'll introduce you around."

Kate looked transformed. Even her hands, usually so busy, remained poised, one at her side and one holding the stem of her glass. Tessa noted that everyone in the room was holding the stem and not the bowl of the glass, and she rearranged her hands to follow suit.

"Julia, Will, this is my friend Tessa."

Following a lukewarm greeting, Julia scanned Tessa from head to toe and then sniffed critically. Will was subtler, stealing furtive glances that ended at her head, where he seemed to wince in confusion.

Had they never seen naturally-curly-blonde hair before? After a few polite questions Tessa was excluded from the conversation, which centered on gossip about mutual acquaintances and club politics. Tessa's feet hurt, her stomach churned, and she was bored.

Just when she felt she might have to leave Kate and hobble back to her dorm alone, two young men approached. The taller one, who had an angular face, blue eyes, and shaggy butterscotch hair, gave Kate a hug. "You're finally here! Glad you decided to follow the family tradition."

"You couldn't keep me away—rah, rah, blue and white." Kate's fist raised in a mock cheer.

"And this is?"

"Oh!" Her palms turned toward the ceiling as she pointed. "Charles Stansworth, Kipp Hawthorn, this is Tessa Mitchell, Tessa—Charlie and Kipp."

Charlie tugged on Kipp's sleeve since he had already stepped into a political discussion with Will and Julia, and he gave Tessa a quick nod.

"Charlie Stansworth, like The Stansworth Academy?" Tessa asked.

"Yes, that's right." He didn't offer anything further.

She wondered if it was his immediate family that ran one of the most prestigious prep schools in the country or if it was a relative. Either way, she was impressed.

"Tessa's my BFF from Haverford. I did a happy dance when she decided on Barnard. Maybe my threats had something to do with it."

"Hmm, that's so unlike you," amusement filled his eyes. He had stunning eyes. "You're at Barnard too?"

"No, engineering, but I'm used to sharing Tessa. She had a whole other life in high school, always at gymnastics practice. I was afraid she'd end up at Michigan or Berkeley."

Charlie fixed his gaze on Tessa. "Barnard, Columbia, there's no gymnastics team, right?"

"No." She felt the emotion rise in her chest, and she glanced away.

"That must be hard for you to kind of go cold turkey out of the sport."

Tessa looked up, hoping for a witty response. When nothing came to her, she went with honesty, "It's not easy. I was injured, so...no choice really. I'm okay though—surviving." She intended that last word to be light-hearted, but it fell from her mouth like a confession.

Charlie's expression softened, and he inched closer.

Her face grew hot. He smelled like soap and musk, and he seemed safe—the kind of guy who wouldn't cheat off you during history tests (that had brought an end to her hook ups with the captain of the Haverford soccer team) or tell you that you didn't need company walking home because you'd only had three shots of Tequila and it wasn't even midnight (she'd already blocked that Short Hills guy's number).

"How many years did you do gymnastics?"

Tessa wrestled her emotion. Gymnastics had taught her never to cry in public. She cleared her throat, "Fourteen years. I began when I was four."

"Wow! That's a long time. Do you dance now?"

"No. It's too...I don't know. Dance doesn't feel like enough of a workout, anyway...." She resisted the urge to play with her hair or rub her hands or act out any of her usual nervous ticks. "What do you like to do? Involved in any sports?"

"I was on crew until this year. That's how I met Kate's brother." He beamed a smile at Kate. "Now I'm taking graduate courses, and something had to give. Lately I'm playing Ultimate Frisbee—how about trying that? Its co-ed, non-contact, we're all a bunch of team athlete wanna bees or retirees like yourself. You'd be in good company."

Kate jumped in, "It's a Saint James team?"

"Yup, and right now we're undefeated." He puffed his chest.

"Well in that case I'm sure I won't be good enough. I think the last time I even touched a Frisbee was fourth grade."

"Are you kidding me? A gymnast, who can fly through the air, can't run and toss a Frisbee? I'll bring you to the quad some time, and you can give it a whirl." He waited for her response to the pun, and she obliged with a snicker. "I'll even throw in coffee at Tom's. That's my final offer. Frisbee, coffee at Tom's, the possibility of joining the Saint James Ultimate Frisbee Club—come on, gym girl, college is time to try new things!"

If he hadn't called her *gym girl*, if his eyes hadn't been that appealing shade of cornflower blue, if the muscles of his shoulders hadn't strained the fabric of his dinner jacket, and if his perfect lips hadn't lifted into a smile, then she might have found a way to say no. "Well, if you put it that way...sure, why not? But no expectations."

His smile contracted at her cool response. Perhaps he wasn't accustomed to women being less than enthusiastic. "None at all. I'll get your number from Kate?"

"Okay, or I could just give it to you—"

"No need. I'll messenger Kate." he turned to Kate and gave her cheek a kiss. "I'll also tell you which professors to avoid. I've heard stories. Even engineering has some losers."

Once Charlie had slipped into a conversation with a circle of men at the bar, Tessa leaned in to Kate, "Why didn't he take my number?"

"Cell phones aren't used in the parlor."

"This is the *parlor*?"

She nodded.

"We have to stay here?" One part of her was curious to learn more about this society and their rules, which seemed so foreign, while another part wanted to escape.

"Yes, we're staying at least another hour."

"I'm gonna need a second drink then."

Kate glanced at her half-full glass.

Turning her back to the crowd, she lifted the stemware and gulped down its contents. "My next drink is going to be whatever it is Sam is serving with the olives in the center."

"That's a martini. They'll put the olives in automatically unless you ask for a twist which is lemon. There's gin or vodka."

"And what do I want?" She laughed, feeling the wine move to her head.

Kate's face darkened. "You sure you want a martini?"

"Yes. Don't worry, I'll nurse it."

She approached Sam. "A vodka martini...please."

Sam winked. "One vodka martini coming up."

Though it took him a few minutes to mix the drink, Tessa resisted her urge for small talk. She drummed her fingers on the linen-draped table, then scanned the room. Kate had moved on to a conversation with two young men who appeared to be identical twins, and they were both speaking with their torsos, their bodies leaning from side to side while their hands cupped drink tumblers.

Sam placed the brimming drink on the table. "One vodka martini."

The familiar timbre of his voice was comforting. "Thank you." She lifted the wide-rimmed glass by the stem and caught his eye before turning. Her mind whispered, *God, give me strength—I am grateful for your gifts.*

The rest of the evening dragged as she and Kate moved through the room of pampered strangers with stellar futures. They spoke of summer internships with U.S. Senators and at hedge funds, planned ski trips to Aspen, spring breaks on islands she'd never heard of, and the best private tour companies in Thailand. Once the vodka kicked in, Tessa could nod politely, and even laugh at their quips. But by 11 pm, when the buzz from the alcohol was wearing as thin as her patience, she convinced Kate to leave. Tessa followed her like a shadow through the room saying goodbye, then stumbled out into the cool night air.

"Let's change clothes and head to 113th Street," said Tessa, ignoring Kate's surprised look. "I hear there is a party at Sigma Chi."

Jasmine

The Rutgers Newark campus was not beautiful, but since Jasmine had spent her life moving through city streets, she felt at home. The grassy quads were comfortable places to read on mild days, and the scattered trees offered shade and a show of colors in the fall. The place seemed to buzz with activity and determination. The student body was diverse, and Jasmine believed them to be a group that was gathered from the corners of the earth to achieve something meaningful and was grateful to be among them. For her, college was like an ocean unmindful of the past. Jasmine believed she could sail forward with the tide, abandoning the buried shipwrecks of her former life.

Before leaving the cafeteria each morning, she'd grab a small carton of milk, a few sausage links, and a Styrofoam bowl. Back at her dormitory, she'd set the breakfast out in the side alleyway for a family of calico cats that had taken up residence next to her own. She'd watch them eat the meat and lap up the milk; all crowding in with their noses touching, vying for space. Family—even these cats had what she didn't. She shook the thought away. After several days of feedings, she held out the sausage and waited for the first kitten to take a tentative swat at it. Soon they were all brave enough to come and eat from her fingers or crouch next to her as she knelt down on the pavement. When one of them decided to climb over her, pausing for a few moments in her lap, she felt a warmth rise up in her belly.

Jasmine's work-study assignment was in the library and seemed a perfect fit for her temperament. She enjoyed being around books and liked the hush that came over the building in the evenings. When there was down time, she'd leaf through the volumes that students had returned, trying to get a sense of what they were studying, what things were out there in the world beyond Irvington and Newark, beyond her own narrow slice of existence. And when boredom set in, she'd put pen to paper and loop her ink across the page, releasing the hurt that pricked her insides and gnawed at her confidence. She'd scratch away, cross out, and rewrite. There was a spoken-word poetry club on campus. If she had something good enough, maybe she'd find courage.

In the streets—where I lived and a piece a me died,
The pulsing pain, permeates posses
Bound for revenge, for rage that never, ever repairs
What's lost.
Sticky gravel, garage grime
On my knees I service, hands gripping my hair,
Leaning back, mouth open, I swallow
A pill that makes no pain part,
No wound heal, no wrong right.

It was a work in progress.

Rutgers was full of new experiences. Her roommate, Padma, had gone to the Clubs Fair, and come back with handfuls of pamphlets and flyers. She dragged Jasmine to the first meeting of the Pre-Med Society, where they listened to a talk about new stem-cell therapies and signed up to hear a panel discussion on job opportunities in health care. Jasmine hadn't yet decided on a major. She spoke with Miss Raymelle about becoming a social worker and working with kids, considered becoming a veterinarian so that she'd only have to deal with animals and not crazy humans, and tossed around the idea of becoming a scientist and working in a lab. Perhaps she could discover something important like a new cancer treatment.

"You should become a doctor," Padma said. "Then you can help people *and* make great money."

Jasmine smirked, "I think you just want a study buddy for when you get to organic chemistry."

"That's not true!" Padma raised an eyebrow, "But didn't you get some science awards in high school?" She closed her biology text and sighed. "If you *can* be a doctor, then you *should be one.*"

"Is that some kind of rule?"

"It is where I come from. Anyone with the ability to become a doctor, well…it's expected."

"Really, I'm glad I didn't grow up with you. That's a whole lot of pressure. And isn't medical school super expensive? How about we get through freshman bio and chem and leave the whole life plan thing for later."

"All right, but let's go to the next Student Outreach Council event. I think they're serving at a soup kitchen."

"You have time for that?"

"Medical schools like to see community service. I'm also going to volunteer at Beth Israel."

"No play time for you, P?"

"Of course, we'll play! We're going to a party Saturday night."

"We are?"

And with that, Padma packed up her books. "I'm off to the library."

Once she was gone, Jasmine scrolled through a list of campus clubs on her laptop. "Rutgers United for Furry Friends; now there's a club I'd like," she told the empty room and noted the time and location of the first meeting.

The next afternoon, Jasmine sat bent over her computer watching YouTube. "Having unlimited internet is the best part of living on campus," she told Padma as she perused a column of Bernie Mac and Chris Rock videos. She looked up and caught her roommate's pouty face. "Except for having you as a roommate...that's really the best part of dorming."

Padma smiled, "Nice save! You do need a Facebook account though, and then Instagram." She didn't wait for an answer, "How else are you going to keep up with people and know what's happening?" Padma moved through their cramped room, putting away her folded laundry that made the whole room smell of lavender.

Jasmine leaned back in her desk chair and opened her email. "I'm not so sure I'm into all that connecting."

"Why not? You have to try new things and grow."

"I'm with you on the growth part, but I don't want people creeping on me, looking at my pics." She kept her eyes glued to her screen, hoping Padma would move to a new subject.

"So, use the privacy settings so only friends can look at your pictures. But let people see your name, a profile picture, and at least your school so that kids at Rutgers can find you. Here, I'll help you—" And with that, Padma commandeered her computer and started clicking away, choosing her password—Jasmine spelled backwards with *18hot* at the end—and filling in a skeleton profile. "There! Now you're all set. I'll be your first friend, and I'll send requests to the girls on the hall." After a few more clicks, she pushed the computer back toward Jasmine, satisfaction pinned to her face. "Just go on it at least once in the morning and once at night, and you'll know what's up."

"Do I have a choice?"

Padma's face dropped.

"It's cool. I'll give it a shot. Don't be looking all doggy-eyed on me." Jasmine clicked around other people's pages and admitted to herself, if not Padma, that it was an easy way to get to know people.

From then on, whenever she could find time, Jasmine went online, and after scrolling through whatever her classmates had posted, she'd follow link after link, learning about the different countries where her friends had lived, bizarre hobbies, off-beat music, and modern art. She researched happiness, infidelity, and incest. She could have spent hours each day surfing but resisted. Miss Raymelle had explained how seductive it could be, and now Jasmine saw it was true.

Padma inspired Jasmine in other ways too. Her roommate was more committed to her academics than anyone Jasmine had ever known. Though she shared little with Padma about her pitiful existence before college, she still found her roommate's calm, studious presence reassuring. On most mornings, they'd walk together to the cafeteria and sip coffee with a few other girls from their floor.

Padma made sure she stayed connected. "Some of the girls are going bar-hopping tonight. Want to join?"

"No offense," Jasmine hesitated, "see, I grew up around here. The last thing I want to do is go out drinking and meet the local men."

"What about the college men or graduate-school men? What about the guys from the medical or law schools? They might be nice to meet." Mischief danced across Padma's pretty face.

"I tell you what, you go ahead and check out the crowd. If you meet a bunch of guys from graduate school, you come back and let me know. Then I'll join you next time. Something tells me that those guys aren't hanging out in bars."

Padma fanned her dark lashes. "They have to be somewhere—"

"Go ahead! You call me if you meet some cool guys— especially if they're interested in someone with my shade a skin."

"Jasmine, why so negative? Most of us are people of color."

Half her mouth lifted in a smile, "Just keeping it real—I'm a Newark black girl in Newark. You're exotic, and so is ShuChun down the hall, and Sonja, and Malaya."

"That's so not true! You're as exotic and beautiful as any of us. Come with!"

"You could be right, but I'm gonna chill just the same. Y'all have fun though."

"Okay, but tomorrow there's a party on campus. There's no reason to avoid that one."

The following evening, Jasmine stood with her roommate in a Woodward Hall lounge. Padma was dressed in all black, with a low-cut sweater and gold hoop earrings that accented her shiny plaits of charcoal hair. Jasmine had borrowed her roommate's rose-colored cardigan and let her flat-ironed hair fall to her shoulders. She had rolled on some lip gloss and blush but declined Padma's help with her eye makeup. "I think I'm okay without all that—you know I don't want to get used to your makeup and then not be able to afford it."

The other girl had smiled, "Believe me, it's not expensive. But do whatever makes you feel good. You always look great."

"Really?" she quipped. "You been smoking something?"

Now the area was filling with more and more students who were holding plastic cups filled with beer and finding partners to grind with in the room's center. Jasmine began biting a fingernail, but Padma tugged her through the crowd to the keg. They both grabbed thin cups overflowing with golden liquid and allowed themselves to be shoved forward toward the far end of the lounge.

"Let's down it and dance." Padma's dark eyes glistened.

"No offense, but you're not my type." Jasmine scanned the students around her. "As a matter of fact, there aren't many of my type here at all."

"You're talking about color again?"

Jasmine lifted an eyebrow.

"You're crazy, and anyway, no one can tell what you are…exactly. You could be Dominican, Puerto Rican, South American…besides, there are plenty of hot black guys here. I might go for one myself."

"Oh yeah? You ever been with a black man?"

"Uh, no. There weren't many of them in my village. Anyway, back home, girls couldn't be *with* any guys."

"There were sex police?"

"Yes, they're called parents."

"So…you've never been with anyone at all? Huh, maybe start with a nice Indian boy then."

"That would make my mother very happy, as long as he was the *right kind* of Indian. Her greatest fear is that I'll marry someone who isn't a Hindu with family roots in Uttar Pradesh. Does your mom give you a hard time like that?"

Jasmine hesitated. She hadn't yet disclosed her foster-care situation, and the thought of sharing it made her light-headed.

Before she could respond, a tall middle-eastern looking guy, with a kind face and thick-black glasses, introduced himself to Padma and asked her to dance. With a swing of her hair she accepted, and the two pushed their way toward the make-shift dance floor.

Jasmine stood alone, surveying the crowd. They all looked like they were having fun, talking, laughing, dancing, chugging warm beer. She felt a pang of envy. She wanted to be like them, wanted to let go of her wrecking ball past and stop dragging it behind her. Tonight, the giant iron ball seemed to sit on the crest of her shoulders, weighing her down. She watched a muscular dude with dreads approach a cat-eyed girl. He laced his fingers through hers and then leaned down into her so that her upper thigh was sandwiched between his legs as they swayed. Seeing that sent her mind back to the garage, Amani's man pressing himself against her thigh, and then pushing her shoulders down….

She caught up with Padma and tapped her shoulder. "I'm heading back to the room. Have fun."

"You sure?" Her eyebrows furrowed.

"Definitely—see you later."

Jasmine elbowed her way out to the hallway. Only then did she realize how different she'd felt from the other students, how damaged. As she walked across the grassy quad, it started to drizzle, and she reached for her sweatshirt hood before remembering that she had borrowed Padma's fancy sweater. She ran the last few yards, tugged out her student ID, and swiped herself into the building.

Back in her room, Jasmine pulled off the rose cardigan and folded it on Padma's bed before zipping up her own soft hoodie. Despite flunking out of *college partying 101*, she could still report to Miss Raymelle that she'd tried, and maybe that was all she could do right now. But Padma's inquiry about her mother had revived some long-buried questions. She leaned back on pillows and began surfing the internet. Following a series of links, she explored websites for kids in search of their birth parents, some new, and some familiar from her time with Amani. With unlimited Internet access, she hoped that finding her birth mother would be easy. The idea now took root. What if she had a mother somewhere? What if she had brothers and sisters? How different would her life be if she knew that somewhere out there were people she could call family? Not fake foster-care family but people with the same blood in their veins. She searched for hours, right up until Padma returned with a shy smile glued to her face.

"You had a good time with Aladdin?"

"I did, but why are you calling him Aladdin?"

"You don't think he looked like Aladdin, you know, from the movie?"

Padma thought for a moment. "Huh, I guess he does kind of…Aladdin with glasses and a slight lisp when he says the letter *S*. His real name is Amir."

"Cool."

Padma circled her bed, pulling off clothes and changing into sweatpants and a T-shirt. "So? What've you been up to?"

"Nothing much…wasting time." Jasmine snapped her laptop shut. Maybe if she knew Padma better, or if Padma didn't have two parents and an army of other relatives, maybe if she weren't worried about how any revelation about her life might change Padma's view of her, maybe if she were in a different body—had lived a different life…no, she was not ready to share her truth with Padma.

Thoughts of her birth mother had often flitted through her like humming birds that could be observed but not held. Treasure had mentioned that her mom was a young girl who got herself in trouble, like the teenagers in the neighborhood with baby bellies. Her birth mother had always been a fuck-up in her mind. But since her own life had imploded, the idea that her mother was a good girl who made a mistake, felt more likely. Perhaps all the people she'd been taught to judge weren't so bad after all.

When she imagined her mother now, she envisioned someone who looked pretty much like her. Small, rounded hips and breasts, deep-set wounded eyes, a crease in her forehead, and a fractured heart protected by thick stone walls. That night as Jasmine lay in bed, all she could think about was finding her. Even though it might take some time, she was excited. Perhaps her mother was someone she could connect with, care about, even love. What if her mother had been hoping that she'd search her out? What if she could have something better than a foster family? What if she could make a real connection with someone—someone who wasn't paid to help her. It was after two when she finally drifted off to sleep, with hope weaving through her dreams.

Tessa

The following Sunday morning, Tessa stood next to the well-trodden lawn in front of Butler Library wearing her gymnastics team warm-up pants and a hooded sweatshirt. No one could see that underneath she had tugged on her gymnastics leotard to give her the confidence to try a new sport—something she hadn't done in years. She rubbed her hands together as if she were applying gymnastics chalk but refrained from what she really wanted to do: stretching. Kate had told her years ago that when she stretched in public she looked like someone who had escaped from Cirque de Soleil. The last thing Tessa wanted to do was stand out, but that was exactly what she'd done at Saint James, and she now regretted agreeing to Frisbee. As she stared out toward Low Library, the temple-like structure surrounded by pillars that she imagined to be a shrine to the gods of intellect, she felt a tap on her shoulder and flinched.

"Glad I convinced you to join the early risers." His face was close, his cheeks and chin stubbly. He had the fresh smell of soap and minty toothpaste.

"I thought you'd come from the other direction," she mumbled.

"I live in John Jay." He pointed toward a building at the eastern side of campus, but she was lost, flustered. He was too near and it was too early, and she had no idea what she was doing with this college senior who could probably trace his ancestry back to the Mayflower. "How are you?"

Was that a trick question? Should she answer honestly? Hell no. "Fine, just fine...and you?" She threw in the last part as an afterthought. How could she focus on him when she was having a panic attack! She pulled the silver band from her hair, another comfort item from her team days, and redid her ponytail.

He was spinning a black Frisbee on the tip of his index finger but then stopped, seemingly aware of her nervous energy. "What's up?"

"Nothing much." She was focusing on her breathing, trying to use the mindfulness tools she'd learned from her high school therapist; back when her panic attacks threatened to keep her from competing. "You?"

"Perfect day for Ultimate. I used to play in high school, but only when it wasn't crew season." He looked at her expectantly, but she couldn't find her voice. "So you're from Jersey...do you live anywhere near Montclair? My dad took us there once for dinner. I forget...maybe it was Middle-Eastern fusion."

"Really? I live about twenty minutes away. Why did you go to Jersey for dinner?"

"My father's a foodie so he's always researching new places. Distance doesn't mean much to him. Last summer we were in Italy and he made us drive for hours to go out for lunch in this town called Spello, because he'd read that it's the gastronomical capital of Umbria. The only problem was that he'd underestimated the drive time, so when we finally arrived, the restaurants were all closed for the afternoon and wouldn't open again for hours. We managed to find one hole-in-the-wall place that was willing to serve us "snacks." My father was so disappointed, he was practically in tears. He told the waitress, *just bring us whatever you want.*"

"So how was the food?" Her body relaxed. He was just a person with a family that struggled on vacation just like hers...though her family never did so in Italy. Still, he was real and open.

"It was the best meal I ever had in my life."

"No way!"

"That hole in the wall served us different types of *toast* that tasted better than anything else I've ever eaten. It was all incredibly fresh—the olive oil from the vineyard down the road, the tomatoes, the mushrooms, the herbs and cheeses. I don't think I was much of a foodie before then, but that trip might have converted me."

"Wow, toast in Spello—I'll have to remember that."

He nudged her shoulder with an open palm. "Are you mocking me?"

"No, no," she laughed. "I really mean it! Toast in Spello, I'm there! Next time I go to Italy, it's on my list."

"We might go back next summer. If you're travelling in Tuscany and Umbria, we could try to meet." He said this casually as if there was no difference between a few weeks in Italy and going *down the shore* in Jersey. "So, ready to toss the Frisbee?"

"I honestly don't know if I even remember how, but I'm willing to take a lesson." The sky was gray and foreboding, but the air had a certain fall crispness to it that made her want to run around. On days like this she used to want to drag her family outside to play touch football, just like the families she saw in movies. That never happened. Her father had a bad back, and her sister had always been too busy.

Maybe it was her nerves, but Tessa managed to fumble every toss. After her fifth attempt landed in the hedges, she was ready to give up, but he wouldn't allow it. Instead, he repositioned her and commanded, "Now, do it again."

This time, miraculously, the Frisbee sailed through the air, right into his awaiting hands. A fleeting smile crossed her face.

"You see? Now you can do it. Your body just has to be facing the right way." He flicked it back to her and she caught it in one hand, pivoted her body, and gave the disk a spinning toss. It flew through the air, and again found its target.

After a few more tries she began to feel at ease, but when she managed to drop a throw that came right to her stomach and sent another one whizzing into some border shrubs, she'd had enough. "Have I earned my cup of coffee?"

"I think maybe even a full breakfast. Have you eaten yet?" He walked toward her, and she again played with invisible hand-chalk. "It wasn't a trick question."

"I had a protein bar. Does that qualify?"

"A protein bar is not a meal." He was now an arm-length away, his gaze resting on her while she examined her palms.

"I suppose in Spello it wouldn't even be considered a snack." She glanced up, squinting as the sunlight peaked through the clouds.

"No, definitely not. In fact, they're probably illegal."

"Well in that case, I think I'd better go with you to breakfast. I don't want to be in violation of any laws, here or abroad." They began strolling together toward the western exit of the campus and the diner.

After a quick meal during which Tessa managed to find her voice and have a coherent conversation about her coursework, they made their way back up Broadway and paused at the black-iron gate where they'd part ways.

Charlie turned to her and she felt his gaze on her skin. "I like to study at the law library, where no one knows me. Come look for me if you need a break. I'm usually on the third floor in a comfy chair near the western windows."

"But if you go there to be left alone...." She saw it then, the warmth in his face that made something inside her ache.

"That's usually true...but not always."

"Are you saying I don't fall into the *do not disturb* category?"

His head tilted. "I believe I just told you where to find me."

In that moment, he looked beautiful to her. Then he was touching her shoulder and hugging her in that *we're just friends,* kind of way. "See you," he said, and then he was gone, taking off in a half jog toward his dormitory.

It was hard for Tessa to keep herself from watching his athletic body move away from her, but fearing he might turn around, she forced herself to cross Broadway and return to her books.

The day dragged on as thoughts of Charlie snaked through her brain. Tessa muddled through an essay, met with her lab partners and Sam, reviewed her bio notes, and then grabbed a tempeh salad sandwich at the local health food store. This she ate as she walked across Columbia's campus to the library. She paused for a minute next to the entrance, finishing the remainder of her whole-wheat pita, before tugging on the ancient wooden door.

Tessa found her preferred place among the many students who sat at rectangular wood tables beneath warm-incandescent lights. She opened her Calculus II text and began working through a problem. When her mind drifted to Charlie and the color of his eyes or his broad shoulders, she tried again to refocus, to banish his soapy scent, the perfect stubble on his chin, his strong legs running to retrieve her Frisbee toss gone wild.

He had told her where to find him. If she sought him out, would he think her needy or desperate—like the way she felt? She made a deal with herself; she'd work hard for another hour and then consider walking over. It would be after 5:30 p.m. by then, a respectable hour for a break if one had been working all day.

When she left the building, she found that the weather had shifted, the air grown misty. She tucked all her hair up inside her hoodie trying to protect her curls from the humidity. Like everyone else on campus, she walked as if time were of the essence. Tessa knew the law school library was on the other side of Amsterdam Avenue but had never been there. She was relieved when it was visible right beyond the main campus gates. Even more fortuitous was catching a glimpse of someone who looked like Charlie, sitting next to a floor to ceiling window on the third level.

Her pulse raced like she was about to try a new tumbling run. Then she saw him, his legs crossed beneath a large text. She felt a rush of adrenaline, "Hey, Charlie."

His eyes widened. "Tessa!" He rose to hug her as he had done with Kate at the party, as if they were old friends. "I didn't know if you'd come." He ushered her to a seat across from him and added, "I'm glad you're here. How was your day?"

"Brutal—just not a good day for focusing." Immediately she regretted this admission.

He put her at ease, "Me too, must be the change in weather. Did you come here to study, or do you want a break—because I sure could use one."

Then they were walking together through campus to his room; a nice-sized single in a four-bedroom suite. She sat cross-legged on his bed while he went to the kitchen and returned with two glasses of club soda with lemon wedges floating on top.

His room had three shelves of books crammed together in a haphazard way. On the floor was an intricate Asian rug with deep reds, blues, and gold tones, and the wall had two framed photos of villages and vineyards in Alsace, and a large photo of a bare-chested Columbia Crew team competing in a race. Though she tried, Tessa couldn't make out which of the athletes was Charlie.

He sat down across from her and began answering some question she had posed about his studies, but she was only half listening. Back home, hookups were straight forward, and she knew what to expect, but with Charlie the lines were blurred. Without thinking it through any further, she placed her drink on his desk and reached for his free hand, braiding her fingers between his as if she had done this a hundred times before, as if this was a simple gesture between friends—or not.

Charlie stared at their laced fingers like he had been presented with a difficult logic puzzle. As his moment of contemplation dragged on, Tessa started to pull away, convinced that his intentions must be brotherly, but he tightened his grasp and placed his drink on the desk next to hers.

He reached for a tendril of hair that had fallen loose into her face and placed it behind her ear. Then his index finger traced the line of her jaw before cupping the base of her head and guiding her glossy mouth toward his. His kiss was tentative at first, and Tessa wondered if it was something he wanted, but then decided it didn't much matter. He tasted like peppermint, lemons, and cappuccino, and smelled like sports deodorant and expensive leather. She was lost in him.

Her need swelled inside her, refusing to be contained. She rose to her knees, pressed her torso against his, and in slow motion, eased him backwards onto the bed. A beat later, Charlie rolled her onto her back in one fluid movement and assumed the dominant position. Tessa exhaled relief. At least he wanted her, perhaps not as much as she wanted him, but he still wanted her.

Their lips and finger tips explored each other, like new terrain, each curving muscle a new discovery. She wondered at the beauty of his body, the mass of muscle that hid beneath his sweatshirt. When he took off his tee and she saw his carved chest and abdomen, her breath caught in her throat.

Charlie moved with intention, not allowing her to rush ahead. He stopped before removing her pants and touched her plump lips with his index finger.

Tessa's eyes were closed. She was lost in the moment until she felt him relax his grip on her thigh, and the hand that had been exploring beneath her bra moved to her jaw and cheekbone. "You can take off my pants," she whispered. When he made no move toward her zipper, she opened her eyes to find him gazing at her, examining her features as he traced them.

"I know," he said.

Tessa was stunned. She had never been refused before. Her limbs stiffened, and her mind raced; she wanted to escape. She closed her eyes and tried to shift away from him.

His response was quick, "Tessa, open your eyes."

She did what he said but would not look at him.

"It's not that I wouldn't love to take them off."

Every syllable stung.

"In fact, at this moment, I can't really think of anything else in the world I'd rather do. It's just that I don't want to be that guy to you—you know, the one you go to when you need a break from studying, the one who you hook up with so that you don't have to bother with a real relationship. You see I've been that guy, I've had that girl. If that's what you're looking for, I'm not that person—at least…I don't want to be that with you."

Her eyes moved to the ceiling and she swallowed hard. He wanted something more, might actually feel something. This was a first. Her first—

"What are you thinking?"

A tear escaped the corner of her eye. She was flooded with emotion; conflicted and complex. But the overwhelming sensation was of falling off a cliff and fearing he wouldn't catch her, wouldn't feel the same. He didn't want to hook up with her—this thoughtful, Columbia University prince, he wanted something else.

"Tessa, what's wrong?" His eyes caught hers in a look so intense, it was disarming.

She almost laughed, "What makes you think that's what I'd want you to be?"

Tessa watched as her own emotion seemed to rise in Charlie's face; her own anxiety and elation jumbled together and reflected back. He encircled her with his arms, his legs, his protection, and held her until all fear abated and she was left with a tenuous belief in what could be.

Jasmine

Jasmine spent time every day searching for her mother. She even found a birth mom looking for a girl with her date of birth, but then learned through email exchanges that her daughter was born in Houston. Her birth certificate, which social services still held, had *Ward of the Court* printed on it. While Padma went to parties on the weekends, Jasmine spent her time stooped over her laptop, scrolling through listings, reading blogs, and researching how to get the courts to release her adoption records.

The courses at Rutgers were challenging, or at least that was the word her tutor at the Learning Center liked to use. Jasmine thought them ridiculously hard! She'd always been a good English student but was shocked when her first essay was returned with corrections to nearly every sentence. She'd slogged through the changes and tried to read the professor's scribbled suggestions. Her biology and calculus classes were more straight forward, but there were so many hours of homework that she felt perpetually behind. The only easy class seemed to be Introduction to Social Work, primarily because she had had so much experience with social workers. Her grades were not yet the high marks she was used to, but she was managing.

At her next meeting with Miss Raymelle at Starbucks, she set aside academic issues and discussed the thing that managed to creep into her dreams and occasionally hijack her study sessions. "I want to find my birth mother. I need to know if there's anyone around that I can call family. Do you think it's crazy to try? Any of your other kids ever done it?"

Miss Raymelle frowned. "Yeah, I've known a few. It's not hard to get the birth records released, but the names will be missing. I can help you with that first part. Finding your birth mother or birth father is another story. Sometimes it seems like a person up and disappeared off the face of the earth. Other times it's as easy as googling a last name if it's the same as yours. It all depends."

"I won't let it get in the way of my school work, in case you're worried. I'd never let that happen." Jasmine could feel the hope blooming in her chest. It was like a wild weed that threatened to overtake the neat practical rows of seedling self-worth that had recently taken root.

"I know you won't, baby. The thing is, you have to be prepared for whatever you find. Your parents could be dead or in jail or drug addicts. There could be no record of your parents' whereabouts or it might be easy as pie. Either way, they may not want to see you. They gave you up for a reason. That reason could be distressing, and they may not want to go back and relive it. You get me? On the other hand, they might turn out to be great people, excited to meet you…it's hard to know. I'm ready to help, but don't do it unless you're really ready to face the reality, *whatever* it is."

"I'm not counting on anything; I promise, I'm not."

"Your birth mom might be a drunk who sends you walking."

"I hear you, and I can deal with it—all of it, whatever it is, because if there's some chance that maybe…I just gotta try. I need to know if there's someone out there that's a part a me."

"See, that's what I'm saying; that probably won't happen. It almost never does."

"And if it doesn't, it doesn't! I'll be okay either way, I promise." She pulled her lips into her mouth, waited.

Miss Raymelle leaned in, "Okay then, you're an adult now and can do it yourself, but I'll guide you through the process. It'll be relatively easy to get non-identifying information about your birth mom, meaning the circumstances that led to your being put up for adoption and any health history that was known at the time."

She gulped down her coffee, and said she had to run to her next appointment. "Getting your mom's name is something else. You'd have to present a pressing reason as to why you'd need to contact her. So, for example, if you had some kind of genetic disease, and there was nothing in the health background that she gave at the time of the surrender, you could request her identity to contact her to get more information about your family's health history. Since that's not the case, I doubt they'll release any of those identifying details. Of course, you can register with the state, saying that you want to find her, and if she also registers, they'll make the connection. I'll email you the paperwork." She stood, and her palm brushed over Jasmine's shoulder blades. Then she was gone.

It took about six weeks for the report to arrive in her college mailbox. Jasmine tore into the envelope and tugged out the few sheets of paper. Skimming through the pages, her jaw dropped. That her mother had been a teenager was no surprise; she could have guessed as much. But there was a paragraph titled, *Circumstance of Child Surrender*, which took her breath away. Jasmine's legs felt weak, and she slid onto the cold lobby floor. She straightened the letter and re-read the paragraph.

Jasmine finished reading the first document and then looked at the next sheet of paper. It was a copy of her original birth certificate, and on it was her mother's name, covered haphazardly by thick black ink. She tried to make out the letters. Was that an *L*? It was no use. Her mother was still a mystery.

At their next meeting, Jasmine leaned over her steaming coffee cup. "Have you seen the report?"

"No baby. It went straight to you."

The crowd bustled around them, but when she was with Miss Raymelle, she felt as if they were in their own private bubble. "I have a twin sister!"

"Really? Not identical...."

"No, not hardly. It said that one of us was light skinned and the other was dark. Which one do you think I am? I mean, I'm not very dark. I'm light for someone who's black. You think I'm the light one? I don't know why that matters to me, or why the fact that I have a twin at all and no one bothered to tell me makes me so friggin' pissed off."

Miss Raymelle swayed in her chair. "That's a whole mess of mystery—that light/dark thing, why no one told you that you're a twin, or why you two aren't together. Wow!"

"Someone can just write shit like that, with no explanation? And what happened to her...this sister of mine? How could it not say?" Miss Raymelle's brow was pulled together. Jasmine waited for a response that didn't seem coming, so she plowed ahead. "And my mother was only sixteen years old. I know it happens all the time, so not a shocker. But then I started to think about it, what it would be like to have a two-year-old right now."

Miss Raymelle nodded.

"Okay, so I get that she was a kid, and it would be hard to have a baby and all...but then I read on. It said the pregnancy was the result of a sexual assault." She looked up at Miss Raymelle as if searching for an explanation.

"So, that tells you a lot."

"It explains why she gave us up. She didn't want to keep some attacker dude's babies. Report said he was a Caucasian drug-addict." Jasmine's mind churned with violent images; a pale man ripping clothes off a dark-skinned girl—her father a rapist, an animal. She tried to shoo these thoughts, but they stuck to her mind like insects on fly-paper. "Shit."

"Hmmm, how are you handling this?"

"Huh, what am I supposed to do with it? Now I can't even really be angry at her for giving me up. Though I still am—a little bit anyways. I mean, if she had parents that could have taken me in, or a grandma or something, I just know my life would've been a whole lot better. It was like she took something mad awful and then made it worse."

Miss Raymelle raised a questioning brow.

"Maybe I shouldn't judge, but I can't help it."

"You're gonna feel what you feel. This is a lot to take in. Your feelings might change with time, you'll see. There's no right or wrong here."

"Why not? There should be something that's right and wrong, 'cause I sure as fuck was wronged! Excuse my language, but it's true."

"You can see her as wrong. No one's stopping you...." A student walked by with a big backpack that brushed against Miss Raymelle's head and seemed to jolt her into action. "You could petition the court to unseal the record. You'd have to make a compelling argument—maybe something about having absolutely no family in the world, being unjustly separated from your twin sister, sexual abuse, the failures of the foster care system—a case could be made for unsealing your record."

"Sounds like I'd need a lawyer and money and time."

"A lawyer and time for sure. But maybe we could get someone to take your case pro bono. That means—"

"I know what that means. I didn't have internet growing up, but I had TV. I watched *Law and Order*." Her jaw clenched and her teeth ground together. Why did everything in her life have to be so difficult? Still, she shouldn't snap at Miss Raymelle. Jasmine sat back in her chair thinking about how she'd possibly fit this into her crazy work and school schedule. "You don't have some wand you can wave to find me one of those pro bono lawyers, huh?"

A sad smile lifted Miss Raymelle's cheeks. "I'm a lot of things, but not a fairy godmother."

"Fairy godmother?"

"I'm not Dumbledore either."

"Okay, I know you do what you can."

"Listen, don't let this distract you from school. Your sister will still be around at Christmas break."

Jasmine's mind was buzzing, she was desperate to learn the whole truth and fearful just the same. "Um, do you think I should be upset because I got a rapist's blood in my veins? You think that's why my life is so shitty...because of what he did?"

"We're talking *sins of the father* now? Like you're being punished because of him?" She looked at Jasmine and shook her head. "Not hardly. My God don't work that way. My God takes pity on children like you. My God sends down people to help them."

"So, you're an angel now?"

"Well, that's a lot truer than God punishing you because of your mother being raped."

"But isn't that exactly what happened? Who got punished here?"

Miss Raymelle thought for a beat. "You, your sister, your mother, even your rotten dad; y'all had bad stuff happen to you. But that doesn't mean that God decided you deserved it. I'm no pastor, but if you want to know how I see it, people have free will. Your father made a choice and did a terrible thing. That's on him. I'd look to God for comfort. Life isn't about punishment, it's about learning something and using that to make yourself a better person." She thought a moment longer. "Life's about making it through to the other side, and then helping others do the same."

"Really? Which church says that? I thought God was up there moving us around like chess pieces."

"You're old enough to find a belief that works for you, but if they start blaming you for everything bad that happens in your life, I'd get me a second opinion. You feel me?"

Jasmine nodded.

"Okay, so let's do it. Let's see if we can learn something about your twin sister and birth mom."

Tessa

Tessa and Charlie got together every day after classes, often meeting in the law library. With heads bent over their books and laptops, they'd steal glances. Tessa learned that despite his air of confidence, Charlie was not without insecurities. Stansworth Academy was one of the most prestigious private schools in New York, if not the entire country. If he followed the path set forth for him, he'd have some of the most powerful, influential and, in some cases, brilliant people in the city placing their children's education in his hands. He'd confessed, "I'm just not sure I'm exceptional enough to keep the Stansworth educational machinery churning out super stars."

When Charlie's mood travelled to these dark places, Tessa felt lost. She tried to use her father's brand of encouragement, "I believe in you. You have more talent and drive (she'd added in the word talent, since her dad never said that to her) than anyone I know!" Still, her words seemed to fall flat. It was hard to encourage someone else when she herself was equally insecure, and as the semester progressed, that was increasingly the case.

Then there was Charlie's prominence in the city's social scene. She learned that he'd often been featured in the society pages standing next to some collegiate heiress at a charity benefit. It was his brief relationship with a certain Hollywood star attending NYU that first landed him in the gossip columns. From then on, attending any public event caused tongues to wag about whose hand he held, and what girl would be joining him in Rome or Madrid.

When Charlie entered the next Saint James gathering with Tessa glued to his side, no one even tried to hide their shock. Kate reported that the conversations were peppered with inquiries about her background, her family, and how she came to be so cozy with a man who'd been labeled one of the ten most desirable bachelors under twenty-five by *City Beat*. Many wrote her off as a passing fancy, a brief affair that would be forgotten as quickly as last year's obsession with Chilean pinot noir—nice for a change but can't replace France or even Napa Valley.

As the two made their way into the center of the parlor, a dark-haired woman with high-heeled Gucci boots clicked toward them. She tossed her glossy mane over sculpted shoulders. "Madeline Warner, nice to meet you." Her face was bright with a smile, but there was a sharpness in her eyes that made Tessa shiver. She felt Charlie's hand move to her back. "Tessa, correct? So, where are you from?"

Her question felt adversarial. When Tessa was younger, her mom had had a job that sometimes involved arguing cases in court. In preparation, she'd present her arguments to Tessa who acted as both judge and jury. Her mother had told her, "You have to believe you can win. Everyone in the room must see you that way." Tessa now tried to channel her mother. "I'm from Maplewood, New Jersey. You?"

Madeline tittered, "Why I'm from here: Manhattan, just like Charlie." She had a speech pattern that sounded pretentious. Her Ts were soft, her vowels a tad elongated. "Maplewood—a commuter town? I've driven through Jersey…on my way to D.C. Now where is Maplewood exactly, closer to Newark or The Short Hills Mall?"

"If those are your only points of reference, then I'd have to say it's in the middle, about forty minutes from the city."

"I suppose it's good to be in the middle. Someone has to be." Her eyes flashed mischievously above her straight nose and bleached-white teeth. "And what do people do there in Maplewood?"

Charlie intervened, "They do just what people in New York do, Madeline."

Tessa took a step away from Charlie's protective hand, "My father's an obstetrician, and my mother's an attorney. Are we done here?" Her tone came out harsher than anticipated.

"I think you've misunderstood—Charlie and I are old friends. I just wanted to meet his latest interest and welcome you. I don't know how things are done where you're from, but here at Saint James, we make polite conversation...even with those who've been less than honest."

Tessa's brow puckered, "And in this scenario, who's lied?"

Her razor eyes shifted, "Still keeping secrets, Charlie?" then returned, "Nice to have met you...Tessa." Madeline pivoted like a model on a runway and made her way to the other side of the room.

"Sorry, Tess," Charlie's words were soft against her ear.

"What was that about?"

"Madeline was my girlfriend last year. It ended over the summer...that is...I ended it. I think she was expecting that we'd get back together. She wanted to talk at the first fall party."

"Oh...the one where we met?"

His arms reached around her, and he pressed her center to his. "How could I have considered her again, once...." The rest of his sentence fell away as he fingered one of her curls and kissed the top of her head.

Tessa wasn't comforted. She glanced across the room— Madeline was statuesque, poised, and of course, beautiful. She understood why Charlie was attracted to her. She knew nothing of her family, but assumed, judging from her arrogance, it was upper crust.

When Tessa tried to pull back from Charlie, he strengthened his grip. "I don't care what they think," and then his lips were on hers, tender. She was filled with warmth and light, an ecstatic joy mixed with a nagging fear that it could all be lost.

She nudged him away, "Let's not give them a reason to throw us out."

"It was one kiss," he murmured near her ear. "I've seen people do a lot worse."

Later that night, Tessa brought Charlie back to her room where they undressed each other and fell into bed. She tried to keep from obsessing about his wealth and family history. *It shouldn't mean anything,* she told herself. His fingertips brushed her breasts, her hands explored his soft hair, the expanse of his shoulder blades. By now they had a rhythm, and he knew how to make her shake with pleasure. Before he entered her, when she was lost in herself, he'd pull her back, "Open your eyes." Then he'd move inside her saying, "This is how much I love you." His cornflower eyes held her. In that moment, she was both lost and found.

Later that night, as he slept, Tessa inched away, picked up her laptop, and settled herself down on her roommate's bed, grateful that she'd left for the weekend. She caught sight of Charlie's watch, keys, and wallet tossed on her desk with her faux diamond necklace and earrings. Something made her grab her phone and snap a picture of their belongings mingled, as if to validate that it had happened; Charlie Stansworth had spent the night in her room. When he made love to her, she imagined their spirits leaving their bodies and dancing together overhead. What was God if not love? And what was love if not making love, especially the way they made love? Tessa wanted to crawl back into bed and doze in his arms, but the encounter with Madeline had sent her mind racing.

She tugged on Charlie's sweatshirt, one that had *Columbia Crew* across the chest. A few nights earlier Charlie had pulled it over her head while studying in his room, and Tessa now viewed it as her second skin. It still smelled like a mixture of his soap and deodorant, toothpaste and sweat. She could often stick her nose in it and feel comforted, but not tonight. She opened her MacBook and entered, *Madeline Warner* in the search bar.

Her eyes grew wide. She wasn't a true celebrity, but Madeline certainly was a minor one. She was sometimes mentioned on the blogs and websites that shared gossip about the city's high society. Her life was chronicled, beginning with her coming out party, continuing with her role in an off-Broadway play, and on through her long relationship with Charlie. They had often been photographed together. There was a picture of her and Charlie in front of the Metropolitan Museum of Art. It was taken just prior to the dedication of the museum's new *Warner Wing*, a gift from her family's foundation. Madeline wore a white beaded gown with a sheer black wrap and her long hair was lifted into a satiny chignon. Charlie looked stunning in a black tuxedo, his arm wrapped around her waist. The caption read, "Madeline Warner and Charlie Stansworth: A Powerful Match."

Closing her computer, she felt her stomach twisting. She took a few deep breaths to calm herself and crawled back into bed, pressing her back into Charlie's chest so that he instinctively embraced her.

In his arms, beneath the comforter she had picked out with her mother, she was both happy and fearful. This burgeoning love felt magical, but it was also fragile. She wanted to protect it—surround it in bubble wrap and stick it in a Styrofoam box.

Her last thought was of Charlie's blue eyes and of tumbling into them. She dreamt that night of falling through space and awoke with a start right before she hit the ground. Charlie was already up and dressed. He was sitting at her desk looking at a phone. She sat up, now realizing that the phone he was holding was hers. "Hey, you're up early. What's going on?"

His eyes were glued to a photo. He turned it toward her, "What's this?"

She felt flustered, "That? You know what it is."

"I mean, when did you take it...why?"

"What are you, the photo police?" she started to laugh but saw that he wouldn't join her. "It's just a shot of our stuff that I took last night. No big deal. You can trash it if you want." His face remained rigid. "What's up?"

"Why did you take this—what will you do with it?"

"I wasn't going to do *anything* with it. It's just a picture, I take them all the time. Anyway, why are you trolling through my phone?"

"I wanted to see the pictures we took before last night's party. I was going to send one to myself...who cares! You still didn't say—"

"What's the problem? I guess I took a picture of our stuff together, so that I could remember it; the first night you spent in my room."

"So that you could remember? Or show your friends? Or post it on social media?"

"It was for me! Just for me! Why would anyone give a shit about your watch and wallet and my jewelry and—"

He cut her off, "City Beat would love this! The headline could read, *Stansworth Looks for Love in Jersey, or Prince and Pauper Pair Up!*"

"Are you kidding me? Is that how you see me?"

"No, of course not!" He was on his feet now. He tossed the phone on her desk and began to pace.

"What's going on?"

"Tessa, are you so naïve? That watch, the watch I wear all the time, it was my grandfather's. It's a Patek Philippe."

"Is that supposed to mean something?"

"You took a picture of it next to your fake diamond necklace and earrings. What was that about?"

"My fake diamonds? How do you know they're fake?"

He cocked his head.

She stood up on her bed outraged, "What difference does it make! The picture was about US, not our THINGS!"

His expression softened, "Okay, okay, I see now you didn't know...just...don't do it again. Don't photograph my stuff. I don't want headlines, and I don't want people knowing that I walk around wearing that watch on campus. We can delete it and forget it, all right? Maybe I'm over reacting."

"You think?" She remained standing, king of her bed; a warrior who was pumped full of adrenaline, prepared for a battle that had already ended. Who had won? She wasn't feeling victorious. It was more like he had decided to give her a free pass. "I don't want a free pass," she said out loud, before recognizing that it made no sense.

He glanced at his watch, his very expensive, heirloom watch. "I have to get going. I'll see you later. Sorry, I gave you such a hard time." He took her hand, and she stepped down to his level. "I'll meet you at the library after dinner."

"Why do you get to just walk out now?"

"Tessa, let's cool down and text later. Okay?"

It wasn't okay. How could it be? But what else could she say? She looked down and shrugged. For some reason that seemed good enough for him, and he walked out the door.

Lakisha

While TJ remained in the hospital awaiting confirmation of his diagnosis, Lakisha, Theo, and the kids tried to maintain some semblance of normalcy—not an easy task. Lakisha would spend most of the day with TJ, go home to have dinner with her other children and put them to bed, and then sneak back to be with TJ overnight. The hospital staff was kind and found a narrow recliner that Lakisha pushed up next to TJ's bed so that she could get a few hours of rest. She'd been asked to judge a collegiate poetry slam on the weekend, and Theo said he'd find a way to manage without her. At moments like this, when Theo displayed the depths of his devotion, Lakisha knew the grudge she carried against him was wrong—that she had been wrong in many ways. And yet the seeds of her anger remained, buried so deep, it would take a seismic shift to unearth them.

Since going back to the hospital where she'd been treated that night, memories of the twins had resurfaced; the soft curl of tiny toes, a scrunched-up face that seemed just as unhappy as she was, and later, their peaceful cocooned slumber. For those first few days after giving birth, the staff had insisted she do the feeding, claiming that regardless of her emotions, they were understaffed. She later understood—they wanted her to be sure, wanted her to feel the weight of them in her arms, inhale their scent, touch the silk of their skin. And she had done it; she'd done all of that and then cut the cord connecting her heart to theirs. But now she wondered if that bond could ever truly be severed.

Her doll from Maizy, the raggedy black and white one that she'd washed and mended over the years, was now dragged around the apartment by Shonda, discarded in sofa cushions or block houses, and then redeemed back into her bed for sleep. Today, in a rare quiet moment, Lakisha picked up the raggedy treasure, stroked the yellow-yarn hair, then reversed the skirt and fingered the brown-fabric face. She pictured the moon-shaped birthmark above that daughter's cheekbone and couldn't help wondering; had she grown into it? Had her adopted mother kissed that spot and said, *you're beautiful*—the way Lakisha would have if she'd raised her? Had her adopted mother kept her safe, taught her to be strong, set her on a good path? Did she grow up with her twin—that other one, with the hair and skin of an attacker? Maizy's gift turned out to be as complex as the woman herself. Had Maizy meant to send a clairvoyant message? Lakisha sniffed in emotion, sat the rag doll on the sofa, and finished her chores.

On a rainy Saturday morning in October, just days into TJ's hospitalization, Lakisha slipped away from Beth Israel, and made her way to The Paul Robeson Campus Center at Rutgers Newark. Lakisha had walked past the campus a hundred times on her way to Essex County College. She'd always hoped to go back and get her four-year degree, but that would take time and money, two things that were in short supply. When she was asked to judge this collegiate event, she almost laughed out loud at the absurdity. But when they offered her a one-hundred-dollar honorarium, she quickly agreed.

Lakisha followed signs to the Essex East Room and chose a seat on the end of the long, draped table at the front. Behind them were several hundred chairs waiting to be filled by college students.

Once she settled her sweater onto a seat, she stepped out into the hallway and phoned Theo.

"Hey, Kisha, how's it going at college? You teaching those kids something?"

He could still make her smile. "I haven't taught them anything yet, but I'll keep you posted. What's up with our crew? How's Auntie doing at the hospital?" Just then she heard a crash and a screech on his end of the phone.

"We're all good here."

"Don't sound like it." Now Kai was crying.

"It's nothing. Shonda knocked a toy off the table, and it landed on the baby's foot. He's fine, surprised is all. Dottie says TJ is the same. We just spoke." Kai was still screaming in the background. "I gotta go, but don't worry. Have fun!"

"Wait, Theo?" he was already off the line. She'd have to leave it be.

Lakisha returned to her seat in the auditorium. Other judges arrived and introduced themselves, and a half hour later, the room was filled to near capacity. This was the first time the Brick City Arts Society had sponsored a collegiate poetry slam, and they were as shocked as anyone by the response. Poetry groups from all over the tristate area had been invited, and the majority had accepted. With a week to go, the venue had to be changed to a larger room. Lakisha turned and scanned the crowd. It looked like the United Nations. She realized she'd never heard someone recite poetry who didn't live nearby. She knew there were loads of readings in Manhattan and Brooklyn, but who had time for all that? She was happy to make the library meetings and find a few moments here and there to scratch out her own words. Fortunately, the readers of her column were none too discerning. If it touched their hearts or made them think a moment, it was good enough.

The audience buzzed with sound and motion until the Arts Society president got up and recited a sweet poem to welcome them all. Then he explained the competition's rules, and the poets began taking turns at the microphone. Lakisha tried to take a few careful notes about each one and drew a small related sketch to refresh her memory later on.

Some of the poems were humorous, but many were expressions of despair, depictions of injuries so fierce, she was grateful when they took a short break and she had room to shake off the images. The students from Rutgers circled through the restless crowd selling food and collecting donations in exchange for poetry chapbooks.

When the audience was summoned back to their seats, Lakisha stifled a yawn. She hadn't been able to sleep more than a few hours a night for days. She took a few sips of coffee from a travel mug and looked up at the next contestant. Lakisha held her breath. It was all she could do to keep from rushing the makeshift stage, for there, right there just a few feet away she saw her—her mother.

Jasmine

This was the largest crowd she'd ever read for, and her extremities
went ice-cold. She surveyed the sea of faces, all waiting for her to
take them someplace, somewhere far away from their own lives.
Perhaps she would bring them to an emotional home that seemed
just that much more poignant than their own, or a place where one
single moment in time became clearer. These were lofty goals,
beyond mere entertainment, but wasn't that the point of poetry?

Her choice for today's reading was purposely short, both because
of her nerves and because she feared revealing too much of her
disastrous life—even through poetry. Jasmine began, "This is for my
roommate, Padma, who pushes me way beyond my comfort
zone...and sometimes, just sometimes, into the light."

She took a few deep breaths and placed her open notebook face
down on the floor. Her eyes closed as she recited the first few verses.

The man approached on the street,
Eyeing my hair, my lips, my skin.
His mouth munched Twizzlers, his thick brow bunched confusion.
"What color are you?" His head cocked quizzical.
I thought on it—scanned past and present;
Things that scorched my blood,
Things that still echoed in my bones.
I touched my skin, nodded.
Me?
I am the color of life and the color of loss,

I am the color of promise and the color of pain,
I am the color of denial and the color of faith,
I am the color of God's tears
And the color of love.
Me, mister?
I am the color
Of a tattered heart.
You?

The applause vibrated through her. She made a quick scan of the room, allowing her gaze to linger on a female judge. Was she crying?

Lakisha

Her mother, or apparition, or whatever it was, had spoken. Yes, it was her mother's voice, or at least something similar to the rounded tones she could recall after close to thirty years. *Jesus, she can't be real...or can she?* She studied the young woman before her, hoping, and at the same time wondering if she'd lost her mind. As the applause thundered around her, the girl at the microphone paused for a split second and tucked a lock of hair behind her right ear, exposing the blushing skin of her cheek, and something else. There, near her temple, almost at her hairline, was a darkened birthmark in the shape of...it couldn't be. A wave of panic passed through her. Now she saw the difference; this girl's face was rounder than Maizy's, her eyes larger, her limbs less spindly, and above her cheekbone was the half-moon that confirmed it. This girl; she was Lakisha's daughter.

The feelings of elation and loss, longing and regret, shame and relief, all came at once—jumbled, conflicted. She missed her mother, had built Maizy up to be a larger-than-life, beautiful, loving, fucked-up, and tragic figure, who now seemed to have returned from the dead as this girl who was a part of her—and yet, not.

The guilt of what she'd done to the twins bloomed. She saw on the stage not only her past, but a piece of herself that could have been her future, something that was now forever lost. She did this to herself and to them. She was the one who told Theo they died, who convinced Aunt Dottie to sign the papers, who murdered the future.

Still, Lakisha couldn't suppress the whisper of pride that circled in her chest as the crowd cheered. It was her flesh and blood they were applauding.

"That was Jasmine White, of Rutgers University, Newark," said the MC.

Lakisha recorded her name in rounded letters. This was one poet she would remember.

As the afternoon wore on, it was hard for Lakisha to pay attention, for her mind kept drifting to Jasmine. During the final break, she craned her neck, searching for her, but Jasmine was lost in the sea of people stretching and smiling, laughing and laying down money for chapbooks. She glanced at her phone and saw a text from Theo.

Doctor says results of the bone biopsy are in. He wants to meet us at 3. Can you sneak out early? Dottie's on her way here, and I'm heading to the hospital.

Please Lord, let this be something treatable. On my way!

Tessa

Sam walked to the microphone, and Tessa, along with about a dozen other Columbians, whooped. Tessa had never heard Sam's poetry, and was happy with her decision to ditch her work and join him. His poem described working for a car detailer in high school and finding a note tucked beneath a seat. Reading it was the only way to know whether or not it was trash, or so he said, and what he discovered was a love letter. When he handed the note to the car's owner, a lithe blond with a southern drawl, she responded with a full-lipped kiss that left his mouth lipstick-pink for a day and his mind in a blonde cloud for a week. When he finished, Tessa and her group were on their feet cheering. Tessa jumped into the aisle and embraced Sam as he approached, and she felt an odd sadness when he released her.

Tessa knew she loved Sam, loved him like she loved all her friends, though there were times she sensed he was interested in something more, and there were even moments when she questioned this in herself. She tried to banish those thoughts. She'd never want to wreck their friendship, and nice as he was, he didn't compare to Charlie. Sam was a regular great guy, but Charlie—he was a prince.

Back in the city, Sam convinced Tessa to hang out in midtown for an hour, rather than heading right back to campus. They flashed fake I.D.s and huddled in a corner booth at an Irish pub. There they reviewed the poems that were memorable and joked about almost getting on a train headed to the Jersey shore. Everything seemed funny after a few shots of tequila. In the midst of it all, Sam reached across the table and touched her forearm. *He must be drunk.* "Sam...."

"I know. I know you're with Charlie."

Sam was sweet and kind, and he was a deep thinker in that way that artists or people who've suffered often are. He'd shared bits and pieces with her about his father walking out when he was a kid and going shopping with his mother using food stamps. His gentle chin was usually covered in three days' worth of stubble, and that, along with the persistent dark circles beneath his eyes, gave him a look of perpetual depression. She tried changing the topic, "You were awesome today. You must feel great."

"Is that what you'd say to Charlie?" He grabbed the full shot glass sitting in front of her and downed it himself.

"Sam, are you okay? I'm just trying to be supportive." She pulled her arm off the table.

"I know you are. I accept it. I accept whatever the hell you want to give me."

"Talk to me. Why just accept it?"

He lifted mournful eyes, "What are my other options?"

PART THREE
The Color of God's Tears

Lakisha

Though God had disappointed her in the past, Lakisha found herself praying as she inched her way through traffic. "Lord, I know I haven't always done right—far from it, but my TJ, he's a good boy and deserves a future. Please heal him and let him recover from this—whatever it is. Don't let this mess with the rest of his life." She was quiet for a beat. "Back in the day when grandma died, and I had to live with Dottie, who was hell bent on blaming me for not calling 911 soon enough...well anyways, I made you a promise that if Mama came back and took care a me, I'd do the right things, go to church regular and all. I didn't think I was asking for that much, but it must have been too big a deal on your end." A Jeep cut in front of her and she slammed on the breaks. "Shit! Excuse my language, Lord. So, I'll make the same deal again, and see if you're listening this time. Whatever you need me to do, I'll do it...just please heal my sweet boy. I know I don't deserve it, but he sure as...he sure does. Amen."

Lakisha and Theo sat opposite the doctor who would give them the verdict. Theo was planted in his chair, passive and resigned. Lakisha was already missing the doctor with the hazel eyes who gave her hope for something that wasn't too serious. Dr. Liu, on the other hand, was a pediatric hematologist-oncologist, and when he chose to have a sit down with you, it was a clue that you should bring along a box of tissues. There was a dying bonsai tree on the windowsill behind him that made Lakisha wonder, *if the man can't even save a house plant, how could he be trusted to save TJ?*

The doctor didn't waste time; she'd give him that much. He opened TJ's record on the computer in front of him and said, "We have treatment options," then he lifted his gaze to meet theirs, "but it's leukemia."

Theo reached for her hand and Lakisha collapsed into his side. Leukemia, something people died from—even children. Not her TJ though, no sir. They'd find a way, they'd just have to. She gathered herself together, so she could hear the rest.

"I'm recommending a round of chemotherapy. We'll begin tomorrow. I've already put him on the list for a bone-marrow transplant, but the best matches are often family members, so I'd like to begin collecting samples from your relatives. Hopefully we'll find someone who's a close match."

"What does that involve?" Lakisha hoped it wouldn't be as brutal as the biopsy that TJ had endured.

"The first test is a simple cheek swab. Then if we find someone who has a few matching markers, we'll do further testing on the sample we already have, then blood tests. We don't have to worry about that right now. What I'd like you to do is compile a list of relatives, and we'll set up a date, probably a Saturday. We're moving TJ to the Pediatric Oncology unit. Treasure, my nurse, will go over all the details of the chemotherapy with you and set up the schedule. Any questions?"

Lakisha's mind was racing. "What's the…what's the prognosis? Can you say?"

Theo dropped his head, upset by the question, but she was a realist. She wanted to know just how much of a miracle they'd be needing.

"The five-year survival rate for children diagnosed with what TJ has, Acute Promyelocytic Leukemia, is higher than 80 percent.

Here at our treatment centers, we are averaging even higher. So this is a serious illness, but we have treatment options and are going to do our very best. You should try to stay optimistic and keep TJ's spirits up. The social worker will be by to speak with you later. There are also support groups that many people find helpful. Treasure and the social worker can give you all that information."

"Doc, TJ is a fine boy, a real loving...." Theo's voice was broken, his street-stance stripped away. "He's so good—I know lots of parents must say that about their kids, but with TJ, it's the God's honest truth."

Lakisha glanced at Theo and understood why she would never leave him: he could voice what was trapped in her heart.

Dr. Liu's expression softened. "Mr. Michaelson, we have a strong program here, and we are going to do everything possible to help your boy."

There was a long silence, and Lakisha was reluctant to get up from the chair. Maybe if she just sat there, Dr. Liu would give her more assurances.

Theo stood, "Thank you. Thank you for taking good care of him." He wrapped an arm around Lakisha and she made herself leave with him.

Out in the hallway, Lakisha dissolved into a puddle of tears. She clung to Theo, sobbing for what felt like hours but was probably only a few minutes. She would have to wipe her face and return to TJ. She'd have to act as if it would all be okay. It surely had to be okay. *God, please, make it be okay.*

They found TJ sitting up in bed and playing cards with a teenage volunteer. The girl looked to be about seventeen and she had a wide-toothed smile. "Hey there, TJ was just destroying me in poker. He said he was up to it."

"Thanks for keeping him busy," said Lakisha. She cleared her throat, trying to dislodge the remnants of sorrow, and closed the door behind the teen.

She sat down at the foot of the bed and Theo took his place on the recliner. She began, "We met with Dr. Liu and he told us that you're going to be moved to another unit and then you'll start chemotherapy. That's where they pump strong medicine into your veins to kill the bad cells that are growing. In the meantime, we're going to start looking for someone to donate bone marrow. No need to talk about that until we find a match."

"Okay, son? You get what we're saying?" Theo placed a hand on TJ's shoulder and the boy looked to Theo in a way that made emotion gather in Lakisha's eyes.

"I guess I'm pretty sick, huh?"

Theo's voice was slow to come. "It seems that way."

"I got cancer?" TJ looked only at his father, as if looking at his mother would bring too much suffering to the both of them.

"It's a certain kind—leukemia. It's in your blood. Once we find the right donor, we'll get you fixed up good as new. You'll just have to be patient while we make that happen."

"So, you want me to be a patient patient."

"Yeah, something like that." Theo's eyes looked misty, and Lakisha swiped at her own.

TJ, on the other hand, was unflappable. "I knew that's what it was. I didn't want to say, but I knew." TJ's lips looked dry, his face, pale. "I knew it had to be real bad, because I feel so tired and I keep bleeding and coughing."

"Don't worry, you'll get better. It'll be okay."

A jagged fault line ripped through Lakisha. "We got an army of people who will pray for you. And Dr. Liu says your chances are excellent of beating this thing."

"I'll get better. At least I'm gonna try."

At that, Lakisha couldn't keep her tears from spilling. "I know you will!"

She wiped her face and offered TJ a half smile.

That night, Theo stayed with TJ while Lakisha sat at home, her notebook out and her pen in her hand. She had listed the names of all their close relatives. There was Aunt Dottie and her two girls and their children, Theo's brother and his brother's kids who lived down in Camden, and of course she and Theo would be tested along with their four other children. Theo had a few cousins with whom he'd lost touch—she'd try and rope them in too. Lakisha read the names out loud. Blood relatives, they were the most likely candidates.

Then there was *Jasmine White*. She whispered the name, felt it in her mouth. She was there at Rutgers, and her twin might be close by. Tracking them down would be a violation of their adoption agreement. The thought of it made her head ache. Even if she were to find the girls, how could she ask them to help a brother they'd never met, one that their mother chose to keep? And what would Theo say if he learned the full story? Though he had nursed her after the attack, she'd kept the rape a secret, had been too afraid he'd seek vengeance and wind up dead or in jail, or be too distressed to stay with her. Theo thought the twins were his, and so did she, right up until the moment wisps of blonde hair told her otherwise. Saying they'd died seemed the best way to spare his emotions, his life. And with all their current heartache, what if learning the truth put him over the edge? No, she couldn't do it. TJ had Nikki, Devon, Shonda, Kai, and a long list of relatives. One of them would have to be the match.

That night, sleep escaped her. She couldn't let go of an image: TJ lying listless in bed, his mind dull from depleted blood, and his smile waning. Chemo would make him even sicker, at least for a while, and there was no guarantee that even a transplant would heal him. It seemed too much to bear: the uncertainty, his distress, the pressures of caring for her healthy kids, her job and column—all of it. Theo had just started his own medical transport business and couldn't take time off. Lakisha could take a family leave from work, but they needed the money. *God, how we need the money.* In recent days, God had become her closest companion. It seemed she spoke to the heavens more than Theo.

After chewing on the facts for a time, Lakisha abandoned the bed and slid onto the carpet. She grabbed her laptop from the hood of the hamper and followed links to articles on Acute Promyelocytic Leukemia. She read them all, learned everything, yet nothing that would help. It wasn't even a common childhood disease. The research said it was just rotten luck, a non-genetic chromosomal mutation. But why TJ? Why their family? *Haven't we suffered enough?*

And why did the diagnosis arrive on the same day as her mother's ghost, Jasmine White? When she pictured Jasmine at the microphone, Lakisha's pulse quickened. She had buried the memories of those babies—tried to forget, as if that could erase the past. Was this some cosmic sign that needed interpreting or more bad luck? She curled into a fetal position, hugging herself, and fell asleep. She dreamt of Maizy joining her at TJ's bedside and wrapping an arm around her waist. Lakisha leaned against her mother, felt her warmth. When she lifted her head to check on TJ, she noticed something dangling from Maizy's delicate fingers; it was the topsy-turvy doll.

Jasmine

Miss Raymelle handed an official-looking envelope across the Starbuck's table. "It's a letter from a law firm agreeing to take your case."

"Is it a good firm?"

Miss Raymelle shrugged, "I don't know, but it's a law firm anyway."

"I guess beggars can't be choosers."

"I don't think it's a complicated case. They'll make the argument before a judge and hopefully some portion of the file will be released. Okay?"

"Yeah, definitely."

"How was the poetry slam?"

"It was mad cool! There were so many readers, and some of them had this deep, powerful stuff, more sophisticated than anything I've ever heard. Some were funny too! There's supposed to be another one in New York next semester that I wanna get to."

"Fabulous! Anything else going on?"

Jasmine looked down at the floor. "Padma convinced me to go to this festival in the Ironbound. A bunch of us are going."

"Is there a Portuguese theme?"

"I think it's Brazilian. I'll stop by for a bit...probably won't stay."

"Might as well have an open mind."

Jasmine rolled her eyes and glanced at her watch. "Is it okay if we end now? We're supposed to meet up and figure out costumes."

"Sure, enjoy yourself!"

Jasmine felt her face blush. It was odd to have good news to share with Miss Raymelle. Walking across campus, Jasmine realized that for the first time in as long as she could remember, she felt happy. It wasn't the kind of good feeling that came from pills or whiskey or sex. Instead it was something quiet and calm; it was peaceful. She didn't want to do anything to mess with it. She'd developed an ache in her jaw, and the dentist at the clinic said it was from grinding her teeth at night. "Your teeth are in good position, so it might be caused by anxiety. Try reducing stress," he'd said. It seemed that even in her sleep, her body was bracing for the next disaster.

Tessa

Tessa was one of the last to find out. It was Homecoming Weekend at Haverford Academy, and she arranged with her mom to spend a day at home. She didn't share her plans with Charlie, wanted to avoid seeing his look of disappointment. Even if he disapproved, sometimes she needed to get away from school. There were moments when he seemed to transform into her mother; tossing out criticism that masqueraded as *helpful suggestions.*

In her haste to finish her assignments before the weekend, Tessa forgot to charge her phone, and by mid-day Friday, her battery was dead. When she arrived home, she opened her MacBook and scrolled through what she'd missed. There were several texts from Kate telling her to phone ASAP. They included words like *situation* and *damage control.* There were also several from Charlie saying, *Hey, it's important we talk,* and *please call.*

What could be so urgent? She wondered if someone had been in an accident. She decided to phone Kate first.

She answered immediately, "Did you see the Facebook page?"

Tessa exhaled, relieved no one had died. "No, what's up?"

"Someone put up a new page about you and the so called *truth,* and sent the link to everyone at Saint James."

"Seriously? It must be all bullshit. There's no big truth about me. What could they write—that I like to chew the tops off of Pez dispensers?"

"I didn't want to miss the homecoming game, so I'm in Millburn. I'll be right over."

Tessa opened Facebook and typed in her name. Her eyes widened as she read through the new page several times. It was so crazy, completely absurd—and yet...*Is this why Mom never wants to talk about my birth?* It was beginning to make sense; not having pictures of her as a newborn, not wanting to tell her anything about her birth mother, not wanting her to even think about where she came from.

I came from a sexual assault—I'm the child of a rapist. I have another sister—a twin! She and my birth mom are African American. That means I'm also....

Her thoughts raced around each other like a dog chasing its tail and her heart tighten into a fist. She stood and paced the length of her bedroom, kneading her hands raw. *What will people at Saint James think? And Charlie...and Charlie's parents?*

"Mom!" When there was no response, Tessa grabbed her computer and began stomping through the house. "Mom! Dad! Where are you?"

"Down here, Sweetie! In the dining room!"

She ran downstairs, and came skidding into the room, almost colliding with the table.

"Careful!"

"Read this. Both of you read this." She shoved the screen in front of them.

"Tessa—" her father started.

"What's this about? Is it true?"

"Look...we wanted to tell you..." her mother's voice emerged in halted gasps.

"Are you kidding me? How could you keep this from me? A twin sister? You didn't think I should know that?"

"Well...we didn't...you knew you were adopted—" Alice was wringing her hands.

"Right...."

"But the sister and the color of your mother, we felt there was time for that."

"Like when were you gonna tell me? When I gave birth to a black baby? Was that gonna be the right time?"

"We didn't think it made any difference. We're open minded; we live in an integrated community; what does it really matter?"

"I guess I'm about to find out, aren't I. Black people sure seem to think it matters! But to find out on Facebook—in this humiliating way, that my mother was a black girl who was raped by some white dude strung out on drugs...I don't know, Mom, I kind of think that those things would be important to know before they were posted on the fucking internet!"

"Tessa, let's sit down." Her father approached and placed a tentative palm on her shoulder.

"I can't believe you did this to me!"

Her mother's eyes were frantic. "Tessa, please! We never imagined anyone would find out and post it—"

"Surprise! Your little world isn't quite so perfect after all, and it seems I'm not either!"

"Can we sit down and talk?" asked her father, but she ignored him and pounded up the stairs.

In her room, she took a few deep breaths and phoned Charlie. "I guess you've seen Facebook."

"Tess, I don't know what to say. I never thought Madeline would do something so awful. I...I don't have words. I'm so sorry."

"You're pretty sure it was her? I mean there really isn't anyone else I can think of who'd want to hurt me."

"Yeah. I just got back from her place."

"And?"

"She denied it of course. She said that anyone could dig up that information if they knew where to look—even her father's assistant."

"What does that mean?"

"Her dad's a real estate developer. There's this woman, Mrs. Parker. They call her The Magician because it seems there's nothing she can't make happen. She's been with them for years, is like family. Madeline must have gone to her."

"Would she break the law?"

Charlie exhaled. "There are ways around the law. Her dad is an attorney and maybe Parker is too. I doubt we'd be able to prove they did something illegal. Besides, she said she'd see if Mrs. Parker could get the page deleted."

"Who gives a shit? The damage is done!"

"I'm so sorry."

"I didn't know any of it. It's not like I was hiding it from you."

"I didn't think that. None of it matters."

"And your parents? Will it matter to them?"

There was a long silence. "I don't know."

"I...I need to go now. This is all too much."

"All right, but can we talk later? I'll text you."

By the time Kate arrived, Tessa lay curled on her bed, her cheeks blotchy and wet, her hands fisted at her chest. Kate edged next to her. "We'll find a way to get Madeline back for making up this garbage. Maybe your mom can sue her for slander and get some of that Warner fortune. There must be a way to trace it—"

"Kate, hold up a sec. My parents say it's true."

"What?"

"It seems *The Truth About Tessa Mitchell* is actually...well, the truth about Tessa Mitchell."

"No shit—umm…okay. But it's still invasion of privacy, harassment, identity theft…. How did she even find this stuff out? We have to be able to get her on something."

Tessa sniffed and wiped her eyes and nose on her sleeve. It was the sleeve of Charlie's crew sweatshirt and it made her feel small, like a child wearing her father's clothing. She propped herself up on an elbow. "I don't care about Madeline; it's Charlie—Charlie and his family. I'm center stage in this internet drama, not to mention the fact that they might not have envisioned their son with the daughter of a friggin' rapist. I have no idea how open they are to having Charlie cozied-up with a biracial girl. For sure, they're gonna tell him to dump me. If I were them, that's what I'd probably do. Wouldn't you?"

Kate took a moment to answer, and Tessa threw herself back on the bed. "You see, even you agree with me!"

"No, no, I was just thinking about the question. The most important one isn't what the Stansworths are telling Charlie, it's what Charlie wants to do, how he feels about it. What does he say?"

She tossed her arm across her forehead. "I don't know."

"You didn't talk yet?"

"We did, but he just kept saying he was sorry and that it didn't matter to him. But what else was he gonna say?" There was a knock on the door. "Not now, Mom!"

"Tessa, your father and I are both here. We need to talk."

Kate nodded, and Tessa acquiesced, "All right."

Her parents entered, their faces grave. Rob moved a desk chair next to the bed, and Alice signaled to Kate and perched near Tessa's feet.

"Why can't she stay?"

"This is the way it's going to be, Tess. You'll call Kate later." Her mother's voice was firm.

At the doorway, Kate touched her fingers to her lips and threw Tessa a kiss.

"This wasn't the way it was supposed to happen." Her mother's voice cracked with emotion. "We had thought about telling you, but then no time really felt like the right time." Her warm palm travelled from Tessa's knee down to her toes.

Tessa pulled away from her and sat up cross-legged on the bed.

Her father cleared his throat and she saw sorrow in his eyes. "This is what happened. We're going to tell you everything, so you'll understand." His voice was soft and reassuring. She imagined this was what he was like when he delivered bad news to patients; *I'm sorry, you have ovarian cancer* or *I'm sorry, your baby has died.* "We were on several waiting lists for a baby, and one day we got a call from an agency in Newark. They said they had a pale-skinned baby girl who needed a home and we rushed down there. The case worker told us a teenager from Irvington had delivered twins. Both girls were born small but healthy. No signs of drug use."

"So I do have a twin!"

Her mother's eyes brimmed, but her father continued, "One infant had darker coloring. The other was light, with fine hair the color of buttermilk. They had a policy back then of trying to make same-race placements, and they weren't optimistic about finding a biracial family who'd take both babies. The mother was African American."

"And the dad?"

"They didn't know much about him. The mother didn't know him. He was white and he'd...attacked her. The birth mother reported that he was high at the time."

Retreating beneath her comforter and pulling it over her head, Tessa moaned.

"Sweetie, you were beautiful and perfec—" Alice bit back the word. "We saw you as innocent and deserving of a good life, a loving family. We didn't care what your birth father did while on drugs. Back in eighth grade we explained to you that your birth father was an addict and you had to be careful."

She lowered her covers. "And you thought that was enough to know?"

Her mother hesitated, "Please, we love you and—"

Tessa threw her arms up, "Shush! Will you just...Dad, get her away from me. Now I know what's been wrong with me, why I feel like I never fit anywhere. And now I'll never fit with..." her voice trailed off, the last word was barely audible, almost a prayer, "*Charlie.*"

"Look, if he doesn't think you're good enough—"

"Go away! Please, please—just...go."

Rob stood, "Come on Alice."

When Charlie phoned later, she didn't answer. On day two, Tessa texted him, I need some time to pull myself together.

Let me come out there and help you.

No. I can't see you now, not like this.

The Facebook page is down, and I love you.

The page is up in my heart, and I don't love myself. That was her final text.

Tessa spent the rest of the weekend holed up in her bedroom doing nothing: no texting, no Facebook, Instagram, Snapchat, or talking. Kate arrived bearing Tessa's favorite mix of ice-cream from Cold Stone Creamery, but in less than an hour she was headed for the front door.

Tessa did venture down to the kitchen a few times. There she stood in her flannel pajama bottoms, t-shirt, and Charlie's sweatshirt, her hair now a tangled, oily mess. She opened both the refrigerator and freezer doors and stared, looking for something that might tempt her.

Alice's worried eyes were on her, "Want me to make you a nice grilled-cheese sandwich?"

"No thanks."

"You want to take a shower? It'll make you feel better."

"I don't think so, maybe tomorrow."

She spent hours lying on the carpet next to Riley, but no amount of doggie snuggles seemed to make a difference. The weekend passed, and on Monday morning she refused to pack up and get ready to go back to school. "I feel like I can't go on," was the only explanation she offered.

Cradled in her childhood bed, Tessa took some solace in the few things she knew to be true—this had been her room, her bed, her island of refuge, and she clutched her favorite stuffed animal in her fist, a well-loved panda bear, named Henry, whose hair had been rubbed away in patches so that his skin resembled the bark of the Sycamore tree that grew large and strong outside her bedroom window.

Her mind buzzed with tormented thoughts about her biological parents. She conjured up a series of scenarios to explain how her father could have come to rape her mother, and why her mother chose to give birth rather than abort the pregnancy. Her head ached from the possibilities. She'd lost a piece of her identity, as well as her grounding in the world. She even feared herself: the ugliness that might be lurking inside her, the attacker waiting to pounce, and the addiction preparing to blossom.

Now she knew the truth. She knew why she often felt the weight of the sky, ready to collapse upon her head. She was raised to believe that if she did everything her parents instructed: worked hard and excelled at school, took on leadership positions, achieved success in and out of the gym, and dated a good man, then she would have a wonderful life, and the sky would stay pinned to the heavens. But despite everything she'd done, it had fallen down.

There would be no winning over Charlie's parents. The Upper East Side was not Maplewood. Why would anyone want to be related to her? She didn't even want to be related to herself, at least not the part of her that had the DNA of a rapist.

It was all a muddle in her mind as she stood before the bathroom mirror and stared at her features; now recognizing her full lips as African, her fair skin and hair as inherited from the attacker. She wondered if he had served jail time. And who the hell was her sister? Where was she?

On Tuesday morning, Alice marched into Tessa's room, opened the blinds and announced, "You're either going back to school today, or you're going for a psych eval."

"What? Why?"

"If you can't function, then I'm taking you to be evaluated. You can't fall apart and expect me not to help you."

"Jesus, mom—"

"Your choice."

Tessa sighed. "I just don't know how I'm going to…survive it."

Alice took a seat on the edge of her bed. "Talk to me."

"Everyone will look at me and know…they'll know my father raped my mother! You've never been to Saint James! You don't get what it's like!"

Alice had been stroking Tessa's leg, but she paused. Tessa looked at her mom, saw her face toughen, her eyes glisten. "Fuck them!"

"That's your solution?" Tessa couldn't suppress her smile. Her mother never used the "F" word.

"Yes, it is. I say, fuck them! Who the hell do they think they are, judging you? You think they don't have skeletons in their closets?"

"They have them, but no one knows. That's the difference. In my case, the contents of my closet were photographed and posted."

Alice cocked her head. "The way I see it, either you'll go to school and no one will say a word, and things will be right back the way they were, or…they won't be. Either way, you need to go back. You're not going to leave school because of it. That makes no sense."

Tessa listened, but she wasn't accepting this logic, not yet anyway.

"Shower and pack up. If next week you still feel like you can't finish the semester, then we'll make a new plan. Let's go. Out of bed!"

During the drive into the city, one that included both her parents because her father had the day off, Tessa decided to google herself one more time. Madeline's vicious Facebook page was nowhere to be seen, but she couldn't seem to banish it from her thoughts.

Arriving in the late afternoon, Tessa told her parents to drop her at the Barnard gate. She had her hood up in a feeble attempt to mask her identity, but soon realized that there was no invisibility cloak for her. Some of the other students seemed to be eyeing her with curiosity, or maybe that was just her own paranoia. The real test would come when she returned to Saint James.

Tessa was only alone in her room for a few minutes before Kate showed up carrying a basket of snacks and wearing a wide grin. "Welcome back, my Contessa!" She caught her up in a tight embrace.

"Hey, good to see you!"

Kate released her, and they fell onto her bed with the basket between them and started unwrapping chocolates and stuffing them in their mouths.

"Thanks for the gift. Any word from Kyle on how the guys at the club are viewing this drama?"

Kate grew serious. "I think the responses were mixed, like everything from *who cares? It shouldn't matter*…all the way to, *it shouldn't matter, but it does, so let's get as far away from this hot mess as possible."*

"Not so comforting."

"Haters gonna hate?"

"You're quoting me pop songs?"

Kate shrugged. "Come on, let's get to the library."

Tessa hung her head and reached for more chocolate.

Lakisha

The scent of dirty diapers and antiseptic, balloons and Playdoh, aging food and fear hit Lakisha as she passed through the doors of the pediatric oncology unit. Before TJ became ill, she wasn't aware that fear had its own pungent odor, but now she could recognize it on herself and other parents around her. They were internally frantic, pumped full of panic, while outside they tried to maintain placid façades for the sake of their kids. She saw it too, in their wide-eyed expressions, like they were deer caught in the headlights of an oncoming tractor-trailer and had no clue which way to move. The doctors always had plans in place to avoid the oncoming calamity— that's what they said. More than once, though, Lakisha had seen staff members wiping tears from their cheeks at the nursing station. There were plenty of good reasons to be scared.

Sitting opposite Dr. Liu's nurse, Treasure, Lakisha handed over her list of family members and waited as she reviewed the names, asking for their ages and then tallying the total number. The wide bulletin board behind her desk held rows of crayon and magic marker drawings, presumably made by sick children. *How many of those kids are still alive?* A shiver slid down her back.

Treasure lifted her heart-shaped face, "Is there anyone else?"

"I don't think so, unless you want second and third cousins."

"No, just...." Treasure hesitated.

"I'll do whatever you say, just tell me."

Treasure squinted at the floor. "Any other kids around, like maybe from previous relationships?"

Lakisha exhaled relief, "Oh, that's where you're going. Theo and me, we been together forever. Nope, those are all the kids we got. Five is plenty!"

Treasure's eyes darted around the room like she was trying to solve a puzzle. "Let's set up a Saturday date for them to come in and be tested. If anyone can't make it, then we'll find another time. I'll use email, but you might want to follow-up with phone calls."

"Don't you worry; they'll all be tested." Lakisha would make sure of it. On second thought, maybe Aunt Dottie would take charge of that. No one could refuse Dottie—she'd harass the hell out of them until they agreed.

Less than a week later, more than twenty family members milled around the hospital lab waiting room, greeting each other with hugs and firm handshakes, wide grins, and little mention of why they had all come together. The mood in the air was that of a weekend cookout, and Lakisha was torn between inviting them all over to her house afterwards to thank them and yelling at them for being insensitive asses. When a lab technician appeared with a printed list and a no-nonsense attitude, Dottie stepped up next to her and admonished, "Y'all are here because our TJ needs a transplant. Don't even think about leaving before this here nurse gets a swab of your cheek. And if any of you turn out to be a match, you better know you *will* be donating. You got that?"

As Dottie stared them down, Lakisha's heart filled with gratitude.

"Go ahead, then," Dottie motioned impatiently to the woman in salmon-colored scrubs. "Let's get this show on the road."

The next time Lakisha sat in Treasure's office, her limbs were twitching with nerves and the two extra cups of coffee she'd downed in the parents' lounge. She was impatient for the results and found it difficult to wait as Treasure pulled up TJ's file on the aging desktop computer. Her hands fidgeted in her lap as her mind whispered silent prayers.

"I see," she said clicking through screens, "we haven't yet found a good match."

Lakisha groaned in frustration. "What now?"

"Now we finish the chemo and hope we get a match from the public registry."

"That's it?"

"Unless you can think of other relatives. If you'd like, you can also organize a donor drive in your community. It might help others as well. Some folks find it gives them something meaningful to do while they wait."

This nurse was pressing on her last nerve. Did she understand that Lakisha had five kids, a partner, a full-time job, and a poetry column, along with rent and car payments? If her life was any more meaningful, she'd be Mother Theresa! "You got kids?"

Treasure hesitated and then shook her head.

"You get yourself a few kids, and then you get back to me about making things meaningful." She regretted the words as soon as they'd left her mouth. She knew Treasure was trying to be helpful. She waved her hand in the air like she was shooing away her words. "I'm sorry. It's the stress talking."

"I didn't mean to upset you. Why don't you see if you can dig up a few more family members? Think on it some more."

That night, Lakisha leaned back in the recliner, counting the clouds on the curtains and waiting for sleep to arrive. As she drifted into slumber, she again had a vision of her mother. She was young and healthy, wearing a lemon-yellow tank top and flowered skirt. She extended her scarred arms, placed something in Lakisha's hands, and then disappeared. Only then did she look down and see it—the topsy-turvy doll. Lakisha awoke with a start, her heart pounding. She wanted to shout, *I know I should look for those girls, but I just can't bring myself to do it!* Spending every day on the oncology unit and watching TJ's torment felt like more than she could bear. What if those abandoned twins put her over the edge? What if the white one looked like *him?* She pictured the poet with the moon-kissed face. She had seemed strong and intelligent, the kind of person Lakisha hoped her younger girls would become. Maybe she could reach out to her first, or even wait a week to see if the public registry found a match. There was no rest for her that night.

When the sky outside the window turned the color of steel and sleet began pelting the glass panes, Lakisha opened the curtain all the way so that TJ could view the flashes of lighting and storm spectacle. Was this biblical-like deluge an omen? When the plague of hail came down in Egypt, it meant that redemption was on the way, but when poor Noah saw the skies open, it was anything but. Lakisha chose to focus on redemption. If her world was coming to an end, it was too late to build an ark.

She spent the next Saturday playing Battleship and reading with TJ like they used to do when he was small. When the book cart came around, he'd chosen a thick volume of Harry Potter. Lakisha had never read the first three books, but in a short-lived flash of energy, he described the plot line, making faces as he described the Dementors and waving an invisible wand in the air while painting pictures of duels between good and evil. Then, they took turns reading aloud, TJ reciting Harry's lines and Lakisha reading the rest.

They had fun until exhaustion set in and TJ slept. Lakisha was then left with nothing but the tempest raging in her own head. The twins: one would be easy to locate, the other one—hard to say. And how would a letter to them read? *I know I gave you away, but, hey, could you do me a favor anyways?* Or maybe she'd tell them the truth, *I was attacked and that's how you came into the world. There was no way I could look at your face every day and be reminded of that. I'm sorry, so very sorry. I tried to make up for it by having more kids and loving them. But now one of them is sick and he may need you. Can you find it in your heart to help?* She'd have to work on it.

Then there was the issue of Theo. How could she ever explain to him that the twins hadn't died; that they had lived, but weren't his? How would she tell him that she had hoped and prayed that they were his, but in the end, one had emerged into the world with another man's telltale coloring? He would demand an answer for why she never told him she was raped, and to that she'd have no response. That decision was made by an immature sixteen-year-old who was scared that her boyfriend might up and leave her, just like everyone else she'd ever loved. Worse than that would have been him taking revenge and ending up in jail or even dead. She'd done the best she could, and up until now it had all seemed to work.

By the end of the day, forecasters were predicting gale-force winds in some parts of New Jersey. Lakisha already had them whipping through her mind. The confession of her lies to Theo was lodged in her throat and showed no signs of budging. On Saturday night, Theo stayed at the hospital and Lakisha went home. She let Shonda and Kai sleep in bed with her but still found no rest. Rising before daylight, she decided to sneak off to church before anyone had stirred. Nikki and Devon were old enough to handle the younger ones. Though paralyzed by indecision about the twins, at least she could pray for TJ. The early service at Christian Love was mostly attended by seniors, but the choir was still powerful, and the preacher full of faith. It was faith that she so desperately sought.

Walking down Springfield Avenue, Lakisha passed a few trees ripe with glistening leaves that were beginning their show of brilliant color. Every year at this time, she promised herself that she'd bring the kids to the South Mountain Reservation to collect pretty leaves that would later be pressed in the pages of thick, hard-covered books. A few times she actually made that happen. This year, they'd have to make do with the few hardy maples and red oaks that dotted the local park.

Lakisha entered the church and was surprised to find it almost full. *There must be a lot of people with problems*, she thought, and slid into the last pew. The other congregants seemed to be moved by the spirituals that vibrated through the room, but Lakisha felt nothing. And when the preacher boomed out his words of encouragement, Lakisha allowed her head to droop. She dozed until a man used his cane to bang the back of her bench. Feeling dejected, she waited until the sermon ended and then moved toward the exit. It was then that she crossed paths with Dottie's childhood friend.

Before Lakisha could even say hello, the buxom woman had her caught up in a hug that lasted several seconds longer than Lakisha felt was necessary. Then the woman remained uncomfortably close, her hand resting on Lakisha's shoulder. She gabbed on about things that seemed trivial given TJ's situation, and Lakisha nodded politely. Then the woman became quiet, and Lakisha could feel the power of her gaze. She'd heard that some of the church ladies developed a kind of clairvoyance as they aged. There was a woman who had warned her neighbor to start wearing his seatbelt, and later that week the man miraculously survived a five-car pileup on the Garden State Parkway. There was another who told a friend that it was time to make amends with her estranged sister and get her affairs in order. Not long afterwards, the friend had a massive heart attack. Lakisha braced herself for what she imagined might be a poor prognosis for TJ.

"Lakisha?"

She reluctantly looked up.

"Ain't but God and your heart know the truth. Your grandma used to say that to me and your Auntie. You've got to trust God and your heart. God knows what's right, and if he's not speaking loud enough for you to hear, then you best depend on your heart to give you his message. You understand? Those words came right from your Grandma Louema, so they must be meant for you—right? It sure does feel like it to me. Ummm-hmm."

Lakisha didn't want her to be right, didn't want to tell Theo the truth, didn't want to face those two girls—the ones who made her remember. But if TJ died…. "Yeah, I guess so. I get you." Lakisha glanced at the cracked plaster ceiling, trying to suppress her emotion. She couldn't keep that Oreo-cookie set of twins, but she was damn sure not going to lose TJ as well. No matter what the consequences, she wouldn't surrender without a fight. The woman caught her in a hug again, but this time it didn't feel awkward. It was like an embrace from her grandma, sturdy and certain. She felt the storm inside her head calm.

"Sit with me for a few minutes." The woman didn't wait for a response. Instead, she held Lakisha's hand and walked with her down the center aisle to a row near the front. There she nudged a few people sideways, and the two squeezed into the pew and began swaying to the music. The singing here was loud and joyful, and it had a force to it. It was the sound of her childhood, back when her grandmother was alive, and it was the call of faith that she had somehow lost…a belief that everything was going be all right. In these melodies, she found her comfort. When the next song began, Lakisha's lips moved with the words, "Oh happy day…."

After church, she went straight to see TJ, and told Theo that she'd be spending the day with him. She convinced him to listen to gospel music on the radio, hoping it might lift his spirits. As he dozed in the late afternoon sunshine, she composed an email to Treasure explaining that she had two more important names. *I need your help,* she concluded, *in finding my eighteen-year-old twin daughters; the products of a rape.*

"Theo, we gotta talk." Lakisha was leaving their bedroom after putting their 1 year old to sleep in his crib. Theo sat with Devon on the sofa, watching the boy play on a handheld Nintendo game. He looked exhausted, and Lakisha felt bad about making things worse for him. She told Nikki that they'd be outside, and she and Theo stepped past the front door and sat down on two milk crates that they kept handy for this purpose.

As they huddled together, Theo's body seemed to brace, his brow creased. "What is it Kisha? Just say it. Are we losing him?"

"No, no!" Lakisha waved away the negative thought and planted her hand on his knee. She was sorry she'd frightened him. TJ's illness was aging Theo. The creases that had been barely visible on his forehead had deepened, and his cheeks were now sunken. He must have lost weight. "It's not about TJ. I need to tell you something that happened a long time ago."

"If it doesn't have anything to do with TJ, I'm really not up for it tonight, Baby."

"I wish that were the case."

Theo's kind eyes held hers, his brows lifting like question marks. A group of teenage boys walked by, laughing and shoving each other. They both glanced up, wishing TJ was out strolling the neighborhood with his friends rather than lying in a hospital bed.

"That first pregnancy I had—the twins, I didn't tell you everything." She was wringing her hands, searching for the right words. "The year before, when we went to that party and I ran out—"

"I sure as hell don't want to think about that mess again. I was fit to be tied."

Lakisha stared at him, hurt.

"Not at you, Kisha. I wasn't angry with you. Lord, just spit it out. Why we gotta go back thinking about that now?"

She blew air out through her mouth. "The guy who attacked me, he…." Theo was right, she had to just spit it out. "I was raped and then…I was pregnant. I didn't think the babies were his, but when one of them came out with his light skin and hair…I knew."

Theo was silent for long moment. "What are you saying?"

"I couldn't keep them, Theo. I just couldn't, so Aunt Dottie helped me give them up, and I told you…I told you they didn't make it."

Theo was quiet, his eyes pinned to the pavement. Finally, he looked at her, "You for real here?"

"I knew the truth would hurt you, so I lied. But now we need to find a donor for TJ."

"And so you need to find those girls."

"If they could help us save TJ, then yes, I have to."

The front door cracked open, and Nikki poked her head out. "Mama, Devon and Shonda are fighting, and I'm done playing referee. I got a history test tomorrow."

"We'll be right in." She waited for the door to click shut. "Theo, talk to me."

"Hah, what am I supposed to say?" He ran his fingers over his head and then clapped his hands on his knees. Lakisha recoiled at the sound. "I would ask why you didn't tell me this when it happened? I would get busy thinking about what this says about our relationship, that you didn't think you could tell me about the rape, and then the babies, that you made such a big decision without talking to me, and that you let me think that my first two children had died. You know I mourned those babies, cried over them. I didn't want you to see it, but I did."

"I'm sorry I lied to you. I didn't know what to do and—"

"I say a prayer for those girls every year at Christmas. I know it's not a Baptist thing, but I do it anyway. Do you know why?"

Lakisha braced for the answer.

"I do it, or I should say I did it, because I wanted them to know they were still loved. I wanted them to see that they still had a Daddy down here. And maybe I even did it as a reminder…so that I'd never make the same mistake."

She waited for more, but he didn't continue. "What mistake? You didn't do anything wrong."

"That's not true." He averted his eyes. "I was a full-grown man when Dottie set those doctor appointments, I should have made you go. I should have taken you there myself. I thought the twins died because, well, I didn't take care of you."

"Baby, I'm so sorry we never spoke about it. I feel terrible."

His expression hardened, and his eyes met hers. "And now you say those girls are alive…and they aren't even mine? Jesus, what do you want me to say? Find them! Go ahead!" He stood up, towering over her. "I'm gonna go on back to the hospital and spend the night with TJ."

"Wait…Theo…." She stood and reached for him.

Theo shook himself free and walked off.

Jasmine

There was a knock on the door and Jasmine swung it open, expecting to find a friend of Padma's. Instead, standing next to the hand-painted banner that read *Scarlet Knights Rule!* was Treasure. Jasmine felt like she'd been sucker punched. She blinked, wondering if she'd stayed up too late the night before and was just hallucinating. Yet there she was, wearing her navy scrubs, trailing the scent of antiseptic. Why had she come? *Is William dead?* A piece of her hoped so. After an awkward moment, Jasmine found her voice, "What are you doing here? How did you find me?"

Treasure's face brightened, "I looked you up on Facebook. Almost all the freshmen are in this dorm, so I just walked in behind someone who held the door. Your name is right there, next to…" she looked around Jasmine to the taped-on construction-paper sign, "Padma." Treasure looked hopeful. The parenthesis around her mouth had deepened, and her eyes looked tired. Her body had also grown a bit stooped, as if she'd been carrying something heavy on her shoulders. Maybe it was guilt. If she had shown up soon after that night when the cops took her away, perhaps Jasmine would have found a way to forgive her. But the way things were left, Jasmine couldn't see forgiveness coming—ever. Treasure was talking, "This strange coincidence happened; I was thinking about tracking you down, and then someone actually asked me to do it."

Jasmine wished she would slither back to wherever she came from, but Treasure seemed oblivious. She plowed forward, with no mention of the anguish she'd caused, as if she had some God-given right to be heard. "I'm still working at the hospital—I'm on the pediatric oncology unit now, and a family came in with this sick boy whose mom had the last name White. Now I know White is a common name, but his mother looked so familiar. Then it came to me, I saw her back when I was fostering you! I was the one who took you from the hospital. Once your birth mom had signed away her rights, she was supposed to be out of the picture, but for some reason she hung around and watched me take you from the nursery. It reminded me of that story in the bible when Miriam is watching baby Moses get rescued from the basket in the Nile. It was like she wanted to make sure you'd be okay. Once I figured out who she was, I realize that I was treating your half-brother! Then it was like something hit me, and I knew it was time. I had to find you!"

Jasmine saw her face trying to radiate caring like it used to, and for a split second fell under her spell. Then a steel door outside the hallway stairwell slammed shut and jolted her back to reality. "Too bad whatever hit you didn't knock you down." The words tumbled out of her mouth, but once they were in the air, she didn't regret them one bit. Then she refocused on the part about her birth mom and brother. "Who's my birth mom?"

Treasure looked like she was weighing the question.

"You showed up here on my doorstep, so you better give me an answer."

Treasure touched her lips as if trying to keep them shut, but then released the name. "Lakisha White," she said, soft but clear. "Your birth mom is Lakisha White." Treasure looked down at the scuffed-up floor and the corners of her mouth drooped, "I understand; it's hard my turning up like this."

Jasmine felt her insides swirl, the deep wound of rejection twisting into rage. If she weren't careful, she'd blow the roof off the building. "No, I don't think you do understand, because if you really understood, *Treasure*," she said her name with ironic emphasis, "then you would know that showing up like this...." her head and limbs were shaking, as if the PATH train was rumbling beneath her. "This here, was a mistake."

"Honey, please give me a chance to apologize. I've wanted to, really." Her eyes were pleading now, her features all bunched in a knot.

There was a tiny piece of Jasmine that wanted to forgive her. Yet, her stronger urge was to smack the woman hard—hard enough to leave a permanent mark, one that would remind her of what she'd done. Then maybe she'd have some idea of what it's like to wake up every morning and realize that you're damaged and won't ever be fixed.

"No, I don't think so. I don't think you get another chance. You had your chance when they asked you to put William out, just until they could investigate. But no, you wouldn't do it—even for a day, even for an hour!" The roof was ready to blow, the train set to jump the tracks. "You made your choice. You could've done the right thing…you could've, but you didn't. You wrecked it all! It was like you cut my heart out, tossed it on the ground, and then stomped on it! You get that?" She stared Treasure down, daring her to speak. Treasure opened her mouth but then shut it before uttering a sound. "So, don't think you can show up all these years later and expect me to give you some kind of absolution."

"I don't expect you to forgive me, but at least let me say how sorry I am. That's all—I'm very sorry. But there's something else; you're gonna get an email asking you to help your half-brother."

She couldn't tolerate one more minute with her. "You don't get it—the time for you to speak up was five fucking years ago!"

"You could maybe save a boy's life," Treasure's pretty eyes pleaded. Jasmine hated those pretty eyes.

"Get the fuck away from my door! I'm about to call campus police!" Jasmine raised her hand, wanting to strike, but then thought better of it. Instead, she shoved Treasure backward into the hall and slammed the door.

Jasmine stared at the flat wood before her, trying to remember how to breathe. She took in big gulps of air as if she had just finished doing ten laps around the high school gym, and then began to punch her thighs and shoulders. "I hate her, I hate her." Each syllable was punctuated with a fist. The walls of her room closed in. She was coming undone and was glad Padma wasn't there to see it. But being alone didn't feel good either.

Jasmine grabbed her bus pass, her wallet, and the pocket knife she still had from her days with Carlina and ran out of the dorm. At the edge of campus, she stood beneath a graffiti covered shelter, and when a bus arrived, she boarded it and took a seat in the back. Glancing around, she wondered how it was possible for the other passengers to appear so calm and content, with necks bent into books or bobbing to music flowing in through ear buds, while she was falling apart. She felt the way she did that first night—the night they took her. She spent hours on the bus, travelling on her journey to nowhere. Perhaps that was emblematic of what her life had been up until now, a journey that seemed like it would have a good ending but was actually just circling her right back to the place she'd started. Whatever this pain was in her chest, it might lay dormant for a while, like a cancer in remission, but then it returned: no explanation, no justice, no reason for fate to demand a recurrence.

It was close to midnight by the time Jasmine arrived back at her dormitory, and she was longing for relief. If she had a best friend, she would have talked to her about what happened and downed a few shots of Jack Daniel's, but nice as Padma was, she had always been sheltered. She'd have no understanding of Jasmine's suffering. She considered phoning Miss Raymelle or Champaine but didn't want to worry them. Besides, they might think her a fool for even opening the door to that bitch. Still, Treasure had given Jasmine the name of her birth mother: Lakisha White. She had to wonder why Lakisha had kept her half-brother and not her? She guessed he was somehow worthy, perhaps his father wasn't a rapist. No, there was no one to call, no escape.

She walked into the hall bathroom, entered a narrow stall and slid the lock shut. Then she pulled out her pocket knife and stared at her exposed wrists, the tender skin covering tendons and veins that disappeared into her fleshy forearm. There was nothing to do with her deep-seated anger, no place to put her raw feelings of worthlessness, the bitterness that churned in her belly, the pounding pulse that made her head ache. "I hate…." she spoke out loud, then hushed herself. The last thing she wanted was for someone to hear her thoughts—crazy as they were.

It would be so easy to run the blade down the length of her blue veins. It would be so easy to let her life drip out of her and finally be at peace. Who would even miss her? She touched the knife to her wrist and waited. Perhaps there would be some sign that would make the decision clear. Tears pooled in her eyes and she blinked them free. If only she too could be free. She stood perfectly still, suspended in time. One of the faucets dripped water into a porcelain basin, a girl walked into an adjoining stall and gabbed into her cell phone while peeing and flushing. There was a crash and then laughter on the floor above her, and someone turned up an Usher song so loud that the almost-empty toilet-paper roll danced on its ring.

Then, beneath the music, Jasmine heard a soft voice, *Uh-uh— not on my watch. You're not doing that. You wanna kill me too?* There was no mistaking who it was. Miss Raymelle had given Jasmine so many lectures about life and how to live it, that at times, her voice echoed in her mind of its own accord.

Okay, Miss Raymelle, I don't want to hurt you, of course I don't. She silently mouthed the words up toward the tiled ceiling and wiped her cheeks with a balled-up wad of toilet paper. *You're the last person I wanna hurt.* She sat down on the toilet, waiting for her pulse to slow, and when it did, she blew her nose, gave her eyes one more wipe, and then stepped out of the stall, back into the world.

The counseling center hadn't changed since the last time she'd been there, and Miss Maggie greeted her with that warm-crooked smile. A piece of her felt defeated by having to be back in therapy, but after Treasure showed up at her door with her apologies, and with her birthmother's name on her lips, Jasmine had found it difficult to sleep at night and make it through each day without thinking about reaching for her blade. The nightmares had returned, the ones with the recurring theme of Treasure and William tossing her in a dumpster too deep to climb out of.

"You were busy looking for your birth mom, and then Treasure just appeared out of the blue and gave you your mom's name?" Miss Maggie's fingernails were bitten down low, and she still jiggled her foot as she spoke.

"Yeah, that's pretty much how it went down." Miss Maggie's office seemed more compact, perhaps she had just piled more books on the shelves. "I keep waking up at night, I think I lost a few pounds, and sometimes my mind feels fuzzy, like it has cotton in it. When that happens, it's tough to understand the class lectures."

"Lack of sleep will do that, so will depression…and worry. Have you tried any of those relaxation techniques we used to do together—slowing down your breathing, relaxing each body part? I'll send you a link to a guided meditation." The clock on the wall said they were out of time, but Miss Maggie hadn't finished. "Try not to feel bad about coming back here. It's just for a little while. Sometimes things happen; triggers can bring back the sorrow like it never left. It's normal and not a failure. We'll get you through it."

Lakisha's email arrived without fanfare. When Jasmine had imagined reuniting with her mother, she always included a dramatic revelation of sorts; perhaps her birth mother would show up at her door, like the Karmic opposite of Treasure's appearance, and she'd have emotion in her eyes, and compassionate words on her lips. In reality, Lakisha's note had few hearts and flowers.

Dear Jasmine,

My name is Lakisha White, and I am your birth mother. Someone from The Children's Hospital told me you were at Rutgers Newark, and I was lucky enough to find your email address in the college directory. I mention luck because it feels like much of my life has been devoid of it. Now I try to appreciate every good fortune, perhaps to counteract the horrible things, the things I can't and couldn't control. When I was sixteen, a man jumped me and did something horrible. I hope you haven't experienced anything like that. One of the reasons I gave you up was to make sure you never would. If I couldn't even protect myself, how would I protect you? There were many other reasons for my decision, and they weren't all selfless, I'll admit that. But in the end, I thought it would be best for us both.

That said, giving you away is something that has haunted me every day since. I pray you've had a good life, that you're happy, that I did right by you. I fought with my conscience for days before finally sending this email. I don't want to make your life complicated or cause you any grief. The thing is, I feel terrible asking, but I may need your help. I have a thirteen-year-old son, Theo Junior (TJ), who was recently diagnosed with leukemia. There's a good chance a bone-marrow transplant could save his life. We're trying to have all blood relations tested as potential donors, and it's only a swab of your cheek. I apologize for having to ask, but would you be willing to be tested?

We are planning to have a round of testing on Saturday, November 3rd at 10:30 a.m. at the Children's Hospital of New Jersey in Newark. If you can't make it, you can come another time. This email is being sent by the lab's scheduling office, so you can write to them to make that arrangement.

If you have any questions about our family's health history, or if you need more information about this first test, or if there is something else you need that I can provide, please let me know. I'm including my email address below.

> *Wishing you a Blessed Day and a Blessed Life,*
> *Lakisha White*

Have a blessed day and a blessed life? Was she for real? Her life had been the exact opposite of blessed. For years she'd been wishing for some contact with her mother, and when it finally came, she was asking for a favor. Jasmine's compassion for Lakisha was waning. The rapist (she couldn't think of him as her father), the drug dealers, even the drug manufacturers, they were all guilty. But the more she stewed, the more the blame shifted to include her birth mother. She could have turned it around if only she'd kept her and raised her. Could living with her have been any worse than what she'd had with William or Carlina? Girls in her high school had done it. Most people had a mother or grandmother or aunt who could help or even take over the mothering. Did Lakisha imagine that all babies were adopted by wonderful families and none of them ever fell through cracks in the system?

A day passed, and then two. Jasmine still struggled to focus in class, and her mind wrestled with itself. In the heart of a sleepless night, when a hush had finally fallen over the dormitory, and only the clang of the aging heating system was heard, Jasmine made an uneasy peace with herself. She was simply not ready to forgive Lakisha. Was there some justice in Lakisha needing her help? She couldn't turn the other cheek. She was no saint, far from it. As the darkness gave way to a rainy dusk, Jasmine curled up in her bed, buried her head, and let herself move to the world of dreams—a place where hope was still possible.

On the morning of November 3rd, Jasmine woke before dawn and once again tossed and fussed beneath a tangle of sheet and blanket. *Damn her.* Why couldn't Lakisha have reached out because she wanted to know Jasmine or had realized that giving her up had been a mistake? If only those had been the reasons, she would have done anything to help her boy. She was not about to forgive Lakisha, hell no. But this kid with leukemia—maybe, just maybe, he deserved some pity. A month ago, she would have done anything to meet her half-brother, would have offered up way more than a swab of her cheek for a chance to meet Lakisha. Then it dawned on her; her twin sister might be there at the lab. She was afraid to hope, didn't know if she could handle another disappointment. But if Lakisha and her sister both showed, and she didn't, she'd surely regret it.

Jasmine pulled on black jeans and a white sweater. She shoved her feet into canvas slip-ons, grabbed her jacket, and left the dorm. The air outside felt thick and damp, and strangely welcoming. Walking across the quad, she noticed white clouds of mist hanging beneath each lamp-post. Jasmine was the lone customer in a massive cafeteria that had just opened. She took a seat near an eastern-facing window and squinted at the morning light. The aroma of coffee and cinnamon buns wafted by. These were signs of everyday college existence. Perhaps if she focused on them, her knot of indecision would unravel.

After spending a good long while watching the rush of colored leaves swirling in the breeze, Jasmine went to the kiosk, bought a sweet-smelling bun, and made her way toward a bus stop. Bumping through the city streets made Jasmine feel like she was doing something, heading somewhere; even if that somewhere turned out to be nowhere at all.

When the bus pulled up to the Children's Hospital, Jasmine understood. She'd had a plan all along, and it included trying to help TJ. She took a deep breath and disembarked. She was an hour early, so she sat for a time in the lobby, watching the workers in their scrubs and lab coats, and the parents with anxious faces and urgent strides. She strolled to the gift shop window and wondered what Lakisha would have bought for TJ, perhaps something classic like a Rubik's Cube or Mad Libs game. She compulsively checked the time on her phone and chewed off a fingernail while wondering how she'd recognize her mother or her sister, and what she could possibly say to them. She glanced again at her phone and shuddered. Her heart was a church bell on Sunday—it was time.

She tried to ignore the tremble in her hand as she pushed open the lab door. Inside, the waiting room was empty. She took a seat against a celery-colored wall and began thumbing through People Magazine, looking at pictures of film stars with bleached-white smiles and designer clothes. After a few minutes she questioned whether she had the right day.

A woman in light-blue scrubs with panda bears dancing across the top, entered from an interior doorway. "Hello, are you here for Theo Michaelson, Jr.?"

Jasmine nodded.

"We've got half-sisters down for today. You are…?"

"Jasmine White." She stood and took a tentative step forward. Maybe she wasn't going to meet anyone today. It looked like her twin sister bailed. Just then the lab door swung open and a white chick tripped her way into the center of the room.

"Careful!" The tech glanced at her paper and she looked confused, "Tessa Mitchell?"

"Yes! That's me!"

Jasmine bit her lip. She had longed for this moment, dreamt about finding her sister—her mirror image. This girl wasn't exactly her reflection, but she was her sister anyway. Tessa was clearly the *light-skinned* one. She wanted to touch her and make sure she was real, wanted to finger one of those blonde curls. *How could they be twins?*

"Sorry I'm late." Tessa tried to shove her keys into a little purse and they clattered onto the floor. She knelt to grab them, and then jumped up like a jack-in-the-box. "I got a little lost, and then I couldn't find a parking spot." She was obviously nervous. Wearing that on her face, she made Jasmine think she hadn't grown up in the hood. She had a pampered look, like she'd never worn tight shoes because someone had regularly pressed on the toe box of her sneakers to see if she needed new ones, or like she never had to go to the library because her parents bought all her books at Barnes & Noble. Her legs looked strong in those tight jeans, but it wasn't from running the streets.

The nurse smiled. "We've got time."

Tessa's gaze flitted across the room. When their eyes met, her creamy cheeks lifted. "You're...my twin sister?" The air was still.

Then Tessa's delight radiated across the space between them. Jasmine felt it like a warm breeze after a harsh winter. "Uh-huh. I'm Jasmine."

Before she could say anymore, Tessa caught her up in a swaying hug. "It's so great to meet you! I didn't even know you existed until a few weeks ago!"

Jasmine wasn't used to being hugged. She tolerated it, and after a moment gave in to the feeling. When Tessa stepped back, she felt a small pang, like she was watching Miss Raymelle's red pea coat disappear in the night. "Me too, I just found out."

The tech interjected. "Why don't you both come with me and we can get this test out of the way? Then you'll have time to catch up."

They both followed the dancing pandas down a short hallway. If it wouldn't have seemed rude, Jasmine would have stopped and studied this girl. They were close to the same height, but this chick was definitely a gym rat. Jasmine didn't know whether she should feel bad about her skin or her hair or anything else for that matter. Miss Raymelle would tell her to be proud of herself. Miss Maggie would say be in the moment. Treasure would say…it didn't matter what Treasure would say.

She followed Tessa into an office and they were each given a piece of paper to read, but Jasmine was too distracted to absorb any of it. She did whatever the tech said: filled out a form, signed her consent, and opened her mouth to have it swabbed. Then she and Tessa were dismissed.

Once the thick lab door closed behind them, Tessa turned around to face her. "Jasmine, wow…." Her smile flashed, and her arms reached around Jasmine's back, pulling her into another hug that began as awkward as the first but ended feeling pretty damn good. "I'm soooo happy to meet you! I mean, I feel bad for TJ, but this is still so cool."

"Mad crazy." They stepped away from each other and Jasmine drank her in. Tessa had golden-brown eyes, the kind that were big and brooding. She imagined they made the dudes lose their minds.

Tessa clapped her palms on her thighs, "I've seen you before! You were at that spoken word slam last month at Rutgers, right? I was there!"

"You write poetry too?"

"Ha, ha! No, not me—I was there with a friend. But, how random is that? You, though, you were really good! You told a story about a guy who walked up to you and asked about what color you are or something?"

Jasmine couldn't conceal her surprise. She'd heard stories about kismet, fate, serendipity—had a vague belief that it was possible but had never imagined it would happen to her. "Yeah, that was me. Since Rutgers was the sponsor, I spent a lot of time running around. I don't know that I saw you."

"There were way too many people to remember everyone. What you read though, it stuck with me."

Tessa was so nice, Jasmine wasn't sure how to handle herself. She was even more expressive than Padma. Jasmine wanted to get to know her better, this girl who put so much of herself out there for the world to see.

As if peering into her mind, Tessa asked. "You have time for coffee?"

Tessa

Tessa easily fell into step beside Jasmine. They both had long legs for their bodies and walked with their toes pointed slightly inward. "How do you like Rutgers?"

"It's a great place. I felt some kind a way at first, being with kids from all over the world when I'd never been more than fifty miles outside of Newark, but that passed quick. I grew up here, so at least I know my way around. The girls I hang with are mad crazy about getting their work done, way different from most kids I knew growing up. Classes are challenging, I'll say that. But I'm liking it. You? You grow up around here?"

Tessa hesitated. The stark differences in their lives were becoming clear and an edge of guilt took hold. "I grew up a few miles west of here in Maplewood." For the first time in her life, Tessa felt bad saying this. She believed she knew the reason her parents had adopted only her and felt ashamed.

"And where are you for school?" Jasmine didn't seem upset.

"I'm at Barnard in the city...New York City, I mean. Of course, this is a city too...."

Jasmine looked amused, "I get you. Even in Newark, people call New York, *the city*. Barnard, that means you're smart."

"More of a hard worker."

"No, you're smart."

"Smart about some things and stupid about others."

"Yeah? Maybe it's genetic then."

Tessa glanced over at Jasmine, expecting to find some trace of humor on her face, but her sister betrayed nothing. Her sister—she had two sisters now. "You got that same thing going on?"

"Yeah, but I'm not gonna talk about all that now. If I did, you might leave saying, *maybe I don't really need a twin sister after all.*"

Tessa laughed, "Had you tried looking for our birth mom?" The word *our* felt strange in her mouth.

"Someone helped me petition the courts, and that's how I learned about you and what happened to Lakisha—why she gave us up. Then someone else showed up at my door and gave me Lakisha's name."

"Who knew her name?"

"A nurse who's working with TJ. She knew me from…years ago. I was just about ready to track Lakisha down when I got her email. They sure do put up a shit-load of road blocks to keep kids away from their birth parents."

"Yeah, right? Although I would've preferred to find out about you and Lakisha by writing to the courts."

"Why? How did you find out?" They arrived at a Dunkin Donuts, stepped up to the counter and both ordered coffee with skim milk and a Splenda.

"I would've gotten around to the whole courts thing, but I didn't have to. My boyfriend's ex did it for me."

"For real?"

They both grabbed their coffee and slid into seats that were bolted to the floor. Tessa studied Jasmine's face and noticed a birthmark near her temple. "Yup. She pulled something shady and got the redacted adoption record. Then she took all that info and posted it on Facebook."

"Whoa, major bitch! How'd that go over?"

"Not well. It was like my whole world imploded."

"What happened?"

Tessa hesitated. She didn't want to try to explain other people's fucked-up views, or even her own. "Um, well my boyfriend's family, they weren't so crazy about me, even before the whole Facebook revelation."

Jasmine cocked her head. "Oh, they're not cool with you being related to ghetto chicks."

"No, no! I think it was more the circumstances of...our conception." The last thing Tessa wanted to do was to insult Jasmine. She glanced at her, caught the sadness that lived in her eyes. She'd have to be careful. Meeting her sister felt surreal, even magical, but somehow tragic too. It was hard to believe they'd been twins raised apart. She was just beginning to understand how different their lives had been. Tessa looked out on the now bustling Newark street. Like Jasmine, she was born here, but she'd left. She'd left her black mother and sister and been raised as a white upper-middle-class suburbanite with every privilege and advantage. All along, she'd been just a few miles from them, but worlds apart. They were quiet for a few moments, and Tessa worried Jasmine had taken offense.

As if sensing her discomfort, Jasmine changed the subject. "You have a major yet?"

Tessa and Jasmine discovered their mutual love of fantasy fiction and Cold Stone Creamery, their common disdain for anime and gaming, and their differing views on JK Rowling's attempts at post–Harry-Potter fiction. After spending several hours bonding across an orange-Formica table, Tessa and Jasmine returned to the hospital parking lot, and Tessa gave Jasmine a lift back to her dorm.

At the curb, they exchanged phone numbers. "Let's get together again soon," offered Tessa, feeling hopeful.

"Yeah, okay. Over winter break for sure. I don't always have minutes on my phone, so don't be upset if I don't respond right away."

Tessa tried not to let her face register shock. They had avoided the heavy topics like who had raised Jasmine, and Tessa hadn't talked much about her own parents. That seed of guilt had taken root, and she felt bad about all she'd been given.

After returning to Maplewood, she chatted with Alice over blueberry-acai smoothies, and told her all about meeting Jasmine. Ever since the Facebook fiasco, her mom had dialed back her constant critique, so when she said, "I'm proud of you for trying to help TJ," Tessa exhaled relief. She was happy to jump on this new wave of parental acceptance and ride it for as long as possible.

Spending time with Jasmine was a healing balm that helped Tessa feel more grounded. She was part of a duo, and she liked her other half. Tessa found Charlie in the law library, sneaked up behind him, and threw her arms around his shoulders. She kissed his scruffy cheek and inhaled the scent of his hair product. "Hi!"

"Hey, how did it go?"

Tessa plopped down in a padded armchair across from him. "It was amazing, and surreal." She shook her head, hoping her thoughts would organize themselves.

"Did you get to meet your birth mom?"

"No, but I met Jasmine, my twin sister! I got to hang with her, and she seems like someone with a lot of layers, but really bright and with this dry sense of humor. We were both tested to see if we can help our half-brother."

Charlie's expression grew serious. She'd been so humiliated by Madeline, she wished he'd find a way to be supportive. "Tessa, I know you want to do the right thing, but donating bone marrow isn't risk free. Things happen…infections, complications."

"You wouldn't do it?"

"I probably would—for the right person."

"You think my half-brother isn't the right person?"

"Your half-brother—now he's your half-brother. A week ago, you didn't know this kid existed. Now your birth mom creeps out of the woodwork, only because she needs something from you." He sat up straight as if he were presenting at a colloquium. "She didn't reach out to you because she wanted to get to know you; it was only when she needed something—and that something is a pretty big thing. She doesn't just want blood from your veins, she wants to dig into your bones! I researched it; there's MERSA, there's discomfort, recovery time, low blood counts, even general anesthesia is dangerous. So, if you're asking me, then no, I wouldn't do it for him."

"You know there are people who donate bone marrow to strangers, just to be nice."

His eyes held hers. "There are people who waste their time doing a lot of things."

Her heart began beating a war drum, "Saving someone's life is a waste of time now?"

Charlie cocked his head, visibly irritated. "You're not going to get this time back. If you want to keep running to Newark whenever your birth mom decides she needs something from you, then go ahead." He rearranged his books and laptop. "You say you want to be a doctor, a job where you'd get to save plenty of lives, so why not just focus on that?"

"I do; I am focused!"

He held up his hand and began counting days on his fingers. "After you had that little breakdown, you missed a day of classes, then you took a day off from studying to go to Rutgers Newark with your *poet* friend, now you just missed another entire study day going back and forth to Newark trying to help some half-bro that you've never met." His look cut her.

"Umm, it's not like this can wait until winter break or summer vacation." Her hands balled into fists.

Charlie just shrugged. "My mother agrees with me."

"Shit, Charlie! You discussed it with your mother?" Tessa leaned forward in attack mode.

"It just came up. She asked me what you were doing today. Did you want me to lie to her?"

She'd had enough of this. He was acting *worse* than her mother! "You know what? You can tell her whatever you want. I'm sorry I'm not living up to your standards. I'm sorry you think I'm not committed enough for you and your mom." She felt tears rising in her eyes but forced them back.

"Tessa...." He reached out to take her hand, but she pulled it away.

"You don't get to hold my hand right now. You don't get to hold any part of me. Me and my precious bone marrow have someplace else we need to be." As she made her way back to her dorm, she pounded her thumbs against her phone, texting Kate.

A week later, Tessa received an email asking permission to run further tests on her cell sample, and soon after that, a woman named Treasure phoned and asked if she would come back in for a blood test. Tessa phoned Jasmine to see if she was also asked back.

"No, no one called or emailed. It sounds like you might be the match. Are you down with that?"

"More or less. My boyfriend, Charlie, tried to veto it. He thinks I should focus on my courses and not get *distracted*. He also tried to scare me about possible complications. I didn't even tell my parents about the blood test."

"No?"

"My mother is a hot mess on any given day. She's such a friggin worrier, I thought I'd wait until it's confirmed. Otherwise she'll have too much time to think and make us both nuts."

Jasmine was quiet for a beat. "Huh, maybe next time she wants to do some worrying, you can give her my number. I might like someone caring about me like that."

"What, your mom doesn't worry?" She had asked the question without forethought, but as the silence between them stretched on, she wanted to suck it back into her mouth. She could feel Jasmine measuring her response.

"Here's the thing; I don't exactly have a mother. I have a foster mother at the moment named Champaine, but I was never adopted."

"Oh my God...I'm so sorry. I'm such an asshole for complaining."

"It's cool," she said. And maybe it was, but not really.

Tessa struggled with her words, afraid of another misstep. "That's crazy! How could they never have found an adoptive family for you? I'll understand if you don't want to talk about it."

Jasmine took a few deep breaths. "I had a family, but things were never finalized in the courts. My case worker, Miss Raymelle, says there were years when the whole agency was understaffed, and things just slipped by them. But even if I had been adopted, there was...." She paused then.

Tessa could sense her suffering; thick and raw, as it reached across the miles between them. It had a weight to it that made Tessa slump in her desk-chair, and she braced for something awful.

"There was abuse. That's all I'll say about it now." She paused for a long moment. "So, 1 landed for a few years somewhere else—until I got kicked out, and then finally moved to Champaine's house. Maybe we'll just leave it right there."

Tessa knew she had to speak, but her words were slow to come. "I feel terrible. How could the state let that happen? How old were you when you left that first family?"

"I stuck with Treasure and William until I was thirteen."

Tessa thought back to her conversation with the transplant nurse, and then her mind ticked through the bits and pieces of Jasmine's life that she'd been willing to share. "Treasure isn't a common name."

"Nope."

She now understood; this thing with TJ had reopened something. "The nurse in charge of TJ's case, she's the one who showed up at your door: she was the one who gave you Lakisha's name." Tessa waited for a response that wasn't coming, so she plowed forward, "That nurse, she was your—"

"It's done and buried. I'm trying...trying to let it be."

A vacuum formed between them and Tessa rushed to fill it. "Over winter break, you'll come to my house for a while. My mom will be happy to get busy worrying about all your problems. It's more than a hobby for her; it's a vocation."

"Ha, sounds good. Let me know what happens with the blood test. If it's cool with you, I'd like to be there if you donate."

"Absolutely! And you should call or text me whenever."

"I don't always have minutes."

"Borrow someone's phone! Most people have unlimited talk and text." She could hear Jasmine's soft laugh.

"Okay, princess—later."

Tessa became excited about the prospect of donating. Who knew if she'd ever become a doctor, but TJ meant something to the woman who gave her life, and if she could, she'd save him. With the help of Jasmine and Kate, Tessa figured out a way to fit another trip to Newark into her schedule. She would never be like Charlie, could never imagine putting herself first. Her parents had made their share of mistakes in raising her, but they had instilled certain values, and chief among them was saving a life.

Lakisha

Treasure peaked into TJ's hospital room, "We think we have a match!" She strutted in, grinning like they'd won the lottery.

Lakisha was on her feet, "Who is it?"

Treasure glanced at her clipboard, "Tessa Mitchell."

The plastic cup Lakisha was holding clattered to the floor, and she dropped back into her seat. TJ was smiling and whooping, his fist pounding the air. Lakisha's heart beat a kettledrum against her ribs. *It's Tessa Mitchell; the white one, the rapist's seed, the child that I couldn't even set my eyes on, she's the only one who can save TJ.* Her throat tightened, but she managed to mouth, *Thank you,* toward the ceiling. She held TJ's shoulder, steadying them both. "What happens now?"

"We'll try to get the procedure on the schedule as soon as possible. We'll need to keep TJ here in isolation, even for some time after it's done, because his immunity will be compromised. Right before the procedure, Dr. Liu will also order another round of either chemo or radiation. It'll be very strong." She spoke to TJ, "It'll make you even weaker, but will get your body ready for the healthy bone marrow. What do you think?"

TJ grinned, "It's great! Let's get it done, the sooner the better. I've counted the clouds on that curtain about a million times, and I've watched every DVD you got on that cart that comes around and read every decent book too."

"Well, we're gonna get you through the process as quick as we can."

"I want to speak with the transplant team," said Lakisha. "Who is in charge?" There would be no mistakes. She would micromanage this thing every step of the way if she had to.

"The team will sit down with you. Don't worry."

"When will—"

"We should know for sure next week."

After Treasure left, Lakisha and TJ sat in silence, their thoughts swimming with the news.

TJ spoke first. "Who is Tessa Mitchell?"

The question hung over them like a bruised cloud: dense, ominous. Lakisha hadn't thought it all through, didn't know how to frame things. Should she tell him about the rape, or was it better to protect him from that and let him think that she'd had a previous relationship? The kids knew she and Theo had been together since she was fifteen—TJ would do the math. He'd understand that this wasn't before Theo. He'd think that she….

"Mama?"

"Let me think for a minute about how to explain." He was growing into his adult self. He'd been testing the waters of maturity, then stepping back into childhood. There was a part of her that cherished their extended time together, the moments when he'd act younger than his years—let his head rest on her arm or close his eyes as she hummed and stroked his back. These pockets of pleasure left her conflicted. More than anything, she wanted him to grow up, to live long enough to leave her. Emotion pricked her eyes. Soon enough he'd be a man, and he'd need to know the truth of the world.

"I'm gonna tell you all about Tessa Mitchell and her twin sister, Jasmine White. It won't be easy on the ears or the heart, but I believe you're old enough to understand. Aunt Dottie says you're an *old soul.*"

"What's that?"

"It's someone who seems wiser than their years, a person who maybe had prior lives and figured some things out already." He looked like he had more questions, but she didn't want to get side tracked. "Here's the thing: when Daddy and I were first dating, we once went to a party down in the South Ward, on one of those bad blocks. I was young and had poor judgment, and your Daddy…well, he wasn't much better. I wanted to leave the party, and he didn't. I got upset and left without him. It was a dangerous thing to do, but I didn't understand that. I got jumped and it was…bad. He beat me near unconscious, and I was sexually assaulted." She let that sink in, "Nine months later I gave birth to twin girls. They were the children of that monster that jumped me. When I set eyes on them, all I could think of was him." She took a deep breath and spit out the rest, wanting the telling of it to end. "I gave them to the state."

"For adoption?"

She nodded.

"Then Tessa Mitchell, she's my sister?"

"Half-sister, yes." Lakisha waited, unsure of how to help him digest it all.

"Does Daddy know?" He watched her nod. "Nikki?"

She shook her head, "You're the first of the kids to know." She supposed everyone would be told soon enough.

"Can I meet her?"

Lakisha felt a wound that was sewn up long ago with a broad-stroked stitch, begin to expand and pop. It had a familiar ache. She glanced down at her torso, half expecting to find a red stain, a black and blue mark, or a frayed thread in need of knotting. She looked up, "Yes, when you're feeling better, after the transplant. When your immunity is strong, then you can meet her." He seemed to turn these things over in his mind.

"Will the transplant hurt?"

She smiled, relieved he didn't want to know more about the rape or the twins. "No. It's just like a blood transfusion. It'll go in through that port you have in your chest."

"How about Tessa, will it hurt her?"

"No, sweetheart, it shouldn't hurt her much. They'll take it from her hip bones, with a thin needle, but she'll be asleep and won't feel it. I don't think she'll even spend a night in the hospital."

"Still, that's really nice of her."

"Yes," Lakisha agreed, "it surely is."

Tessa

Treasure phoned while Tessa was busy quizzing herself on the structure of nucleic acids and the mechanics of protein synthesis. Biology notes and handouts were fanned out around her on Charlie's bed, and he sat at his desk, tapping out a term paper and chewing his bottom lip.

Now that she knew something of Treasure's relationship with Jasmine, she couldn't help bristling when hearing her voice. She had hurt Jasmine, and no amount of kindness to TJ would change that. She'd keep her interactions with Treasure limited to what was absolutely necessary. "Yes, I can come to an information session, but it'll have to be a Friday, when I don't have class. If possible, I'd like the procedure on a Friday too." She stood and paced into the corner of the room, wishing there was a way to talk out of Charlie's earshot. Once the appointment was set, she pivoted toward the desk and Charlie's critical gaze.

"So, you're donating."

It wasn't quite a question but she responded like it was. "Yes, I am."

"Your parents? They're on board with this?"

"Not...completely sure."

"You haven't told them."

What could she say? She hadn't wanted them to worry—that's what she told Jasmine, but there was more. Unlike Charlie, she wasn't the *golden child* in her family, she was actually the one they always compared to the golden child and found lacking. Lately, being with him didn't feel much better. She rolled her eyes, "I'll tell them tonight. I didn't want to worry them unnecessarily. It'll all be fine." That's what she hoped.

She procrastinated much of the evening, hoping that if she phoned late enough, her parents might be too tired to give her trouble. After she told them, there was a long silence—too long.

"Sweetie?" It was her father, the voice of reason. "You're a good person for wanting to do this. Mommy and I support you...."

She held her breath.

"I'd just like to research the risks."

"They gave me information about it."

"Yes, but a transplant center wants to do transplants. They'll always paint a rosy picture. It's better to look at the statistics and know what to expect. Will it be surgically removed from your hips, or will they do PBSC from veins?"

"From the hips. The nurse said that's what they usually do when it's for a kid." She pictured Alice sitting next to him on the bed, shaking her head, imagined the long discussion they'd have deep into the night. She was glad she wouldn't be there in the morning to see her mother shuffle into the kitchen with bruise-like circles under her eyes and a look that said, *you did this to me.*

"I'm not on call tomorrow, so let's meet for dinner. Mommy and I will come to you."

She sat across from them at a restaurant on Broadway, inhaling fragrant samosas and crunching on papadum. Her fingers worried the edge of the tablecloth, and she noticed her mother doing the same.

Her father wasted no time, "The most serious risk in donation is going under general anesthesia. As you've probably read, about 2.4 percent of donors have serious complications from anesthesia or some other type of damage to the muscle, nerve, or hip bone."

"Yes, I know. That's a statistically small number."

Her mother pounced, "It's a statistically small number unless you're one of the two or three people in a hundred who are left with a serious problem."

"The other thing to consider," her father spoke slowly, "is how accurate that number is. Unless a donor lives locally, they're unlikely to return for medical treatment to the donation center, so unless they do careful follow up research, the numbers might be underestimated. Will the donation be at Hackensack?"

"Yes, the Children's Hospital there does the actual transplants. I looked them up and their ratings were almost all above average, especially regarding infection." Tessa fidgeted while she waited for her father's response. She wished he'd hurry up and speak his mind instead of measuring each sentence, as if he was in a chemistry lab and feared setting off an explosive reaction.

He unfolded a sheet of paper and handed it to her. "I printed an article for you. The side effects of general anesthesia are usually mild: a possible sore throat from the breathing tube, nausea, maybe even vomiting. Then for one to three weeks afterward, you'll have mild to moderate pain and fatigue. Occasionally that lasts up to three months, but rarely with someone your age."

Tessa nodded. She'd skimmed over this information online but hadn't read it carefully. She didn't want to turn into her mother and start to panic.

"You'll be tired because of reduced white blood cell, neutrophil, mononuclear, hemoglobin, and platelet counts. Your blood will regenerate of course, but it could take a month, and your hemoglobin could take up to six months to reach your baseline level."

"So, I'll be a little tired and sluggish for a month. I get it."

Her mother chimed in, "That means you'll be anemic; you could feel sick, have heart palpitations, hair loss, shortness of breath.

Read the article. We're talking a few months of that, Tess, during your freshman year."

Had Charlie spoken with them or was the universe just conspiring against her? "Are you suggesting I tell TJ that I'll save his life, but it'll have to wait until next summer to suit my academic calendar? Or why don't we ask him to wait until I've finished medical school or residency? After all, I'll have to work in a research lab every summer, and I'll need energy for that too." Her eyes were darting between her parents, daring them.

"We only wanted to make sure you understood the risks."

Her mother added, "If you go into it with your eyes open— we'll support you. We'll be worried," her lip trembled, "but your desire to help this boy…it's noble. We can't fault you for that. If you do it, we'll be with you."

"Thank you," she exhaled, "I feel better now," then added, "I hope I don't lose my hair." They all smiled. What she didn't tell them, was that she wasn't being completely selfless, for in the back of her mind she hid a growing wish to meet Lakisha.

Jasmine

The evening before Tessa's bone marrow donation, Jasmine took a train to Maplewood. "Nice wheels," she said, as she slid into Tessa's passenger seat. Tessa looked embarrassed, which made no sense to Jasmine. Why be shy about having a new car? "What's up? Nervous?"

"Sort of, but I'm trying not to think too much about it."

"All right, and Prince Charles? He all on board now?"

"Eh, not sure."

Jasmine held back her laughter. Tessa couldn't see what was right in front of her. "That means he's not on board at all. But who gives a shit, right? It not his body going under the knife. You're still in charge of your own body, right sister?"

Tessa shot her a half smile.

When Jasmine saw Tessa's house for the first time, her mouth fell open. It was like a mini-mansion from one of those feel-good family movies. She hated those movies—they seemed so far from reality. Yet Jasmine couldn't help thinking of what it would've been like to grow up in Maplewood and have Tessa's parents as her own. The question of why they didn't adopt her along with Tessa loomed large. She walked past the double-wide carved-wood door, and into a vestibule that was as big as Champaine's whole living room.

A lady who looked to be Tessa's mom trotted down the stairs in workout clothes that had never seen a grimy gym, and a tall man with bushy eyebrows and reading glasses followed behind her. When the woman reached Jasmine, her face lit, "Hi, I'm Alice. It's great to finally meet you! Tessa's told us wonderful things about you!"

"She must have been talking about some other sister then."

Alice grinned and pointed, "And this is Rob."

These people were a bit too happy. Maybe it was that kind of nervous happy; she'd seen it before in a few young teachers. "Jasmine, it's a pleasure," said Rob. "Should we sit down in the living room for a chat?"

He said this to Jasmine, but Tessa answered, "Do you think it would be okay if Jasmine and I hang for a while on our own? Tomorrow night, we can all have dinner together. Would that be cool?"

Rob looked a little dejected, but Jasmine was relieved. "Big day tomorrow. Do whatever you'd like," he said.

"And make yourself at home!" Alice added. "We have leftovers from dinner in the fridge in case you haven't eaten."

"No, I ate. Thank you, Mrs. Mitchell."

Alice was waving her hand in the air like she was shewing a fly. "Please, call me Alice. We have snacks too. Tessa can show you."

"Okay, thanks, Ms. Alice." Calling someone older by just their first name was disrespectful. She wasn't about to start doing that right out of the gate with Tessa's parents.

Rob and Alice moved toward the stairway, then hesitated. She couldn't blame them for wanting to know their daughter's twin. She followed Tessa into the giant kitchen that sat at the back of the house and overlooked a wide yard. Tessa pulled two bowls out of a fancy wooden cabinet and filled them with chocolate ice-cream. At the kitchen table, Jasmine chowed down on ice-cream and envy.

As if she could read Jasmine's thoughts, Tessa said, "I can't help wondering why my parents didn't adopt you too."

"What made you ask that now?"

"It's a natural question, isn't it?"

"I know, but I was just thinking the exact same thing. Is that cool or creepy?"

Tessa shrugged.

Jasmine looked around the kitchen, taking in the Mexican-tile floor, the stone counters, and the shiny-metal appliances. This kitchen probably cost more than Champaine's entire house.

Alice entered the room humming to herself, "Hi, girls...I'm just here for a seltzer."

"Hey, Mom. You have a minute?"

Alice didn't miss a beat. She took a seat at the table and began picking at her nail polish.

Jasmine braced herself, because if she was still on Tessa's wavelength, this wouldn't be pretty.

"When you were adopting me, why didn't you adopt Jasmine?"

Jasmine stood to leave. She didn't want to get on Alice's bad side by participating in the interrogation.

Tessa lifted a hand, "Hold up, this is about you too."

"It's okay, you guys can talk."

"Your life would have been so much better if you'd grown up in this house. Don't you get that?"

Alice had moved her finger tips to her hairline, as if trying to banish a migraine. "Oh my God, Tessa, it was so long ago. Things were different. We had a social worker helping us, and she didn't encourage it."

"And you thought it would be better for us if you tore us apart?"

"We didn't tear you apart! You were barely together."

Jasmine started walking, but Tessa motioned her back.

"We were together since conception, Mom. That's pretty significant!"

Rob joined them. He must have been listening on the steps. "Maybe we need to take a break before things get said—"

"Things like what?" Tessa was on her feet. "Things like you didn't want a dark baby?"

"Tessa! That's absurd. You know us!" Her mother was now standing too.

Jasmine inched away from them and moved toward the edge of the room.

"Do you know what kind of hell she went through? She was never even adopted, never had a family she could depend on, but you both...." Tessa's voice was desperate, "Why didn't you take her?"

Alice's eyes looked hurt, "Can't you just be happy that you found your sister? Why do you have to spoil it?"

"I'm not spoiling anything; I'm just done with the secrets, completely finished with all of that! I've found my sister, and now I want the truth. I want to know why we spent the last eighteen years apart. I want to understand why she had to suffer when we were here in this giant house—plenty of room for one more kid, Mom."

"What?" Alice pushed her hair from her face and Jasmine saw a vein bulging on her square forehead. "You have no idea what we went through—none at all. We were waiting and waiting for a baby. We had pretty much lost hope, and then you came along. We wanted you so badly!"

"So why didn't you take us both? Isn't two better than one?"

Alice looked like she was crumbling, her face twitched, and Jasmine wished there was some other way to learn the truth.

"Alice," Rob's arm moved around her shoulder, but she elbowed him away.

"I just couldn't take you both!" She was sucking in air like she was having trouble breathing.

"Why not? Why couldn't you?"

Rob made a half-hearted attempt to reach for Alice, but then let his arms fall helpless at his sides.

"Mom?"

Rob tried to interject, "Tessa, I can answer you—"

"How dare you! I always gave you everything; waited on you day and night!" Alice's hands moved to the base of her neck.

"Why just me, Mom?"

Her mother bent over like she couldn't breathe.

"Stop it, Tessa!" Rob moved to Alice's side, held her upper arm, stroked her back. "Try to take deep breaths. Where's your Xanax? In your purse? I'll get it for you." She nodded, and he left for a moment, returning with a small white pill and a glass of water.

It was then that Jasmine understood—it was a panic attack. She felt pity.

Tears streamed down Alice's face. "I...I...I couldn't handle it!" A deep groan escaped her throat. "I just couldn't do it! I couldn't handle twins!" Her sobs echoed against the high ceilings. "I have too much anxiety. I take medication; don't you know that about me? I couldn't take you both...it...it would have been the end of me!" Her knees seemed to give way and she knelt down on the tiles, clutching her chest. Rob squatted next to her. "They said it was okay if I took just one," she looked up at her daughter, "and I chose. I chose you, because you had the same color hair as my aunt Sophie, and yes, because our skin is similar."

"Mom," Tessa crouched down too.

"We thought another nice family would adopt the other baby. If we had had any idea that that wasn't the case, we would have found a way. I have to believe we would have found a way. How were we to know?" Her eyes searched out Jasmine. "I'm so sorry. How was I to know?" She took the glass from Rob, swallowed the pill.

Tessa looked moved by her mother's words. Her voice softened, "You couldn't have known. Okay, okay, Mom. I didn't mean to…to…." Her voice trailed off.

"Tessa, you've got a big day tomorrow, emotions are high." Her dad was clearly the peacemaker in the family. How great would her life have been if she'd had Rob as a dad instead of William? Her mom really wasn't bad either, thought Jasmine.

"Yes," sobbed Alice. "I should have found a way."

"It's all right, Sweetheart." Rob put both arms around her.

"It's all right, Mommy."

This scene felt overwhelming. There were things Jasmine could say, forgiveness she could offer to Tessa's parents. But those kind words were wedged deep down beneath a maze of emotions. She moved toward the hall, "Hey Tessa, it's been a long day, and I'm mad tired. I'll meet you upstairs."

Jasmine left Tessa and her family to sort out their feelings, and she went to figure out her own. These folks seemed to make their own drama when they could just as easily be happy. Alice and Rob should have adopted her, but Alice was too fragile, and Rob was busy bringing other people's babies into the world. There was no end to the irony. God must have a wicked sense of humor. She entered what looked to be Tessa's private bathroom. *But if I'd grown up in this house, unlike them, I'd have found a way to be happy.*

She used some of Tessa's face wash and began poking through the medicine cabinet in search of Advil. Her head was pounding. She found something labeled Migraine Relief and swallowed two capsules with a handful of water. By the time she heard Tessa's footsteps on the stairs, she had already brushed her teeth and tucked herself into Tessa's feathery bed. Her sister entered the room looking like she was returning from a street fight that she'd lost. Her eye makeup was smeared, and her face was blotchy.

"Hi. How's your mom doing?"

Tessa collapsed onto the bed and tossed her arms over her head. "She'll be fine, I guess. Seems like she's in her own private hell, but I think it won't last long. She accepted everything before. She'll just have to find a way to live with knowing the consequences of her decision. What a day."

"I'm sorry my coming over started all this. Your mom seems like a really good person. The whole thing sucks."

"Not *all* of it." She patted Jasmine's arm as if to confirm her solid presence.

Jasmine and Tessa stayed up talking late into the night. There was so much to catch up on, years' worth of stories. Finally, Jasmine said, "Princess, you best catch some Zs. Like your dad said, you got a big day tomorrow. Maybe shut off the lamp and we'll talk more later on."

"I'll shut the light, but I'm still wired. Besides, there's a lot I still don't know about you." Though they were in Tessa's queen-sized bed, Jasmine kept inching back, unaccustomed to closeness. "If you scooch any farther away, you're gonna fall off the mattress."

"Scooch? Is that a word?"

"Jasmine…."

"What do you wanna know, Princess? I'll see if I can tell you. I'm very private."

"Yeah, I figured that one out!" She gave Jasmine's shoulder a playful shove. "I just want to know the whys; why didn't things work out for you?"

"You mean other than the fact that I have brown skin?"

"Come on, why didn't you stay with Treasure and William? Then, why didn't you stay at the second placement? And why didn't you phone anyone when Treasure showed up at your door?"

Jasmine sat up. "It's a long story, and I don't know how you'd feel at the end of it."

Tessa got up too and leaned against the headboard. "Try me; I'm not about judgment. I keep that for myself."

Maybe it was the lateness of the hour or the absolute feeling of comfort that had sneaked in as they spoke. Or perhaps it was the small sliver of hope that she could be like other people and put her trust in someone. But whatever it was, something shifted inside Jasmine, realigned in a way that made room—a safe space to share herself with someone other than Miss Raymelle and Miss Maggie.

Jasmine exhaled, letting go of a breath she didn't know she'd been holding. "I told you about Treasure and William. I knew that they were only my foster parents, but they said that I would always be theirs, and I believed them. Why wouldn't I? Up until the bitter end, I thought that the name Treasure was fitting for her, because that's just what she was to me. I felt her love—always. William might have started out that way, but then things changed. Treasure got a night shift and William started drinking. He lost his job—then his mind."

After she described William's night-time visits, she glanced over at Tessa and was glad that the room was dark so that she couldn't read her expression. "Things only went down from there. The state took me away from them and put me with this woman who didn't give a shit about me. I felt like garbage and started acting like I felt: smoking weed, using, doing whatever it took to get the weed and pills...if you get me." She looked away, transfixed for a few moments by the trees' shadows dancing on the wall. "I was hanging with the dealers, the bangers. That became my life."

"Then one day I got caught by my friend with her man. I didn't know he was hers at the time, or maybe I did. Who knows? She showed up and caused a mess with my crazy foster mother, who swept her off the front porch with a broom. That was a sight. Later that evening, the girl came back and set a fire on the wooden porch. I put it out fast, but that was the end of that home. Bitch put me right out on the curb."

"Oh, my God."

"Yeah. By some miracle, I got lucky after that. I landed in a decent home with my foster mom, Champaine. Miss Raymelle, my caseworker, found it for me. That's when I managed to turn things around. I put my nose in the books, got my grades way up, volunteered, and what not. When I got into Rutgers, I felt like a conquering hero, the poster-child for foster care. They practically erected a statue of me at Champaine's." She wished her story ended there. "I was doing great until Treasure showed up on my doorstep. Then I started hating on myself again, couldn't sleep, barely ate, couldn't concentrate. I landed right back in therapy, trying again to let go of my shitty past. So, Princess…there's probably no fixing this mess I got inside me."

PART FOUR

The Color of Love

Tessa

As the shadows skipped through the room, Tessa was a tangle of emotion, her organs feeling shattered into sharp shards scraping her insides. Her first thoughts were of vengeance: making William pay for what he'd done, making the whole fucked-up system pay. Her mind churned with anger, but there were so many people to despise, she didn't know where to start. Then, in a sudden realization, she was overwhelmed with shame for her own self-pity about the Facebook page and fighting with Charlie, feelings that now seemed absurd when suffering of such magnitude was happening right next to her.

She felt her mother, Alice, stirring inside her and she reached for Jasmine, wrapping her in her arms, holding her despite the other girl's initial stiffness. Her fingers moved over her sister's back with loving strokes, her words a gentle salve. "Jasmine, I don't get how all that could've happened—I mean why it wasn't stopped. But I know for sure that William is sick; he's a predator."

When Jasmine's voice came, it was raw and bitter, "He said it was my fault, and I guess it's easier to believe that than think...." She moved from Tessa, reached for a box of tissues that sat on top of a dresser, and wiped her eyes and nose, "If it wasn't my fault, then that means that either they were really messed up or else...."

"Or else what? You weren't lovable?"

Jasmine's face contracted.

"Jasmine, they were really messed up! You're this rockin', intelligent, kind person, and they were crap. Don't go romanticizing them because they took you in. They never adopted you, he abused you, she probably covered it up and then took his side to keep him out of jail. Did he go to jail?"

"No, he didn't. I don't think there was enough evidence."

"Well he belongs in jail! As soon as the semester ends, you'll come and stay here for a while."

"Thanks, Tessa, but you don't have to do that for me. You have your family."

"You don't get it—you *are* my family. Besides, this house is big enough for at least one more kid."

Jasmine was crying and laughing at the same time. "It sure as hell is. You could fit about twelve kids in here and still not have a line for a bathroom."

"My parents may not be up for that many, but you are for sure welcome." She picked up her phone, glanced at the time, and then snuggled into her down comforter.

Jasmine joined her, "Let's go to sleep." A blanket of silence settled on the room. "I was just thinking...."

"Hmm?" Tessa's eyes popped open.

"Not that I'd wanna be you or anything, but those parents you got...."

Tessa touched her shoulder, "Things will get better for you, you'll see."

"I wouldn't want that piece a shit prince of yours."

"Really? You don't think he's a keeper?"

"Not hardly. He doesn't think you should help TJ. For me, that's pretty much a deal breaker right there."

"I know, but it's really his mother."

"I'm probably wrong then."

Thinking about Charlie was exhausting. Tessa felt a wave of weariness roll in as she closed her eyes, her back parallel to Jasmine's, her body curled in a mirror position. She fell into a dreamless sleep, her mind resting before the difficult day ahead.

Tessa's alarm sounded at six in the morning. She shut it off and flopped back on the bed, accidentally hitting Jasmine. Her sister didn't even stir, so she nudged her awake.

"What time do we have to leave the house? Wake me fifteen minutes before."

"That's all the time you need?"

"I'm used to a house with six kids sharing one bathroom so I'm quick, and I know you're not eating breakfast, so I won't either."

"How do you know I'm not eating breakfast?"

"I researched it, just like your parents and your prince."

"Really? You did?"

"Yes, now let me sleep."

"You can try, but my mom will be in here any minute to hurry us. She likes to have a cushion of time."

Almost on cue, Alice poked her head in the room and started talking.

It wasn't long before they were all in the car and on their way. National Public Radio filled the air with calm voices, and Tessa gazed at a bank of cotton-candy pink clouds that edged against an indigo veil. Travelling at dawn always made her think of the early flights they'd taken to visit her grandmothers, and she was filled with a similar nervous anticipation: a fear of the unknown laced with excitement for TJ, her mysterious half-brother. More than anything, she wanted this transplant to work.

Once she was registered at the transplant center, it didn't take long for her to be called into a curtained cubicle. It wasn't the first time she'd ever been asked to change into a hospital gown, but it was the first time she'd done it without her mom at her side and she missed her presence. Once her IV line was in place and her vitals were recorded, the nurse said her family would be allowed to wait with her. Lily had phoned the night before to wish her well and said she'd come by over the weekend to visit. She wondered what Lily thought of her having another sister—then realized she probably wasn't thinking about it at all. There was a thin line between driven and selfish, and Lily often seemed to be on the wrong side of it.

She worried about the low backache she'd have after the surgery and hoped it wouldn't be as bad or last as long as the pain from her gymnastics fall. When she'd attended the transplant center's lengthy information session, she'd asked if her father could scrub in and be with her during the procedure, but they'd assured her that she wouldn't be awake and so she'd have no need of him. But what if she did need him? She was being irrational. *Lord, let this go well for TJ and me. I am grateful for your gifts.*

Her parents pushed aside the curtain, and Jasmine trailed in behind like the caboose of train. They surrounded her propped-up gurney with soft smiles and gentle pats that made her feel both precious and fragile. After a sedative was injected into her IV, her body relaxed, and her mind grew placid. Then their tender faces were leaning in, covering her with a warm blanket of encouragement. The anesthesia and their waves of love soon enveloped her and carried her to a sandy bed beneath a tranquil sea.

When she woke, her throat was scratchy, and she still felt sleepy. Her mom and Jasmine entered the room.

"Hey, Tessa," her mom brushed a hand over her forehead. "How are you feeling?"

"Tired, but fine. Where's Dad?"

"They only allow two people at a time in recovery, so he let Jasmine come in first."

"Hey there, sister." Tessa reached out, and this time Jasmine met her halfway and took her hand.

"You're a good woman." Jasmine had emotion in her eyes.

"Not really."

"At least today, own that you're good." Alice touched her lips to her daughter's cheek.

The combination of drugs, feeling she'd made a difference, and finally winning Alice's approval, brought up happy tears. "Do you think Lakisha will come by?"

"TJ probably just finished a round of super strong chemo or radiation, that'll make him feel lousy. I doubt Lakisha will leave him."

"When will he get the transplant?"

"Daddy thinks it will be tomorrow. Why don't you give Lakisha a few weeks?"

She felt her eyelids grow heavy again. "That's cool, I'm probably too wiped anyway. But maybe soon."

Lakisha

TJ looked worse than she'd ever seen him. He had almost no hair on his head, his eyes had sunken into craters on his face, his mouth was dotted with sores, and his skin had taken on an ashen hue. Even more disturbing was his flat expression; his optimism now replaced with a grim acceptance. Lakisha and Theo sat with him while the room was readied for the transplant.

Ever since Lakisha told Theo the truth about the twins, the two of them hadn't spoken unless it had to do with TJ's treatment, the kids, or bills. She felt shattered beyond repair, held together by kind words from hospital staff, strong cups of coffee, fleeting bedtime cuddles, and a few poems and prayers. She didn't know how she'd make it through the day without knowing her relationship with Theo would heal.

She stroked TJ's leg and tried not to stare at the central venous catheter that had been inserted in his chest after his transfer to the pediatric oncology unit. Lakisha wondered how he could put up with all the needles and prodding. Of course, that was only what was happening on the surface. The real torment was going on in his veins and arteries, and inside his bones. She hoped the side effects from the chemo hadn't weakened him too much to recover. Though she'd never speak the words out loud, he looked like someone sitting on the stoop of death's door.

"This is going to be like your birthday, TJ! This is the beginning of a new life for you." A heavy-set nurse with large hands and an ear-to-ear smile was cleaning the catheter, preparing it for the transplant. "Like the doctor said, this will be similar to a blood transfusion—no cutting, no needles, none of that. You can relax now. The doctor will be in soon to get things started. Mama, Daddy, Birthday Boy, can I get you anything?" They shook their heads and she beamed at them, as if they'd soon be getting a giant birthday cake or a visit from a clown who did magic. "I'll be back with the doctor."

Once they were alone in the room, Theo took Lakisha's hand and gave it a squeeze. Their eyes met, "Are we ready team?"

That was all she needed. She reached for TJ's hand and the three of them made a prayer circle. Lakisha's voice was calm, "Lord, thank you for the blessing of finding a donor for TJ. We pray for your continued support. Please show compassion to this loving boy. Please bless him with a full recovery and grant him a long and happy life…and please bless his generous donor, Tessa, with the same. We are very grateful for all of your gifts. Amen."

Once the bone marrow, which looked just like blood, was moving down the tube into TJ's chest, Lakisha kept her eyes trained on him and tried to read meaning into every subtle movement. If he sandwiched his lips, did that mean his body was rejecting it? If his hand relaxed, was that the beginning of healing? He was on antibiotics to prevent possible infection, but since his body was so depleted, there were many other things that could go wrong. She'd kept her darkest fears hidden from Theo, understanding that he liked to keep his mind flush with optimism.

The transplant took over an hour, and then their long wait began. The following morning, TJ developed a fever. Lakisha huddled next to him in his isolation room, worrying the bed sheets until the air filtration system hummed them into naps. He had little appetite, and she resisted the urge to spoon food into his mouth, though she wasn't above putting a can of chocolate Ensure in his hand and guiding it to his lips. She made a nuisance of herself at the nursing station, until the charge nurse sat her down and made it clear that infection and fever were common transplant side effects and were not indications of rejection. "They've added IV antibiotics, which should help. I know the waiting can be torturous. Do you need a shower? A few hours of shut-eye in a real bed? I could sneak you into your own room until my shift ends."

Lakisha appreciated her kindness but stayed with TJ. She'd couldn't rest until his fever finally broke more than a day later. Once he was well enough to eat a light meal, she called in Dottie and went home to sleep. She collapsed into bed, half delirious, and woke ten hours later in a panic, worrying that something awful might have happened in her absence.

The next few weeks seemed to crawl by. TJ remained weak and uninterested in the board games and books that she offered. He'd even lost interest in watching the Nature Channel on television. Days stretched into weeks, chipping away at their hope. Neither Lakisha nor Theo spoke of feeling discouraged, but the pretense was exhausting, and the whole family was struggling. Shonda and Kai needed her at home, Nikki had started staying out past her curfew, and Devon had been acting up at school. Lakisha felt like a piece of salt-water taffy being pulled in many directions at once. She struggled to prioritize. Though TJ found Aunt Dottie grating, he had to put up with her some nights, so that both she and Theo could spend time at home.

Then one morning, TJ woke up hungrier than he'd been in months. He plowed through two trays of food and still asked Lakisha for more pancakes. "I think I could eat the world!" he said, and she saw that light had returned to his eyes. The doctor soon confirmed the change—his blood levels were rising!

While he dozed, she tugged freshly laundered sweatpants and t-shirts from a vinyl tote and put them on a closet shelf. They smelled like home, and she felt her heart flutter with the possibility, *maybe he'll be home soon*. She reached into the bag and withdrew her changeable doll from the bottom. After Theo had left with the kids, she'd grabbed it off the floor. Lakisha sank into her recliner and her mind travelled from Maizy to Jasmine, the moon-kissed poet, and then, to Tessa. After recovering from the crushing physical pain of the rape and making her decision to surrender the twins, she'd sealed away some part of herself; placed it in a weather-proof box and used thick packing tape at the seams. She'd always imagined that what she'd placed inside was the bitter past: poisonous, lethal. Perhaps that's what she needed to believe to make peace with herself and what she'd done.

She turned the doll so that the yellow hair caught a slice of morning sunlight. She fingered a braid, straightened the blue dress, and hugged it to her ribs. Tessa had turned out to be a good person. Despite her biological father and being abandoned, Treasure said she'd lived a nice life—a life that Lakisha had missed.

TJ moaned and rolled over. "Why did you bring me a doll?"

Lakisha's heart grew heavy, like a bag filled with tears. "It's not for you—it's for me."

On a Sunday in December, Theo and Lakisha strolled down Springfield Avenue beneath the mid-day sun. Lakisha looked at Theo through jubilant eyes. She had waited until they were alone to report, "The doctor said TJ should be able to be home by Christmas. He'll have to wear a mask outside the house, but he's looking so much better." She felt grateful to the medical team, her family, and even to God, who somehow managed to come through this time.

Theo rested a hand on Lakisha's shoulder. "And his last blood counts were solid. I don't wanna speak too much more about that, because I'm afraid I'll jinx it. I know we're not out of the woods yet."

"Yeah, but I may have just enough room now to fall apart."

Theo stopped walking. "Kisha...."

"I won't really, but all the anxiety and the stress of running back and forth to the hospital—it just about killed me."

"It's been a little slice a hell, I'll give you that, but the worst is over."

"I hope so, because I can't take much more." She pulled a cinnamon drop candy from her coat pocket and offered one to Theo. They walked on a few more paces, "I wrote her a long thank you note—to the donor, I mean."

"I knew who you meant. I was hoping you'd do it. It's better coming from you."

The unsaid words hung between them. Although years had passed, Lakisha still carried that night with her, like a collection of stones in her pocket. There was a stone with the word *regret* on it, one with *blame*, one with *fear*. There was a rock with the word *anger* penned in big block letters, and then one more. The last one had fuzzy-looping letters spelling *grateful.*

A brisk chill in the air sent a shiver through Lakisha, and Theo wrapped his arm around her jacketed back, pulling her close to him in a way that reminded her of their early days as a couple. Even his idea of leaving the kids at home and taking a walk together was unusual. They rarely walked anywhere without a specific purpose: the bank, the supermarket, church. Just the thought of taking some time for themselves felt a bit self-indulgent. Still, she had to admit that she was relishing being outside after the recent cold snap and was loving the feeling of Theo's strong body touching hers, their steps in sync.

Theo took her hand and they continued walking. When they arrived at an intersection two blocks away from where Lakisha had lived with Aunt Dottie, Theo paused and turned to her, "Do you remember this street corner?"

Lakisha felt the right side of her mouth curl into a smile. "Yeah, baby, I think I know this place. I wonder if folks still slam poetry here."

His arms encircled her waist, and he pulled her close. "When I saw you, all them years ago, your voice shaking as you read—so determined to speak your peace and be heard, even though you were so goddamn young...I knew."

"I was too young for you."

"Yeah, that's what your aunt thought, but she was wrong. She was so wrong. You were older than your years—"

"You made me older than my years! I remember that first poem you read to me—the one about your brother. For a long time, I kept it folded up in a compartment of my wallet. It may still be stuck in there. "My brother was the moon, he was king of the streets. Others tried to play him, slay him, but he had them all beat."

Theo's eyes crinkled up, "I guess you were listening."

"Sometimes. That poem stayed with me. It made me think of my mother."

"I know. I know you pretty well by now." Theo released her and took a step back. "It's been good, hasn't it? I mean, most of the time. I was good to you—least I tried to be."

"Hmm, I suppose." She was unsure of where he was heading, but she wasn't above giving him some trouble.

"If I could go back in time and change one bad decision in my life, like if I got a *do-over*, I'd go back to the night of that party, and I would stop you from leaving alone. I would have stood up and listened to what you were saying. I would have protected you. I swear, for the rest of my life, all I care about is protecting you, you and the kids both."

Lakisha felt her brow relax, and her jaw stopped its incessant clenching. Without that night, where would TJ be now?

"You and me, Kisha, we're a good team; you know we are."

She looked at his dark eyes, now so intense. They had been together close to twenty years, more than half her life. She had endured the worst trauma imaginable—partially because of him. Still, she had remained—they both had. "You're making me nervous."

Theo took her hands in his and knelt down on one knee. "Lakisha?"

She laughed out loud, "Oh, Sweet Jesus!"

"Lakisha, will you marry me?" His eyes squinted up at her.

"Get up off the dirty sidewalk!" she pulled at his arms.

"Not until you answer me."

"Have you lost your mind?" She took in the darts poking out around his eyes, the lines beginning to take up residence near his mouth, his still stunning smile.

"No, I've found it."

She was tugging at him. "Get up here!"

"Answer me."

"Yes, the answer is yes! Now stand up!" Once he was closer to her eye level she continued, "What's gotten into you? Why now? Just answer me that. I wanted to get married years ago, and you said, *We ain't ready. We don't have the money.* So why now?"

"I'm tired a waiting. There's never gonna be a good time, and I saved up a bit. I think we should start the process, get you a ring. Let's make it legal!"

"Oh yeah? You wanna make it legal?"

"Mrs. Klein, you know, the lady I drive three times a week to her dialysis appointments, she set me up with her son who sells diamonds. We got an appointment there in the city this afternoon, so we can pick out a ring. I even got your cousin to babysit, so Nikki won't have a meltdown. Come on Kisha, don't go giving me a hard time now. Let's go buy you a ring." His eyes were fixed on her, unwavering.

How could she disagree with any of what he was saying? Of course she wanted to be his wife, but that was her eighteen or twenty year-old dream. At thirty-five it wasn't so easy to switch gears and reconnect with it. "Okay," she said and couldn't contain her grin, "Let's go shopping." As they started to walk on, she added, "Proposing on the street corner where we met was all right, but don't go thinking we're gonna get married there too."

On the way into the city, they stopped at home so that Lakisha could phone the hospital, check on the kids, and pick up the ruby ring that had been Maizy's. She had decided to take the stones and divide them into three separate rings; one would be for her, and then the other two would be for the future—perhaps for her daughters.

The diamond Lakisha chose was just shy of one carat, and had a good round cut, several small inclusions, and grade J color. "Put it in the least expensive gold setting," she said to the middle-aged, bearded man standing behind the display case. "A stone that beautiful doesn't need a whole bunch of metal to make it stand out." She turned to face Theo and brought her lips to his ear, "Thank you. You did great."

"You deserve it, Kisha. This ring isn't even good enough." His eyes smiled, and he grabbed her up in his arms.

The day of her wedding arrived, and despite feeling a bit foolish about squeezing herself into a floor-length ivory gown, Lakisha had to admit that she was happy—happier than she'd been in a long time. The dress had a simple cut, but it accented her curves and pushed up what little cleavage she had. The sleeves were elbow-length lace that matched a strip of Chantilly at her waist. She'd shopped reluctantly with Aunt Dottie and did her best to ignore Dottie's remarks about her gown being too ordinary. "It's a sample, it's on sale, and it looks good on me, Auntie. That's more important than fashion."

Dottie had bobbed her neck, "Well you can have both, I'm just saying."

"Not at this price, I can't. This dress will be just fine." And so it was. Her relaxed hair was pulled back into a high-twisted chignon, and pearl earrings hung from her earlobes. Around her neck, she wore a black and cream cameo on a ribbon, and her grandmother's watch was fastened to her wrist. Theo had taken the kids to dress for the wedding at a friend's house, so that Lakisha could get ready in peace and quiet.

"You can't wear that watch with a wedding dress," insisted Dottie when she arrived at Lakisha's apartment.

"Grandma is with me when I wear the watch. I need her here today." Her eyes grew moist.

Dottie shifted uncomfortably and then dropped her gaze. "You know she loved you—my mama did. She wasn't much for saying the words, but you had to know it."

Lakisha nodded. Her grandmother was not a warm person, but she was dependable. She had given Lakisha a solid home right up until the day she died.

"And it wasn't your fault…when she died. You were young. It wouldn't have made a difference if you'd gotten to a phone sooner."

"I know that too." Lakisha felt the tears spill over. "Shoot, you're gonna wreck my makeup." She reached for a tissue and blotted her face. "It would've been nice if you had said that earlier, like maybe when I was eleven or twelve. But I'll take it now anyway."

Dottie cocked her head. "You know mothering ain't my strong suit."

"Yup. That I know!"

Dottie opened her sturdy arms, and Lakisha fell into them. "Don't you be getting makeup on my outfit."

Lakisha pulled back from her, scanned Dottie's apple green silk dress, and laughed, "You still look nice."

"Come on then, I'll help you fix your face."

During the ride to the church, Dottie flipped between radio stations, searching for a song she liked.

"Can we listen to the news? Changing the stations is making me nervous."

"What you got to be nervous about? You been together almost twenty years!" She glanced at Lakisha, huffed air out of her mouth, and then switched stations.

After the weather forecast, came a story about thirty-year-old twins who were reunited with their birth mother.

"Oh, Auntie."

"What's the matter? It's just another block. We'd be there already if it wasn't for this Saturday traffic."

"Did you listen to that story?"

"What? What was it about? I never listen to the news—too damn depressing."

Lakisha decided to keep quiet. But even when Dottie let her out at the curb in front of the church and she entered the chapel, taking in the fragrant rose, lily, and baby's breath arrangements that decorated the pews, her mind still swirled through the past. Maybe she should have spoken to the twins when they came to the lab to be tested. Perhaps she should have asked to see Tessa on the day she made the donation. She could have left TJ for a few minutes. What made her think she was so fragile that she couldn't handle seeing some piece of that night reflecting back at her through Tessa? Though she tried to resist the next question, it rose into her consciousness. *What if giving them away was a huge mistake?*

She turned toward the door and saw her kids filing into the chapel, peeling off their winter coats and straightening their dress clothes. Those girls that she gave away—they had beauty in them, just like the two daughters here now. That dark one, the ghost that haunted her at Rutgers, she was the spitting image of Maizy. Lakisha felt the echo of her mother's abandonment, but then questioned how she could have spent so many years mourning Maizy, only to then give away her clone. And the white girl—even the white girl, at this very moment, a part of her was inside TJ, helping him fight off the cancer. If he lived to adulthood, it would be because of her. How could she not find love in her heart for a girl who was willing to do that? The twins were a part of her family. She allowed herself to know this truth—to understand the damage she'd done. They were innocent babies, and she took no pity on them. The room was spinning. Lakisha reached for a pew and slid into it.

"Kisha, you okay? You look…I don't even have words for how good you look." Theo was beside her, leaning over in his new navy pinstripe.

She reached her hand up, and once he took it in his firm grasp, she felt better. He had a way of centering her, helping her remain grounded no matter what storm was brewing. Her son Devon clattered down the aisle in his Sunday best, and her little girl trailed after him, her patent-leather Mary Janes already beginning to step on the wide sash from her dress that had loosened and fallen to the white carpet-liner. TJ, Nikki, and baby Kai followed close behind. TJ's suit jacket was boxy, his belt cinched in tighter than the last time he wore it. Over his mouth and nose was a blue medical mask, but even that couldn't camouflage his smiling eyes. Kai was walking now, but Nikki carried him on her hip, and her face was hardly recognizable—she looked cheerful.

Lakisha rose to her feet and corralled the group. "Come on now, don't get messed up before we even get started! We're gonna go down to the social hall and wait there. Try to keep yourselves neat—at least until after the ceremony!" And with that, she herded her five children to the stairway.

Less than an hour later Lakisha walked down the aisle, surrounded by her children. TJ was at her side, looking frail but steady. Then Theo took her hand, and they stood before the pastor, exchanged vows and rings, and listened intently to words about fidelity and family, compassion, courage, and faith. At the end, Theo sealed it all with a kiss, then leaned back and twirled her around. The small crowd cheered.

Together, they bundled into their coats and walked three blocks to a restaurant with a party room on the second floor that had been decorated with white and silver balloons, and bud vases with roses. Dottie assigned her two daughters to keep an eye on Lakisha and Theo's younger kids, during the party. A disc jockey pumped music into the room, and Lakisha and Theo sat down with their guests and toasted their future.

When Joe Cocker's voice filled the room with *You Are So Beautiful*, Theo stood and extended his hand. As the two swayed around the cramped dance floor, Lakisha took in the faces of her children, Dottie, the cousins who had helped her so much, and the small sea of other family and friends who gathered to help them celebrate. She felt so much love in the room, and her heart was so full of gratitude, she feared it might burst. Perhaps everything was going to be all right, and her life would be calm and secure now that she was married. She had achieved what Dottie never did; she had a band of gold on her finger. But then the people who were missing flashed through her mind: her mother, her grandmother, and even her two eldest daughters; that sweet Oreo-cookie pair. Her eyes reached up to Theo's.

He pulled her closer, "Happy?"

Tessa

Tessa sat at her desk bent over a complex calculus problem. The ache in her back had disappeared after a week but the fatigue stubbornly persisted. As finals approached she questioned how she'd get through all the work. A few weeks ago, she would have texted Charlie, and asked him to come over, but something in their relationship had changed. Since her bone-marrow donation, he didn't ask to see her every day, and when they did meet, he seemed withdrawn. Still, she needed him, felt desperate to see him. If only she could curl up in the comfort of his arms, then perhaps she could get through the next week, the next day, the next hour.

Her phone was heavy in her hands as she texted. Hey, I went for my last medical follow up today and I'm back ☺.

Glad to hear it, he responded, but nothing more.

Miss you.

Me too.

Any chance we could meet? She held her breath.

Not a good idea. I've got so much work. Just can't.

That was it? Not a good idea? What did that mean? Who cared how much work he had? Time to talk?

Maybe tomorrow?

OK, g'night, xo.

G'night.

There was no xo, no hugs, no mention of love. Maybe she was just making herself crazy. He was busy. It was the end of the semester and he was under tremendous pressure. It was true that he had no free time, none of them did. But in the past, he'd always made space for her. He'd said that being with her helped to calm his stress.

She wished she could get together with Kate and talk it out but knew that neither of them could spare the time. She thought of knocking on Charlie's door and demanding answers, but that would be a mistake. She had to respect his need for space, at least for the time being.

The next week passed in an academic-overdrive blur. There was little sleep and even less socialization as the students made their final push to complete their papers and ace their exams. Tessa slept only when the caffeine stopped working, and then only in five-hour increments. She was determined to do well and prove herself. Besides, she didn't want to give Charlie the satisfaction of being right about her. Sam stopped by her table in Butler Library a few times dropping off energy bars and fleeting words of encouragement, and there were brief conversations at meals before Tessa and her friends speed-walked back to their work. Tessa made a final dash toward the finish line of the semester, and the freedom to focus on her future—on Charlie.

Before leaving for winter break, Tessa tried again and again to reach him, but he didn't respond to her calls or texts. She remembered that during midterms he had turned off his phone and stuck it in a drawer to reduce distractions, but finals were over, and he was still unreachable. *Could he have been in an accident? Did his appendix burst?* That had happened to a kid in high school, and he was stuck in the hospital for days. But if that were true, someone from Saint James would have texted or phoned. No, it had to be about her. *He's ghosting me.* Angry tears flooded her eyes and she blinked them away. She still wore his sweatshirt, now stained from coffee that splattered during an all-night study session. Stray hairs clung to her shoulders, reminders of the time she'd spent mindlessly tugging at her head while worrying.

After a semester-long romance, she'd not allow it. She deserved an explanation—*either that or he better have been hit by a city bus!* She ran gloss over her lips, patted some concealer beneath her eyes, and headed out the door. When she arrived at his dorm, his suite mate told her he'd already left for winter break. Tessa scrolled through old texts, found his home address and trotted toward the subway, driven to see him—even if it was for the last time.

Charlie's mother answered the door, made a feeble attempt at masking her surprise, and then invited her in. Tessa waited in the foyer, willing herself to calm down.

He appeared on the staircase, his face confused. "Tessa, nice to see you." His lips barely grazed her cheek, with a ghost of a kiss. His wide shoulders filled out his cotton Henley, which was unbuttoned just enough to allow a few soft chest hairs to show. She ached for him. "Tessa, I'm sorry, I wasn't expecting—"

"No, I know I shouldn't just show up here, but…you weren't picking up my calls."

"Oh, the sound might be off." He shifted his weight between his legs. "My family is just sitting down to brunch, and my parents have a few colleagues over. Would you like to join?"

"No, no! I don't want to crash the party. I just thought maybe we could have a few minutes to talk." She bit her lip and tasted blood.

"The thing is, they're waiting now. Please, if you could just join us, then we can talk afterward. It's our end of semester celebration brunch. We do it twice a year. Come on." Charlie tugged her sleeve in the same brotherly way he had when they played Frisbee together that first day.

The last thing Tessa wanted to do was sit down to a meal with the Stansworths, but what else could she do? "I guess…I could…." She inhaled courage. "Okay, I could sit for just a few minutes."

Tessa followed Charlie downstairs to the ground level. The meal was set around a massive wooden table in the kitchen. Bagels, spreads, cheeses, pastries, smoked fish, salads, and fruits were all laid out on decorative painted platters, cloth napkins were nestled in wrought iron rings on top of each plate, and milk was being frothed by Charlie's father at the brown and cream-colored granite island.

The other guests greeted her with reserved warmth and she was ushered into an empty seat at the table. A place setting was added, and she was handed a short steaming cup of cappuccino. Tessa glanced down at her dirty sweatshirt and felt embarrassed. Brunch wasn't at all part of the calculation when she dressed that morning. She had just wanted to speak with Charlie, had needed to get some clarity, to put an end to the obsessive thoughts that held her captive. She wanted to win him back, convince him that she was still the same person, that they could have differing views, and still have a future together. She pulled the sweatshirt off, revealing a fitted striped T-shirt that was thankfully clean.

Tessa was too upset to make small talk, so she drank some phenomenal coffee and waited for Charlie to finish his first bagel. Then she turned to him, "I don't mean to interrupt, but I actually have to catch a ride home soon. Do you think we could speak for just a few minutes? Then I'll get going."

"Of course," he was on his feet. "Please excuse us," he nodded toward his parents.

Polite responses abounded along with obligatory holiday wishes. Charlie led the way up two flights of stairs to his childhood bedroom, a room Tessa had never seen before and sensed she would never see again. She scanned the high school sports trophies, and the academic awards that were framed and nailed to the wall. He was president of his high school's student government and salutatorian of his class. Why did he never tell her these things? She didn't bother to sit down, "I tried to reach you."

"I'm sorry, I guess I forgot to turn my phone back on after finals."

She knew he was lying and felt anger heat her face. "What's going on?" Her eyes searched his for some truth, but he couldn't or wouldn't hold her gaze.

"Nothing is going on. I just...I don't want to hurt you. It's been a rough semester for you."

"How would you know? You haven't even spoken to me in like a week. Just say what you want to say."

Charlie appeared to be carefully choosing his words. He ran his fingers through his hair. "Okay, Tessa, it doesn't seem like it's going to work out with us. I'm sorry, I really am, but I just don't see it happening."

"You don't see it happening because...."

"Okay, well...Jesus, it's all of it—it's just all of it. First there was that time when you just shut me out for a few days—"

"You're talking about after the Facebook fiasco? I was in a crisis! You know it's not like I knew all that dirt and kept it from you—I really didn't know any of it—none at all! It took time to process it."

"Yes, but then it just kept getting worse and worse. It wasn't just that single drama, because then you started spending all that time in Newark, doing—"

"Saving my brother's life!"

"Trying to save the life of a stranger—it's really irrelevant." His hands were on her shoulders, "Listen, I still care about you, but there has just been too much...I don't know." His eyes scanned the ceiling, "I know that Madeline started the trouble. It's not your fault, but the rumor mill and gossip—it never ends with you. I don't want to be connected with all of this, and I can't have it associated with my family. What you're involved in now seems like a story ripped from the pages of *The Enquirer* or *Star Magazine*. Someone from *City Beat* actually phoned me and asked if I could confirm certain rumors about you, and that's a publication that people I know read."

"Huh? What did you say?"

"I said nothing, but it won't end there. Look, I don't know how else…this just doesn't work for me. It has nothing to do with New Jersey or you being bi-racial or not having a strong work ethic—"

"My work ethic? Really? You don't know anything about me, do you?" She was incredulous.

"Look, I'm sorry, truly I am. But this is just the way it is. This is just the way it seems it has to be."

Tessa tried to bite the words back, but they tumbled from her mouth. "I thought you said it didn't matter what they think! I thought you said all that was important was how *you* felt!"

What followed was a brief silence, the air thick with regret. It was then that she understood—when his gaze fell to the floor and his arms reached around her back to encircle her for the last time. His feelings had changed. There was nothing left to say. After a few anguished moments, she ran out.

She held her tears in check until she heard the heavy front door click-shut behind her, and then allowed them to trail down her face, streaking her burning cheeks. She shivered all the way back to the dorm, not even bothering to put on the sweatshirt she clutched in her fist.

Alice drove into the city a few hours later to retrieve her, and found Tessa lying on top of her soft comforter, a puddle of tears collecting on her tie-dyed pillowcase. Her mother helped her organize her belongings, gathered her daughter in her arms, and guided her down the steps and across the brick walkway to her double-parked car.

Sitting in her bedroom and gazing out at the giant Sycamore tree, Tessa reached for her phone and almost dialed Kate, but then chose a different number.

Jasmine picked up on the fourth ring. "Hey, Tessa, what up?"

"Nothing much. How are you?"

"I'm cool. I'm at Champaine's church doing some Christmas decorating."

"Oh, okay, I don't want to bother you."

"It's no bother! Let me sit down a minute. Hold on. Hey, Danny, don't be throwing that garland, it's gonna tear! Sorry about that."

"You're busy, maybe we should talk later."

"You sound like shit. What happened? The prince decided to bounce?"

"Yeah, how could you tell?"

"I know you."

In a defeated voice, she shared a few facts about the way things had ended.

Jasmine didn't miss a beat, "I'm coming over. I don't have the train fare, and I'm too tired to figure out the bus connections. Can you pick me up?"

That night, Tessa and her parents drove through the narrow one-way streets of Newark, looking for a poorly lit, brick row house, home to Jasmine's foster family.

Jasmine

The car that Tessa's father drove reminded Jasmine of the dealers' cars: big, shiny, expensive, and almost new. Inside, the seats were smooth leather that made everything smell like the designer handbags at Macy's. It was a waste of money, sitting on leather when your butt would be just as comfortable on fabric. It did feel good, though. "Thank you for picking me up."

Both of Tessa's parents tried to respond at once. Her mother won out, "We're glad to do it. We've never been in this part of Newark."

"No, I imagine not."

Tessa nudged Jasmine, and the discomfort of being in the flashy car with the rich white people faded. She caught Tessa's eye, "That boy in New York is a fool."

She'd spoken softly, but Alice chimed in. "We completely agree." Rob stayed quiet, but she saw him nod. Her parents were so nice, Jasmine had to fight off the blade of envy that poked at her side.

When they arrived at the house, Jasmine followed Tessa up the slate path.

In Tessa's room, they took off their shoes, and Jasmine watched Tessa plop down on the bed and then motion for her to do the same.

Jasmine leaned back against the headboard, "So what did that fool prince say exactly?"

"He said it was just all of it—all the drama, the way it went down. He made some lame excuse about his family and not wanting to be linked up with—"

"A bi-racial girl?"

"Not in so many words, but, yeah, a bi-racial girl, a crazy girl, a lazy girl...."

"What?"

"I know! Right? I mean, I didn't get all As this semester, but I got all As and Bs —not bad, all things considered. He gave all kinds of excuses, but I just knew—I could tell...things had changed." Tears gathered and leaked from her swollen eyes.

"Listen, that man is *young and stupid.* There's not much you can do with young and stupid. He thinks he's gonna find himself another rich, fine girl like you?"

"Compared to the people he's used to, I'm not rich or fine."

Jasmine lifted her chin. "You may not have the money they got, but I know he won't meet a finer person."

After swiping at her cheeks with a pillow, Tessa grabbed a few tissues and honked her nose. "Well, I don't think that's true, but it's nice of you to say."

"What's that bitch's name? Caroline?"

"Madeline."

"Madeline has nothing over you. All she got is a fat checkbook to stand on, and her daddy in her back pocket. That stuff will only take you so far. You think her parents would be touring around Newark to pick me up?"

"No, they'd probably send a limo." Tessa's fist began tapping against her cheekbone, and Jasmine swatted it away.

"You know there's something about doing things yourself, having a big enough heart to really care about someone. A person who does shit like Madeline? I'm not buying that she got something beating in her chest like you got."

"Maybe not." Tessa sighed. "All right, I'll try to quash my self-pity."

"Good, because that Columbia prince, he ain't worth it; you feel me?"

Tessa nodded, grabbed another tissue and wiped her face. "Okay, it's vacation. Let's focus on that. What should we do tomorrow?"

"I'm down for whatever."

Pulling out her phone, Tessa began researching movies, but then started texting and laughing.

"Who are you texting?"

"It's Sam."

"The poet, Sam?"

Tessa smiled, "Yes."

"You seem awfully pleased with what he's writing."

"He's just a friend."

"Time will tell."

Tessa gave her a shove with the ball of her foot. "Tomorrow is my half birthday…I mean it's *our* half birthday. I used to celebrate it instead of my regular one because so many of my friends would already be away at camp by the end of June. Maybe we could do something together to celebrate."

Jasmine's mind had drifted. She surveyed Tessa, assessing their similarities. Maybe Tessa's cheekbones curved at a similar angle. Perhaps her hair framed her face in a heart-shaped line just like Jasmine's.

"So, what's your favorite color?" Again, Tessa seemed to be on the same wave-length.

Jasmine rolled her eyes, even though she was happy to play. "Purple."

"Me too! What's your favorite cookie?"

"For real? Chocolate chip."

"Me too!" said Tessa.

"But everyone likes chocolate chip best."

"No, my dad is obsessed with peanut butter cookies. What's your favorite ice cream flavor?"

"Last crazy-ass question, okay? Are we talking grocery store?"

Tessa smirked. "What does it matter? Yeah, okay, grocery store."

"Well, there's a difference. So, grocery store, I'd say, mint chocolate chip."

"Ha! Come with me." Tessa jumped up and grabbed Jasmine's hand. "Come on!" Jasmine followed her trotting sister down the stairs and into the kitchen. There, Tessa tugged open the freezer. "Ta, da!" she sang as she danced her way to the kitchen table carrying a container of mint chocolate chip ice cream. "Me too!"

"Baby, what was that thing you were doing with your butt?"

"What, this?" Tessa made a figure eight with her hips. "That's my ice cream dance. You don't have an ice cream dance?"

"Naw, I think we're different there. If I was to do that in my old neighborhood, I'd be in deep. We danced for sex or money or maybe to celebrate a touchdown, that's about it."

Tessa looked pouty. "Just for that, you only get two scoops instead of three." She began dishing brown-speckled green mounds into mugs.

Later that night, they lay in bed together, each lost in thought. Jasmine heard Riley's bark and her tags tinkling as she bounded up the stairs.

"I think we're getting a visitor."

Just then Riley scampered into Tessa's room wagging her tail and nosing against Tessa's legs. "Hey, Riley! How are you, Lovey?" She rubbed Riley's side and gave her a kiss.

Jasmine reached out a tentative hand, and Riley gave it a sniff and then a lick. Jasmine stroked her soft fur, "Oh, she is something!" Riley lay down on the carpet and the two girls moved next to her and rubbed her belly. After a few minutes, Jasmine's eyes began to droop.

"Okay," said Tessa, "I'll let you sleep." They both got into bed, and Tessa began rearranging the two pillows on her side of the bed. She made a whole commotion and grunted as she burrowed into a side-sleep position.

"You ever quiet?"

"Usually not. G'night."

"G'night."

"Sweet dreams...I love you."

Jasmine's body tensed. This sister of hers was caring and frightening all at the same time. Jasmine fidgeted a moment, but then found her voice, "Me too." She pressed her back close to Tessa's, felt her warmth, and then focused on the sound of her calm breathing. Only then did her thoughts float away, releasing her to a world of dreams.

The next day, Jasmine and Tessa walked into the kitchen wearing sweatpants, T-shirts, and sleepy eyes. Alice jumped up from her chair, leaving behind her laptop. "Breakfast? You girls want eggs, pancakes, cereal?"

Tessa replied that they'd just make their own coffee and the girls moved through the kitchen, like two dancers, their motion in sync. When they had their hot mugs in hand, Tessa started toward the staircase, but Jasmine looked to Tessa's mom, "Thank you, Ms. Alice, for having me over." She thought about saying other things too, like how good a mom she seemed to be, and that she shouldn't feel bad about not adopting them both. But the thoughts weren't forming into coherent sentences, and she didn't want to upset her.

Alice brushed some invisible dirt off her yoga pants. "First off, just call me Alice. Then, you should know that you are always welcome here—*always*. And if there is anything Rob and I can do to help you, please, let us know. Whatever it is, talk to us. We'll do our best. You're part of our family now."

"Ms. Alice, I mean, Alice, I don't need anything from you, really, but thank you." Her face grew hot. She didn't know what to do with all this kindness. It felt as if she had slipped into some alternative universe.

"Well, you'll let us know." Alice took a step toward Jasmine and moved her long fingers over the girl's shoulder blades. Jasmine felt Alice's affection travel into her body and take up residence. *Maybe I could get used to this.*

After they had downed their coffee, Tessa suggested they go out for lunch.

"That'd be great if I had any money, but my budget is beyond austerity."

"You taking history or economics this semester? You're talking austerity?"

Jasmine gave Tessa a sideways glance. "You think you're the only one who studied for the SATs? I didn't take any fancy prep course, but Miss Raymelle got me one of those big fat books, and I put my nose in it every night for months."

"My parents made me go to tutoring twice a week. There was homework for that on top of everything else. It was *brutal.* Anyway, lunch is on me. We can get whatever you like: sushi, Chinese, Indian, salads, sandwiches...."

"I'll eat whatever, as long as it's cooked."

"Awe, have you tried spicy tuna rolls?"

"Not today, Princess."

"No?" Tessa's eyes glinted. "Have you tried wrestling?"

"What?"

Tessa grabbed the other girl's upper arms and shoved her backwards onto the bed, and the two tussled around for a few moments, shrieking and laughing before collapsing onto their backs, their chests rising and falling in unison, matching smiles pinned to their faces.

Jasmine felt like she'd just smoked a blunt. This insane light-skinned chick had a way of lifting her up, even when she didn't know she was down. Everything in this massive suburban house was beginning to feel amazingly, out-of-control, good to her. "I guess you're all healed now, your hemoglobin and what-not."

"Maybe they need to do a study of how high school athletes recover from bone-marrow donation, because after a week or so, I felt completely fine." That's what she said, but Tessa still lay there, catching her breath.

"Hey, Cinderella?" Jasmine sat up.

"I don't get it. Why do you call me Cinderella? I mean if I'm Cinderella, who are you: Princess Jasmine? The Little Mermaid?"

Jasmine considered this, "You know there are two versions of *The Little Mermaid:* the original, by Hans Christian Andersen, in which she has to kill the prince to survive but can't bring herself to do it, and so she's turned into sea foam, and the Disney version that ends with her marrying the prince."

"I don't remember that first one, but you're definitely the mermaid who gets the happy ending."

"Yeah? How come?"

"I don't know, I just don't think that turning into sea foam is in your future; sand between your toes at the Jersey shore—maybe, but not sacrificing yourself for a man who doesn't love you."

"Uh-huh, I guess you're right. I've been down that road."

There was a space then, and Jasmine took a leap, "Did Lakisha ever come by or phone to thank you?" Jasmine had wanted to ask this ever since the surgery but resisted. It needed to be said without a whiff of envy, without letting Tessa know that she'd discovered where Lakisha lived and had staked out the place a few times just to catch a glimpse of her.

"She wrote an email. I've been wanting to read it to you, since it's kind of written to us both."

Jasmine felt her stomach clench. If only Lakisha's words could end the solar eclipse of her life. What would it be like to feel a mother's warmth again or to live as Tessa did, surrounded by dappled sunlight and love?

Tessa tapped at her phone, "I wish we could meet her! I think it's her guilt that gets in the way. Here, tell me what you think." Tessa's voice filled the room with their mother's words.

Dear Tessa,

There aren't enough letters in the alphabet or words in the dictionary for me to convey how grateful I feel. TJ is slowly, miraculously, thanks to you—recovering! We don't know what the future will bring, but you've given him a second chance at life, and in doing so, you've changed everything for our entire family. Your donation was the most selfless thing a stranger has ever done for us, and it makes me think differently about the world, just knowing that there are people like you in it. Yet even as I write this, I know I'm bending the truth, a piece of me revising history. We aren't really strangers, you and me. I'm no stranger to your sister, Jasmine, either. It's as if we've all been tethered together somehow, circling around each other on the same Jersey streets, connected, but not.

When you girls were born, I hadn't seen my mother in years, and I never did get to meet my father. Truth be told, my mother, Maizy, never even spoke his name. Grandma Louema passed when I was eleven, and Aunt Dottie, well, let's just say she wasn't much interested in raising me. At sixteen, all I had was a tattered heart, and a wavering conviction that life could be different. I didn't set out to abandon you and your sister, but giving you away was the only path

I saw to save us all. My love of family is something fierce, so what I did has been hard to live with.

But your generous spirit says that someone must've loved you growing up. I find that thought comforting and hope it's true. I hope that you and Jasmine have had good lives. I don't want to disrupt whatever peace you've been able to carve out for yourselves, so I'll just say that I will keep you both in my prayers, and I'll think of your kindness every time I see TJ's face spread out with joy.

With Grateful Blessings,

Lakisha

Jasmine felt her throat tighten. Tessa *had* been raised by loving parents, she'd gotten that much right. For Jasmine, Miss Raymelle and Champaine were more like placeholders until something real came along. Lakisha's kids and Tessa all had what she didn't. Whatever was choking her, moved down and formed a knot in her stomach. It was a familiar pain, one that she knew as intimately as breath itself. Still, Lakisha hadn't shut the door on them. No, she had not. She'd left it ajar, in need of just a push to open. An idea came to her, "We should try to see Lakisha on Christmas Day." It tripped out of Jasmine's mouth as a statement instead of a question.

"Really?"

"She goes to church at Christian Love."

"Have you been stalking her?"

Jasmine didn't answer. It was unimportant how she knew. All that mattered was getting Tessa to agree with what had to be done. This is what she needed, and perhaps Tessa needed it too. "I know when the family service starts. We could catch her on the way there. It's close by, so I'm sure she'll walk it. Maybe we can even check on TJ."

Tessa stood and began to pace. "You really think she'll want that?"

"We could try—who knows? It's Christmastime; maybe she'll grace us with a few sentences. Or maybe it'll just be closure for her. In that letter, she seemed to want some closure."

Tessa kneaded her hands, and her face looked like she was deciphering a calculus problem. Finally, her eyes grew resolute. "Okay, I'm in. Let's go see Lakisha."

PART FIVE
The Color of a Tattered Heart

Jasmine, Tessa, and Lakisha

Tessa awakens early on Christmas morning and shakes Jasmine's shoulder.

"What? Why are you waking me up?"

"We're going to go see Lakisha, remember? We have to leave time to drive there and find parking."

"Okay, okay, I'm getting up." But she doesn't move a muscle.

"Come on, Jazzy." Tessa gives her a strong nudge.

"No one calls me Jazzy, Contessa. And you're very annoying in the morning."

"My friend, Kate, actually calls me Contessa, and I don't mind it one bit. Come on, I don't want to miss her."

The drive into Irvington is an easy one, with very few cars on the road. After circling two blocks, they find parking, and stake out their spot within easy view of Lakisha's front door. The two are bundled in their winter jackets, and Tessa's knit gloves and scarves. The weather forecast calls for snow in the late afternoon, but so far there is no sign of a white Christmas. The parked cars on the street are covered in a glistening film, and the dirty remnants of the last snowfall are mounded at the curb.

"We're in luck. There's a donut shop open across the street." Tessa squints and holds up her gloved hand to shade her eyes against the morning sunlight. "Do you think there's time to grab a cup of coffee before she comes out?"

Jasmine looks at the *Princess Jasmine* watch strapped to her wrist, an early holiday gift from Padma. "We have time. I don't think they'll start walking before 10:00, and even if they do, we'll see them through the store window."

The sisters cross the street, and each orders a coffee and cinnamon bun. They return to their corner and begin sipping their drinks. The street has an eerie silence, with almost no traffic moving down the double wide avenue. A few shrieks of pleasure pierce the air, followed by deep-toned laughter.

"I guess someone got what she wanted." Jasmine glances at Tessa, but her sister's eyes are fixed on Lakisha's door, as if willing it to open and end the suspense.

"When do you think she'll be out?"

"I guess patience isn't your thing." Jasmine takes a bite of bun and licks a stray piece of frosting from her lips. "This sticky bun is good; you should try it."

Tessa shivers.

"You cold? Drink the coffee; she'll be out soon."

Doors on the block begin opening, and the neighborhood comes to life. Some families head for cars and begin scraping ice off windows, but most seem to be making their way on foot. Though they are all bundled beneath coats and jackets, some women wear fancy hats decorated with colorful feathers and wide ribbons. The parade of pedestrians distracts Tessa until Jasmine grabs her arm. The door to Lakisha's basement apartment is ajar and people are emerging into the frosty air.

Shonda grasps the topsy-turvy doll in her hand, but when it begins to drag on the pavement, Lakisha takes it and presses it to the handlebars of Kai's stroller. In his canvas seat, her youngest kicks his feet while singing to himself. Lakisha walks a few yards before bending down to adjust his safety buckle, and from the corner of her eye she spies her mother's ghost coming from the opposite direction.

Once upright, she realizes that there is not one ghost, but two; two young women who are approaching arm in arm. What is most striking to Lakisha is their eyes. They are large and seem to peer inside her, and she fears that they'll see her turmoil, her profound regret. She blinks repeatedly, half expecting them to evaporate into the air, like breath in winter—visible and then gone.

The mother and daughters stand rooted to the pavement a few feet apart, while the little girl plays with a knotted piece of purple yarn, and the baby hums. Lakisha takes in the sight of them, noting their pretty faces and slight frames, the blond one's warm expression and readiness to smile, and the brunette's stoicism so like her own. Anticipation flurries in her chest, and for some reason she is overwhelmed by Maizy's sweet and spicy scent. The absurd words trip from her lips, "Do you smell cinnamon?"

The one who looks like her mother, holds out a bakery bag, "Maybe it's the bun."

By this time, Theo and the rest of the children have caught up, but they stand back several paces—waiting. One corner of Lakisha's face lifts into a fleeting smile. "So, if you're holding a pastry, I'm guessing you two aren't ghosts."

The dark one shakes her head no, while the light one says, "Flesh and blood," and offers her a forearm to touch.

"Flesh and blood," Lakisha exhales. She doesn't want to touch this girl's arm, but she can't help herself. She lifts her crimson-gloved hand and places it on Tessa, but then pulls back as if scalded, and her fingers move to the matching wool scarf at her neck. "I never got to thank you in person...for TJ. We're incredibly grateful. He's doing great." Emotions buried so many years ago are now unearthed and they tear at the bag of tears in her chest. There are many things she should say, but she can't stop staring, her voice has gone missing. She swallows hard and chokes out, "You're both beautiful." She's searching for something but can't tease it out of the turmoil in her head. *Is it Jasmine's resemblance to Maizy that is making me crazy, or is it the shade of Tessa's hair? No, I won't think that way anymore.* Lakisha longs to mother them; with words, with hugs, with time. So much time has been lost; they're no longer hers. They probably just came to meet her, curious about the mother who gave them away. She begins to resign herself to this, prepares to wish them well and walk on when Tessa reaches for her.

"I just want to say…I forgive you. I know what happened, and I don't blame you."

This absolution is too much for Lakisha, and regret leaks from her eyes, dotting her new wool coat. She had never imagined forgiveness, wasn't even aware that she desperately needed it. But now that it's offered, she is gripped with gratitude, as well as a primal sorrow woven with possibility. Her legs grow weak and she leans against the stroller. The light one, the daughter who wears a rapist's skin, that's the one who forgives her. Her eyes lift with hope toward the other girl.

Jasmine looks hard at Lakisha, sees her anguish, recognizes it, as if she were viewing her own mirrored reflection. After a few moments she mutters, "I'll think on it."

Lakisha lets out a sigh and wipes her face with the doll she's holding. Perhaps she deserves no better. "Thank you both, for—everything."

"Mama, you all right? Who these ladies be? I wanna get to church early cause they're giving out candy to the kids. I don't want them to run out!" Shonda is tugging on Lakisha's hemline.

"Okay, we're going," Lakisha strokes her daughter's neat braids. "Merry Christmas, girls. Perhaps…" there are many things she wishes to say, but she's got no claim to them. She's not their mother. "Thank you for giving me the chance to meet you. Your parents must be very proud. I know I'd be." She takes them in for a moment longer, trying to commit every detail to memory. "Merry Christmas."

"Merry Christmas," their thin voices trail disappointment.

Lakisha tightens her grip on the stroller and takes a few steps away from these two pieces of her past.

Shonda yanks on her coat sleeve, "Are they our kin, Mama?"

"Hmm?"

"Those ladies? Are they our kin?"

Lakisha stops the stroller and takes in her youngest daughter. "What makes you ask that?"

Shonda looks back at the twins. They're still standing in the middle of the pavement, and they give her a wave. "They look a little like Aunt Dottie's girls or like...I don't know. Can we just get to church?"

"Like who?"

"Maybe, sort of...like you."

By this time, Theo and the other children have reached the girls, and they all stand in an awkward group, eyeing each other. *What should I do now?* Lakisha looks up to the heavens and then turns back to her family standing a few feet away.

Her eyes latch onto Jasmine, now understanding that she's the one who needs mothering. "My Grandma Louema used to say, *Ain't but God and your heart know the truth.*" She shakes her head, "I guess it's about time I listen to them—God and my heart that is."

Jasmine nods and bites her lip.

"You know which house is mine?"

Jasmine responds with another shy nod.

"I serve Christmas dinner at three o'clock this afternoon. Bring your sister if y'all are free." Then she says to her younger children, "Let's get going. Our little expert here says they're giving out candy." And with that, Lakisha leaves behind her ghosts now transformed into daughters, and pushes forward down the avenue. When she's walked half a block, Lakisha looks back, fearing that perhaps it has all been imagined, but there they are, standing together at the corner. Dappled sunlight dances on their faces. They raise their entwined hands up into the air and wave toward Lakisha.

Their mother responds by lifting the doll skyward and motioning in their direction. The heaviness in Lakisha's center lifts, and is replaced with something that feels foreign, but pleasant.

Theo sidles up to her, and as his arm encircles her waist says, "You invited them to dinner? Good for you, Kisha."

Lakisha peeks back at Jasmine and Tessa who are holding hands and swinging their arms like delighted children as they stroll away from her.

Lakisha then remembers the ruby rings she had made up from the one that was Maizy's. In that moment, she decides who should have them.

At 3:00 p.m. sharp, Jasmine and Tessa press Lakisha's doorbell. It is Theo who swings open the door. "Come on in!" He has a jubilant smile on his face. "We've been waiting for you." Then in a conspiratorial tone adds, "I think Santa left gifts for the two of you under the tree. Something special from your Grandma Maizy."

"Welcome!" says Lakisha, approaching the door while wiping her hands on a dishtowel. "Don't be shy now. Come on inside and visit with TJ."

Together, Jasmine and Tessa cross over the threshold.

Acknowledgements:

I view this story as an urban fairy tale, one grounded in emotional truths, but woven with threads of resilience that most often require support from people like Miss Raymelle, Champaine, Theo, and even the Aunt Dotties of the world. Sadly, many of those I met in my inner-city work had virtually no social network. Still, I witnessed first-hand the power of caring, and our innate ability to rescue each other. This book was written as a wish, as a prayer, as a profound hope that the young women I tried to help will find their own quiet strength, peace, and happiness.

Thank you to the members of Women Who Write Watchung Hills Novelists' Group and New Providence Library Group, and the New Providence Writers' Meetup who provided feedback early on. Editors Alice Peck and Marlene Adelstein helped me along the way, and Julie Mosow guided my manuscript to completion. Thank you to literary agents Ellen Geiger, Jane Dystel, and Sue Armstrong, who offered moral support and sound direction. Thank you to my publicist, Mary Bisbee-Beek for your advice and hard work on my behalf. To Joan Leggitt, my publisher, and to her incredible team, thank you for believing in this book, offering editorial insights, and making it possible for me to share Lakisha, Jasmine, and Tessa with the world.

To my wonderful friends who were kind enough to ask about my book over many years, and then perceptive enough to stop asking when I'd nearly lost faith in the project—thank you. Special thanks to Nancy Gerber, who read the first and the last drafts and offered that unique brand of compassionate encouragement that can only come from a friend who is a fellow writer and a therapist. To Treasure Cohen, you are the polar opposite of your fictional namesake, and have always been my mothering role model. To everyone in my spiritual, professional, parenting, and writing communities, and to my extended family, I am grateful for your support.

To my sisters, Marla and Jodi, who read the awful first draft and said things like, "It would make a great movie!" and "It's the best book I've read since The Time Traveler's Wife!" — thank you. Thank you to my mother and father for all of their love and faith in me, and for teaching me to cherish every blessing. To Sam, who offered his marketing expertise and professional connections, Jared, who gave me writing advice and encouragement, Hannah who allowed me to borrow liberally from her life and said that college kids would like it, and Marisa, who shared her knowledge of social media and branding—I'm in awe of you all, and love you beyond measure. Lastly, to Jacob, who listened intently to every hope and fear, wiped my tears and applauded my happy dances. You've given me wings and made my universe safe enough to follow my dreams. In your arms, I'm home.

A few organizations that help girls in Newark and Irvington and would gladly accept your donations:

Girls: Live Love Laugh: www.girlslivelovelaugh.org
Butterfly Dreamz: www.butterflydreamz.org
Sadie Nash: www.SadieNash.org

About the Author

Lisa A. Sturm is a clinical social worker who sees couples and individuals in her private practice in Springfield, New Jersey. She's had several short stories, novel excerpts, and essays published in literary journals and newspapers. *Echoed in My Bones* is her debut novel, inspired by her work as an inner-city psychotherapist. In the summer of 2013, while visiting a dying client in the hospital, Sturm asked how she could help. The woman's eyes grew sharp, her voice certain, "Bring more love into the world!" *Echoed in My Bones* is part of this author's commitment to do just that.